BOOKS BY P.S. MERONEK

A Lifetime to Die

Stay Another Night

Purchase these titles at:

www.ponytalepress.com

Ponytale Press

P. S. MERONEK

THE JOSHUA EFFECT

www.ponytalepress.com

Ponytale Press

ISBN 978-0-9857096-3-1
ISBN 978-0-9857096-5-5 (ebook)

Printed in India

Author's Note

Again, another cleverly disguised love story about a guy who has to find out how to love himself before he can appreciate the love of another. It's nothing new. Jesus may not have said it first, but he certainly said it more eloquently than the rest of them.

This one is for you, Mom. You're one half the reason I'm here. Thanks for that night of June sixteenth, so long ago. I hope you guys had fun. Ever since, I know I have.

Special thanks to contributors Ken Hunt, Nicole Pucci, and Dr. Duke Mojib. Thank you for your valuable contributions in helping to make this manuscript a reality.

Chapter 1

What I called my field office faced the Hudson River. I lived in the top floor of an eighteen story renovated apartment block in Westchester. The building was originally completed in 1923. When the real estate market in New York had rebounded in the eighties, Westchester had been pulled along with it. In the early days my father had almost starved meeting the mortgage payments. I don't remember how many times we had eaten rice and beans every night for a week at a time just so we could stay in the game. I never complained. I was more into the books: accounting, finance, reverse mortgages – all this while I was still in high school. So by the time I was old enough for college, it was a no-brainer: Pop sent me to Wharton. I was almost halfway through when his heart gave out. The funeral was small, but the friends and family were close.

I finished out the semester and quit at the end of my second year. Wharton's professors had taught me enough to carry on where Pop had left off.

A sculler came into view. I lost him in the glare as he rowed like a hunchbacked beetle in the middle of the pale gray water between where I was standing and the two o'clock October sun.

"We're supposed to be there in an hour," Gary reminded me, ripping my thoughts away from *her* and back to the present.

I shrugged unconcernedly, my back to him and the big table, my hands in my pockets.

"Mostly it's for the politicians, Gary. Personally, I could live without it." The edge in my tone wasn't lost on him. Gary and I went back almost to the beginning. He knew me almost as well as Charlie. No one knew me as well as she did.

I finally turned away from the bank of glazed plate glass windows and faced him. The lawyer sat in his usual place, four seats down from mine. He faced the windows, which were fifteen feet or so away from the heavy, egg-shaped rosewood table which when fully attended sat sixteen. That was rare. I made sure I owned at least fifty-one percent of everything I touched. If there were ever any problems and I needed to act fast, I didn't want to be encumbered by any arguments. At the end of the day my signature alone was all that was needed in order to move mountains.

At three o'clock this afternoon we were having a press conference on the roof of my latest tower, a sixty-three story office-condo project in midtown. The Mayor wasn't going to be there; he was busy out of town. But some significant others from his office would be attending the exclusive ceremony. I had agreed to make an appearance because in New York it was still very much a game of politics. If I didn't show up to one of my own cap parties, I might offend somebody. They'd keep the chit and I would have to pay later, at my most vulnerable. Lately, City Hall had been like my own little Swiss clock. We were getting pretty much whatever we wanted in the way of easements and variances, within reason. It seemed all I had to do was show up, smile for the cameras, and toss back a glass or two of expensive wine. I could almost always get in and out in under an hour. It wasn't that I didn't want to stay longer; sometimes I did. It was just that lately my time had become a precious commodity. Everyone wanted a piece of my action. I had to admit; these days there was more than enough to go around. I had to be careful not to get bogged down. I had to constantly be alert and on the move. And as for Charlie…Charlie was a big girl. She knew what she'd signed on for. There had been no secrets, none. Maybe that had been the problem, I had been too open and up front with her. What had she called it the last time? "Brutally honest", I think was the exact phrase she'd used.

"Next time don't ask," I remembered I had turned on her.

"Alright, I won't," she had thrown back at me.

I'd been sitting on the edge of the bed trying to get my new left shoe onto my foot. The leather was hard, not supple like the upholstery on the pair I had bought from the Italian last month. To make matters worse, I didn't have a shoe horn. I made a mental note to speak with Giovanni next time I was downstairs in his store. I'd paid him a thousand dollars for these shoes and I didn't want him shaving quality for profit. Not in any of my buildings. That wasn't how it worked in the 'Empire', as it had come to be known.

If there was one thing I couldn't stand it was uncomfortable shoes. I grimaced as I was finally able to force it on. I'd buckled the new leather heel in the process.

"Black, red, what does it matter? It's only a dress. You look great no matter what you're wearing. Or not," I added as she moved into the framed doorway of the walk-in closet.

She was wearing a pair of white lace panties. Nothing else, save her matching high heels. She folded her arms across her bare breasts and stared at me, not saying anything at all.

"Finish getting ready, will you?" I was losing patience now. I stood up. The shoe was so tight my foot throbbed like my arm did when I had my blood pressure checked. Now I was really getting pissed. "I can't wear these," I complained to myself. I sat back down in a chair beside the bed and wrestled the damn things off. I threw them against the bedroom wall, but it didn't help matters. I could feel her looking at me, her stare boring a hole through the top of my head. I sighed and looked up at her.

"The red one," I said. I tried my best to sound sincere. "It really shows off your figure." I added what all women wanted to hear.

Her stare grew colder. I guess she could never fully appreciate how she looked to me, and to most other men for that matter. She'd turned twenty-nine last month. Charlene Leigh Bakersfield. Charlie had it all. Blonde, originally from California, she was as ambitious as she was beautiful. She was five and a half feet of oozing sensuality no matter what her disposition. Like now. I couldn't help smiling. She made a smart package.

"Everything is a joke with you, isn't it, Jonathan?"

"What, I can't smile anymore?" I played innocent.

"From the first time we met, you've never taken me seriously. Have you?" She demanded.

"Of course I have," I replied truthfully. "And I don't think it's very fair of you to imply otherwise," I added.

She stared at me. Her features had softened somewhat. I wasn't smiling anymore.

"Come over here," I said quietly.

"No. See, that's just what I mean, Jonathan."

"Charlie –"

"Every time I have something serious I'd like to talk about you trivialize it and most of the time we just end up in bed together. I'm tired of it, John. There's more to me than that. And if you can't get past that…" She trailed off, and then began again. "I wanted this to work. But I'm scared, Jonathan. I'm really scared that this is all there is. Don't get me wrong. The sex is great. Fantastic. But, there's more to a relationship than just sex all the time."

"We don't just have sex all the time," I protested.

"We don't?"

"We go to receptions, openings, concerts, dinner, the movies…"

"Yes and what's behind everyone of them?"

I shook my head in disbelief. "It's like you're describing a drug addict who needs a fix. Having intimacy with the one you care about is normal, Charlie. It's what people who love each other do. It's not supposed to be a chore. It's not supposed to be something obligatory."

She walked across the tile floor and sat down on the bed across from me. She reached for my hand and held it.

"I never said it was a chore," she said in a softer tone. "With you it's always fireworks. I…I would just like more, Jonathan. I want more of you."

"You've got all of me now," I said.

"It'll be one year next week."

"No way," I reacted. I had no idea we had been seeing each other for that long. As usual, I was terrible at remembering anniversaries.

"And I don't have all of you. You've never given all of yourself to anyone. Lately I've been wondering if you have that in you."

I sighed. She was probably right. No one had to tell me that my time was spread thin. But what Charlie was implying was that she had become little more than an afterthought, mortar between the bricks of my life. Wasn't that what she was supposed to be? Without the mortar everything would fall apart. I thought about telling her this, and then I passed. I realized from her perspective it would sound like more of the same. However inadvertent it may be, it would sound to Charlie as if I was not only trivializing our one year relationship, but her role in it as well. I felt relieved. I had almost made the horrible mistake of comparing her to mortar. She would not have been happy.

"I'm not happy," she said, seemingly reading my thoughts.

"Things will get better between us. I promise, Charlie."

She sighed. "This isn't easy for me, Jonathan."

I stared into her eyes. My heart suddenly tightened into a fist of ice. "What isn't easy for you? Now you're scaring me, and I don't like it."

"I'm not scaring you," her tone didn't change. It was soft and sonorous, like the rest of her. But her eyes bored into mine. Nothing but conviction there. I could see she had made up her mind about whatever it was she had been thinking about. How long had it been coming? "Nothing scares you, Jonathan. You are courageous, you are strong; you are invincible."

"Why do I hear a big but on the end of this?"

"But, I think we need a little space for a while."

I felt woozy. "Space? Awhile? What do you mean, awhile? How long is awhile? I need you Charlie, now more than ever."

She smiled reassuringly and patted my hand like an owner pats a dog's head. "You've never needed anyone, Jonathan. You see, you can do it all by yourself. I can't. We're different that way."

"Oh, so you're better than me because you need a partner," I attacked her.

"Jonathan, this isn't a competition. It isn't about being better or worse than another person. You know that. I don't want to hurt you. I don't want that."

"You could've fooled me," I said flatly.

"Now you're acting like a teenager." She got up and strode briskly toward the closet, then stopped in the frame of the doorway and looked back at me. "I'm moving out for a while," she declared. "Tomorrow. I think it's best."

"How long?"

She looked at me.

"Alright," I held up my hand in defeat and swallowed the lump in my throat. I hadn't lost at anything for so long that I couldn't remember the last time. It was a strange, unpleasant feeling. I sucked it up as best I could, determined to take the high road if she was leaving. "If there is anything I can –"

"I'll be fine." She stopped me.

"Tonight…" I hesitated. "After the reception…"

"A sympathy fuck?" She feigned concern. "That's so unlike you."

Now it was my turn to look at her. "You are so wonderfully beautiful, Charlie. I'm going to miss you terribly. You are a wonderful person."

As I watched her she seemed to decide something. In a quick, deft movement she slid out of her panties and kicked them to the side with a high heel.

"That got you a blow job." She smiled seductively. "And I don't feel like waiting."

Later, she wore the black dress. She left the next morning and I hadn't seen her since. That was three months ago. I had screwed up big time. If only…if only.

A thousand, thousand regrets I thought I'd never have to deal with haunted me every minute of every day since she'd been gone.

"She called me," Gary said out of the blue. "Yesterday."

I examined him more closely as he stared at me from where he sat hunched over the table. It looked as though he'd just chased the table down and killed it for his dinner. He was a big, beefy guy who tipped the scales at two-fifty, and was a shade over six feet, the same as me. I thought I was pretty trimmed out at two hundred pounds, but at forty I worked at it. For some reason unknown to me, Gary didn't have to do anything. To the untrained eye he looked chunky, but when he had to he moved like a big cat. Gary Stanick was dangerous to his enemies; a better friend would be tough to find. I liked him from the first time we met in Corporate Finance class at Wharton. He had switched to law school a year later. We stayed in touch and I hired him right after he graduated.

"She had forgotten some files is all." His chunky baby face betrayed no more than what he'd said. "I told her to call you about it."

I stared at him and he stared back at me. The beautiful autumn sun dropped a little lower in the sky. The sculler was gone now. The river looked cold and empty behind me.

"Thank you, Gary," I said at last. "I'm sure I'll hear from her soon, then." An awkward silence followed.

Gary finally said, "I think we better leave soon, Jonathan. They've got some very strict rules now about the air space over New York. David mentioned to me that they weren't too happy about your flight plan."

"They're never happy about a whole lot of things. It's their job not to be happy. It's their problem, not ours.

But," I sighed, more for the disturbing memories of the Charlie fiasco as I was beginning to call it, "I guess we better not make *them* any less happy than they already are. Time to rock'n'roll Gary. Give David a call and tell him to light up the helipad. We'll be down in a few minutes. We'll leave right after I use the john."

David Atwell had the front of the Sikorsky facing the back lobby of the building. The blades were already turning when the back door swung open. Although we had plenty of clearance under the blades, we instinctively ducked as we came near them. Gary and I clambered aboard. David took us up and steered us out over the river. He angled the aircraft toward Manhattan and hit the turbine, sinking us back into the plush leather upholstery. The feeling I usually got from flying was exhilarating. It terrified some, especially when David was flying, but it always put a smile on my lips. Now I felt nothing as I stared at the empty seat across from me where Charlie usually sat.

Pop would have thought I was crazy. He would have said I had rocks in my head, and he would have said it with love in his heart. He'd been a bricks-and-boards, old school kind of a guy, and would've wondered what the hell a helicopter had to do with building towers. I would've told him that America was a different country. The old ways he'd grown up with didn't work anymore. Now it was all about marketing and how savvy you could be. It was about who could make the guy shelling out the two and a half million clams for a sixth floor condo feel like he was a somebody. The Empire was good at that. A lot of people said we were the best. They didn't always know it, but being the best didn't come cheap.

On the water below us the sculler came into view and just as quickly fell off to the rear of the aircraft. The big buildings of Manhattan began to rise up in front of us. I forced my mind to shift gears. Enough of this foolish and self indulgent melancholy, I thought to myself. Tonight I was determined to put this baby to rest. I was right. There were plenty of other fish in the sea. Maybe I'd hang around on top of the roof for a bit. Like fine wine, there were always plenty of fine women at these events.

David Atwell was showing off. He banked steeply off the Hudson, and then, prudently, slowed to a crawl as we skimmed the taller structures of New York. We slowly moved inland.

We had already landed on top of the roof a few times during construction, so David knew the drill. His voice came over the headphones: "I have visual on the building, Mr. Strickland. Touchdown will be in about three minutes."

"Take us in, David," I spoke into my microphone. "Slow and easy. Can you see anyone on top of the roof?"

"Looks like a full house. You want me to bank it so you can have a look?"

"Negative. Just take us in. Keep us between the sun and them. Nothing fancy, David, but I don't want anyone to see the chopper until after they hear it. This is supposed to be a surprise. They think we're using the elevator."

"Nice surprise," said the pilot.

"Hopefully," I said back to him. "That's the plan, anyway."

"Alright," David announced as we slowly approached the building's roof. "We've got land."

I saw immediately what he meant. The elevator shafts conveniently sectioned off the roof. About sixty percent of the roof was on one side and forty percent on the other of the concrete motor house. Someone had run a temporary fence as a partition on the far side of the motor house, between where the guests were now gathered and where we could land. The motor house, below which the elevator shafts ran through the guts of the building, would shield the guests from most of the rotor wind. We would set down in the middle of the forty percent side, which gave us a landing pad of about eight thousand square feet, the whole roof coming in at just under twenty thousand. The Sikorsky's rotors would have ample room between their tips and the parapet walls, which created a four foot tall perimeter around the entire roof. For something to do, David would have probably agreed to land it blindfolded.

We were probably just over two hundred feet out from the roof when someone must have guessed it was us.

As we hovered and carefully eased our way into position for a rooftop landing, I could see most of the guests pointing our way. Some of them were laughing; others held their glasses over their heads in our direction, a mock toast. They weren't that far away by now. I recognized some of them: politicians, news media scrambling in front of their lenses, contractors, subcontractors. They were all there. They looked like they were having fun, too.

"What the..?" It was David's voice. We were softly sinking to land from about fifteen feet off the roof. I didn't like the tone of his voice. It sounded strange in my headphones – scared.

"Fuck me!" he shouted now, and I felt us stop, but something else. It was like David had suddenly changed his mind and was now taking off instead of landing. My heart suddenly leapt into my throat as my mind tried desperately to assimilate what my eyes were seeing. It could not be happening. We suddenly began to ascend. My eyes registered this as the rooftop began to fall away from us. Only the chopper wasn't moving. It was still hovering in one spot, so what I was seeing was impossible. It was not happening.

I screamed, "David, the antenna!"

The pilot was thinking even faster. He throttled up hard and fast. In the same instant I felt the helicopter lurch sideways as if we had been kicked in the guts by a mule. I saw a blur of steel girder flash by outside the window on my side. The fifty foot steel communications antenna which a second ago had stood like a rigid sentinel on the top of the motorhouse missed us by inches. I realized in horror that if David hadn't twisted the aircraft around when he did, the steel antenna would have sliced the Sikorsky's tail in two.

I saw people below us, screaming. For a brief second or two I saw the white terror in the many faces of my friends and acquaintances. Then they were gone. They just fell away, their hands and arms groping and flailing helplessly toward us as they went. Everything: the tables, the chairs, the bottles of wine, disappeared beneath us, swallowed whole by an ever growing, monstrous cloud of dust, debris, and soupy roiling clouds of impenetrable gray smoke. The huge building was going down. Sixty-three stories were collapsing in on themselves, and all those people with them. We watched from above it all, but none of it seemed real. None of us spoke. We just stared down in horror, our mouths agape in disbelief.

Chapter 2

We set the Sikorsky down on the rooftop of another tower I owned not far from the one which had just collapsed. I didn't want to chance flying out of the city. I knew from 9/11 the jets our military already had in the air wouldn't hesitate to shoot us down on the slightest suspicion the chopper had something to do with what just happened. They wouldn't give a shit that I owned the tower that was now a pile of smoking rubble. They would have every justification for it. I realized right away we were the smoking gun. We were there. We were a few feet from landing as the tower had gone down. We were suspects. A wry thought occurred to me as David cut the engine. If I hadn't gone to the john before we left Westchester, we'd all be dead right now.

No one had said much since I had directed David to land further up the Avenue. Now, on the roof of the fifty-seventh floor, Gary looked across at me and said, "Do you think we can see it from here?"

"Yeah, I think so. From the south side. Let's have a look."

All of us left the chopper, dazed, and wandered over to the parapet on the building's south side. Even before we looked, we could hear the sounds of chaos on the streets below us: sirens, horns, screams, police, fire trucks, you name it.

We stood side by side, staring down the block. Giant, mushroom shaped clouds of smoke completely obscured what was happening where my tower had collapsed, about a half mile to the south of us. We could see forms of what were obviously people emerging from the edge of the roiling dust storm. A weird kind of black soot had filled the air, making it difficult to breathe. Some of those emerging from the dust were helping other people. Some ran, while others, unable to breathe, stumbled and collapsed in the street. Emergency vehicles were already flooding the area. The cops were quickly throwing a net around the macabre scene. The whole thing had a surreal quality to it.

"I've seen this before," Gary whistled softly.

"Eerie," Was all David muttered. "Fucking eerie."

I said nothing, instead dissecting what I had seen from the aircraft. I knew there was a reason for what had just occurred. I knew we would eventually find the cause. But I also knew we were right there. We had seen it from only a few feet away. I searched my mind for a clue, hoping for something – anything. Something I had seen, innocuous at the time, but which would lead us to an answer for this carnage.

"Did you guys hear anything?" I demanded. "See anything? Anything at all?" I was scared. Who wouldn't be? I shivered all over as it occurred to me how close we had come to dying.

"I couldn't hear shit over the rotors," David said. "Besides, we all had headphones on."

"Our mics were open, too," Gary added.

I nodded. "Did you see anything? A flash of light, maybe? A puff of smoke just before it went down?"

"I saw something from the corner of my eye. It was just a blur." Gary was thinking now, too. Our minds were clearing.

"Out my side?" I asked.

He nodded.

"The antenna on top of the motor house," David answered for me.

"It's why he jerked the chopper sideways. Otherwise it was coming down on top of us," I said.

Gary looked at the short, balding pilot with a renewed respect. "Thanks, David. You saved our lives."

David nodded. "We're lucky I caught it in time."

I looked at David. The wind whipped the few, thin wisps of hair he did have across his furrowed brow. "You saw it begin to fall?"

He shook his head. "I was concentrating on the landing. But I always look for something so I can gauge my distance to the ground."

"The elevator house," Gary guessed. "Your point of reference."

"That's right," said David. "I've used it before. That's when I saw the son-of-a-bitch twist. The metal just suddenly torqued. Steel does that when it's collapsing."

"He's right," I said to Gary. "I've seen a crane buckle before. The boom twists like a pretzel."

"Takes a lot of stress to cause that," confirmed David.

"Like a sixty-three story tower going down," Gary said, clearly shaken.

"That would certainly be enough to do it," I agreed. "So you saw it begin to fall?" I pressed David.

"The com tower, yeah. Not the building. That part of it," he paused. He was searching for the right words. "I felt that part. I can feel when the landing is going right. As soon as we got close…" He shrugged, and then continued. "It didn't feel right. The next thing I knew…" He looked at me now. His eyes were intense. "What the hell just happened out there Jonathan?" David jerked his head to the street below. The noise was getting louder by the moment.

My cell phone suddenly went off.

"Don't answer that," Gary advised me.

I glanced at the number and recognized it immediately. I could guess why she was calling now. A lot more people would be calling soon.

"It's okay," I overruled Gary. "I know who it is." I flipped open the phone and said, "We were there. We were on top of it in the helicopter. We almost went down with it." I could hear my own voice. It sounded hollow and strained.

"So that was your helicopter. Thank God you're all right." Charlie was on the verge of hysteria. "If you hadn't answered –"

"I'm okay, Charlie," I cut her off. "We're fine. Gary and David are with me. Where are you?" I was thinking about how good her voice sounded to me after three months, especially right now. I was also thinking about the friends I had just lost, of all the people who never stood a chance, who never saw it coming. I was thinking how close Gary, David, and I had come to being among them. I felt cold and clammy, but I held it together. I had to. Pretty soon, I realized, a lot of eyes were going to be on me. People would be demanding answers to some hard questions.

"I'm here, in New York," Charlie said. "I was meeting with my agent about the book. I'm right down the street from where it happened. We're all watching it on CNN. There was a report of a helicopter. It took off right before the explosion."

"Took off?" I was stunned. "We were landing, Charlie. What explosion?" I looked at Gary and David to make sure they were catching all this. "There was no explosion. We didn't see anything, and we were right on top of it." It sounded like the media was already pumping the numbers. What they didn't know they were making up.

"I'm scared, Jonathan. I'm really scared." Charlie was on the verge of tears.

"It's alright, Charlie. Everyone's okay. Calm down."

"I'm calling my father."

"Why? What can he do?"

"He can help, Jonathan. I...I think you're going to need some help. He's on the inside. I couldn't tell you before," she hesitated, "and I probably shouldn't say this now, but he has the highest attainable security clearance possible."

"Are you telling me he's in charge? FBI, right?" I remembered Charlie had always been vague whenever the subject of her family had come up. She was the only child. Her mother had been killed in some kind of an accident, and I thought she had once told me her father worked for the Bureau. Or had she?

"He's Homeland Security now. He's not in charge, but he might as well be. He's the liaison between the field operatives and the Office. He reports straight to the Director."

"You think this has something to do with terrorism?" I was following her train of thought.

"Something brought that tower down." Her voice trembled slightly when she spoke.

"And CNN said there was an explosion?" I repeated my earlier question.

"They've been interviewing eyewitnesses: anyone they can find who saw anything. Early reports seem to indicate there was an explosion at ground level. Jonathan?" She was calmer now. She had regained her composure, but I could tell she was still scared. I turned my back to the parapet wall. I moved a few yards away from the sirens and bullhorns in the streets below us.

"Yeah, I'm here," I spoke softly into the mouthpiece.

"I miss you." Her voice cracked.

"I miss you too," I said. "But I wasn't the one who left, remember?"

"I've been doing a lot of thinking," she continued.

"And…?"

"And I think we should talk, Jonathan."

"Now?"

"Soon. After I speak with my father."

"Are you saying you want to come back?"

I heard her breathe into the phone. "I miss you."

"That's not what I asked," I pressured her.

"You shouldn't be alone right now."

I thought about it. I could trust Charlie with my life. I had no idea what had just happened, but I knew she was right. I had always considered her my friend, and only a fool would pass on an olive branch from a friend. Especially one he was in love with.

Another call was waiting. I glanced at the phone to see who it was. I didn't recognize the number. It had started.

"Call me on Gary's private cell from now on," I instructed her. "They already have my private number. They'll have his soon, too. They'll check all the records and start calling everyone I know."

"Are you hiding?" She was somewhat taken back

"Avoiding. I don't have the time to talk right now. Once the government dogs clamp onto their bone, I won't be able to pry their jaws loose. I think I need some time to process and collect myself. When you talk with your father, why don't you set something up so he and I can speak? Somewhere quiet."

"He might not agree to it. He might not be able to," Charlie elaborated. "But I'll try. I'll call you back after I speak with him. Jonathan?"

"I'm here."

"Be careful."

"Always," I assured her. "Call me as soon as you know something."

She said she would and then she hung up.

I looked at Gary and David over by the parapet of the roof. David had lit a cigarette. They had given me the space I needed. They weren't just employees; they were my friends, too. Both of them looked at me to see if they could read my mood. I walked back over to where they were standing. When I spoke this time, my voice had an edge to it. "I won't mind if you pass on this one, but I'd appreciate the help from both of you. We're going to need a few other people, as well."

"What are you planning?" David threw what was left of his cigarette onto the flat roof and ground out the butt with the toe of his boot.

I looked past them, down the now completely clogged streets below us. Cops and firemen were everywhere. The streets had turned into sections of a giant, crammed parking lot that stretched out like the spokes of a gigantic wheel in all directions. Only now, as the swirling air currents began to clear some of the dust and smoke away, could I begin to make out the mass of twisted steel and rubble which only minutes ago had been sixty-three stories tall. The air had an odd coolness to it I hadn't noticed earlier. Reflexively, I wiped my brow with the back of my hand and realized I was sweating. I saw ambulances, their flickering emergency lights announcing their positions. They weren't there to help the people I had known who had been on the roof. My only consolation for them was the knowledge that their end had been sudden and quick. My gaze shifted back to Gary and David. There was a steel glint in my eyes that hadn't been there a moment before. Now it was growing, like the sun rising off a clear still lake first thing in the morning. I measured my words carefully, because I had a pretty good idea what was probably coming down the pike for all of us.

"The plan is I'm going after the sons-of-bitches who did this to us." I looked past them again. I'd been right earlier this afternoon. There was no doubt about it. We'd make the six o'clock news, all right.

Chapter 3

Death is final. It doesn't discriminate. Sooner or later, it takes everyone. It's in the contract. There is no exit clause, no way around it.

The people in that tower had done nothing to deserve the horrible fate that had befallen them. They had simply been in the wrong place at the wrong time, and I'd almost had my own ticket stamped along with theirs. It took me a while to compose myself after that realization, but once I did I realized that it changed me. On some level I understood I'd be different for the rest of my life. I hated to think I'd be less kind, but I wasn't so naive to think otherwise.

The enemy was silent and invisible. I feared what I would probably have to become, and tried to convince myself for a long time that the building's collapse had been a design flaw, that perhaps the engineers had made some kind of mathematical miscalculation. As horrible as this implication was – because that would mean it could have been prevented – it was preferable to acknowledging the alternative: that the tower had been deliberately brought down, and all the people I knew had been murdered.

"And murder isn't a word I'm accustomed to using. At least not in a context such as this," I confided to the fourteen men and women around the table listening to me. For the moment, we were off the record.

"I don't think any of us will ever be entirely comfortable with a situation like this." Clifford Wallace leaned forward, lacing his fingers together on top of the table as he spoke. His pale, bony hands reminded me of a lizard's claws. "But our own personal feelings aside for the moment, we'd like to explore the feasibility of all possible scenarios." His eyes were slits instead of holes. I could barely see into them.

"Where are you going with this, Mr. Wallace?" Gary sat directly across from Wallace. The lawyer leaned forward onto the table as well and stared down the smaller man, his own hands like heavy metal wrenches. I let the discussion continue, but I didn't exactly appreciate the direction the questions had moved in, either. I wasn't stupid. None of us were. It had become obvious in the last few minutes that this so-called 'informal fact-finding security commission' was nothing less than a thinly-disguised panel of government hatchets hell bent on a witch hunt. But I had a surprise for them I knew they weren't going to like. Even Gary didn't know what I had up my sleeve. I was biding my time, just waiting for the right moment to use the information in a way that wouldn't compromise the promise I'd made to Gus.

My tower had been brought down on Monday. It was now Saturday.

I had met Charlie's father, Gus, in a secret meeting on Wednesday. Tony Mourning had buzzed my office from the building's security desk downstairs. Although his voice betrayed no emotion over the intercom, I knew Tony was on high alert. I had briefed him earlier that afternoon to expect Gus Bakersfield at six, and then to forget he'd ever seen him.

"He's on his way up now, sir."

"It's a pleasure to meet you again, sir." I shook hands with Gus, half lying. "I'm glad you could make it on such short notice." I pretended not to notice how damp and cold his hand felt to the touch. The clamminess of it belied a confident, almost severe countenance which seemed to say, 'I'm on top of you, I know your every move, and you'd better watch it. Especially where my daughter's concerned.'

We had met only twice before, both times in passing. I hadn't completely made up my mind about him then, as he had carried himself in a way that made me nervous. To his credit, I knew this might also be partly my fault. I had a natural aversion to spooks, which is what I thought he might have been.

"Have a seat," I said guardedly. I had ushered him into one of our medium-sized conference rooms. The chairs were covered in green Naugahyde, coordinated with the room's pastel green ceramic floor tiles. The walls, too, had been painted with a soft-tone, an art deco green color. We were forty floors up, inside the same building we'd gone to on Monday, after the other one had collapsed.

"Thanks." It came out more as a grunt. Was it me, or was he this congenial with everyone he met? He couldn't have been more different than his daughter. How had his wife died, I wondered? Maybe that had something to do with the way he acted. I looked at him more closely. Charlie was twenty-nine. I put Gus at no more than what, fifty-five? His face had the lines of a man much older. His hair was still all there. It was thick and bushy, but neatly trimmed, graying at the sides, of course. His eyes were small black holes that held my own with a stare that said, 'Try anything, anything at all, and your ass is mine.' Only this time I realized he wasn't making me nervous. With a mounting satisfaction, it confirmed to me I was somehow different now. I guess watching my friends plunge to their deaths from the rooftop had indeed changed me.

"Thanks for agreeing to meet with me," I opened.

Nothing.

I continued, "Charlie tells me you're number two at Homeland Security."

Still nothing.

I stared him down. He stared back at me.

I got up and walked over to the bar. I fixed myself a strong vodka and seven.

"Make mine a scotch. A Glenlivet if you've got one," he said to my back, startling me.

"A double, if you don't mind, Mr. Strickland. Over ice."

I glanced back at him, mixed it, and returned to the table. I set the glass down on the table in front of him.

"Thank you," Gus said, without touching the glass. "Did you –"

"I had everything turned off, Mr. Bakersfield," I knew where he was headed. "No mics, no cameras. That includes the parking lot, lobbies, elevators, and all the hallways. A technical black hole is what we will call it. You're not here. We'll log it in as an IT malfunction or some such thing. And don't worry about Tony. He's been with me forever."

"The front desk security officer, can you trust him and his partner?"

"All my people are extensions of myself," I assured him. "Tony and Javier included. They're part of Gary Stanick's team," I explained.

"Stanick? Isn't he your lawyer?"

I smiled. "That, too. A pretty good one, as a matter of fact." I was purposefully evasive. "You're not here, Mr.

Bakersfield," I repeated. "You never were."

He weighed it for a moment or two, then nodded, making up his mind.

"Okay, Mr. Strickland," he decided.

"Jonathan. I've been sleeping with your daughter, for Christ sakes."

He gave me that stare again. I gave it right back to him. I wasn't buying whatever he was selling and I wanted him to know it right up front. If he didn't like it, he knew where the door was.

"So I've heard." He seemed to relax. We both knew what it was to be a man. "But I didn't come here to talk about the two of you." He implied that would come later.

"Why are you here, sir? Why'd you come? You're risking a lot." If I opened the windows I knew we could hear the noise of the heavy equipment clearing the rubble not more than a half mile from where we sat. I had immediately volunteered my people for the job, but the feds had nixed my offer as quickly. They had said something about a conflict of interest. It didn't matter. I knew everything anyway. No suit and tie would stoop so low as to get their hands dirty clearing the site. Those guys were union, and I knew every last one of them. Maybe not by name, but I knew the site. I'd done a hell of a lot of building in New York. I had always paid everyone fairly, from the contractors on down to the little guy who operated the backhoe. They respected me for that, because they knew I respected them. I had never forgotten I wouldn't be here if it wasn't for the guy behind the shovel. So nothing was happening down the street I didn't know about five minutes later.

"Why don't you call me Gus?" For the first time the corners of his mouth turned upwards into what had to pass for a smile. It wasn't much. But right now it was a good beginning.

"All right, Gus," I emphasized his name. "My question stands. Why'd you come? You should have said no."

"Because we have a problem," he answered, "and you're not the only cowboy at the rodeo."

"I'd say that's the understatement of the year."

"You don't know the half of it."

"That almost sounds like a threat, Gus. Why don't you tell me?"

"First you've got to give me your word you won't repeat any of this discussion to anyone. Nothing we talk about today can leave this room. If you'll agree to this then we can move on."

"How do you know you can trust me?" I asked.

"You come with good references. My daughter tells me you're an honest man. Charlie's a good judge of character. She got that from me. I would like very much to trust you."

"All right," I conceded. "I'll agree. Nothing leaves this room. If things change, I'll run it by you before I open my mouth."

"I can live with that," Gus said. I was beginning to like him. Maybe he and Charlie weren't so different after all. Both were direct and both could let out a bit of seam without unraveling the entire cloth.

"We knew about your tower." He said it like he was telling me the temperature outside, like it was no big deal.

It took a moment for this revelation to sink in. In my mind I saw my friends toasting our arrival. Then I saw their smiling, laughing faces contort with the terrible realization that they only had a moment left to live. I shuddered. It must have been absolutely horrible.

I slumped into the chair opposite him. I was suddenly drained of all my strength. My head swam with confusion. I fought a sudden urge to throw up.

"You knew?" It was an accusation.

He held up his hand like a cop stopping traffic. "Not which tower. But we had picked up some chatter. The NSA advised us. We had been listening to some talk out of Syria. We only heard it once. Someone said something which turned out to be a confirmation."

"What'd they say, Gus?" My heart was racing.

He sighed. "We didn't have time to confirm it. I only learned about the conversation three days later, on Sunday."

"The day before," I stated flatly. "So why the fuck didn't you do something about it, then?"

"Our intel was too general. They never got specific. Only that the target was somewhere in New York. Everyone I know did everything humanly possible to stop it, Jonathan."

I knew he was right. I knew it was next to impossible to interpret what most of the time was coded, cryptic conversation picked up over the ether. Most of it would be bravado. When it wasn't bullshit, it was usually a couple of nuts: some wannabe zealot thumping on the Koran, or another McVeigh. We had a lot of enemies to keep track of, and thanks to some botched foreign policy we seemed to have fewer and fewer friends. Still, our guys were getting paid good money to stop this kind of shit from happening.

"Confirm it?"

"I beg your pardon?"

"You said you didn't have time to confirm it. The conversation?" I waited. I had sensed there were more details he didn't want to get into. But I also sensed he was on the fence about it. A part of him wanted to tell me.

"There was a letter," he admitted.

"The conversation you picked up in Syria confirmed the contents of that letter," I guessed. I watched him closely. I was looking for a flinch, a harder than normal blink, any tiny piece of body language which might tell me how hard I could press him before he clammed up. There was nothing. Gus was a pro. He would tell me, or he wouldn't. I still was wondering why he had agreed to meet me. Surely not because Charlie had asked him.

"Yes," he said. His voice was almost a whisper.

"When did you receive the letter?"

He swallowed half his Scotch before he answered me.

"We didn't. *The New York Times* did. It was more of a communiqué, a manifesto of sorts. *The New York Times* thought it prudent they contact us before publishing. We...didn't want a panic."

"So you asked them not to print it?" I guessed again.

"Let's just say we made them an offer they couldn't refuse. Everyone cheats on taxes."

"Not me. But that's beside the point. What was in the letter?" I urged him to continue.

Gus cleared his throat. He finished his Scotch. I moved to get him another. He waived me off and I sank back into my chair.

"The letter contained a list of demands. The final demand was for publication. They wanted 'to have a dialogue with the ordinary American people' was how they put it. They seem to think there is a difference between the American people and our government. They don't seem to understand we have elections."

"It's me and you now, Gus." I was suddenly pissed. "Tell me you don't really believe that horseshit. Tell me you know different, that you know the special interests have everyone on the Hill bought and paid for. I don't believe for one second you're that ignorant. And the last time I checked you weren't running for public office." I wasn't here to play games. He had to know that now, before we went any further. Maybe he and his boys could sell that one to the rest of the country, but my boys and I hadn't fallen off an American turnip wagon yesterday. There was what they fed to the masses, and then there was the truth. What was really going on out there was too ugly to look at. A little commercial here and there, usually disguised as the six o'clock news, had always proved more than enough to keep people afraid. I knew most people would agree to just about anything when they were afraid. "And you must realize by now I'm not a stupid man."

He nodded. "I apologize. Old habits die hard."

"Kill them, quickly. Or one of us is out of here." It wasn't what Gus was used to, but I figured neither of us had time to fool around. I was right. This time.

"It was not target specific," he began again.

"I believe you, Gus. How about the time?"

"When we first learned of their demands?"

"That, too. I was referring to when they would take out the tower, though."

He was nodding. "The manifesto, three months ago."

"You knew about this three months ago?" I was incredulous.

He ignored me. "As for when they would take out part of the skyline, they were very specific."

I recalled the alerts. Security around the country and especially in New York heightened to unprecedented levels. Everyone boarding a plane, bus, train – anything that moved – had been getting checked and rechecked. Someone had made the comment that lately we looked more like North Korea than North Korea did. I was beginning to agree with them. Seeing machine gun toting police blanketing New York City wasn't something I would soon get used to. If it was like this now, I reasoned, then where was it headed? Where would this madness end? Or would all we have to look forward to be more of the same? Certainly now, living here was more like living in an occupied city. That brought another disturbing thought to mind that I hoped wasn't true.

Gus continued, "And I'm afraid they were extremely accurate as well. We tried to stop it, but we were looking in the wrong places."

"I know."

Normally expressionless, Gus raised his eyebrows. "You know what caused it, then?" he surmised.

This time I sighed. "I've got a pretty good idea. We're running some tests on some steel and concrete fragments. We may know for sure in another day or two." I noticed his disapproval. Nothing the government didn't authorize was supposed to come off the site. I didn't care. I had my own agenda. "They were my friends, Gus. I knew them. Like you said, I'm just one more cowboy at the rodeo."

"You work fast, Jonathan," he conceded.

"I'm motivated," I said. "I can help."

"We said no."

"Yes, well, call someone who cares and then shove it up their ass."

"You could be charged," Gus pointed out.

"We're both on the same team, Gus." I pointed out the obvious. "My tower, my people. My fucking city."

Now he was shaking his head.

"I want to help," I said. "I'm an American, too, Gus. What has this country come to if you throw me in jail because I'm looking for the truth?"

"Leave it to the pros, Jonathan."

"I've never asked anyone for permission in my life, Gus. I'm not going to start now. Especially not now. Arrest me. I'll be out in an hour."

"Not under the new Patriot Act."

It wasn't a threat. It was a fact. Most Americans didn't know it, but the Act would do it. I could be taken away under suspicion. I wouldn't be allowed to see a judge, and I sure as hell couldn't talk to a lawyer.

"Try it," I dared him. "You'd be in more shit than me for just coming here."

"Remember that, and take a breath." His tone was sharp, but it softened as he continued. "I'm not the enemy, Jonathan. I want to help, too. You'll get your test results a full day before ours." His candor surprised me.

"I'll make you a deal," I said. "I won't get in your way if you don't interfere with what I'm doing."

"Two heads better than one?"

"Something like that."

"I have to be in that loop."

"That sounds like an order. I don't work for the government. It's one of the reasons we work faster."

"You're a loose cannon, Jonathan."

"I get results," I argued.

He agreed. "Yes, you do. At least that's one of the things my daughter told me about you."

"What else does she say about me?" I was filled with emotion. I wasn't thinking with my head now. Gus had baited me, and I had taken it. "In case you haven't heard, we haven't seen each other in three months. She moved out on me."

"You're seeing her later tonight. You've spoken with each other several times a day since your building collapsed." He read my thoughts. "It didn't come from her,

Jonathan. Get yourself another cell phone. Sometimes we can be fast, too."

"I'm a suspect? You think I'd bring down my own tower, people with it? You're all out of your fucking minds. No wonder you couldn't stop it. You're all too busy chasing ghosts." I was breathing hard and fast. I felt like hitting him. He suddenly smiled at me, a full and wide grin.

"You son-of-a-bitch." It dawned on me. "You've been gaming me, haven't you?"

"She also told me that sometimes you could be a real bastard."

"Is she putting that in the book?" I managed to ask him.

He shrugged. "I suppose that's up to her. And you. You're a bit of an enigma, you know. We dug up your gravesite, your past. All the stats are there. But I suspect Charlie knows more about Jonathan Strickland, the man, than anyone. You are one of the wealthiest people on the planet, and one of the most secretive. Quite frankly, when she first told me you'd agreed to the project, to allow her to write this book about you, I had my doubts. I thought you'd reconsider and back out of it."

"Yeah, so did I. But something funny happened on the way to the zoo," I said sourly.

"You fell in love with each other," he ventured.

"I fell in love with her. I'm not so sure about the other half of the equation, though." I never would have imagined I'd be talking about these kinds of private matters with him. But who better, I thought, than Charlie's own father? After all, this was the first time we'd spoken at length. I understood now why Gus did what he did. He was crafty. I thought I was going to learn some things from him. Now I began to realize it was the other way around.

He must have known about me running my own investigation into the tower's collapse. No one would ever learn which individuals were helping me; I had people everywhere. That's what money could do: I protected my sources, and they protected me. I was quite sure Gus, the NSA, Homeland Security – all of them – didn't care. They'd probably written me off as an amateur, an eccentric, or both. If I proved a liability, they would deal with me differently. What they had clearly failed to recognize, however, was how motivated I was. Never underestimate a man with a motive, I thought. Gus had already done so by telling me they had managed to locate and listen in on my calls, even though I'd replaced Gary's cell phone with another unlisted number that first night. I'd gotten Gary to take Charlie one as well so we could talk. Obviously it hadn't worked. In the future I'd know better. In their world a mistake like that might cost someone their life. I had to turn up my game, but that was okay by me. I was a fast learner.

"We've got more important things to worry about than my love life, though." I steered away from the topic of Charlie and I. "I want to know more about the letter to *The New York Times*, Gus. You said the letter, this manifesto, contained demands other than one about publishing it?"

"Yes. There was the usual rhetoric that comes with that sort of thing. Rambling, mostly. We're the infidels. They're not. We're all going to die. They're not. We took it seriously, of course, especially when it spoke of bringing down another tower. Sadly, it would appear we were no more able to stop them this time than we were the last time. The list of demands appeared at the end of the letter. There were three. Firstly, they called for the immediate forgiveness of certain international indebtedness."

"We did that with Afghanistan," I said.

"Correct. We pretty much had to in order to deal with the Taliban."

"Nothing like a fresh start. You might as well include Iraq, too. Neither of them worked."

"They listed countries. I could go on, but you get the drift. We've convened a think tank. It would never agree on anything, but it's normal to at least conduct a feasibility study into something like this. It keeps everyone fresh. We want our people on edge. Maybe we can learn something along the way."

I didn't say anything. My worst fears had just been confirmed.

"Their second demand was for the immediate release of all prisoners taken in the War on Terrorism. This would include virtually everyone at Guantanamo Bay."

"Did they specify?"

"Names? A few, yes. Places? Their knowledge was very impressive. They know more than we thought they knew."

"Let me guess." I followed a hunch. "They know about our private little air force. How we snatch certain individuals from around the world, drug them into oblivion, and toss them into the back of one of our Lear jets. They wake up in a secret location with a set of electrodes attached to their gonads."

"Far worse, believe me, Jonathan." Gus confided.

"And they knew the location of these little houses-of-horrors?"

"Some of them. Not all."

"You said three," I said.

Gus sighed. It was a rare display of emotion. He leaned forward in the comfortable green chair before he spoke. His voice sounded strained when he said, "They indicated certain individuals had been tried in absentia. These individuals had been found guilty of crimes against humanity. They were to be executed."

"Americans?" I managed.

Gus nodded. "They provided us with a short list, the President among them, as well as the VP and a number of other high-ups."

I was beginning to figure this out. "And the demand for the dialogue with the 'ordinary American people?' It wasn't a demand, was it, Gus?"

"No."

"It was an ultimatum: give them up or my tower's toast. Let me ask you a question, then." My eyes were on fire. "If you had let them, if they had been allowed to speak through the media..." I wanted him to finish.

"Jonathan, we did everything possible to stop –"

"Not everything, Gus." I snapped. "Those people, my friends, didn't have to die. If you had allowed these bastards to publish their diatribe – if you'd given them a voice – my friends would still be alive." I was breathing hard again.

Gus didn't answer.

"They wanted to talk, and you wouldn't let them. So they killed some of us. That about it? Another question: what happens next? And don't lie to me." I was fuming.

"Another letter," he allowed. "*The New York Times* got the e-mail yesterday. They'll print on Saturday."

"Or?"

He drummed his fingers lightly on the table.

I answered for him. "They take out another tower, right?" I suddenly saw why they needed me.

Gus stared.

"Only this time it involves a lot more people," he

finally volunteered.

"New York again?" I asked, calmer. One way or another we had to deal with what was now in front of us.

"They didn't say. We assume so. But not one."

"Excuse me?" I felt like I'd been hit in the head with a baseball bat.

"This time they said they would take out two high-rise buildings."

"When?" My voice was barely above a whisper.

"Publication on Saturday will buy us a month. I'll have that second drink now, if you don't mind."

Chapter 4

A sudden question brought me back to the present. It was Wallace the lizard again, calm as the eye of a hurricane. The ten other government agents were hanging on his every word.

"How many buildings do you own, Mr. Strickland?" His gaze was as casual as his question was loaded.

The answer to that question was the reason why they needed me. They absolutely didn't want me along for this ride, but they had no choice. By now all of us knew nothing had hit my tower. Like Gus had said, they got their test results a day after we'd gotten ours. No jet aircraft had slammed into it, no five-ton truck filled with fertilizer, nothing so obvious.

Our beefed up vigilance was working. We weren't asleep at the switches anymore. We were watching, listening, and in a twisted irony we were all a lot less free. We were catching some of them as a result. That's the main reason people were letting it happen. In theory, we could extract information from small fish who would lead us to the bigger sharks. We were into torture now. Murder, too. Whatever it took. It was them or us. At least that's how the lizard saw it. I wasn't so sure I agreed with him.

I attacked. "What brought down my tower?"

"That information is classified, Mr. Strickland." This from Gene Ambrosie, Special Assistant, Homeland Security.

"How many did you say, Mr. Strickland?" Wallace kept coming, referring to the number of properties I owned.

"I didn't." I looked from one to the other, then scanned the rest of them. My tower, my people. My fucking city. "How long are we going to dance? I don't know about you people but I've got a plane to catch. I'm not into bullshit. The only reason I agreed to this little confab was in the hope we could work together."

"We don't share information with the public in these matters, Mr. Strickland."

"National Security?" I was being sarcastic. They pretended not to notice.

"Something like that." Wallace was like a machine. He had ice in his veins. "Assets, Mr. Strickland?" His spook credentials were showing in spite of himself.

"You don't have to answer that," Gary jumped in.

I nodded my appreciation. "I know," I said.

"Mr. Stanick is correct, of course." Ambrosie confirmed. "We could reconvene in front of a grand jury if you wish."

"I wish." I waved off Gary, who was about to speak. "Therefore, since it's obvious we have nothing else to discuss..." I stood up and made a show of shuffling papers together in front of me. The room went silent. It wasn't going the way they had anticipated. I wasn't the kind of guy they could intimidate. I shoved some of the papers into my briefcase. Gary, too, was making a show of leaving. We had rehearsed this earlier.

"Perhaps we should begin again, Mr. Strickland." The voice was unfamiliar, imbedded among their team. I looked up, my hand in my briefcase. I feigned surprise. Inside I was smiling. The plan had worked. We'd just flushed out their boss.

"I'm not so sure I want to, Mr...?" I played hard to get.

"Smith," he said. "Derrick Smith."

"It seems to me we've got nothing to trade, Mr. Smith." For the moment I stopped stuffing my briefcase.

"Sit down, Mr. Strickland. Please." His voice softened slightly.

I hesitated, glancing at Gary, then shrugged. "I only have a few minutes," I checked my watch and sat back down. So did Gary. Everyone in the room sighed with relief.

"The tower that came down —"

"My tower," I corrected Mr. Smith. I knew my hand was filled with trump cards. I could use their blessing, but I was also confident I could do what I had to do without them.

"Your tower," he conceded, "was rigged."

"With high grade C-4 explosives. It was imbedded between the rebar in the foundations over a year ago, when we put them in."

"Is that a confession?" Wallace quickly jumped in.

I turned on him. "The only thing I'm confessing to, Mr. Wallace, is that I think you've got shit for brains. Our people have been murdered. More will be. We should be working together to try and stop it. All you want to do is find a scapegoat. Anyone will do, just so you can deflect the spotlight away from your own incompetence. You've been in the office too long. You've lost your edge. That little contract you and your knuckle-draggers performed for the agency in Damascus is old news." His eyes narrowed even more, causing them to appear closed. "Yea, I know all about that one. I know a little something about everyone in this room, in fact." A bluff. Gus had heard things, but Smith was still a mystery. He was a shadow who operated behind the scenes, brought in when they needed results. Like now.

"Don't look so stunned," I goaded. "I have more resources than you." I knew this wasn't entirely true. Money could buy information, most of the time. I was a delicate surgeon when it came to using a dollar, and I had them beat there. But I recognized I couldn't match their ruthlessness. I was convinced some of these spooks would be on death row somewhere if they hadn't picked up this gig with the government.

Some of them were sociopaths. I'd been told the stories. Gary had witnessed an interrogation in Bosnia. The spook had been slicing small pieces of flesh from his victim's chest and arms. It wasn't enough to cause the captive to bleed to death – they needed to keep him alive long enough to talk. But he didn't know anything, and that had presented a problem.

Gary had told me that even he couldn't stand it after a while. The victim was no more than a Serbian farmer who had wanted to be left out of the conflict. Too often, though, the conflict finds the innocent.

They had grabbed this guy in a sweep of his farm. The spooks had convinced themselves he was a go-between for the Serbian Army who gave away sensitive information responsible for American deaths. The spooks had used this perverted logic to intimidate Gary into compliance.

They'd gotten a national to do the actual dirty work, just in case it ever came back to haunt them. The interrogator had tried stuffing a wet cloth in the farmer's mouth to stifle his screams, but he somehow always managed to work it loose. After a while they knew he was innocent. But they also knew they couldn't let him go back to his wife and family. It was too late for that. Casually, like carving a turkey for Thanksgiving, the spook had finally drawn his ten inch blade across the farmer's throat. The guy gurgled and bled out. Gary had told me he had watched as the spook rinsed off the blade under the room's only tap. Then he went into the next room, where they'd been eating. He used the same knife to cut the cheese for his lunch. That, in hindsight, became a defining moment in Gary Stanick's life. Up until then he'd been a fairly regular guy. He'd had a propensity to see the good in people. So much so that he had volunteered six months of his time to help oversee the peace keeping efforts in Serbia. The up-close-and-personal encounters with the faces behind the stories brought out what he'd later call 'instincts'. He would remain a kind man, but now he understood and fully appreciated how malevolent the dark heart of man could be, and he conducted himself accordingly. He became more capable.

"I must say I'm impressed with the depth of your knowledge, Mr. Strickland," said Mr. Smith. "We may have misjudged you. You must want something. Do you want something? Yes, you must." Smith answered his own question, trying a new tact. "What is it you want, then, Mr. Strickland?"

"I want either for us to work together, or for you to stay out of my way. I've got some killers to catch."

"We want the same things, then," Smith continued. "Let's talk."

"I don't trust you." I stared directly into his eyes.

"Quite frankly, we don't trust you either." Smith's candor surprised me. "Jonathan...may I call you Jonathan?"

"I've been called worse. Go ahead. But are we getting somewhere?" I asked derisively.

He shrugged, feigning nonchalance. "Time will tell, don't you think?"

"Time is a luxury we can no longer afford." I pointed out the obvious.

"I see you know about the evening edition. What else do you know, Jonathan?"

"Why should I tell you guys anything?"

"Because we can arrest you. Now. If it suits our purposes." Wallace spoke again.

I ignored him. The threat was a tired old club. I knew they would have already used it if they felt it would have done them any good.

"No one is going to be arrested, Mr. Wallace," Smith instructed his minion. I glanced at Wallace. I could swear I saw him flinch, as if he'd been hit across the face. I got the feeling he wouldn't be saying anything else for the rest of the meeting.

"You must understand we always work on a need to know basis, Jonathan. It's best no one be aware of the entire situation. For reasons of security."

The vision of a farmer strapped to a bare metal chair in an interrogation room, bleeding out, came to my mind. He couldn't say what he didn't know.

"I understand," I began. "But you must understand I don't dance to your drummer. I'm a private citizen of the United States. You work for me, Smith. Not the other way around. I think you guys get that confused from time to time."

"Touché, Jonathan. But this gets us nowhere."

"You started it. You called me here. You want to change the rules of engagement? It's your move, Derrick." I waited, weighing my options. I knew he was doing the same.

Finally, after what seemed an interminable silence,

Smith turned to Wallace and said, "Mr. Wallace, why don't you give Mr. Strickland and me a few minutes." It may have sounded like casual politeness, but everyone knew it was an order.

"My staff and I will be down the hall if you need me," Wallace replied immediately, rising from where he sat. He and eight other people shuffled toward the room's only exit.

Suddenly Gary and I were in the room alone with Derrick Smith and one other person, a female. Her name was Maya Todos. She looked to me like a librarian. If she turned her head a little sideways, her thick glasses magnified her eyes until she looked like a goldfish. Appearances, though, could be deceiving.

"Ms. Todos is my personal assistant," Derrick Smith explained. "I confide in her."

I nodded. Everybody needed one.

"How much do you know, Jonathan?" he asked with a sincere face. He wore his hair short, in a crew cut. I guessed him in his mid to late thirties, well preserved. He looked after himself. He was slim and angular. When we'd been introduced earlier, I'd guessed his height at six-two, a couple inches taller than my own. Everything about him had seemed average, until I had looked past the obvious. Then, I realized, Derrick Smith was like a relaxed cobra. Get him riled up, and he'd be trouble. Still, in a pinch, I felt I could be trouble, too. In his case, I'd just as soon like to avoid the confrontation. I knew if it came down to some kind of matchup between us, things would get ugly. My advantage, if I had one, was the ounce of arrogance I'd seen in his eyes when he'd told Wallace to leave. It was his Achilles' heel. He underestimated Gary and I.

"As much as can be determined from the forensic

examination of the samples." I was cagy.

"So you know how they did it?"

"We know, yes," I conceded. "We know how. We know approximately when. I'm convinced in time we'll learn who as well."

"We looked for your log books, Jonathan." Smith was referring to the log books every construction superintendent was required to keep. These log books, if they were accurate, recorded every day's progress while a building was being constructed. Everything that happened, from site clearing to the cap ceremony was spelled out in detail. It was a diary. The main purpose was to match the actual work to the architect's critical path. If the diary stayed in sync with the path laid out by the architect during the planning stage, then chances were excellent the project would be completed on time. Incentives in the form of financial bonuses or penalties could be integrated into the construction schedule. By comparing the log books to the construction schedule, the owner – in this case me – could see at a glance if the project was on time. Smith had gone after the paper trail the day after my tower had collapsed not to see if we'd been on time, but to ferret out who the players had been. Who'd done the foundation work? Which companies were contracted? Who bonded them? Who leased them the labor? He needed to find anything that could lead to the identity of the brains behind what happened.

Because more destruction was coming. In a month two more rigged towers were coming down. Smith hadn't found anything. I was, above all, a privacy nut. There had been a small fire in our records department on Monday night which had conveniently destroyed all the hard copy records of my tower. We hadn't had time to put any of them on disc. That was our official story. I'd done this before they had tapped into the phones as well. I still had everything; they knew it and were furious. Wallace had mentioned the Grand Jury, and Smith knew I didn't care. Besides, it was my word against theirs. If they hauled me in front of the Grand Jury they would never learn a thing. I had a reputation and I could be very stubborn. There just wasn't enough time. The clock was ticking, and every second counted.

Smith had done his diligence. He knew the only way to those records was through me. I wasn't in the way, I just wasn't going to risk more lives. Our own lab was progressing at light speed and it already proved that someone had infiltrated the building and planted the C-4 when the foundations were going in. It was brilliant when I thought about it. They had destroyed the building before we'd even built it.

The explosive was like a cancer. No one knew it was there until it was too late. I had shivered when my lab guys had told me what they'd learned. If they had managed to rig my building, then how many others had been compromised? I could picture other hollowed out footings in other towers, filled with C-4 explosive, sleeping, waiting. Two next month. How many after those ones? We had to stop it. We had to work together, before it was too late.

Conceptually, it was possible they'd rigged a hundred buildings or more. We just didn't know. It had been many years since 9/11, and we'd stuffed that drain hole. It appeared they had found another way. I didn't like to think about stopping them the other way, by capitulating to their demands. Kill the President? Hell would freeze first. This was my country. Our country. We'd find them or we'd die trying.

"Yeah, I know about the log books. We had a fire in

our records section." I eyed Smith warily. Todos' eyes bulged at me through her coke bottle lenses. I felt like throwing some fish food her way. "We never had time to put them on disc. The contracts were with them. Check stubs, deposit slips, you name it. Everything was destroyed. There are no records, other than public, on that tower."

We both knew how easy it was for someone to forge adequate credentials in order to pull the permit necessary to put in the foundations. It would have been a cake walk to bribe someone at the Contractor's Licensing Board to type in a fake license. The rest would be easy. Whoever handled that job was no doubt gone or dead. By the time Smith found out, the two next towers would be history. Again, there just wasn't time. I looked at Smith. He stared at me, thinking.

"You win, Jonathan," he said matter-of-factly. "We could do this without you."

"Eventually," I gloated.

"I could probably throw your ass in prison for the rest of your life for this. I'm still thinking about it."

"We don't have the time," I said earnestly. "You might make it stick. I'd be willing to bet you'd lose. I'm not a millionaire. I'm worth billions. You can't fuck with people like me. We've got too much power. Meanwhile more people will die. None of us would benefit by such a clash of egos. Fortunately, there's another way."

"Terrorism makes strange bedfellows." He cringed at the admission.

"These are crazy times," I admitted. "But I don't see that we have any other choice for now."

"We're stuck with each other."

"Stuck is your word. I prefer to look at it differently. I think we can find these guys. But..." I paused to get his full attention, "Don't for one second take my kindness as a weakness."

"The little I've seen so far, that would be a mistake. I've clearly underestimated you, Jonathan. I used to think you rich fat cats had more luck than brains. Either that or you lied your way to the top."

"Or both." I smiled.

He smiled now, too. For the first time I began to think this might actually work. We could use my information, my mobility, and his resources. He had plants in most of the hot spots around the world. His eyes and ears were already in places I could never access.

"You would have made a good spook," he said.

"I still don't trust you, Derrick."

"Nor I you. It's the sign of a good spy. Now are you going to tell me what you know?"

I thought about it. "Yeah, some. I usually deal on a need to know basis," I gave it back to him. Before he could reply I said, "We're going in the same direction. Don't worry. I'll keep you informed, *if* you reciprocate. I will know if you lie to me."

"I have little doubt."

"Don't play me, Mr. Smith. Ever. If I for one second believe I'm not getting straight goods I'll pull the plug so fast you won't know it until it's too late."

"Agreed."

"Good. Now you tell me what you know. I'll fill in the blanks." I glanced at the design on the wall above him. From where I was sitting it looked more like a crown than the American Seal.

Chapter 5

I didn't tell Derrick Smith everything, but I didn't leave out much, either. I wager he did the same. I stalled him when it came to the tower's records, and stuck with my story about the fire destroying them. He grunted when I told him I was certain we could retrieve data from other areas that would match the destroyed information. He knew I had the originals. He also knew I was stubborn.

My logic was sound. We had to move quickly with the information we had. I figured if the government got involved they would only clog the works; they might even come to the dangerous conclusion they had enough to go it alone, and that meant I would be frozen out. As long as they needed me that wouldn't happen. It wasn't an ego trip on my part. I was confident that when it came to finding out who did it, I was the best man for the job. I'd been in the construction business most of my life, and I had learned it all from the best. Pop had taught me things most structural engineers wouldn't even know. I knew what to look for. If I needed any help, I could pick up the phone. In less than five minutes I'd have the best in the world on the other end.

I looked up from the log book. "Did you know someone died putting those foundations in?"

"Interesting," Gary said. "Doesn't surprise me, though. Who was he?"

"A guy named Mojab. He was in New York on a work visa from Israel."

Gary contemplated this for a moment. "Something doesn't fit."

"I'll say," I agreed. "Mojab is an Arab name. Find out what they did with his body. I'd bet last year's pay his death wasn't an accident. I'm sure Mr. Mojab wasn't alone."

"Family?" Artie McKenzie postulated.

"That, too. Maybe they're pissed off at Mr. Mojab's severance package," I said.

"They just might feel like talking," said Gary. "It's been over a year."

"If there's any family left to speak with," Artie said. "When it's all said and done, whoever these guys are, they're pros. I'm absolutely certain they would not leave any loose ends."

"That translates into no witnesses," Javier Gonzalez said.

All of us were in agreement. Apart from being the best demolition expert in the country, Artie was also street smart. We had first met twenty-five years ago. By the time Pop had reluctantly switched from knocking down old buildings with a ball and crane to using dynamite, Artie had already built a name for himself. At fifty-seven, he was thin and still a handsome ladies' man. He wore Versace and drank old, expensive wine. When he showed up on site, though, it was all blue jeans and business. He could blow a ball bearing off a baby's butt without waking it.

"I hope this works." He was talking now as he tampered with a projector, trying to hook a wire up so it would work. The screen was about ten feet in front of him. The light was working, but so far he hadn't been able to get a picture.

We were in a secured townhouse beside Central Park. It was big, with a floor area that exceeded twelve thousand square feet spread across three levels. We had moved my offices out of the fifty-seven story building on the Avenue of the Americas. Who knew what was coming down next. I'd crammed the executives and my office staff into every nook and cranny of the townhouse. There were some frayed nerves as people tried their best not to trip over one another. Everyone understood it was better than taking the chance of dying. It was Monday; a full week after my sixty-three story had been brought down. *The New York Times* had run the story, with the demands, in Saturday's evening edition. Thirty days didn't give us much time, not to mention what was in store after that. Everyone, moving companies included, had pitched in for the move from floor forty to the townhouse. We had begun last week, right after I'd met with Gus. Somehow we had managed. The basic infrastructure for everything from satellite communications to broadband had already been installed, so it became an issue of logistics more than anything else.

Artie swore, slapped his laptop, and a picture magically appeared on the screen. "There we go," he said, mollified.

"Good job, Artie." This from Tony Mourning, our erstwhile main floor security – the same guy who had earlier last week showed Gus the way to my office on the fortieth floor. The bulge under his suede leather jacket was barely discernible, I noticed with satisfaction. I couldn't even see anyone else's. We were all armed now. I carried two weapons: a Smith and Wesson thirty-eight in a shoulder holster, and a smaller twenty-two long around my ankle.

I had the townhouse swept for bugs twice a day. I'd done the third floor conference room a half hour ago. It had come up clean. I knew the spooks didn't bug offices much anymore, but if Smith and his boys were going to listen to us, they'd have to work for it.

"This is the original footprint of the tower," Artie said.

I recognized the old building Artie had demolished to clear the site. It was big and clumsy, twenty-two floors of a mix of office and records storage. I had bought it for the land. Artie clicked through a half dozen shots from different vantage points around the old landmark. He progressed into some shots of workers drilling horizontal holes through interior columns. A few shots of the basement, labor doing the same thing. A shot appeared of a concrete beam with what appeared to be a row of bird's nests running along an edge of it. The holes looked to be evenly spaced, six of them, each a foot from the next. Artie hesitated on this shot. Then he clicked the presentation pointer device once more. This time he could be seen in the image, pointing to the first hole. Its diameter was now scaled to his hand.

"All right," he said at last. His voice was low, belying his occupation. He sounded a bit like a bored college professor about to begin a lecture.

I leaned over and whispered to Gary, "Start with the Coroner's Office on Mojab. Soft pedal my name around."

Gary nodded his understanding. "They'll know where we're looking," he whispered back.

"That's the idea," I confirmed. I didn't know if it would work, but we had absolutely nothing to lose.

"As you can see," Artie raised his voice slightly, "the bore holes are drilled with a two and a half inch rotating jack hammer. Simple enough. We call them the hands that rock the cradle. In essence, they are sleeves for the explosives."

"How do you determine where to drill?" Javier asked.

"Experience, mostly. We find the soft spots and work our way out." Artie clicked through more shots. Most of them showed workers drilling more holes. He stopped on one showing a small group, himself among them, standing at a desk in the building's basement garage. Everyone was examining some large papers laid out across a drafting table.

"We were actually very fortunate. We found an old set of blue prints on a dusty shelf in what was once probably a caretaker's office. We were able to use these drawings to pinpoint the structure's weak points. The plans were dated nineteen forty-six, in case anyone is interested."

"What if you can't locate any prints?" asked Javier.

Artie didn't hesitate. "Like I said, most of demolition is about experience. Everyone works from precedence. The American Institute of Architects, or AIA, has been building upon the same standards they used before Christ. Of course they weren't called the AIA back then, but we use the same principles in construction now that they used to build the Pantheon. Columns supporting beams supporting floors, or some such variation. In the case of the magnificent architecture of the Coliseum, the columns supported the very distinctive front portico. Today those same columns, reinforced with steel, might support say, sixty-three floors. No offense, Jonathan."

"None taken," I waved it off.

"Today the math is superior," he continued. "We use computers to figure our load calculations on bearing walls. Bringing down a tower is about reversing the construction process. Think of it this way: If you stand up and put all your weight on one leg, I can tell which leg is supporting your weight by looking at the way you stand. If I go around behind you and suddenly kick you behind the knee of the leg that is supporting your weight, you're going down.

"A tower is no different. They're all built to the same mathematical specifications. Humans have a singular anatomy, towers have theirs. The rules of physics apply to both. There are no exceptions, unless, of course, you believe in miracles."

"Miracles don't pay the rent," I said flatly.

"No, they don't," Artie acknowledged. "Otherwise I would have used them by now." In spite of the somber mood we all chuckled. It relieved some of the tension. The room seemed to relax some. I felt better knowing I could put these people together as quickly as I had. My confidence grew every time I listened to them speak. This was another huge difference between my men and Smith's. My guys searched for solutions. I was convinced guys like Derrick Smith were far too busy identifying problems. That might be okay, unless you spent the other half of your time looking for someone to blame instead of trying to fix the problem. Artie clicked through a few more pictures. He stopped on one that showed him smiling, a switchbox held out in front of him like a prize cake at a bake sale.

"This lights the fire," he said almost reverentially. "All the holes have been drilled, and all the charges have been placed and are hot. When I press that green button you see right there, a current runs through the charges. All of them are set off within about a half second of each other. Hopefully, the building falls in on itself." He sighed. "Which brings me to my next point. Someone ask me what happens if either some charges don't fire, or are intentionally delayed."

"Please continue, Artie." I didn't like his tone.

"The building doesn't fall down, or worse."

"Worse?" Tony's curiosity was piqued. I already knew the answer. I had a sick, sinking feeling in my stomach just thinking about it.

Instead of saying anything, Artie suddenly lifted a rigid chair up onto the table. He placed it in such a way that one leg was suspended in the air a few inches away from the table. The remaining three legs supported the chair. Everyone watched him carefully.

"Presto! Instant high-rise," he said, gesturing to the chair as if he was some kind of magician. "Javier, would you hand me three or four of those books beside you, please? Yes, those will be fine, thank you. That heavy one, too."

One by one, Artie gingerly stacked the three smaller books onto the corner of the chair above the leg suspended over the floor. "And now for the coup de grâce," he said as he edged the fourth, heavier book into place on top of the others.

He didn't even have time to take his hand away as the chair collapsed out over the floor. It made a solid thumping sound when it hit. The books scattered onto the carpet around it. "I will explain what happened now," Artie left everything where it fell. "The chair, of course, was our tower; the table its pilings, footings, and maybe even a slab or two. The chair's legs were the tower's supporting columns. Pretend a charge had taken out the column which the leg not on the table represented. A controlled charge, if you will. Properly taken out, the chair – the tower – fell sideways. It hit the floor. Its direction of decent was predetermined by the placement of the charge." He was quiet, to drive home his point. The conference room was as silent as a morgue. The implications of what Artie had just explained were chilling. He continued.

"The chair is every building that's been rigged. Whoever did this is an expert. As good as I've ever seen. The first one, your tower, Jonathan, was only a warning. It was a calling card. My guess would be it was some kind of a warm up. A test, to see if what they've done would actually work. The tower came straight down. It collapsed in on itself. This would indicate a standard demolition. Equally spaced charges were placed throughout the foundations. No holes needed to be drilled because they planted the detonators with the explosives in the forms and then poured the concrete. Perfect. No one would ever know they were there, imbedded in the columns, until after the explosions, which were basically simultaneous. That's why the sixty-three floors came straight down, exactly like the Twin Towers. The structure failed everywhere at the same time. The second reason I think it was a test was because they did it to a new tower. It was all but empty, forgive me, Jonathan. I know you count your friends among the dead. I knew some of them, too. We've been going to the same memorials. But many more people would have perished if the tower had been occupied. As it was, the loss of life, fortunately, was limited. Next time, it will be far worse. Because the same way this chair tipped sideways, that may well be the way the next building comes down. And if that happens, there may be a domino effect. Conceivably we're talking what? An entire city block of Main Street U.S.A."

No one spoke. I'm sure in our minds everyone had the same mental picture. It was of a large metropolitan downtown area. Suddenly a massive explosion followed by one of the central area's giant towers falling sideways into the one next to it. Perhaps it would fall into another one across the street. That would give it momentum. That many millions of pounds of concrete and steel allowed to build up speed as it fell over the empty air of the busy street beneath it would give the building enough force that whatever it came into contact with would no doubt fall as well. Who knew when the carnage would stop? Even the worst quakes in California had not so far been cataclysmic enough to have tested Artie's scenario. How many would die?

"Can we x-ray concrete?" This from Tony, who'd let out a quiet whistle when Artie had spoken of how an entire city block might simply vanish in a heap of smoke and rubble and lots of dead people.

"I know where you're headed," I answered. "Theoretically, yes. From a practical standpoint."

"There isn't the time," Artie finished for me. "We use mobile x-ray units on our demolition sites all the time. It makes drilling those holes a lot easier when we go around the steel rebar rather than through it. But in this case?" He shrugged his shoulders in a gesture of defeat.

"We'll use it," I said. "We'll give that bone to Smith. It'll keep his people busy."

"Where will he start? Where will we start? Finding these guys is like finding a needle in a haystack." Javier sounded frustrated.

"Smith will start with the new towers. Everything that's been developed since 9/11," I said. "Size matters, too. Whoever is behind this has gone through a lot of trouble and expense. My guess is they've rigged only big ones. I think they've used local labor, especially here in the States. Larger developments have to use union workers in most places. Even in right-to-work states labor on the kind of scale needed has to be organized. I think we should be looking for bodies; deaths which occurred in the early stages of construction."

"When the foundations were going in," Tony said. "Makes sense."

I agreed, "That's their window of opportunity. It's the only time the buildings are truly vulnerable. It's the front end of the project where the least number of people are involved. If anyone tripped across someone inserting the C-4, they would have been eliminated."

"Mojab," Javier reiterated.

"A very dead Mojab," said Gary.

"Mojab was one of them," I said. "I'm convinced he was with them. It's too much of a coincidence that he was here on an Israeli work visa. Think about it. He was an Arab. I'm not buying any other explanation."

"So they made their first mistake," said Tony.

"Maybe," I said. "We'll follow it up. That's your job, Tony. Let me know as soon as you find out anything. It's a lead. Also," now I turned to Praveen Chirumamilla, the Empire's IT architect, "I want you to scour every database you can get into, Praveen. Find any new tower constructed after 9/11. Make sure it's more than..." I hesitated, looking at Artie.

"Make it anything over thirty floors," he jumped in. "I'd say more, but we might miss something."

I nodded and turned back to the soft-spoken computer scientist. He was from Bangalore, India. He'd gotten his Masters at Berkeley. Gates had grabbed him even before he'd gotten out of school. After that, he'd become a busy genius. His reputation and marks had been off the charts. I'd managed to steal him several years later. I'd offered him complete autonomy and let him bring his friends along for the ride. It was what had finally changed his mind. He didn't need the money. By then he was already worth a few million.

"Anything over thirty floors," I repeated.

Praveen, who hadn't said one word until now, spoke softly. "Yes, Jonathan. How large must the city be?" His question was insightful.

"Search the fifty largest cities in America. Unfortunately, the rest of the world will have to look after itself. If we find anything concerning another country, we'll turn it over to Smith or Gus. We've only got so much time. Once we have a compilation of every tower over thirty floors built since 9/11, we'll work backwards, starting with the smallest. We'll probably be able to eliminate over half the towers immediately because of logistics."

"What about the ones constructed before 9/11?" asked Tony.

I was shaking my head. "Necessity is the mother of invention. After we beefed up airport security, they found another way. I think our tower proved that. It wouldn't have occurred to them before 9/11. Or if it did, they had an easier way that they decided on. Airplanes filled with jet fuel. This took more planning, more time. They didn't do this before the Twin Towers. I'm certain of it."

I turned my gaze back to Praveen. "Look for a central database. I'm sure one exists. New construction starts are forwarded and compiled into statistics that help determine the growth of our GDP. Do you think you'll be able to get behind it?" He knew I was referring to the firewall securing the government's database.

Praveen quietly replied, "I have friends who wrote the codes for the applications concerning these areas for the American Government."

"Did anyone from India *not* write our codes?" I asked in mock seriousness.

It brought a grin to his cherubic countenance. "Outsourcing, Jonathan. Thanks to this wonderful land of opportunity we now have a middle class. We are very grateful to our American friends."

"Maybe I should pay you in rupees."

His grin grew wider. He said, "I will have the information in a few days. Perhaps a week at the latest. I may need to trace the federal files back to their point of origin." He was referring to the planning departments of the counties which would have issued the building permits for any new tower construction.

"Do it anyway," I instructed him. "That way we can check the local coroners' offices for any deaths that may have occurred while those buildings were under construction."

Praveen nodded his compliance.

"What about us?" Gary asked about himself and Javier.

"Pack," I said.

"Are we going somewhere?" Javier asked, not surprised.

"Damascus," I said. I checked my watch. "We fly out in four hours."

Chapter 6

I left everyone in the conference room. They knew what had to be done. Normally, Gary would be responsible for arranging the away team that would receive us when the jet landed overseas. This time I told him to leave it alone. I wanted anonymity. The fewer people who knew our movements, the more I felt we could accomplish. Sheila Collingsworth, my executive assistant, was uncomfortably crowded into a cramped corner of the second floor of the townhouse. "Any calls?" I asked her, leaning through the door of her makeshift office.

She peered over the bridge of her horn rimmed glasses and smiled when she saw me, in spite of what we'd all been through the last week. I appreciated her immensely. She insulated me from the insanity.

"You want the short list?" She asked. Sheila's stolid control in the midst of the chaos around us amazed me. She not only represented the epitome of composure, but demanded it from everyone in the office who came into contact with her. She was ten years older than me; I wasn't running a beauty contest. I had hired her a dozen years ago for her competence. Sheila may have looked to some like a matronly librarian, but she brought that much more class to the Empire.

I nodded. "That would be nice." I smiled my thank you.

"Derrick Smith, Gus Bakersfield, and Charlie Bakersfield, plus about fifty more calls and an equal number of e-mails since you last checked with me yesterday. I've catalogued them in descending order of importance for you, all according to the instructions you left me with last week."

"When did Charlie call?" I had my own order of importance.

"Twenty minutes ago." Sheila's brow furrowed as she re-read her own printout. "She said she'd be waiting for you under the moon, if that makes any sense."

"Thanks, Sheila. It does." I knew exactly what Charlie meant.

"She didn't leave a number."

"She wasn't supposed to. Call David Atwell. Ask him to meet us at the airport..." I glanced at my watch again. It was already four o'clock. "At nine sharp." I added an hour's margin for the always unexpected. "Tell him to have the Gulfstream fueled and ready to take off, and that I said to top off the gas tank. That's all I want you to say."

"Gotcha, Jonathan. Anything else?"

"Are you religious?"

"I go to church," she conceded.

"Then a prayer or two wouldn't hurt. Shuffle all those messages to Gregory. Tell him I said he's officially in charge while I'm away." Gregory Tenille was my Senior Vice President of Marketing. "Just give me Smith's and Gus's numbers. I'll call them on the run."

"Where are you going?"

I sighed. "Into the lion's den. I'll call you from time to time on the satellite phone. It's the most secure line we've got. Be careful what you say if we talk. They'll probably be listening."

I turned to leave and she called me back. "Jonathan?"

I looked at her. Her eyes were worried. Like a mother's eyes, I thought. Something tugged at my heartstrings.

"Be careful."

I smiled reassuringly. "Yes, always. Now I really must be going."

She shooed me away.

I passed four people on my way out. One was our doorman, the other three blended into the scenery near the front portico. I only saw them because Tony had mentioned them to me yesterday. One looked like a hundred other tired salesman, the other two had squeegees in their hands. Anyone who watched these two closely would have noticed them spraying the ground floor windows with a bleach solution. Then, bored, they would tiredly wipe the windows clean. But they kept doing the same windows over and over again, making sure they worked opposing ends of the front entrance to the townhouse. The doorman was where you'd expect, at the door, in the middle. The salesman trolled up and down the two hundred feet of the townhouse's front facade, trying to look busy. He carried a black briefcase. Good. I was satisfied. Tony had done well. I felt the people inside were safe. I wouldn't put anything past the people who were responsible for the turmoil around us.

I walked briskly south down Fifth on the wide sidewalk across the street from Central Park. I couldn't help but notice the fear in the normally complacent eyes of my fellow New Yorkers as I passed them. It was almost something I could touch. Everyone felt it. It hung in the air like noxious fumes. I gazed upwards to the tops of the skyscrapers further down the street. Would it be one of these? Two of them? Which ones? Thank goodness not anything older than 2001, I thought wryly. No more jet airplanes exploding into fireballs, thank you ma'am. I picked up my gait, and leaned into the slight breeze. The sun was beginning to slide behind the towers, engulfing Manhattan in a gray twilight. A faint haze hung in the air. Winter was knocking on the door.

I hurried. Charlie was waiting.

The Moon was a hole-in-the-wall restaurant Charlie and I frequented when we wanted to be alone. As I opened the spring-loaded door and entered, silver and gold chimes in the shape of tiny crescent moons hanging over it announced my arrival. The eatery was long and narrow. I spied Charlie sitting in a booth near the back. She smiled and waved at me. I made my way over to her. I passed a dozen or so checkered cloth-covered tables hugging the wall to my left and shuffled in opposite her.

"Hi," I said. I leaned across the table. We kissed and I looked into her eyes. She probably looked better than I did. Gus had been right about us meeting last week. We had slept together again for the first time in a long time. I bet the government didn't know about that one.

"Hi." Her voice was almost a whisper.

"You were wrong, Charlie," I said seriously. She raised her eyebrows, and I smiled. "About me not needing anyone," I answered her raised eyebrows. I smiled, and said, "I'm glad you called me. Right after it happened, I mean. Your timing was perfect. I...I've been having nightmares." I don't think there was anyone other than her I would have admitted it to. Not even a shrink.

She reached across the narrow table and pressed my hands between hers. "I know. I heard you talking in your sleep. But it's okay to be scared. It's..." She searched for a word. "Natural. I'd be worried if you didn't have any nightmares. Don't worry. They'll go away."

I swallowed hard, more because she understood. "These ones are bad, Charlie. I'm afraid to fall asleep. They're like ghosts. I see all the people I knew up there on the roof. Only they're not waving, like when we first saw them. They're pointing at me. It's like they're accusing me. And then I start to wonder about everything." I held up my hand to stop her from interrupting me. "I could have stopped a long time ago, Charlie. I had more than enough. Pop left me everything. I could have stopped back then. I don't even know how much money I've got. Everybody knows how much they're worth. Everyone." I didn't even notice I had raised my voice. "But I don't. All I do is buy more land. Build more buildings. Those people – my friends – would still be alive if it wasn't for me. Am I that greedy? Have I become someone I don't know? This morning I asked myself who I was and I couldn't come up with an answer. And now what? I want to find out who did it. Then what? Turn them over to the authorities? What if I can't do that? What if circumstances aren't so convenient as to allow that? These people won't come gift wrapped, that's for damn sure. What do I do then? Kill them? To appease my guilt? Who the fuck am I becoming, Charlie?"

"Stop it," she cried. "Stop right now, Jonathan."

For the first time since I'd sat down the silence allowed me to listen to my own breathing. It was fast and labored. As I listened I suddenly realized this whole thing might be affecting my judgment. I squeezed Charlie's hands between mine. "Please don't leave me. I do need you." I breathed deeply, trying desperately to force myself back under control. She squeezed my hands back.

"I'll always be with you, Jonathan." She looked from one eye to the other, and back. "It's natural. Everything you feel now is normal. Think about what's happened."

She sighed. "Guilt is a powerful force. Sometimes it makes us do things we'd never dream we're capable of doing. Good things and bad things. In the end history will be the judge of our actions. But during the process of living we're always our own worst critics." Her voice softened as she felt me relax. "You can quit any time. You can walk away free and clear. No one would blame you for anything. You don't owe anyone. You had nothing to do with those people dying. Do you understand me?"

I took a deep breath and let it out real slow. After what seemed a long time, I nodded.

"Good," she said. "Because if you can't, it will eat you up from the inside out. Yes, some of those people on top of that roof were your friends. I'm sure if they could talk to you right now they would tell you the same thing I'm telling you. It wasn't your fault. You had absolutely nothing to do with it, and if you decided to leave it in the hands of people like my father, that would be fine. Justice is ultimately in the eye of the beholder."

I nodded again. I knew she was right. The decision was mine to make. I had the means and the God-given abilities to right this wrong, perhaps even to prevent others from dying. But I knew in my heart there was a fine line between justice and vengeance. It was a line I never wanted to cross. I guess that's why I needed Charlie; maybe she was my conscience. I knew what my guts told me, and I didn't think I could do this without her. Unfortunately to involve her was to endanger her, and that was the last thing I wanted to do.

There it was, finally. Now I knew why I'd been so troubled. That was why everyone in my nightmare kept pointing at me. They were already gone. I knew by pursuing this there was a chance I'd join them, but, God, not Charlie. I absolutely could not do that. Yet I needed her. I sighed again, suddenly drained of every ounce of my strength, and slouched back against the booth's orange leather covering. "I'm going out of town for a while."

She said nothing, waiting for me to continue.

"Gary and some other people are going with me." I left it at that.

"I'm not sure if I like the sound of this." Her voice sounded brittle, like thin ice cracking. "Where?"

"Syria. Damascus. Someone died when the foundations for the sixty-three story were going in. I think he might have been murdered. At the very least, I think there's a connection between his death and what happened at the cap ceremony."

"And you think it's from the Middle East?" Charlie picked up on my theory.

"Yes. I think so. The dead man's name was Mojab. He was here in the States on a work visa. There's nothing odd about that, until you look behind it. It's an Arabic name."

"So?" she said. "A lot of Arabs work here. That doesn't make him part of some shadowy terrorist organization." She was not in a hurry to start accusing anyone. Neither was I, but I couldn't ignore the facts, either.

"He was here on an Israeli work visa. Not to mention the fact he worked on the front end of that tower. And he ended up dead."

"Why would they kill one of their own people?" Charlie asked. "If, for the moment, we assume your theory is correct."

"If I knew the answer to that question, I wouldn't be going to Syria. I know I could be dead wrong about this, but I think it's worth a trip over there. There's too much at stake not to at least take a closer look. If I'm wrong we've lost nothing, and I'll have some time to think on the way over there. The Gulfstream is fully equipped with all the modern amenities as far as electronics go. It's a mobile office and one of the quietest jets built. The remote access is incredible. We're running down Mojab's family. If he's got one, we'll find out who they are and where they live before I'm halfway across the Atlantic. My computer guys will bounce all the information off a satellite in an encrypted transmission. We'll decode all the communications on our side of the firewall. If anyone's listening, they'll hear baby talk. We've got to go after them, it's the only way. They'll never come out of hiding unless we flush them out."

"What if they are here in the U.S.? What if they have already been given orders to destroy more of the rigged super-structures? Wouldn't that be more logical, instead of having to wait for more instructions? What I mean is what if the people in charge were caught or killed? Then who would give the orders? If I was in charge I'd make sure that if I died it wouldn't matter. I'd make sure ahead of time that the plan would still proceed without me."

"Normally I'd say you'd be right. But in this case, I don't think so. I think there has to be a way of stopping it all if we capitulate. I think they honestly believe they can win this."

"By killing the President?" She was stunned. "Jonathan, they can't possibly believe for one second the U.S. would ever even think to meet that demand. They can't be that crazy."

"Crazy has nothing to do with it," I said. "It's the one big mistake the West has always made whenever we've tried to figure out what makes these bastards tick. They have an entirely different mindset than we do. They kill – they die – for their beliefs. We kill and die for money. Life here on earth just isn't as important to them."

"We believe in freedom," Charlie protested.

"Yeah," I said. "The freedom to run roughshod over any country whose resources we covet. If we're so idealistic why didn't we stay in Somalia? It became apparent it wasn't in our national interest to be there in the first place. In other words they didn't have anything we either wanted or needed. Iraq, on the other hand, did. A few thousand lives are cheap compared with seventy-five dollars a barrel."

I didn't like hearing my own words, but I was a billionaire many times over. I knew the power and influence money had over most people. In my experience it seemed the more people got of it, the greater their lust became. We went into Iraq and we never gave a shit about their arms caches until after the hostilities were pronounced over. It only became an issue when our men and women became targets again with those same explosives. The whole thing made me sick to my stomach. The only secure ordinance in Iraq was the pipeline.

When I thought about it, a part of me couldn't fault the bastards who were continually trying to blow it up. I probably would've done the same thing if I'd been one of them. I guess they figured if they couldn't keep their oil, then we sure as hell weren't going to have it. The whole mess became a constant tangled web of deceit and misinformation, and as always those too ignorant to see it for what it was kept paying the steepest price.

"Sometimes you've got a terribly cynical view of the world, Jonathan." I could tell Charlie was getting pissed. I didn't have time for it. I had a plane to catch, though it didn't sit well with me. I knew the moment I boarded the G550 there was no turning back. I'd be at thirty-one thousand feet, heading across a vast ocean toward my destiny at close to six hundred miles an hour. The thought of walking away crept into my mind again. I shoved it back. These were my friends. This was my country.

Sometimes it makes us do things we'd never dream we're capable of doing. Charlie's words. She was right.

"I'm going with you."

I heard the moon chimes jangle as someone either came or went.

"What? No, that's not going to happen. It's far too dangerous. These people play for keeps." I shuddered to think what might happen if Charlie was caught in the crossfire.

"Are you forgetting who my father is?" she demanded. "This is my fight, too."

"We don't even know if there's anything to this Mojab connection. It could be nothing."

"And it could lead to the people responsible."

"No," I said again. "It's far too dangerous. I won't allow it."

"You won't allow it?" She was incredulous. There was fire in her eyes. I had never seen her like this. "Fine. It's your jet." She scrambled out of her seat and stood up beside the booth.

"Charlie, sit down."

She glared at me.

"Please," I softened my voice.

"Why? You're off on your own again. You've just proved what I've been saying all along. You don't need me. Not for anything of consequence. You sleep with me, that's all. You make me feel like a whore."

I reached for her. She jerked back.

Was I really treating her like she said?

Perhaps I understood her perspective. I just wanted to protect her. I feared she didn't grasp the full implications of what lay ahead.

Then I listened to myself think. I sounded like her father, not her partner. Life and love were about sharing. I knew this. If I didn't allow her on the plane with me I knew that would be it. She'd given me a second chance and I loved her all the more for it. Ironically, this tragedy had brought us back together.

I feared my concern for her safety would impede my judgment along the way. If I stuck to my guns now, I also knew she'd walk out of this greasy spoon diner and I'd never see her again. Then what?

"Okay" I said quietly.

Chapter 7

The synchronized humming of the twin BR 710 Rolls Royce engines had long ago faded into the background. We were a little better than four hours out of New York, just after two in the morning. I was wondering if maybe I had made a mistake when the call from Praveen came through.

"I didn't know if you would be sleeping." The satellite relayed the audio-visual stream in real time, and his voice was crystal clear. I looked directly into his eyes as we spoke. He might as well have been sitting across from me.

"The others are." I glanced around the cabin, and my eyes came to rest on Charlie. She had reclined her chair into a makeshift bed and covered herself with a blanket. The plasma screen cast colored shadows across her peaceful face. She looked like a sleeping angel.

"No luck on my part, though." I closed the laptop I'd been working on. "I've been thinking too much. That's not good for sleep. What have you come up with?" I shifted in the soft leather of the captain's chair and glanced into the darkness out of the window nearest me. It was a clear night across the Atlantic. The stars were beautiful pinpoints of light in an otherwise pitch black sky.

Praveen's voice brought me back into the cabin.

"Something interesting. And, I'm afraid, something disturbing as well."

I sighed heavily. "My theory was correct, then."

Praveen said, "Even invisible people leave footprints."

I became aware of movement in the cabin and looked up. Gary and Javier hadn't been sleeping after all. I motioned for them to join me. Javier stifled a yawn, but Gary looked as if he'd gotten a solid eight hours and just finished his morning coffee. He, like me, only needed a few hours a night to refresh himself. I nodded to the empty leather chairs on the other side of the small oak table, then pulled off the headset and punched the speaker button on the conference console. Hopefully, we wouldn't wake Charlie.

"...correlated with the permits," Praveen's voice wafted into the air. "The Workers' Compensation records were then matched to the locations where the accidents actually occurred. I was able to then determine if it was new construction. Mr. Bakersfield was able to help me by providing access to these records through the Homeland Security Department.

"What about rehabs?" Gary asked, now seated opposite me. He had picked up immediately on the content of our discussion.

I was already shaking my head. "In theory it's possible I suppose, but not likely."

"I still think they were only concerned with new construction. It's simpler to plant the C-4 before the concrete is poured into the forms. It is perfectly malleable. The C-4 can be made to look exactly like a part of the natural form casing, color and all. You heard what Artie said. Drilling into hard concrete would take forever. They'd run into all kinds of problems, like hitting rebar, for instance. There'd be more people on site then as well."

"Let's assume you're right," Gary chimed in. "One thing still puzzles me. You've got what? Twenty, maybe thirty guys screeding that concrete?"

"Not everyone works on the pour." Javier was suddenly involved. All appearances of his earlier weariness had vanished. "Even if twenty cement mixers are lined up for a unipour – that's when an entire floor is poured with concrete at once: columns, beams and all. I started on those sites when I first came here from Mexico. My first job was tying rebar. Then I'd screed the concrete after it was pumped into the forms. You might have twenty-five guys, but only eight or ten of them will be in the vicinity of where you're pumping concrete."

Gary picked up where he'd left off. "Okay, let's say ten guys, then. My question is how do you do it? How does someone plant C-4 explosives next to rebar without at least someone seeing it? Especially if they placed it in a number of new towers. Someone had to have seen something. Someone would have to know."

Javier responded, "They probably used casual labor. Most Mexicans know how to work with concrete. There isn't a lot of wood in most parts of Mexico, so out of necessity they learn how to build using cement. It would have been easy to locate highly trained crews. If someone wanted to use only illegals, it would have been easy to find them. They'd be paid in cash. Then they would either move onto the next project or simply disappear. If anyone had seen anything, they wouldn't say a word. They send most of that cash back home. They've got families back there who count on it. No one here illegally would risk deportation."

"That's *if* anyone saw anything." Gary now understood.

I said, "My guess would be if that happened, whoever saw something probably ended up dead. Who's going to give a rat's ass about a dead illegal with a heroin needle conveniently stuck in his arm?"

"No one," said Javier knowingly. "At least not until towers start coming down. And even then, very few would ever make the connection."

"No one but Praveen," I said.

"It was your idea." Praveen passed back the compliment.

"How many bodies?" I asked him.

"Since 9/11 there have been fourteen-thousand, nine-hundred and seventy-one accidents that have resulted in claims with various workers' compensation boards. Deaths resulted in four-hundred and seventy-three of those claims. I factored in the construct variables we discussed, and added some on my own: that they died within twenty-four hours of their accidents, that they never regained consciousness during that time —"

"Meaning they were never able to tell anyone what they saw," Gary added.

"And, most importantly," Praveen continued, "they had to be employed during the initial phase of the new construction."

"The foundations," I said.

"Yes," he affirmed. "Records for illegals, unfortunately, were all but non-existent. Some injuries were reported, but I could find no recorded deaths."

"Makes sense." Javier's voice contained an edge of melancholy.

"Sixteen died under our construct," said Praveen. "One, as you already know, was Abdul Mojab. He was the only man who was ever killed on one of your development projects, Jonathan. I checked. I'm sorry, I hope you don't mind that I did this. I thought you might find it interesting."

My mind was racing. "Good work. I won't ask you how you did it. I'll simply thank you."

"You are welcome. As I said, Mr. Bakersfield's help was invaluable. I believe he can be counted on as an ally. Oh, one more thing. I almost forgot."

"We're listening."

"I was able to check on the movements of Abdul Mojab's body for you."

"Wasn't he buried in the States?" asked Gary.

"No. Not here. The body was shipped overseas. You were right, Jonathan: it was sent to Damascus. The curious thing is not so much where it went, although that proved most difficult to trace."

"Someone didn't want anyone to find out where it was going," I guessed.

"It would seem so, yes. They went to great lengths and spent a great deal of money to hide its movements after it left the coroner's office. But they are not the only ones who have a great deal of money. So we were able to trace the body's movements after it left the morgue in New York. It was shipped to Syria on a commercial aircraft and received in Damascus by the Syrian authorities."

"Why do you suppose the Syrians would be interested in the body of a construction worker in New York on a forged work visa from Israel?" I threw out. Inside, I was doing cartwheels. We had confirmed our first solid lead. My theory had suddenly grown legs. But the surprises weren't over.

"Not necessarily the Syrian government, Jonathan. The remains were transferred in Damascus to a private jet. The aircraft which received Mr. Mojab's remains in Damascus was registered in Saudi Arabia to a member the

Saudi Royal Family. The body was flown home, to Riyadh. So far, I have been unable to track it after the plane landed at King Khaled International. I will keep trying."

"I think I can help." I realized the time had come for a direct call to Derrick Smith. "I'll call Smith at Homeland Security."

"As I recall he wasn't too co-operative at our last meeting," Gary said. "He and his kiss-ass flunkie, what's his name?"

"Clifford Wallace," Javier reminded him.

"That's the asshole," Gary said. "Two peas in a pod as far as I'm concerned; I got the impression Gus Bakersfield isn't his boss either."

"Wallace is horizontal. He's high up the chain of command. He's got parody with Gus. They both report to the Chief, and the Chief deals directly with the President. Wallace is on the technical side of Homeland Security. He's in charge of their gadgets," I explained. Gus had in turn explained all of this to me. He didn't particularly enjoy Clifford Wallace's company, either, but he'd been forced to work with him.

Wallace had started out as a field agent for the CIA. He'd been promoted from there to work as a handler. When the President had formed the new Agency, Wallace had gotten the nod. He was considered a techno-wunderkind. These skills, coupled with a reputation in the field as a guy who could get the job done, had earned him a James Bond reputation – only it seemed that no one liked him. They tolerated him because he was skilled at what he did. Now we needed him.

"I'll call him," I said to Praveen. "I'm almost certain he'll provide us with pictures. I know we had a bird over Syria when that body changed planes. I also know it recorded the transfer on the ground in Riyadh. It wouldn't have meant anything then, but our guys would have kept the images. They would have a keen interest in anything that resembled a coffin. Munitions are shipped in similar containers, so are drugs. It's something we would want to keep an eye on."

"Will the resolution be good enough?" Javier asked.

Gary looked at his friend and smirked. "Our high-resolution cameras can count the number of camel patties in the middle of the Arabian Desert, Javier."

"At night," I added. I glanced out the window into the star-filled void. It went on forever. No one was beyond the new age of high tech surveillance, I thought ruefully. Even now, I had little doubt we were being observed as we crossed the great expanse of the Atlantic Ocean. I turned back to the screen.

"I'll have Wallace send you the satellite images, Praveen. Let me know the instant you have more information. I want to know the final resting place of the enigmatic Mr. Mojab."

I punched the conference exit button. The two foot image of Praveen vanished from the screen. I leaned back in my chair and looked across at Gary and Javier. They were clearly perplexed. To me everything was beginning to make a lot more sense. I smiled; feeling better knowing my guess had been at least halfway right. Riyadh was a curve ball, but one I could live with.

"I don't get it." Gary was the first to speak. "What the hell is going on? How did you know?"

"About Riyadh? I didn't. At least not for certain. That Mojab was from the Middle East? Absolutely. Do you think I'd waste this much fuel on a flight of fancy?" I smiled again.

Gary and Javier traded glances. Both of them had question marks across their faces.

"Access, gentlemen. It's all about access: who gets to go where, when, and for what reason."

I could see they weren't following my line of thinking. I felt a bit like Sherlock Holmes explaining the crime scene to Dr. Watson. I got serious.

"We know this has been put together by some well-heeled, ruthless professionals." I retrieved a colored printout from the floor on my side of the table and spread it out in front of them. It was a map of the United States.

"While you guys were sleeping, I got this transmission from Praveen." They both leaned forward. Carefully, they began to examine the map. "If you look closely you can see circles around ten of America's largest metropolitan areas. Here..." I began to point. My finger worked its way from the west coast all the way across the map to New York. "The sixteen bodies were found in these cities. Praveen was able to determine these men died working on the foundations of a total of thirteen of the newest, largest towers in the country. He's compiling the coroners' reports of each of their deaths. We'll have them before we land. My guess is most of these so-called accidental deaths will be suspicious at the least."

"They took out witnesses," said Gary.

"Probably," I concurred. "Or people who were used and no longer needed. No one will ever prove it, either way. But I think we'll find Mojab is the one who doesn't fit. How many of these guys' remains do you think get sent back to their royal relatives in the Saudi Kingdom?"

"Who was Mojab, then?" Javier asked.

"Who was Mojab?" I repeated softly. "That's what I've been asking myself ever since I found out about him. One thing I do know is that his name sure as hell wasn't Abdul Mojab."

There was a soft rustling sound behind us. Charlie had turned in her sleep. I lowered my voice, and continued.

"I think he had access. I think he knew the people who planned this. And I think he was sent over by some very powerful people."

"Why?" asked Gary.

I shrugged. "I don't know. At least, I don't want to commit one-hundred percent to my theory. Not just yet."

Gary eyed me. He knew me better than that.

"I've got a couple of theories," I admitted. "First is to check on their progress."

"That doesn't make any sense," Javier pointed out. "Why would they murder one of their own people?"

I nodded. "I reasoned the same thing earlier, and that lead me to my second, more plausible theory."

"Please continue," Gary said.

I looked from one to the other. "I think whoever this guy was, he was sent to stop them. I think that whoever started this thing changed their minds halfway through and ordered it stopped. Things got out of hand. For whatever reason they didn't want to stop it. Maybe they couldn't, or just wouldn't. I think Mojab may have been an assassin. I don't think we'll ever know for sure. But I think he was sent to the States to take someone out. Someone who'd gotten out of control. Someone who thinks what they're doing is worth a whole lot more than what it started out being worth."

"They're not asking for money, Jonathan," said Gary. He was referring to their manifesto in *The New York Times*.

"More can refer to something other than money," I pointed out. "Keep in mind, it's just a theory at this point. So far we haven't proven anything."

"It's a damn good one, though." The voice was female. I looked over Javier's shoulder and smiled at Charlie's open eyes.

"Good morning. How long have you been listening?" I asked. My watch read half past three, New York time. The sun was already coming up over the Atlantic Ocean.

"Long enough." Charlie smiled back at me. She sat up, shivered slightly, and retrieved the blanket, pulling it around herself. "Who wants coffee?"

The best offer we'd had all night.

"I'll wake the steward." I reached for the button to page him.

"No," Charlie said quickly. "Let him sleep. I can't. Not after what I've just heard." She shuddered again, rising. "Keep talking. I know where the galley is. I'll be right back." She made her way past us to a chorus of gratitude. I grabbed her arm before it was out of reach.

"How are you feeling?"

"Just fine. A little tired, but the coffee will fix that." She leaned over and kissed me. "Could've used a bit more privacy," she whispered into my ear. I pulled her closer, and kissed her back, longer. Our lips parted slowly.

She purred, "I'll put on the coffee."

"Okay," I said softly.

She pecked me on the cheek and headed for the back of the cabin.

"Where were we?" I turned my attention back to the boys, who were grinning. The interlude with Charlie had been a welcome diversion.

"You were saying something about motive," Gary reminded me.

"Right. Thanks. We can't overlook the obvious," I went on. "Maybe the guys in the States are being paid."

"By whoever wants our President and half his executives dead?" Gary asked.

I was shaking my head. "I don't buy it for one second. I don't think anyone wants them gone. It's a smokescreen."

"What are they shooting at, then?" Asked Javier.

I considered my next thoughts carefully before speaking again. "What is happening all over the United States right now? I mean, all bullshit aside, if you had to describe it in a word?"

I waited.

"Panic," Gary finally said.

"Disorder," Said Javier.

"Chaos," I added. "I could throw in lunacy, too."

We all knew about it. Hell had broken open. It had come from the bowels beneath the sixty-three floors of my building. For once, the media reports weren't exaggerating.

The inner cities of America had taken on the appearance of war zones. The National Guard had been deployed everywhere to keep order. People's nerves were raw. No one wanted to work in a tower. As the terrorists' deadline approached for the destruction of the next two, tension had risen like the flames of an out of control bonfire. Insanity prevailed.

Citizens scurried about the downtown areas like rats about to drown. They arrived to work late, and left early. There was barely controlled panic. Minor fender benders became catalysts for urban warfare. Gun battles erupted in the streets between normally placid accountants, lawyers, and the like. Sanity was slipping away. The death toll was rising. Routinely, it seemed, toll booth workers were being shot for holding up long lines of traffic. In some cases, local governments had sent the operators of their booths home, opening all lanes, unwilling or unable to provide the necessary security. Every police officer was occupied. Worst of all, articles had began to appear in the editorial sections of large daily newspapers suggesting that a part of being a good leader meant certain sacrifices had to be made. Talk shows had taken up the mad debate. Nuts were coming out of the woodwork. The very fabric of American civilized society had begun to show signs of unraveling. Some, regardless of the consequences, simply no longer showed up for work if their offices were anywhere inside or in the vicinity of high-rise buildings. All this happened in just over a week. And the clock kept ticking, louder with each passing hour. No wonder Smith, Gus, and their superiors were letting out our leashes. They had nothing to lose. As a result, I felt strongly that we would get what we needed from Smith.

Taking stock, we had one lead. It amounted to one dead Arab whose identity I was convinced, at least for now, remained a mystery. When we learned who he was it would lead us to some answers. The more I thought about Mojab, the more I knew his hadn't been a murder of convenience. There had been a whole lot more to it than that.

I didn't believe in coincidences. Praveen, had confirmed what I'd thought to be true when I'd first learned of it. Mojab's had been the only construction fatality not only in my history, but Pop's career as well. That went back close to fifty years.

Pop had drilled it into me from the time I'd been a small boy. I'd lost count of the number of lectures I'd gotten on safety. No amount of profit in the world, he'd told me, was worth a single life. Everyone had someone they loved; everyone was loved by somebody. He had drilled that into me until it had become a part of me.

I hadn't been told about a man named Mojab. I felt bad about that. One of the promises I had made myself early on was that I'd always be in touch with the little guy. But I had become too big. I'd lost touch. I knew I couldn't possibly be everywhere all the time, but I should have at least been told about it. Somehow Mojab's death had slipped through the cracks. We knew about him now, though.

It was Gary who interrupted my reverie. "If it's this bad now, what will happen if the next two towers are destroyed?"

Javier added, "Even if the ones Praveen has found are evacuated, there's no guarantee he hasn't missed some other ones. Surely someone didn't die on every rigged building. They'll take one of those out instead. All they've got to do is watch the news. They'll know which buildings still have people in them."

"Yeah, they will," I conceded. "Either way the country's in big trouble. People don't have to be in those buildings. They'll panic anyway. It's our nature to fear the unknown."

"That certainly applies here." Charlie reappeared. She set a silver tray with four mugs and a decanter onto the table with cream and sugar. She filled each mug in turn. We watched, consumed with our thoughts.

"Dig in," she invited as she set the decanter in the middle of the tray. The fresh aroma wafted through the cabin. It smelled good, like home a long time ago. She sat down in the chair next to mine.

"Can I ask a stupid question?" Charlie looked at me across the top of her mug.

"There are no stupid questions. Only stupid people," I said.

"If we don't stop it...If the other buildings are

destroyed, I mean. Aside from the horror of it all, what do you think will happen to the economy? Let's say for one minute you're right and there's money involved. Terror is all about the destabilization of a power structure through fear. It can be rooted in religion, in ideology, granted. But they know us. Whoever is doing this has defined their enemy well. We're everything they hate: big cars, big houses, arrogance, greed, money. That's what they're attacking. That's what they're seeking to destroy. What if they – whoever they are – are in it for the money?"

"Is that your question?" I asked.

"No. That's my premise. You have your theories, I have mine. My question is if the American global economy is successfully crippled, who stands the most to gain from it? Who would benefit?"

"Are you serious?" I was stunned.

"Yes. And I'm asking someone who ought to know the answer. After all, you're the billionaire. You're someone who would be affected most by it. Call this our own private think tank, Jonathan." She gazed around the table. "But from what I know of Washington, I think we're every bit as smart as they are. They're self-serving."

"And we're not?" I was fast becoming intrigued.

She frowned, "Jonathan, if you're going to make fun of me..."

I held up my hand. "I did it again, didn't I? I'm sorry, Charlie. It's late. I'm tired."

"Apology accepted, but my question stands. Who benefits most if our economy goes to shit? I already know who loses." She blew a wisp of steam off the surface of her coffee and carefully sipped it.

We stared at her. She looked awfully innocent for having just set a bomb that size in the shelter.

Chapter 8

Smith had groused about me waking him up. Then he had groused some more about sending Praveen the spy satellites' pictures from a year and a half ago. He agreed to it, but only after I promised to share more information with him. He was pissed I hadn't called earlier, and that's when I hung up on him. I didn't want to hear his bullshit. If it came up later, I told myself, I'd blame it on our computer.

I thought about asking him to call Syria, but decided against it. I called their State Department myself to let them know I was coming. By the time I finished that call I was exhausted. I folded one of the unoccupied leather chairs near the galley into its horizontal position and laid down. The last thing I remembered was Charlie tucking me in. She kissed me goodnight and I went out like a light right after.

I woke up as we touched down in Damascus, sat up groggily, and stretched. It had been a long flight, and the inside of my mouth was dry as sandpaper. Originally I'd thought about refueling in Paris, maybe spending the night in a hotel, but time was of the essence and the Gulfstream had a range of 6,750 nautical miles. David assured me he could make it all the way. If need be he could set the autopilot and snooze over the Atlantic, so we'd flown non-stop to Syria.

I could feel the irregularities of the tarmac as David taxied the jet along the runway. I looked around the cabin. Slowly, the others were coming to life. Charlie, too, had gone back to bed after I had fallen asleep. Now, her hair in disarray, she stirred, rolled over, and pulled her blanket over her head. I pulled up the shade next to me in order to look outside, unsure that I liked what I saw. David steered us toward what in the U.S. would have been General Aviation, the part of the airport away from the passenger gates of the main terminal.

I made my way to the jet's cockpit.

David looked up and saw me enter when he heard the door open. He forced a smile.

"You don't look so good, boss," he said, stating the obvious. His own eyes were bloodshot.

"Have you checked the mirror lately?" I scowled.

"It looks like we have company," David said, returning his full attention to the console in front of him.

I followed his gaze through the jet's front windscreen. A man dressed in coveralls and wearing earmuffs flagged us toward him with a red wand flashlight in each hand. David now had his headset on. They clearly wanted us in a specific location on the tarmac. The man walked steadily backwards, waving us toward him. Fifty feet behind him, a couple of limos seemed to be surrounded by three or four canvas-covered military vehicles. Soldiers with automatic weapons stood beside them.

"So much for keeping a low profile," I said sourly. It had been protocol to let the Syrian State Department know we were coming. I wanted to speak with someone who had clout regarding the Saudi jet that had received Mojab's remains not far from this very spot eighteen months ago. I half expected a bureaucrat with a clipboard; this was something else. Why the fuss?

One of our big pluses was our ability to move across the board quickly without being noticed. Now we weren't just on the radar; we were smack dab in the middle of it. After all, technically I was a civilian. I wondered if Smith had done something foolish. I guessed I would find out soon enough. David finally eased on the brakes, and the jet stopped. He peeled off his headphones and tossed a glance over his shoulder.

"Welcome to Damascus. I hope you had a pleasant flight. Please fly with us again soon."

I grunted.

"What do you think?"

I shrugged. "I think there's a lot more going on in Syria than we know about."

"Do you think they're in on it?"

I looked at him, and then at the soldiers on the tarmac. "They know something. They would have to. The plane with the body landed here. Whether or not they're going to feel like telling us whatever it is they know is an entirely different matter. It's all speculation, though." I smiled at one of the soldiers. If he noticed he didn't acknowledge me. "Why don't we try and find out what information these bastards are willing to part with."

"They could lie to us," David said innocently.

I checked to see if the pilot was being serious, then looked back at the soldiers on the tarmac. "I'd be disappointed if they didn't. But I'm not so much interested in what they do say as in what they don't say. Shut this thing down, David. And don't let these assholes anywhere near this plane without you breathing down their necks. Understood? We're in Syria now. We've got to turn it up a notch. They just did."

David patted the bulge beneath his coat. "I've got us covered, boss. Russ and I will sleep here until you need us. Onboard, I mean, if you don't mind. We've got enough provisions to last a month."

"That'll be fine. I'll leave Frank Ambrose here, too. He can keep an eye on what's going on outside the jet. That will make three, counting your co-pilot."

"You think they'll try something?"

"Expect it, and you'll never be disappointed. Someone out there is blowing up buildings. The Gulfstream's small potatoes in comparison. Keep a sharp eye. The plane's replaceable; you guys aren't. Any problems, call me immediately."

"Where's everyone staying?" David asked.

I said, "I've left that one up to Gary. I thought I heard him tell Javier the Cham Palace Hotel. He'll brief you before we leave."

David nodded. "I'll shut her down. Tell Gary to give me ten minutes."

I nodded.

I began to leave the cabin, feeling confident of the team I had assembled. These guys were with me all the way, no matter what. That had me worried most. I almost slammed into Gary as I left David in the cockpit. His bulk filled the aisle, and he looked concerned.

"What's the matter?" I asked good naturedly, smiling. "Forget your passport?"

"I thought you made a call?"

"I'm just busting your balls, Gary. I did. Last night. Or this morning. Whatever the hell time it was. With all this moving around my clock's all screwed up. But I didn't cause what's out there," I jerked a thumb in the direction of our reception. "Not all by my lonesome."

"That prick Smith?" Gary could tell I wasn't happy.

"That would be my guess. Once an earner always a worker. It's his way of staying involved, I suppose."

"It's his way of fucking up the works."

I could see Gary was in no mood to have the government spook sucking on our side, either. In part it meant we were one step ahead of the boys at Homeland Security. They were good. What they lacked in creativity they made up for in diligence. Smith would allow no stone unturned. He would demand every orifice be checked and rechecked, and then he'd get someone else to check on the guys he'd originally used. Therein lay the rub, because when it came to us, he was out of his element. He hated it. He probably hated me. I know I had a healthy dislike of him, bordering on contempt. As far as I could tell, the only thing his kind were better at than me was killing people. There wasn't much difference between Smith and his cronies, and the assholes blowing up our buildings.

Smith needed us. We had what his people didn't. We had the imagination and creativity they lacked to equal their enemies. Our skills would bring them up to snuff. We had faith in our convictions; we played hunches. Pop had done it his whole life, whether he ever admitted it or not.

And so did I. I had built an empire with it that spanned the entire globe. I owned stuff I didn't even know about, because I had faith in the people around me. I wasn't so sure Smith could ever say that. Everyone in his organization I'd met was paranoid. They didn't trust the enemy, and they couldn't trust each other. They had too many double agents in the closet for that ever to be part of their reality. When it was all said and done, they were salaried employees, hired help. Take away the money and they would all soon follow. No check, no job.

That was the crux of it. That was where a guy like myself, or Gary, or David, parted company with guys like

Derrick Smith.

I had spent my whole life working for the things I believed in. I never worried about what I made or didn't make. Even now I realized it had never occurred to me to wonder about the financial impact of our sixty-three story being destroyed. I only cared about the people who had perished in the conflagration.

Smith knew it. On some level, however dim that light was, he knew we were closer to the monsters in the arena than he could ever be. They did what they did for the very same reasons as us: they believed in what they were doing. It seemed they were lined up to blow themselves to smithereens for those beliefs. If it came right down to it, my way or their way, I'd blow them the fuck off the planet, too. I was Smith's edge, his foot soldier. At least I was pretty sure that's how he looked at us, which was all right by me. Ours was a tenuous relationship at best. That was a funny thing about terrorists: if they did one thing extremely well, it was that they made strange bedfellows of the rest of us.

I looked at Gary. "We're on the same side as Smith. He needs us. We need him. It's the way it is for now. Maybe Washington did us a favor."

"By telling them we were coming?" Gary was nonplused.

"Think about it for a second. Now the Syrians know we have knowledge of their little sleight of hand with Mojab."

"You think Smith told them about that, too?"

"He didn't have to. They knew. Mojab wasn't Mojab. They put him on a wide-bodied jet that flew out of here and into Riyadh. The jet was owned by the Saudi Royals. Of course they knew."

"And now they know we know." Gary was flustered.

"I'm confused, Jonathan. How does that help us? I figure if anything, now they can take steps to conceal further knowledge."

"Ten lies for every one," I smiled. "Let's talk with them, listen closely to what they say. They'll make a mistake. Before we leave Damascus we'll know much more than when we arrived."

Gary nodded, seeing the logic in what I proposed. "I like it," he said, a hint of a smile forming across his own face.

"Yeah, me too," I said. "By the way, David needs some briefing. He's going to stay with the ship. So is Russell Jackson, his co-pilot. I'm giving him Frank, as well. For security."

Gary nodded his approval. "Ambrose is a good man. I'll talk to them all."

We both heard the jet's engines power down as David cut off their fuel supply. Charlie caught my eye from the cabin's aft.

"Be careful," I cautioned Gary. "These guys are not our friends."

Gary's eyes hardened into dark pools. "I'm aware of that, Jonathan. You put me in charge for a reason. Javier and I will handle the security of the team from here on." He was all business now. I felt relieved.

I forced myself to step aside. It was a mind thing. Gary and Javier were among the best in the world at what they did. I reminded myself I'd hired them for a reason. Maybe I wasn't good at killing anybody; thank God I'd never been tested. But with them it was a very different story. They had some blood on their hands. I was glad they were on my side.

Now I was free to concentrate on the things *I* was best at – like finding out who was blowing up our towers, and why. I was convinced the manifesto didn't spell out the real reasons. If I could find out why, I knew it would eventually lead me to those responsible, and then we might be able to stop them. We had less than three weeks before they made good on their promise, less than three weeks before the next two monoliths came tumbling down.

Chapter 9

They took us to the Four Seasons on Shukri al-Quatli Street in downtown Damascus. It was a ten minute drive from the magnificent Umayyad Mosque.

The hotel cost a hundred million in 2005. It was eighteen stories of grand opulence, decorated in Ottoman, Persian, and Syrian styles. It had two hundred ninety-seven rooms, twelve residential apartments, three restaurants, and a beautiful spa second to none – the biggest and best in the entire country.

I didn't give a shit.

I'd stayed in nice places the better part of my adult life, and many people have tried to impress me with lavish gifts and unwarranted gratuities before. Usually they wanted something in return. I thought it funny how most of these same people wouldn't give a homeless guy the time of day, while the more money I got, the more free stuff they'd shove at me. In this case, however, the guy doing the shoving fascinated me. He was Saudi. His name was Prince al-Walid bin Talal bin Talal Abdulaziz, or Prince al-Walid bin Talal for short. He owned at least two hundred hotels around the world, including the George V in Paris, and the Plaza in New York. When I found out the Syrian government was insisting we take their comp I had Praveen run a check for me.

The Prince owned a sixty-five percent stake in what

was called the Syrian-Saudi Company for Tourism and Investment. He was also good buddies with none other than Bashar al-Assad, the President of Syria. In fact, he'd been there during the inauguration. I thought it an awfully cozy relationship, and therefore agreed to the comp.

Gary was less than happy. Now he was worried about bugs. So was I, but I knew if we stayed smart, it could all work in our favor.

Charlie looked at me. "What do you think it means?"

Javier swept the apartment. It was clean, for now. I said, "It means they want to be seen as co-operative."

I'd learned an hour ago that Smith had indeed called the Syrians right after I had. We were official now. We represented a country. They knew which country, and by now they also knew it had been my tower. "I think we have them intrigued. I think they want to know more about why we're here, and who we are."

"They want to know more about you, Jonathan," she speculated.

"We're an odd bunch: me, you, Gary, the others. They also don't know what or how much we know. I suspect they would love to find out, though. This is a great opportunity for them. The place is clean for now, but I'm not holding my breath."

"But it's so beautiful." She ambled across the suite foyer's marble floor to the bank of floor-to-ceiling windows overlooking the pool areas. "And so unreal."

"Yeah, I know what you mean," I said.

So beautiful, and so very dangerous.

There came a soft knock at the door.

"That would be lunch." I walked across the large sunken room and hopped the stairs that led to the suite's front door. They wheeled in the food, set the table, refused the gratuity and quickly left. I noticed an envelope sandwiched between two bottles of wine closer to my side of the table. Gold embossed lettering made it look official. I ignored it for the time being and sat down to eat instead. The food's tantalizing aroma tickled my nose.

"Steak and eggs, with caviar." Charlie smiled with satisfaction.

"Can't very well save the world on an empty stomach." I selected a silver fork and a knife.

"There's a letter," Charlie noticed as she reached for the wine.

I nodded. "Go ahead and open it."

She started, and I looked up from carving my filet mignon.

"It's from the Office of the President. I wonder why they sent two?"

"One's probably a dessert wine," I said quickly, motioning with my hand for her attention. As soon as she looked at me I held my index finger to my lips, telling her to be silent. I'd seen the second envelope as well. It was quite a bit smaller than the one with the Presidential Seal, placed behind and under it. I motioned for Charlie to hand it across the table; she wrinkled her nose in puzzlement, but complied. When her eyes met mine, I drew an imaginary circle in the air in front of my face, then pointed to my ear. She nodded.

"What does it say?" I encouraged her. My voice was light, as if nothing had changed. My eyes, on the other hand, were intense. Good girl, I thought. I could see she'd caught on.

It was true that Javier had swept the place, but I couldn't chance it. In this game, there were no second chances. I assumed someone wanted to talk, and they had found a way to get a message through to us in spite of all the heavy security.

There had been a lot of that. It had started at the airport and gotten worse. The Syrians wanted us under their microscope. I was pretty sure from watching Praveen the last couple of years that we didn't have the technology market cornered. We'd been given this hotel and these rooms because it was easier for them to control the situation this way. If the Syrian government wanted to listen in on our conversations, they would – aside from the encrypted satellite communications from the jet. They had been tutored by Russians, after all.

"I was looking for this." Charlie was playing along. "You wouldn't want me to break a nail." She held up what looked like a solid gold, miniature stiletto. It was a letter opener left beside the original envelope, probably at the front desk. That meant the envelope I held had been placed alongside the other, official one, somewhere between the time when room service had assembled the entire tray, and when they'd delivered it. I tried to remember the faces of the three bus boys who had brought the trays into the suite's dining area, but each melted into the other, forming a blurred, nondescript mishmash of indistinguishable features. It didn't matter, I realized. No doubt whoever had delivered it knew nothing of its contents, or its author. That way, if I reported it and all of them were questioned, the delivery boy wouldn't be able to tell anyone anything – only that he'd probably been paid handsomely to deliver it, and keep his mouth shut afterward.

"I'd never hear the end of it," I bantered with Charlie, referring to the broken nail.

I watched as she sliced open the envelope. She handed me the opener. I nodded for her to retrieve her envelope's contents. Using the rattle of paper for cover, I opened the small one and retrieved the paper inside it at the same time. It was a small card, with a message typed in the center. It read 'Hebrews 11:30', followed by 'Palmyra Theater'. Beside that was a time, '8PM Tuesday'. Today was Monday. I read it over and over again, trying desperately to make sense of it. Where in hell was I going to find a Bible in the middle of Syria?

Chapter 10

Praveen was working overtime. Either that or there were two of him. It seemed information was being transmitted nonstop to the computer on the Gulfstream.

I wanted to stay at the hotel and respond personally to the invitation to join some of the more senior officials in the Syrian government for dinner later in the evening. Gary and Javier had volunteered to drive the fifty minute round trip to the airport and back to courier the material David had called me about. They both looked at me funny when I asked them to see if they could find a Bible along the way.

"I'll explain later," I said.

I also sent a few more queries for Praveen with them for David to send out on the satellite broadband. After, Charlie and I decided to take a stroll along the Barada River. Immediately across the river, on the other side of a similar pedestrian walkway, rose the first four domes of the Great Mosque. I gazed at it in wonder.

"Are you tired?" I held her hand as we slowly strolled along the river walk.

"A little," she conceded. "It's been a long day. I didn't sleep that well on the plane. The nap after brunch helped." Charlie untangled her fingers from mine and clasped onto my arm. She held on like she didn't want to let go and leaned into me for support. I liked the way she felt. We walked a bit, saying nothing.

"Do we have to go to this thing tonight?" she finally said to the stones in front of our shuffling feet.

"Not if you don't feel up to it," I responded. "Are you coming down with something?" I was suddenly concerned.

She squeezed my arm. "I'm all right. A little bit of jet lag. I have a sinking feeling in my stomach about what we are getting ourselves into. It just seems so hypocritical to me. These people could just come out and tell us what they know. Maybe even who they think might be involved. But with them it's always politics." She was referring to what had turned out to be an invitation to dinner. That had been inside the larger of the two envelopes, the one with the President's seal on it.

"And playing politics with people's lives isn't cool," I agreed.

"No, it isn't. Then there's that cryptic note. Why on earth would someone be quoting scripture regarding the meeting at Palmyra tomorrow evening?"

"It's got me intrigued," I admitted.

Charlie tugged on my arm, stopping us in the middle of the walkway. A soft breeze tugged at her hair. It was warm for November, around seventy-five degrees. I couldn't pin it down, but the air smelled different over here. Not unpleasant, just different. She searched my eyes. Concern was etched into her own.

"You're not actually thinking of going to Palmyra?" It sounded as if she was accusing me of a mortal sin.

I sighed. We started walking again. "I'm going to wait and see what the verse says."

I'd instructed Gary that if he didn't locate a Bible to ask Praveen to send it over the secured line of communication. I told him to stay with David until the verse came back off the satellite. There were plenty of copies of the Koran in Damascus, but I wasn't holding out much hope of him actually finding a hard copy of the King James Version of the Bible.

"What if it doesn't say anything?" Charlie mused. "I mean, what if it makes no sense? What if the whole thing is a trick to get us out to those ruins? There's nothing out there, Jonathan. It'll be dark by eight o'clock. The last tourist bus will have already left. That spells no witnesses. What if it's a trap?"

"Stop," I said carefully. "We haven't even looked at the verse yet. Before you go jumping to any conclusions why don't we see what it says? No one's going off half-cocked, least of all me. And as for the collective, who said anything about you going with us? You're right. It could be dangerous. You're staying put at the hotel Charlie. If anything goes wrong out there I don't want you in the line of fire. It's non-negotiable. That's what Gary and Javier and the others get paid for."

She stopped, and whirled me around to face her. There was fire in her eyes. She was breathing hard.

"If you think I came all this way just to sit in some safe haven hotel room, think again. I came for the ride, the whole ride, from start to finish. My father once told me if there's nothing in your life worth risking it for, you don't have much reason to live. He told me that right after my mother had been killed. I believed him then, and I believe him even more now."

"Charlie," I stopped her, searching her eyes. She didn't blink.

"What?" she finally asked.

"I love you with all my heart. Every time I smell the fragrance of a beautiful flower I smell you. Every time I see a bird soaring gracefully on the wind, I see you." I held her by both shoulders. I had to make her understand me. "I know you want to be with us – me. But sweetheart, we don't know who sent that note. We don't even know if it's connected to why we're here. For all we do know it might be from some guy wanting to sell us some smuggled jewels."

"It's connected," Charlie said softly, but pointedly. "The verse from Hebrews will prove it." She didn't give an inch.

I took a deep breath, then let it out slowly between pursed lips. "And if I say no? If I say you can't go out there to those ruins with us? Are you going to leave me, Charlie? Is this how it's going to be every time we disagree? How am I supposed to live like that?"

She suddenly closed the gap between us. We held on to each other for a long time. Neither of us spoke. Finally, I slowly separated us. Both of us had tears in our eyes.

"I'm sorry, Jonathan," she said softly. "The answer is no. I love you, too." We both smiled in unison. "We make a good team, you know."

I nodded. "We do." Then, more seriously, "There's danger in this, Charlie. These people cut off heads." I wasn't pulling any punches. She didn't flinch.

"I know that," she said. "Let's walk some more." Her tears were gone. Mine, too.

We ambled along the stone path in silence. I wished I could freeze it in time, just hang on to this moment and keep playing it back, over and over again. I wished our walk beside this peaceful river would never end.

"My mother's death wasn't an accident." Charlie interrupted the silence. I was more surprised than I let on. We exchanged glances. For the first time since I'd known her, she looked nervous. She continued. "Dad's job...he never brought it home with him. But one time...one time he didn't have a choice because it followed him home. They had been working on a case. It was big, something to do with narcotics from Central and South America. Someone our government had allowed to stay in power to ensure some degree of stability in the region went rogue."

"Noriega?" I guessed. "Panama?"

"Yes." Her eyes fluttered. I could see she was conjuring up some awful and painful memories. "We sent our troops into Panama to 'restore order'. What never made the papers was that he sent his troops – his assassins – to do the same. Mom picked me up from school that day. I remember because it was raining all day. Dad had bought me a new dress. It was the first time I'd worn it and Mom didn't want me walking home in that kind of weather. They were waiting inside our house when we got back. They said they wanted to send a message to anyone who thought they could interfere in their politics. I saw my mother get raped, Jonathan. They forced me to watch. Then they killed her. They cut her throat open and left. My father was still in Panama, but he came back immediately. I still go for counseling. You're the first person, other than the psychiatrists, I've ever spoken to about what happened." Her voice had become almost a whisper.

"That's why Gus told you if there's nothing in your life worth risking it for, there's not much reason for living it." Now I understood. I pulled her closer to me.

She nodded, looking at the ground.

"I'm so sorry, Charlie. But I'm also glad you told me about this."

"I was ashamed at first," she reluctantly confessed. "Imagine, being embarrassed about my own mother's death. All I could think about was what if the other kids found out? What would they say? How would I be able to face them? The doctors assured me what I felt was normal. The feds put a pretty tight lid on it. Nothing ever got out. Now I wish it had. Now the only thing I'm ashamed of was the way I reacted to the whole thing. I wish I could have done better. I try to forgive myself. It took me a long time to get this far."

"I know," I said quietly.

"I'm happy, though." She brightened suddenly. "That I told you, I guess deep down I was nervous about how you might react."

"What I think is that you are the most amazing and wonderful person I have ever met in my entire life. I'm happy you became a writer." I smiled.

"Why? Do you think we still would have met if I didn't?"

I shrugged. "That's the same as wondering what my life would be like if my father hadn't bought that first ramshackle fixer-upper in the Bronx. If I met you as a plumber, would you even notice me? It's a tough question, Charlie. How many people have wondered the same thing? I'm just really happy we met, is all. And the doctors were right. I would have reacted the same way."

"Thank you." She leaned up and kissed me.

"You're welcome," I said. "This doesn't change anything, though."

"I know," said Charlie. "You're always going to be more stubborn than is good for you. I think that can be good sometimes."

"But not now," I said. I wasn't the only one who was a bit too stubborn for their own good. "I'm not going to change your mind, am I?"

"Nope."

"It's dangerous. Not to mention downright

foolhardy. What if it *is* some kind of trap? We may be closer to the people who did this than we realize. Someone might be getting very nervous about us being here. A bullet doesn't care who you are – rich, poor, man, woman; it wouldn't matter."

"Dad taught me how to shoot when I was eight," Charlie said.

I stared at her in surprise.

"I'm an expert markswoman." She wasn't finished with her bag of tricks. "If I level a gun at someone, I see a target, not a person. I'm going to Palmyra. You may need me to watch your back."

I looked at her in a new light. An odd kind of feeling welled up inside of me. I didn't immediately recognize it, but I realized that what I felt was pride.

"Remind me not to get caught alone with you in a back alley when you're pissed off," was all I could think to say to her.

Chapter 11

"I understand that you are a very important man, Mr. Strickland. Your influence is not only felt within the United States, but in other parts of the world, as well. Your wealth is a matter of conjecture at best; presumably into the billions of U.S. dollars. You are a very private person." It was a statement, not an accusation.

"Yes," I agreed. "I'm a lot like the middle eastern oil reserves. There are many barrels, although no one is really certain of the amount."

"Touché, Mr. Strickland." He understood.

"You're a doctor." I'd done my homework.

"I'm a politician," he corrected. "I was a doctor in a former life. It was a long time ago." His shoulders seemed to sag a bit.

"Your English is excellent," I commented.

"I lived in England. I went to school there, until my brother died. That was in ninety four."

"The reason you came back?" I vaguely remembered reading about it.

"Yes," said President Bashar al-Assad. "It is an irony. I did not want this life." His candor surprised me. "Six years after my brother died, I lost my father as well."

"The lot was cast."

"Yes. What did a famous American once say? 'We have one life; it soon will be past; what we do for God is all that will last.'" His smile was disarming.

"Mohammed Ali," I said.

The President of Syria seemed to brighten. "The greatest ever. Unfortunately I never saw him fight. Not in person. It was very unfortunate the way he ended up."

"I don't know about that," I disagreed. "Someone else said that about him once, when he lit up the Olympic torch in Atlanta. He was shaking pretty bad by then. Parkinson's is a real bitch. I remember he almost didn't get it lit. But I never knew Ali not to do anything he set his mind to. Some people felt sorry for him right afterward. I guess they hadn't seen him in a while. When he heard about it I remember what he said." The President stared at me with keen interest. "He smiled. Then he asked those who felt bad for him when was the last time they lit the Olympic torch in front of a billion people around the world to start the Games?"

Al-Assad nodded. "We could all learn much from such a man."

"If only we would listen. If only we could understand." I stared upwards from where we stood on the hotel's outdoor terrace. It was a beautiful night. I found Orion's belt while barely aware of the phalanx of security around us. My guys were there, too, somewhere among the other guests. They'd been forced to give up their hardware. No one except the President's security was allowed to carry.

All of them were sticking to the periphery, trying to be as unobtrusive as possible. As usual Gary didn't like it, but there wasn't much he could do. We had been required to hand over our weapons to the Syrians earlier in the day. We'd get them back from the military after tonight. I felt vulnerable; Gary and Javier felt like deer in crosshairs.

I'd seen Gary earlier. He'd been nervous. But earlier

we had not expected the President, either. The President walked in after we had noticed a build-up in security, and I'd caught Gary's eye from across the room. He was somewhat mollified, and his anxiety was replaced by a begrudging acquiescence. He understood this game. It would have been no different Stateside.

"It was your tower." Al-Assad was speaking. I looked down from the heavens back to him.

"Yes, they were my friends," I said, gritting my teeth. There was no mistaking the anger that flashed in my eyes.

"Sometimes, Mr. Strickland, I am still a doctor. I can still feel the pain of those who suffer," said al-Assad. "What happened last week in New York was a terrible tragedy. Seventy-three lives." He shook his head. "It is nothing short of madness. Now they threaten more."

I watched him carefully. "Whoever they are will do it again unless we stop them, Mr. President."

I was fishing. I had to choose my words carefully.

"As a country, we respect the sovereignty of all nations." I wondered if he was stepping onto a soap box. "As you must know, Syria has condemned this horrible act of barbarism. We are behind the United States one hundred percent in denouncing such acts of terror." Now he seemed to search my eyes, looking past the diplomacy of our encounter. "I am sorry for your loss, Mr. Strickland. I know what you must feel. I, too, have lost friends. Sometimes it seems like this will never end. But you and I must never give up, even when we discover things are not what they seem. Even when our sworn enemies proffer us the dove of peace and our most trusted friends betray us. We must keep moving forward. We must always continue our search for peace and balance."

He lowered his voice. Unless he was wired, we spoke in confidence. I couldn't ask him what I wanted to ask him. I couldn't just come out and say, 'Do you know anything about these crazy motherfuckers, Mr. President? Did you start this? Are these your people?' I couldn't even be sure of what this man was all about. Peace?

Who didn't want to live in peace?

Too many people unfortunately.

"There was a man who worked on my building, Mr. President. He died. He was killed when the foundations for the tower were being constructed. This was a year and a half ago."

The President listened carefully.

"I think he was murdered."

"I don't understand. Does this have anything to do with my country?" He seemed genuinely perplexed.

"He was carrying papers stating he was from Israel. His identification was forged. His body was recovered and then flown here, to Damascus, where it was then transferred to a wide-bodied jet owned by the Saudi Royals – people you know, Mr. President. One of them owns this hotel with you. We have satellite photos of the casket being off-loaded. We have pictures of the transfer. We will find the people responsible, sir, and bring them to justice, and we will not stop until we have done this." I forced myself to stop. I knew I had to remain completely in control, and I reminded myself who I was speaking with. A picture of the tower beginning to collapse spun around inside my mind.

"We would appreciate the cooperation of the Syrian authorities, anything, Mr. President. Anything at all that might help us."

He seemed to change as I watched him. Something in his eyes told me I'd gone too far. He was a politician now, and a Syrian.

"I can assure you we will do everything in our power

to help your country in these very difficult times. In spite of what you may think of us, we do not enjoy this anymore than you do." He straightened suddenly, as if he'd been slapped on the back. "It has been a pleasure meeting you, Mr. Strickland. I hope the rest of your stay is a pleasant one." The President extended his arm. I realized it was over as we shook hands.

"I would like to extend my condolences to your country, and to you." He turned to walk away, but stopped suddenly, and turned back. "How did you know I owned part of this hotel, Mr. Strickland?"

"You told me," I said. "Just now. Thank you, Mr. President."

And that was that. He turned and walked briskly to the open doors entering the hotel from the outer terrace. Immediately, he was swarmed by his plainclothes security guards. I stared after him, not certain how I felt about what had just happened.

I felt Gary move in beside me.

"Short conversation," he noted.

"But not entirely sweet," I suggested. I faked a smile in case anyone was watching. Just as quickly I thought what the hell and dropped it.

"You got face time. That's something. You think he knows anything?"

"I don't know," I said thoughtfully. "He's here tonight for some reason. I don't buy that he just happened to be in the neighborhood and decided to drop in."

"He knew we would be here. He might have thought a one-on-one would mollify us," Gary suggested.

"Maybe," I said slowly. I was still watching the President as he worked his way through the reception area. It looked as if he was leaving. "Politics," I said more forcefully. "I never cared for them. And politicians are a classic example of how the road to Hell works."

"They're always paving it with good intentions." He finished the old cliché for me.

"Amen," I said.

"Did he say anything?"

"About our dead Saudi construction worker? The transfer? The satellite imagery? Nothing. But he liked Ali."

"Ali?"

I looked at Gary. He was befuddled.

"Yea, Mohammed Ali, the boxer. The President and I both agreed he was probably the best athlete ever. In fact, when it came up, he said he thought Ali in his prime could've taken you out in the first round." I remained stone-faced.

Gary was slack-jawed. I let him stew on it for all of two seconds before I couldn't keep myself from grinning.

"Asshole."

"Got you."

"Yeah, you got me, all right." He thought about it. "I think I could've gone two, maybe even three."

"We'll never know."

Gary posed the leading question. "Do you think the President has ever killed anyone?"

I was still watching al-Assad. "You mean directly? No chance. If he has I'd be surprised. In my opinion, he doesn't have the stomach for it. Did you know he wanted to be a doctor? His brother died suddenly. It was a car accident, I think. He was at school in London. In ninety-two he didn't want this job."

Gary watched now too. Al-Assad was almost at the exit door on the other side of the interior pre-function suite. He was smiling, nodding, listening, all the while continuing to move through people all vying for his time.

I noticed that no matter what, he never actually stopped moving towards the exit. His bodyguards flowed with him like a family of ducks swimming together in the same pond, invisible in their roles, as if they were just more guests at the reception. The President of Syria was well protected indeed.

We could see everything through the doors separating the outer terrace from the inner hall. I felt the first chill of evening lick across my face as the breeze picked up. Wisps of it played hopscotch along the tiles. The day had been unseasonably warm, and the night's chill was welcome.

"But he's been responsible for killing. He's ordered deaths. It's part of the job. Every politician in his position does it, some more willingly than others. On a sliding scale..." I hesitated. "I don't know where we would find him, Gary. I think our guy's worse. He's had to be. We live in a fucked up world."

"It's getting more fucked up all the time," Gary said.

"Did you have any trouble getting in?" I asked. I had instructed both Gary and Javier to join me immediately after they returned from seeing David at the airport. It had taken them longer than we anticipated.

"We changed into these penguin suits first. They've already got our guns. They took those this afternoon."

I nodded.

"They found the one I tried to bring in here though."

"You didn't try to bring a gun in here?" I lamented.

"How the hell did I know the President would be here?" he complained. "Besides, it was on my ankle. They found it anyway. The guards outside the lobby scanned us with metal detectors."

I remembered the wands. Every invited guest had been required to go through the procedure. It had been no more bothersome a process than the one required to board a commercial jet.

"They squawked a bit until they confirmed who we were. But we still weren't allowed to carry. I can respect that now that I know the reason behind it."

"Were you able to speak with Praveen?" I wanted to know. So far I'd kept my curiosity in check.

"Yes, we spoke. You want it all?"

"Just give me the verse. We'll go over the rest of the info later." I had to admit, the rest of the information was subordinate to the quote from the Book of Hebrews. The scripture would tell me if there was a connection between our visit here and the anonymous request for tomorrow night's meeting at the ruins of Palmyra.

Gary fished a small piece of hotel stationary from the inside pocket of his suit jacket. He handed it to me to read. "I figured you would want to read this first. I copied it from Praveen's transmission."

I nodded. I looked at the paper and immediately recognized Gary's handwriting:

Hebrews 11, verse 30
By faith the walls of Jericho fell down, after they were com-
passed about seven days.

I stared up at Gary, trembling. The piece of paper shook violently in my hand. My heart pounded against my ribs.

Gary said, "I had the same reaction."

My tower, the first, had been destroyed seven days after the original manifesto was supposed to have been published in *The New York Times*.

Chapter 12

David had been poking around at the airport for the better part of two days. He'd managed to secure a contract on an old military helicopter from the air force's bone yard which had been purchased and converted to private use. The new owner was an accomplished pilot who'd spent the first two-thirds of his adult life flying similar aircraft for the Syrian Armed Forces. Now he made day trips to places like Palmyra for tourists with enough cash to pay for them. He became our new best friend the moment I agreed to pay him double his asking price. I gauged his reaction to my unexpected generosity very carefully. I wanted to know if he and his silence could be bought. In case we got into some unexpected trouble at the ruins, I had to be sure he wouldn't leave us. The only way I could be certain he'd stick around was if he liked cash more than he feared the unknown. Most men had their price. I was relieved when I determined he was no exception.

We had all left the Four Seasons at different times, between eleven in the morning and one in the afternoon, ostensibly to do some sightseeing. We were careful to walk away from the hotel, rather than to take a taxi. When we were certain we hadn't been followed, we paired off into different cabs, again at different times – Gary and Javier in one and Charlie and I in another. We switched cabs twice. A third took us to the airport, where the chopper was leaving at four. I looked at my watch. Everyone was here in the cabin of the Gulfstream. We had at least an hour before the tour chopper was scheduled for take-off.

David and his co-pilot, Russell Jackson, were here, as was Frank Ambrose. Javier supported himself by leaning across the back of the plush gray leather chair where Charlie sat, directly across from where I was. I didn't know Frank as well as the others; I didn't have to. Gary had hand-picked him, and that was all I needed. The first time I saw Frank I thought he must have been who Jim Croce sang about when he quipped, 'And you don't mess around with Jim.' He was one mean looking giant, and he never said much. I remembered thinking he probably saved it for when he needed it, but he always surprised me when he did say something. He was soft-spoken and polite, the epitome of professionalism. His accent pegged him from the South. It had hit me then: put a wide-brimmed hat on him, and he would have made a perfect cowboy.

Gary made eight in attendance. My eyes came to rest on him last. His back was turned to me, screening me from something he was doing. He seemed to be organizing a briefcase. I knew he would hear every word spoken.

"By now everyone knows what Hebrews 11:30 says," I began. "There is no way it could be anything other than what it is."

"A signature." Oddly enough, it was Frank that spoke. His eyelids, half closed, made him look tired. I knew otherwise.

"Yes, that's how I see it," I said to everyone.

"Why?" said David.

"Quote the Bible?" Charlie jumped in. "To identify

themselves. Their note was meant for Jonathan. Him alone. The verse was confirmation. If the note had somehow been intercepted, no one else would know that."

"But we do," I agreed with Charlie. "That verse left no room for interpretation. This leads me to my next observation. Hebrews was written a long time ago."

"A lot older than your tower, Jonathan." Gary finished with what he'd been doing. He turned around to face me. It didn't surprise me he'd put it together as well. The others kept silent as they tried to work it through.

"What Gary means," I explained, "is that this verse is absolute proof these people have planned this for a long time. The story of Joshua's destruction of the city of Jericho is well documented. They sieged the city, and finally, from what I understand, got their instructions from God on how to destroy it. Every day, for seven days, Joshua and his priests marched around the city's walls. On the seventh day, on cue, they sounded their trumpets. The walls of Jericho came tumbling down. They destroyed the rest of the city. A lot of folks died a horrible death. End of story. Seven days after the sons-of-bitches demanded their manifesto be published we all know what happened."

"They sent us a message," David suggested.

"We all heard it," Russell said somberly.

"Now they want to talk?" Javier asked, bewildered. "To you?"

I shook my head. "That doesn't make sense. I've looked at this a hundred different ways since we got that note, none of which add up."

"They sent you the note," David protested.

"They sent jack shit," I said. "I don't have the slightest idea who wants to talk, but I know it's not the same guys who are blowing up the buildings. It's someone else.

The note, well, they knew I would get it. They knew I'd understand it was about the sixty-three floors. I'm here, in town. We made the effort. Now it's their turn. They've got something they want to get off their chests. Maybe they're at war with whoever's taking out the towers. They might see this as a way of evening the playing field."

"They might all be from the same crew," Frank said.

"He's got a point, Jonathan." Gary backed him up.

"Yeah, I thought of that – the idea these guys all started out together. Then, for some unknown reason they had a falling out."

"Mojab." David was catching on.

Charlie added, "It might explain why they killed him. I think we're all in agreement his death was no accident. Someone went through a lot of trouble to claim his body afterwards, too. Whoever he was – whoever was behind this – didn't want anyone having a closer look."

"Why you, boss?" asked David. "There's plenty of spooks floating around here. Whoever this is could've just as easily made contact with one of them."

"My tower. Like I said before, I'm here. We made the effort. They may know the spooks. They may not want to be identified." I shrugged. "All I know is we've got to find out what they want. We have no choice. Right now we're on the point of the sword."

"I don't like the sound of that." Charlie's brow furrowed in that old, familiar way.

"We're running out of time, Charlie." I sighed. Every time I smelled danger my stomach turned to wet pottery clay. I pushed the thought of anything bad happening to her from my mind. I had to think with my head; right now thinking from the heart was a luxury none of us could afford.

"I want to turn the logistics side of this operation

over to Gary. We're not sure what we're walking into. I think it's better if we assume the worst. Anyone wants out, now's the time." I gazed from face to face. No one flinched. "Gary?" I moved out of the way.

Gary used the table between the four leather captain's chairs. He spread the first enlarged satellite photo across most of it, then looked at Praveen's image on the screen embedded in the partition wall in front of him. "I'm showing them the ruins first, Praveen."

Praveen's on-screen image nodded. He still hadn't spoken, but I wanted him to hear everything. He looked his usual, accommodating self. I noted it was just after eight in the morning in New York. As far as I knew, Praveen had been up for over twenty-four hours straight, helping us.

Gary continued, "We'll come in from here, low over the desert floor. Palmyra will come up quick, out of nowhere. The ruins are actually beside Tadmor. That's Arabic for Palmyra. It's a small town, maybe fifty thousand people."

"How can anything live out there?" Russell asked.

"The Ephka Spring," said Gary. "It's the secret to all life in this part of the desert. Palmyra was built because of it. It's an oasis, really, surrounded on all sides by a very unforgiving desert. You've got the valley at Orontes about sixty miles to the west, the Euphrates a hundred twenty miles to the east, and basically nothing north and south of it. Like I said, Palmyra's in the middle of nowhere."

Gary pointed to an object on the image appearing to sit along a road lined by columns on both sides.

"The theater," he announced. "The note indicated this is where the meeting is to take place at eight tonight. The chopper will set down over here, just outside the walls."

"What's that? Here," David indicated a spot on the photo. "It looks blurry. Like the camera was out of focus or something."

"It's been overcast," Gary began to explain.

"The picture was taken an hour ago," Praveen said. "Cirrus cloud cover sometimes interferes with the image quality. We actually have a live feed." He looked at me. "Gus Bakersfield authorized it, Jonathan."

This didn't surprise me. "Why don't we use it?"

"The geostationary satellite might pick up the precipitation," Praveen said. "Besides, a continuous live feed would be redundant. What you needed was a floor plan of the ruins, and some close-ups of the pertinent structures. Mr. Smith argued that the bandwidth did not warrant its use."

I began to fume, but bit my tongue. Criticizing Smith at this point would be counterproductive. I'd talk to him later. I also realized the meeting would be after dark. The satellite photos would be useless then. No one would be recognizable, not even with the Milstar system. 22,250 nautical miles up in a stationary orbit, it still had its limits. Like now. I suddenly remembered what I'd grabbed from the front desk of the hotel right before Charlie and I had gone for our walk along the Barada River yesterday. I was wearing the same pants. I checked my back pocket – it was still there.

"This might work," I said, unfolding the brochure. I spread it out across the table. It was almost as large as the blow-up from Milstar. The detail of the ruins was incredible. The shot could have been the twin of the one we'd been looking at before.

Gary was surprised. "Where'd you get this?"

"The hotel lobby. Every tourist has one – so low

tech it's high tech. They printed a shot from Google Earth to promote the ruins. I suspect by the picture's grain that it's static, about a year old. It's good enough for what we need now, though. They had slightly different software back then. But I'd agree with you, Gary. They're ruins, all right," I smiled, but added, humbly, "Not much has changed out there in the last two thousand years, has it?"

Gary smiled too, seeing the irony the brochure had captured. "They've renovated the place a few times, from what I understand." Then his smile vanished. It was back to business.

"We'll have to hike in from the parking lot."

"How far?" asked David. I'd decided he was coming with us. Russell would stay with the Gulfstream. It was a risk, I knew, leaving only one man with the jet. But I felt it would be even riskier to travel to Palmyra with less than the number we had. We'd be gone for a relatively short time. Russell would be armed. Gary had suggested it in the first place and I agreed.

"This entire area," he swept a flat hand across the image of the ruins, "is about three and a half square miles, less than two miles across. We'll never have to walk that far, though."

"Won't it be treacherous?" David asked. He crowded in closer to the table and pointed to several spots on the photo. "Those look like piles of rubble. We'll have to go around them. It will be dark by eight o'clock."

"No, it won't," Gary explained. "They've got lights all over the place. Some of them are left on all night. Some areas will be in the shadows, true, but we should be fine. We'll land over here, on this spot. It's a parking lot, but it'll be empty by the time we get there. We'll go in through here down what they call the Colonnade, which starts here, at the Temple of Bel. We'll take this short path that branches off to the theater. Then we'll walk in a line, staying at least six feet apart. No closer. If someone gets hit —"

"Hit?" Jackson let out a breath. He wasn't used to finding himself in the middle of what had become a paramilitary operation. He caught himself, and said nothing more.

"If we come under sniper attack it's better if we're not all bunched up. We'll have plenty of cover. The Colonnade is lined on both sides. The stone pillars are huge. When we get to the theater, here, what you'll notice immediately is its size. It's small by Roman standards. Jonathan, you'll come with me."

Gary reached behind himself and retrieved another image, which he laid across the top of the first. It was the theater, six shots from different angles showing every detail of the structure's floor plan. "We'll enter here, at the front of the stage, under the arch and through these pillars. Charlie and Frank will enter at the side of the theater. Stay on your toes at all times and make sure you're not exposed. Stand behind something, if you can. Never stand out in the open, or in front of anything. At the very least, stand beside it. David, you and Javier will also enter at the side of the amphitheater, only you'll go in on the left side, over here. Again, at all times be aware of your surroundings. Think cover."

"Exit strategy?" Javier asked quietly.

Gary looked up at him. "Same as always, my friend, get your package out alive. That includes yourself." He turned his head to Frank, who nodded. From here on in, not that anything had changed, it was all business.

Chapter 13

We lifted off a few minutes after four and headed northeast across the desert. Two hundred feet below the aircraft, a wasteland of sand, rock, and the occasional emaciated shrub slipped past us. Our one-name pilot, Khaleb, had told us it would take a little more than an hour to fly the one hundred and thirty-five miles out to the Bride of the Syrian desert, as Palmyra was sometimes called.

We first saw it as a tiny speck of green on the horizon. Then, just as Gary had predicted, Tadmor came up fast, seemingly from out of nowhere. Khaleb set down just outside Palmyra's ancient walls, in a lot between the ruins and the present day city of Tadmor. I noticed there was a rickety bus and four cars still parked on the other side of the lot. A few straggling tourists gawked at us as we exited the aircraft, not happy with the dust storm we kicked up when we landed. It was five-thirty.

I walked over to Khaleb, who had also disembarked. He was checking something near the exit door. He banged what appeared to be a latch, swore in his dialect, seemed halfway satisfied, and turned when he heard my approach.

"No matter what happens, I want you to get us out of here tonight. All of us."

"Yes, of course." He seemed puzzled. Or had he

taken offense? I saw something flash in his eyes and decided instantly to up the ante.

"Do this, and I'll give you triple what I've already paid you when we get back to the hotel."

Another flash. It was something, almost as if he had caught a speck of dust in his eye. A tick. I wondered what was causing it; whether it was something he couldn't control, or something else.

"Triple," I repeated. "When we all get back safe and sound."

"A man who offers such a sum of money either wishes to get somewhere in a hurry, or get away from somewhere in a hurry. Either way makes no difference to me, Mr. Strickland. I thank you for your generosity. I am, and will always be, at your service." He bowed slightly.

I nodded and walked back over to where the others were gathered, halfway between the helicopter and the bus. The latter was filling back up with tourists for the three hour drive back to Damascus.

I met Charlie first. She fiddled with a digital camera.

"You make a convincing tourist," I said.

She leaned up and kissed me. She was smiling, but I knew inside she was worrying.

"You still tired?" I asked, remembering yesterday. Last night, she'd fallen asleep immediately, and stayed that way until morning. I'd been the one who'd been cursed with a restless night.

"Uh-huh. Now I'm wide awake. But you've got a couple dark circles," she noticed.

"Yeah, I didn't sleep that well last night." I gestured over my shoulder to the chopper. "It might be a good idea if you were to stay with the pilot."

"And miss all the action?" She smiled knowingly.

"Can't blame me for trying."

"No, I can't. But I can love you for it." She took a deep breath and let it out with a gush of wind, looking over to where the ancient ruins began. "So, these are they."

I followed the direction of her gaze. "Yeah, these are they." I felt reverence. I could almost see the robed ancients, hear their voices, as they walked their streets. How different was it back then? The people must have been nearly the same as today. They met, fell in love, had babies. They died. They prayed. They went to war. They bowed to governments. They worshiped the rule of law until something better or worse came along. We had better technology now, though, like C-4 in the base of a building. That thought snatched me back from the centuries. I realized with a start that Gary had his hand on my arm.

"You all right?"

I nodded. "I'm fine, thanks. Just thinking about how it must have been. You know. Back then."

Gary looked over at the ruins. All of us wore sunglasses; he took his off. Already the sun was hanging low. "This place takes you back to an ancient time." He, too, marveled at the spectacle. Then, the moment was over, he returned to the business at hand. "We still have a couple hours. I suggest Javier and I go in, casually. We'll have a look around, turn over a few rocks." He smiled at his pun.

"Funny man," I said, not smiling.

"You guys go into town. We'll meet you in the coffee shop at the first hotel on that street over there." He pointed.

"How long?" I asked.

"An hour, tops. We'll hook up again just before seven. We can all watch the sun go down. From what I've read in the brochures, it's a pretty spectacular sight." He looked upwards. "The sky has cleared up. Should be a good show. See you in an hour."

"Be careful."

"Always." He strode off, Javier immediately joining him.

I kept my eyes open in the café. Everyone did, discreetly. I made small talk with Charlie at a table away from David and the others. The lights came on in the porch area as the sun slipped further toward the horizon. Dusk. Seven.

Five minutes later, just when I began to develop some serious concerns, I spied Javier and Gary as they ambled toward the hotel's front entrance. The café part of it was to the right as soon as we had walked into the hotel. The floor-to-ceiling louvered windows had been opened to the street, but we knew they would soon be closed. With no sun, the desert was quick to cool. Gary came in and sat down in the empty chair next to me. Javier made a beeline over to where Frank was sitting. Frank nodded to him, and leaned closer to Javier in order to hear him without making it obvious they were engaging in a very private conversation. I gazed around the room. It seemed as if nothing had changed. There were perhaps fifteen people in the café, besides us. If anyone had noticed Gary and Javier enter, I couldn't tell. They seemed a contented bunch. Most of them were probably staying at the hotel. They continued to chat with each other, oblivious to us.

"Anything?" I asked Gary casually.

My eyes stayed on the room. Maybe I was paranoid, but I felt like something was different now. I tried to shrug it off. I guess I was an amateur. This must be how it was in a world I realized I had no business being involved with. I should have stayed out of it. I didn't show it, but I was scared. What was out there? Who was waiting in those shadows between the ancient stone buildings? In almost the same instant I was ashamed of my cowardice. Those had been people I knew on the roof of my tower. I was the reason they'd been there. I knew nothing. I could never bring them back. They were gone, but certainly never forgotten. I knew we were racing against the clock, and if we lost this race more innocent people were going to die. No matter what, I was determined to do whatever I could to stop it from happening. Whatever it took. Now I was angry.

Gary faked a smile. A waitress had appeared at the table. We relaxed. He ordered a coffee. It was ten past seven. The waitress went away. Gary said quietly, "The tour bus left. So did the cars. There were still some people in the ruins, but they seemed to be leaving – no one who looked out of place. Back-packing college kids by the looks of it. We followed the Colonnade out to the theater and swept about two hundred yards around it. We didn't see anything out of the ordinary. Whoever they are, they're good."

"Recommendations, Counselor?"

He let out a slow breath. "You and I know that's a tough one. If it was me and my loved ones who were called to this meet, and if I lived in a vacuum, I'd abort. I don't like how it smells. But it's not and I don't. A lot is at stake, so we've got to go in. I don't see we have any choice in the matter. It's all we've got. We have to go for it."

I nodded. "That's how I see it. They're counting on us. Did you read it?" We both knew what I was referring to. No one had had time to catch any television or read any papers. It wouldn't have mattered. They wouldn't have told the full story. We got our report from the Security Office.

"I read enough for it to scare the hell out of me," Gary confessed.

"There's a thin veneer on the so-called civilized world," I said. "Did you read the part about entire cities shutting down? No one's going to work."

"Can you blame them?" Gary kept his voice low. "No one wants to risk dying by having a high-rise building tumble down on top of them. The news media have been replaying the 9-11 emergency calls of people trapped in the stairwells of the World Trade Center right before they came down."

"Talk about throwing gas on the fire. What the fuck makes those people tick?"

"Same old thing," said Gary. "Their numbers are going through the roof."

I said, "I guess everyone can afford a newspaper."

"That is about all they're going to be able to afford. The economy is beginning to look like a flushed toilet. No one is flying. The downtown areas are empty. The first demonstrations have begun to appear demanding the Administration's resignation. Some idiots have even suggested we feed them to these bastards."

I whispered, "Mobs are burning businesses owned by shopkeepers they called by their first names a week ago. I guess their houses will be next."

"I wouldn't want to be olive-skinned, right now." Gary shuddered. "There is a mountain of hate loose in the streets. The people are terrified. They're panicking."

"It's only the beginning. Boatloads will die. It's only a matter of time. This thing is gaining momentum on all sides."

We both fell silent then. As odd as I felt, I understood. Unbeknownst to the rest of the world, we were at ground zero. We had followed the quickest, only lead to have come out of the first downed tower, searching for answers from a man who could no longer speak. Who was he? What more could his spirit tell us? Even now, here, I somehow felt his presence.

"It's time," said Gary.

I nodded, getting up from my chair. The waitress arrived with Gary's coffee. He quickly paid for it. It would grow cold where she'd set it.

All of us gathered in the street outside the front of the hotel. We headed toward the walls of the ruins. It was quarter to eight as we passed the helicopter. Khaleb waved silently to us from across the parking lot where he stood guarding his aircraft. He would wait there for us until we returned. Or not, I thought ruefully.

We spread out. Gary took the lead. I was next. Charlie walked in silence six feet behind me. The others followed in accordance with Gary's earlier instructions. Everyone was quiet.

The sun had all but set as we passed a museum on our left, just outside the walls of Palmyra. We entered through an ad hoc gate and followed a path leading in the direction of the Temple of Bel. Instead of following the path all the way to the Temple, Gary veered to the right, toward the Monumental Arch. I stepped onto the Colonnade for the first time, a few yards away.

There was no time to stop and fully appreciate its majestic beauty. I marveled at the arch, towering in a geodesic formation high over my head. For an instant I felt as if the huge blocks of stone comprising it would suddenly tumble and fall. Then I realized with astonishment that they had been standing, unchanged, for over two thousand years. I could almost touch the ghosts of this city's past. It was wonderful and frightening at the same time.

I wondered how many of our own buildings would stand as testimonials to our accomplishments in the thousands of years to come. They would be here, I realized, in some form or another. We built them to last. Some of them would probably still stand, with or without us to bear witness.

In the penumbra of artificial light, I stumbled on a stone. Gary looked back at me, and kept going. I followed, more mindful now of the path ahead than I'd been before.

I glanced to my left, where the Temple of Nebo had once stood in unprecedented splendor. I was sure it was only the wind, but I could swear I heard the chants of long forgotten worshipers as they exalted their various gods. I stepped on something that gave way and cracked like an eggshell under the weight of my boot. I'd crushed the life out of a scorpion. I ignored it and kept walking.

To my right I peered upon the ruins of what were once the baths of the great emperor Diocletian. I knew from the satellite photos the Roman amphitheater would be located across the Colonnade from these baths. I wasn't disappointed.

Almost straight ahead, beyond the ruins to the west, far up on the side of the mountain, it appeared as if a fire was burning. It was, I realized, the lit sixteenth century Arab castle of Fakhredin Al Maany, a silent beacon of yet another erstwhile empire of days gone by. A ghost on fire, I thought to myself as I followed Gary, who had just taken a left off the decumanus. The theater lay straight ahead. I glanced over my shoulder. Charlie was still behind me, the others in single file behind her. I took a deep breath, and closed in on Gary.

Chapter 14

Shadows seemed to move. Ghosts and phantoms came alive inside the ruins. I thought I saw someone, perhaps more than one person, then shook my head in an effort to clear my vision. My eyes were playing tricks on me in the strange glow of the theater ruins.

I saw Frank and Charlie as I glanced to my right; what Gary had called the left side entrance. They had tucked themselves as tightly as they could into the wall at the end of the bleachers on that side of the theater. To my left, I could see a couple of silhouettes at the end of the stage area, between it and the end of the other side of the semi-circular bleachers. David and Javier hugged the wall near the ground where the stone benches ended. Gary and I hung back beside two opposing columns holding up the portico at center stage. The penumbra of artificial light bathed us in an ethereal glow. We looked like the ghosts I had just imagined.

Now what, I thought impatiently. Five minutes ago the luminescent glow on the hands of my watch had read eight twenty-five. I shifted my position slightly, careful not to make any noise. How long should we wait? When should we call it quits? A half hour? An hour? I was ready to give up and call it off right now, but I knew I couldn't. This wasn't a joke. It couldn't be. If whoever called for this meeting wanted us out of the hotel, or away from the jet, there were other, less melodramatic ways to accomplish it. They didn't have to go to this much trouble. Everything told me this was the real deal. And yet...where were they?

I strained, listening and looking into the strangeness of the night.

It came from in front of the stage: a soft, indistinguishable sound, followed by a slight movement from across the theater floor in the stands, about five rows up in the bleachers. I looked across the floor area of the portico at Gary. He was looking right at me, his finger to his lips. I was relieved he'd heard it, too. At this point, though, we probably could have heard beetles fighting a hundred yards from where we stood.

Gary already had his gun out. He moved swiftly across the stage in a crouch, not making a sound. He stopped for a half second at the front to listen again, then hopped down like a gazelle and bounded across the open area toward the stone bleachers on the far side. I ran as quietly as I could to catch up, noting the others in my peripheral vision moving in our direction from where they'd taken up position. We were converging quickly, and all were accounted for. That meant it wasn't one of ours up there.

There was a stone wall about three and a half feet high rimming the floor of the amphitheater. It separated the floor area from the stands rising above it. Gary vaulted across its rounded top as easily as he would step over a curb. I tried my best to catch up to him as he bounded onto the first bleacher. The rest of us scrambled after him.

"Hey, man!" someone protested.

I could see Gary had grabbed a figure about five rows up into the bleachers. I could see how whoever it was had until now been able to remain hidden. They must have wedged themselves into a space created where the stone ledge of a bleacher met the riser behind it.

Now I heard a woman's protestations. "Get off me!" she screamed. Then, "Help!" as she began to panic.

"Please don't hurt us." The man's voice was pitiful.

By now I began to put two and two together.

"Calm down," Gary said as I climbed up behind him. I was puffing hard, trying to catch my breath. I'd given my all on the sprint to the bleachers. "No one's going to hurt you."

"Then get your hands off us," the guy demanded. He was quickly becoming less timid.

"Stand up," Gary ordered. Now I saw them from over Gary's stooped shoulders. He helped the young man to his feet. They were a couple of kids.

"What are you? A cop? We haven't done anything wrong," he protested.

"We fell asleep," the girl said. They both looked like college students. Everyone relaxed at once.

"We were...we were just –"

"I know what you were doing," Gary said gruffly to the young man.

I stepped forward, trying to be pleasant. "What's your name?"

"Bob." Then more forcefully, "Bob Tucker. This is my girlfriend, Janet Swenson. We were visiting the ruins. We were watching the sun go down. Hey, you're American."

"Yeah, that's right," I said.

"Wait a minute." His eyes seemed to brighten with a kind of recognition. "I recognize you. You're that billionaire. You're Jonathan Strickland. This guy's Jonathan Strickland, Jan."

"Cool." Jan smiled; relieved it was someone her boy-friend recognized. Her eyes were glossy, and slightly out of focus.

Noticing, I said, "If they catch you guys smoking that shit around here you're both going to be in for some serious payback."

He agreed, "So we've been told. It's personal, though. They usually let you off with a warning." He produced a joint from nowhere. "Wanna hit?"

"No thanks."

"If you change your mind..."

"I'll let you know. But thanks for the offer."

"Anytime. Wow. They'll never believe me. *The* Jona-than Strickland." Bob began to take note of the others. "What the fuck are you guys doing in Palmyra?"

Both he and his girlfriend had become relaxed enough to now be curious. I had to end this.

"Seeing the sights." I tried to be nonchalant.

"I saw what they did to your building," Bob pressed. "The one in New York? That was awesome, man. So not cool for those people, though. I guess they never had a chance."

"No, they didn't."

"The media said some of them were your friends."

"Another time, Bob. It still cuts deep. You know what I mean?"

"I feel you, Mr. Strickland. I'm sorry."

"It's all good. But thanks," I said. Bob was a smart kid. He was backing off on his own. "You guys staying at a hotel in town?" I asked in an effort to close the deal.

"Can't afford it," Bob said.

"We're on a budget," Jan admitted. She was smiling now. She was a pretty girl; young, sweet, and innocent. I fished into my pocket for my money clip. I peeled off five one hundred dollar bills.

"Here. Get yourself a room." I handed Bob the bills.

Bob began to protest.

"It's okay." I winked. "I've been there. Besides, what good is money if you don't spend it? And I'm a billionaire, remember? Go ahead, you and Jan enjoy."

He took the small wad of bills. "Thanks, man. This is so cool. Wait until my friends find out about this."

"Uh-uh." I stopped him. He was pulling on the bills. I hung onto them. "One caveat."

"Name it, Mr. Strickland." He realized I was serious.

"Not a word until you get back home. To anyone. You didn't see us. We weren't here."

"I can tell everyone later?"

"Where do you live?"

"Dallas, Texas."

"You can tell the world when you get back to Dallas. But not one word until then." I raised my eyebrows.

"I'd agree even if you weren't giving us any money. I've read about you. I can dig the privacy thing." I let go of the cash.

"Thanks," I said. "I know I can hold you to it."

"I'm not saying it'll be easy," said Bob. "You're one of the richest dudes on the planet. I can't believe we're standing here having this conversation. It's blowing my mind, man."

"If I don't, that other stuff will," I told him. "I can count on you?"

"You can bet the farm on me." I knew I could. He wasn't counting the money.

"Thanks, Bob. Now, uh, we kind of need some privacy," I hinted in a conspiratorial tone.

Bob looked around, then at his girlfriend. She'd pressed into him while we'd spoken. It was going to be a cold night in the desert. "Jan, we got a bed to rent. Let's leave these folks some room to breathe. Later, Mr. Strickland." He proffered his knuckles.

"Later, Bob. Be cool." I rapped the back of his knuckles with my own.

We watched them climb down out of the bleachers. Bob whispered excitedly to his girlfriend most of the way. They crossed the theater floor holding hands, then stopped to wave near the side exit. We waved back. They disappeared beneath a stone archway.

"Those kids nearly gave me a heart attack." Gary dusted off his pant legs.

"For real, man." I smiled. He looked at me. My eyes were serious, even though my demeanor was not.

I shivered. It had probably dropped to fifty degrees. I looked at my watch. The Bob and Jan fiasco had chewed up fifteen more minutes, and it was now a quarter to nine. The note had said eight. They were a no show.

I looked around me. Everyone was in a tight circle, like we were some kind of football team huddling for the next down. Charlie's teeth were beginning to chatter.

"Maybe they're trying to freeze us to death," I said wryly. I winked at her. She moved into me.

"The thought crossed my mind," Charlie said to no one in particular.

"Something must have gone wrong," I said. "I suggest we call it a night. Let's go back to the hotel. They weren't full. We'll grab some rooms for the night and head back to Damascus first thing in the morning. If they want to re-contact us they can try it again from there, unless anyone wants to wait out here for a while longer?"

Under a chorus of no's and one 'not on your life' from Charlie, we began to crawl down the bleachers.

We crossed the theater floor and exited at the side of

the stage, then turned an immediate right, stepping back onto the mile long Colonnade. Gary and Javier led the rest of us up the middle of the dirt path as we retraced our original steps. Bathed in semi-darkness now, we again maneuvered our way past the baths of Diocletian on our left. The ruins of the Temple of Nebo appeared on our right. Here, within a few feet of the Monumental Arch, Gary and Javier stopped dead in their tracks.

"Bob? Jan? Is that you?" It was Gary's voice.

"What's up?" I whispered to him. I'd closed the small gap between us and stood right behind him.

Staring into the darkness beyond the archway, Gary whispered back, "Someone's out there. Up ahead, on the other side of the arch. Whoever it was ducked out of sight post haste."

Javier had already separated from us. He slipped silently to the edge of the road and disappeared behind a circular stone abutment, part of an old column.

"It isn't Bob," I whispered, hoping for another tourist. Nonetheless, my heart was racing.

"Javier will flank him," Gary said quietly. "Wait."

Finally, after what must have only been twenty or thirty seconds but seemed an eternity, Gary began to move again. This time he hugged the side of the ten foot wide path, moving swiftly from cover to cover. I motioned for David to stay with Charlie while Frank and I followed Gary toward the arch. We used the same guarded approach. I watched Gary's back, ten feet in front of me. Frank, on the other side of the Colonnade, had drawn his handgun.

I hadn't quite cleared the arch when I heard the thickly accented voice. It seemed to come from out of the darkness in front of me.

"There is no need for violence." It was now obvious

the man was speaking to Gary.

"Who are you?" asked Gary.

Frank and I caught up to him. Like a deer caught in headlights, a tall man stood in the middle of the Colonnade, directly in front of Gary's drawn pistol. I heard David and Charlie come to a stop beside me and Frank.

"Tell your friend I am no threat to any of you. I mean the one behind me. Please, sir, come forward. Come out. You are making me extremely nervous."

There was a rustling sound as Javier moved out from behind the cover of some ruins twenty feet behind the man. The man himself was dressed in a flowing robe of dark wool, the clothes of the Bedouins. They had been using these same garments for as long as they had traveled the desert, unchanged for thousands of years. The attire kept them cool in the day and acted as a warm blanket to shield them from the cold at night.

I could see the man was no tourist. His face was weathered and deeply lined. His hair was jet black, with a slight wave to it that hid half his ears. I guessed his age at forty. Just as quickly I realized he might also be in his fifties. No Bob, that was for sure.

"Thank you," he said as he glanced at Javier, who approached him warily from behind. He held up his arms to allow us to inspect him more closely. "See?" He smiled. His teeth, I noticed, were clean and even. He'd had dental work done, recently by the look of it.

"Who are you?" Gary repeated. His weapon was still leveled at the man's midsection. Javier had finally reached him from behind. He patted him down quickly and thoroughly. Satisfied the man was unarmed, he said, "He's clean," and backed away a couple of steps. The man seemed unfazed. Gary and I both exchanged glances. Something wasn't right.

"I have no money." The smile never left his face.

"Yeah, well, we didn't come here to rob you," I said. I was nervous that he wasn't nervous. This guy with at least two weapons pointed right at him was still undaunted. For all he knew we would blow him away any second. It didn't make sense.

"You got a name?" I repeated the question Gary had asked him in the beginning.

He looked at me, his eyes absent of malice. Then for the first time he seemed to notice the others. He bowed respectfully, and then gestured with an arm to the ruins, looked downward near his feet at the ground we stood on.

"This dirt path – this road – it is the very same now as it has been for thousands of years. Did you know the most powerful woman who ever lived once walked upon this very spot? She was the great Queen Zenobia, wife of Septimius Odenathus. It is rumored that Zenobia may have been responsible for the assassinations of both her husband and his eldest son, Hairan. Who is to say? One thing is certain: the queen was as ambitious as she was beautiful. Less than three years later she had carved out a vast empire for the formerly tiny Palmyra. Her control extended from Egypt to the Bosphorus. She was by then so powerful that she declared her independence from mighty Rome. She minted her own coins. Can you imagine the temerity, the audacity?" His dark, piercing eyes blinked in wonderment. I didn't think to interrupt him; I, too, found Palmyra's history fascinating. Like a school boy, I continued to listen.

"Rome, of course, could not abide such insolence. The Emperor Aurelian personally led the campaign to destroy her and take back these vast lands which she had claimed for her own. In the end the last battle took place at a location not far from here called Emesa. Seventy thousand against seventy thousand. It must have been glorious. Alas, the Roman legionaries, as they always had been, were victorious. Zenobia was defeated. She fled across the desert, first to Palmyra, and then again to the banks of the Euphrates. It was there she was finally captured, but her life was spared. Some say, like Cleopatra before her, she committed suicide. Others claim she was transported to Rome, where the Emperor paraded her through the streets shackled in gold chains. Later, she married a Roman governor and retired to a villa near Jivoli. Which story to believe?" He shrugged and smiled again, "I much prefer the happier ending. It makes the world seem somehow a better place. Don't you agree?"

I had been transfixed by his storytelling. So had everyone else. Now a deafening silence descended around us.

I broke it by asking him, "Are you a teacher?"

He laughed as if I'd just told the punch line to a good joke. "No. I don't think I am. At least not officially. More of a messenger, I would say."

I eyed him carefully. "What did you say your name was?"

"I didn't, Mr. Strickland." I felt the tension rise with the mention of my name.

"You have an advantage," I acknowledged.

"Yes, I am afraid so. In fact, I have several." His smile suddenly vanished. There was almost a resigned quality to his voice. It was as if he'd been enjoying himself. Now he'd come to some kind of regretful decision.

"Is that some kind of threat?" Gary asked menacingly.

The man looked at Gary as if he was nothing of consequence. "Threats are for the foolish and frightened."

To reinforce my sense of foreboding I carefully

reached out and touched Gary's arm in warning. This guy was too sure of himself. It was all wrong. I'd seen crazy people act this way in the streets of New York, but this guy wasn't crazy. Nothing about him said nutcase. We had to be careful. I began to look more carefully at his bulky garments.

"You seem to know your history," I engaged him in mock pleasantry. "Do you live here?"

"Here?" He looked around. "I suppose for now I do. Yes. Would you like to come to my home? You will be my guest. You and your friends Mr. Strickland; we will have tea together."

"Thanks," I said. "We'll have to pass on that one. We've got a plane to catch."

He looked hurt. "In our culture it is not polite to turn down such an invitation. I am sure your plane will wait for you."

"Sorry. Perhaps another time," I replied.

"Come, Mr. Strickland. Walk the ancient path with me. There is much you can learn from such a journey."

"I've been to school. Goodnight, sir."

"Why did you come here?" His voice took a commanding turn.

"Look," I said. "Whatever you're selling, we're not interested, okay?"

All pretenses of charm left his face. He began to shake his head from side to side, as if he couldn't believe his senses.

"Now I must insist that you accompany me."

Javier jumped in. "Am I missing something here? Or am I just plain stupid? The man said no. And where I come from no means no, sir."

The man glanced sideways at him as if he'd been bothered by a gnat.

"I am afraid I must also insist you all wear blindfolds. Don't worry. You will not die if you cooperate. At least not here, not tonight that is. You have my word. It is for your own protection as much as is it is for ours."

I looked around, not understanding. "What? You want us all to put on blindfolds? And then what?"

"And then I will take you to my leader." He smiled at what he thought was funny.

"That's your message?" Gary said. I could tell the man had exhausted Gary's patience. I wasn't far behind. If he was wearing explosives under his robe, then nothing mattered. We were already dead. But I didn't think so, because Javier wouldn't have missed something that bulky.

"Yes. Among others. I am but a dutiful servant." The man bowed his head slightly. A signal?

"I'm afraid we can't go with you," Gary said, moving his eyes from side to side. He was cleverly looking past the conversation, exploring the shadows around us. The man noticed.

He shook his head again. It was almost a 'tsk tsk' gesture.

"I am afraid you have no choice. You see, at this precise moment there are more than twenty rifles pointed at our bodies." He gestured around him, toward the shadows among the ruins. He turned around in a slow circle, his arms stretched out from his shoulders and stared at me when he returned to his original position.

"If you do not cooperate, we will be killed, Mr. Strickland. All of us, I will die with you. I will become a martyr. That is how it works. I will die so there is no possibility you can use me against my friends, as a shield for instance."

Then I began to see them. And hear them. My eyes

identified tiny holes in the dark. They were indeed, I realized soberly, the business end of rifle barrels hidden among the ruins. We had walked into a trap.

I strained to see past the umbrella of darkness and made out a crooked elbow attached to a barrel protruding from behind a column. Behind it, barely visible, eyes. I saw another one, then another, this time part of a hooded face. I heard a rustling sound and followed the noise to its origin behind yet another part of a Corinthian column. Two more appeared. They were stepping out from behind their cover.

I focused on the man in front of me, our host.

"You've got some friends," I muttered. He stared back at me with a blank, serious-as-cancer expression. He said nothing. It was our move.

"All right, let's do it." I shrugged. For now we were defeated. On the plus side I figured if they hadn't already killed us then maybe we had at least a slight chance of coming out of this alive. However small that chance might be, I'd take it in a heartbeat over the alternative.

"Take us to your leader then, messenger boy."

Chapter 15

Both the blindfolds and the ride were uncomfortable. My last jibe probably hadn't helped our cause any, but I noted with wry satisfaction that it had made me feel a little less helpless, a little more in control. I knew the psychology of our situation would be dynamic. I kept telling myself every time we hit a painful pothole, or an awkward rut, that our survival depended in part on how we conducted ourselves. I didn't know for sure who these guys were, but I had a pretty good notion they were in some way connected with the towers. Who else could they be? Why else would they have blindfolded us, and then thrown us in the back of what must have been some kind of extended panel truck?

The coarse fabric of the blindfold chaffed my skin. I tried to see out from behind the black cloth, but it was useless. They knew their stuff. I kept having visions of the kneeling civilians they used to show who had been caught up in the initial stages of the conflagration in Iraq. Poor bastards, assault files pointed at their heads. The mental torture visited on them had been horrible. And then, finally, the atrocity of being beheaded. I shuddered.

With sheer willpower I drove the horrible images from my mind. I thought of Charlie. She must be terrified. As gutsy as she was, I knew she never bargained for this. None of us had. Cowboys, I cursed myself. Again, I was the one who'd gotten us into this mess. What was I thinking when I'd decided to set out upon this self-indulgent crusade of retribution?

Stop it, I told myself. Look at the bigger picture. This wasn't about me, or Charlie, or Gary, or the others. This was a fight to the bitter end. The very sanity of the world was at stake. It was a global war. In war there were casualties. If we were next, if we must pay the ultimate price, then so be it. At least we tried. We weren't alone, either. These bastards would find this out soon enough. We'd kill every last one of them if we had to. We'd win in the end. I knew that. But I was still scared.

We hit another pothole. I thought I heard David grunt. We'd been instructed to remain silent, but fuck it.

"You all right, David?" I said to the darkness.

"I'll live," he said.

"Silence!" someone hissed.

Underneath my blindfold, I smiled. In the war of psychology score one for the good guys.

It was all about control: who had it, and who didn't. I was okay, I realized with satisfaction. If I was going down, it wouldn't be pretty. They were going to have to work for it. I wasn't rolling over for anyone. I hoped the last thing I did was spit in their motherfucking eyes with the last breath I had after they slit my throat. I'd bet the farm everyone else was thinking the same thing right about now. A strange kind of peace descended over me. I began to think about how we were going to get out of this.

We'd been driving for about a half an hour. I gave up trying to count the number and direction of the turns the driver was making; it was obvious he was putting in time. We weren't really going anywhere. That way it appeared we were traveling a much greater distance than we actually were. The occasional sounds, plus the potholes, told me we hadn't gone into the desert, which I felt was a good thing. Bodies were easy to get rid of out there. We were obviously driving around the streets of Tadmor. I heard at least two other trucks, so now wasn't the time to try to escape. The other vehicles were undoubtedly full of guards. They had taken our guns. Resistance was futile. We had to ride it out.

With a squealing of spent brake pads on worn out discs, we slowed and finally came to a stop.

Up front, I heard the driver of the truck say something in a language I thought to be Arabic. He spoke with someone for another few sentences. Then the other truck carrying Charlie, Javier, and Frank pulled up behind ours. I heard a latch click. The doors on the side of the van slid open. We were herded out and then down a short path. I stumbled; someone caught me.

I still couldn't see anything. We were then halted as we arrived at what I assumed was our destination. There was another short exchange, again in the same, vaguely familiar dialect as before. Then I felt something small and hard press painfully into my back. It was a gun. I didn't argue. I followed the prod through an obvious entryway. I heard commotion and some talking behind me. I breathed easier because then I knew all of us had been brought to the same safe house. I was also aware, given the fact we were now officially kidnap victims, that up to this point we had been treated rather well. So far, the poke to my ribs had been the worst of it.

I was steered across a hollow sounding wooden floor to a spot where I was finally stopped. I was turned around, and the rope binding my hands was removed. No one stopped me when I reached up to remove the blindfold. I rubbed my eyes and blinked as they adjusted to the dim light of the room.

I first noticed the others around me. Charlie was only a few feet away. I quickly approached her and helped her remove her own blindfold. She saw it was me and grabbed me in an embrace.

"You okay?" I asked. She nodded into the front of my jacket. "They didn't hurt you?" She shook her head and looked at me.

"I'm all right." She smiled weakly. "Everyone accounted for?"

I glanced around. Gary was rubbing his wrists, regaining his circulation. He looked thoroughly annoyed, like he wanted to eat a live cow. It made sense. They had probably adjudicated him the worst troublemaker and tied his bonds more securely than the rest of ours. The others didn't look any happier than I felt.

"All present and accounted for," I said in a tone which I hoped would reassure her. "Don't worry. If they wanted us dead they would have already done it."

"This is correct, Mr. Strickland," a soft voice I hadn't heard before said from behind me. I turned to see who'd spoken.

The man I was looking at was in his forties. He looked vaguely familiar to me. His long, angular face was bearded. His eyes were droopy, sunken into their sockets. It gave him a perpetually weary appearance, as if he hadn't gotten an uninterrupted night's sleep in a very long time. But that couldn't conceal the intelligence they eschewed. He contemplated me from where he sat on top of a rug near the back wall of the room. As far as I could tell it had no furniture at all, unless I counted the pillows on the floor around the rug. The six of us stood in the middle: eight men armed with automatic rifles hugged two of the four walls around us. It was a perfect crossfire position. A ninth man, also sitting, leaned close to the man who had spoken. He whispered something in his ear. The man, still studying me intently, nodded. I couldn't tell for sure, but I perceived he was much taller than the others. The man we had originally spoken with on the Colonnade – the messenger – was nowhere in sight.

A door on the opposite side of the room from which we entered suddenly opened. Another man, dressed similar to the two who were seated on the carpet, entered the room. The three of them wore the same traditional Islamic loose cloak, or *bisht,* as the messenger had been wearing. I noticed the garments were nothing fancy; they were stitched from camel hair. This guy was carrying a tray of tea. He dutifully set it with great care in front of the man who I had decided ran things around here. He reached and began to pour. The leader waved him off with a polite gesture. The server half bowed, and then left by the same metal-hinged wooden doors through which he'd entered.

The leader spoke again. "Please, Mr. Strickland. Join me. Your friends, too." His invitation surprised me. Not that we were asked to join him – that I expected. It was more the inflection of his voice, soft and sincere. He gestured to either side of where he and his consigliere sat. "Forgive me for such melodrama. These are very dangerous times we live in. One can never be too careful."

I shrugged. "Why not? It's been a while since I had tea." I moved closer to the carpet.

He smiled. "Here," he offered. "On my right side, Mr. Strickland. In my culture it is the seat of honor."

"Thank you," I said, playing along. Oddly enough, I found I couldn't help liking the guy. In spite of everything, he played the gracious host. I knew, however, it was the relationship of a flute player to the cobra.

I sat next to him. Charlie sat next to me. The others found spots around the edge of the circular rug.

"You know who I am," I opened after everyone had seated themselves.

He nodded. "Yes. You are a very famous man. We have satellite television and CNN here too, you know."

I smiled in spite of myself.

He poured the contents of the large teapot into handmade ceramic mugs. As he finished, each mug was handed to each of us in turn by his assistant.

"Smells good," I admitted. Its aroma had an almost medicinal quality to it. I could feel my sinuses reacting.

"It is Persian. At least, some of the herbs used are. It has been made the same way for thousands of years. I hope you like it," he said sincerely. "It was very popular in the time of Christ."

"I didn't think you acknowledged Him," I said.

He was careful in his response. He thought for a few seconds before he replied, "Religion, like war, makes strange bedfellows, Mr. Strickland." The thought occurred to me that everybody knew my name, but these guys weren't telling us theirs. I guess that was their prerogative. They had the guns.

Charlie finally spoke up. "Do you make it a habit of kidnapping your guests? Or is it just us?" She feigned cordiality. I winced.

But our host simply replied, "It was for reasons of security, Miss Bakersfield. No one has treated you harshly." It was true. "You are not being held against your will, if that is what you think. You are free to leave at any time. Of course we must blindfold you again, and then take you back. That will be the end of it."

"No," I said quickly. "We came because we were invited. Are you familiar with the Bible?"

"Yes," he said. "In fact I find a number of stories contained within it to be quite fascinating." The leader carefully sipped his hot tea. I tasted mine. It was a subtle, spicy flavor. I liked it immediately.

"Very good," I commented.

Our host seemed genuinely pleased. "I am glad you are enjoying it."

"I do. What story in the Bible do you find to be the most interesting?" I looked into his eyes.

They twinkled with life. "There are many interesting stories, of course. Several stand out. But I have always found the story of Jesus and the temple to be the most provocative of them all."

"Which one?" I was curious now. "Christ spent a lot of time around temples."

The leader nodded. "This is true, of course. I was referring to the time when He lost His temper. It is the account of when in an uncontrollable rage He turned over the tables and drove out the money changers at the end of a whip. When He sinned."

"You think Christ sinned?" I found the idea intriguing. In all my experience it had never once occurred to me that the Son of God may have sinned. "I always thought God was without sin, that He was incapable of it."

"Yes, absolutely. God is without sin," he replied emphatically. "But," he waved a long, slender finger in the air, "this was God in human form, subject to human frailties. He loved, He felt sadness, He felt joy, and sadly, He felt indescribable sorrow as well. He experienced everything you and I have experienced, and more. He was here, on this earth, one of us, constrained by the same parameters that constrain us all. God sent him, the infinite trapped inside a finite being. One of us." He smiled knowingly. "You see, if He cheated, none of it would have worked. That single act of allowing Himself to be crucified became the lynchpin of the Christian belief system. Everyone, including one of the thieves who died on the cross next to Him, has always wondered why He just didn't snap His fingers and get out of it. Dying on a cross, crucifixion, is among the most horrific deaths one can imagine. The pain would be excruciating. Over time exhaustion sets in. The joints rip from their sockets at the shoulders. In many cases victims lasted for a week or more, publicly humiliated in their nakedness. Finally, they succumbed to asphyxiation."

"Christ wasn't that strong," I said.

"No, he wasn't. Mercifully, his injuries killed him fairly quickly."

"What makes you think He couldn't have stopped it?" I asked somberly.

"The Bible itself." He seemed surprised at the question. "In His own words, proof beyond any doubt, He honestly believed the Father had abandoned Him."

I nodded. I said quietly, quoting scripture, "Father, why hast Thou forsaken Me?"

"He believed in those last moments He was truly alone. Think of it! He questioned everything, His very faith. Because if He'd been abandoned, then it had all been a lie from the very beginning. None of it was real. He was just another zealot. Perhaps a notch above John the Baptist, but certainly not the Son. At that moment, I believe He knew only what it was to be a human being. He felt every man's pain and anguish. He experienced all the doubts and fears we feel. Are we doing the right thing? Or is what we believe in a lie? Have we been fooled? Who do we believe in if we doubt ourselves? Our own senses? Who will lead us? Who will be our hero?

God was truly understanding the one thing He had never before experienced: what it was like to stand in the shoes of His own creation."

I felt the hair stand up on the back of my neck as I listened to him, feeling confused, angry, and exhausted all at the same time. I prided myself on having an open mind. My initial, knee-jerk reaction to his preposterous theories had been to humor him by listening to them. After all, he was no Christian. His air mile points came from discrediting those Western delights. But the more I thought about what he'd said, the more I began to realize he wasn't saying anything that contradicted what I'd been taught as a kid in Sunday school. He was taking it farther in a way that, if I had to be real honest with myself, did not in any way demean Christianity. His case, I realized, did the opposite. It explained our religion in a way that was respectful. What he was proposing made a lot of sense.

"Your faith is Islam," I guessed politely. "And yet you know much about Christianity."

He chuckled pleasantly, shaking his head. "You Westerners. You live in boxes, work in boxes. You demand all things be defined. It is science you worship more than all else. What is the first thing you ask of another after the exchange of pleasantries? 'What do you do?' 'What is your religion?' Jesus Christ did not die as a carpenter. Even the sign above His crown of thorns told the world He was King of the Jews. The irony lay in the fact that when the Romans attempted to ridicule Him, they inadvertently exalted Him for all of man to see. And so now you accuse me of being Islamic."

"I accuse you of nothing, sir. I only assumed –"

He cut me off, "One of your greatest sins is your arrogance. The West assumes they know everything." I noted the first hint of anger flash behind his peaceful facade.

"I won't disagree with you. You're right. Sometimes we are guilty of being know-it-alls," I conceded. "But I can assure you..." I glanced at a couple of his armed guards. They hadn't moved since taking up positions around us. If they had even blinked, I hadn't noticed, "I'm not one of them."

"You come from a privileged background, Mr. Strickland," he pointed out. He'd done his homework.

"For all I know, so have you," I countered. "But I didn't come here to get into some kind of pissing contest. You're right, again. I've got money. Lots of it. But there's no crime in having money. It's in what you do with it. Therein lies the rub, as Shakespeare put it. I earn a lot. But I also spend a lot. I try my damnedest to give back in places I feel can do the most good. I'm no angel. I've never said I was. I'm just an ordinary guy. I do the best I can with what I've got. And with what I've been given." I didn't need him, or anyone else for that matter, accusing me of being some self-righteous proselytizer.

He considered me carefully for a few moments, sipping his tea as I sipped mine. I tried to hide my nervous shaking by holding my cup with both hands.

"We are not enemies," he finally said after setting down his teacup.

"Someone murdered my friends." I studied the leader's eyes. They gave nothing away. "In New York, we say the enemy of my friend is also my enemy."

The leader smiled. "We say the same thing here."

"Was it your note?"

"Yes," he replied. "It was our note."

I nodded.

"You know who killed my friends, then," I said warily. My tone was intentionally halfway between a question and an answer.

"You have not once mentioned the destruction of your building." His tone carried the same inflection as mine had.

"My only concern at this moment is for the people who died," I admitted honestly. "And for those who will soon follow if we do not stop those who are responsible. The towers themselves are nothing more than molded piles of clay."

"They represent everything which the West stands for," he said.

I shrugged, "That may be true. For me, it's the people. My friends. I'd like to see the killing stop. I like peace, not war."

"You came here armed."

"To protect ourselves. To stop the killing. My friends and I are not the aggressors. This is not something I ever imagined I would be a part of. You might say I'm one hell of a reluctant warrior."

"Do you love your country, Mr. Strickland?"

I sighed. "No, sir, I do not." I felt his surprise. "My country is dear to me, but I save love for the people in my life. My country's like one of those towers I build. In fact, build enough towers, and they become a country. The reverse is true, too. Tear enough towers down, and the result is a different country. Either way, the constant is the change. Empires come and go. Powerful armies emerge from ashes, and in time are destroyed as well. As the human race I think we should always look for a new way – a better way. A way which benefits the most people it possibly can. My view of the world is a bit utopian, I know."

"You and John Lennon," he said.

I smiled. "He was a decent man. Too bad there's not more like him. We seem to kill all the good ones."

"It is the nature of the beast within us all," he agreed.

"Do you know who murdered my friends? Do you know who gave the orders to kill them?"

A deafening silence suddenly enveloped the room. Finally, after what seemed an interminable amount of time had passed, the leader said, "the Joshua Effect. That is the name by which it is known." He stared at me.

"The Joshua Effect," I repeated in a whisper, stunned as I slowly began to comprehend the horrible implications of the two words he'd just spoken. Suddenly I felt sick to my stomach.

Chapter 16

My brain finally stopped swimming inside my skull. Mercifully, the nausea faded. I swallowed hard in a futile effort to remoisten the back of my desert-dry throat.

"The verse from Hebrews," I said hoarsely. "It wasn't just to get us out here to meet you."

"I'm afraid not," the leader stated matter-of-factly.

"It's a plan," Gary chimed in. He looked from me to the leader. "The effect of the monoliths' destruction will have was carefully considered before this plan was implemented. What did you guys do? Have a roundtable on the best way to destroy the world?" The lawyer's eyes were piercing. "Who dreamed up this one?"

The leader didn't give an inch. He remained perfectly calm. He stared back directly into Gary's hardened eyes.

"You did, Mr. Stanick," he said quietly. Then he elaborated, "You write about it. Bestselling authors produce bestselling books; your Hollywood makes the blockbuster movies. Anyone who is inclined in such a direction does not need to dream up anything, as you say. Your culture's unbridled avarice accomplishes this for them. You have become one of the most violent societies on earth. You kill your own. You kill us. You kill anyone who stands in the way of your ideology and then you glorify it in print and film. No room in America with a television is immune to the obscenity. Your culture swims in that pool. That's where *we*," he emphasized the word we, "get our ideas. Whose weapons do you think the world uses? Whose advanced technologies? We don't buy them from you. Quite the contrary, you sell them to us. There is a difference."

"We don't teach people to do crazy things."

The leader's brow lifted in a way that suggested perhaps Gary rethink his last statement. He said, "Right. Guns don't kill people. Neither do bombs. If you are correct, and not simply self-righteous, then how can we possibly explain the world today? The Americans have led the world for many years, but you did not watch your servants very carefully, did you? You slept. And while you were sleeping things got crazy. You once had a democracy."

"We still do, last time I checked," David said petulantly.

"What we have has changed," Gary admitted. "It has had to change to accommodate the changes in the world around us."

"And you have had nothing to do with those changes?" the leader accused. "If you believe this, then I have grossly overestimated all of you." A sadness had crept into his voice.

I stepped into the fray. "You haven't overestimated anyone. Isolationism ended with Pearl Harbor." I was speaking to our host, but admonishing Gary and David at the same time. It wouldn't be the first time pride got in the way of common sense. I realized they were being patriotic. They were defending the flag. But they were dead wrong if they believed for one second the States didn't affect the way people around the world thought about a lot of things.

Everyone respects a leader, some out of admiration, and others from fear. Fear was bad. The West, I knew, had evolved to believe it was necessary. It was an argument of perspective based in part on ideologies. Right now, though, I didn't feel this philosophical discussion was going in a direction that helped our cause. Whoever this guy was, he'd been ready to talk. I desperately wished to hear what he had to say.

"We are your guests," I said. "I sincerely apologize on behalf of everyone here if we have in any way offended you. If this has happened it has been an inadvertent consequence of being raised an American. We are an extremely proud people. We pull together during tough times, but we're not always right. Given enough time, though, we've been known to correct a mistake or two."

"Your apology is accepted," the leader replied with a barely perceptible bow of his head. The room thankfully warmed. Inwardly I sighed with relief. "Unfortunately, as you are well aware, time is running out."

I nodded gravely, "Yes. Of this I am certain." I went for it then. "Sir, you called us here for a reason. Is this reason to help us? What do you know of what you called the Joshua Effect?"

He sipped more tea before he responded, taking time to dab at his upper lip with the knuckle of his right index finger. He would choose his words carefully when he was ready to speak. Suddenly the man who sat cross legged beside him leaned over, and whispered behind a cupped hand into his ear for a long time. The leader nodded occasionally throughout this one-sided conversation. Finally, with one last nod, he held up his hand. The consigliere, as I thought of him, instantly ceased whispering. He leaned away and resumed his original position. I waited patiently, throwing sidelong glances to everyone in a silent order to keep their mouths shut. This was it. I didn't want anyone fucking things up.

"Mr. Stanick was correct," the leader began. "There were people who discussed scenarios. They discussed possible outcomes."

No computer models, I thought wryly. No casualty counts based on which cities got nuked. Those were scenarios from the dinosaur era of the Cold War. This war of necessity had to be fought differently. So far no computer invented could predict how people would react emotionally to terrorism. Their hearts and minds were their own, as unique and individual as fingerprints. No software ever written could capture the 'feel' of mass hysteria. No model I knew about could tell our leaders how to deal with the emotional volatility of what was happening Stateside even as we spoke. The world watched as the most stalwart of all societies disintegrated before their judging eyes. Our allies might in some way empathize, but our enemies? Who knew what they were planning next?

"Outcomes?" I prodded him. "What kind of madmen sit around and discuss what's going to happen when they start destroying superstructures?"

"Determined. Motivated. Patient. But certainly not madmen. They are anything but mad."

"Who's doing it?" As long as he kept talking, I figured I'd keep asking. "How many buildings were rigged?"

"Perhaps two dozen, that I know of. There are probably more."

I stared at him in disbelief. "Why mine? Why didn't they take out one of the other ones first? Wouldn't it have been far more effective if they had killed more people?"

He shrugged. "Perhaps. We don't always know the why. I believe they wanted to see how it would work, how it would play out. I believe their expectations have been exceeded."

Gary asked, "Can you tell us who they are?" His tone, I noticed, was more conciliatory. The lawyer in him was speaking now.

"Specifically? Not the foot soldiers. Those in charge?" He sighed and leaned back, straightening his frame. Sitting couldn't hide his height. "This has changed."

"What do you mean changed?" I asked, bewildered. It was double talk. Gary caught my eye. I let him continue his subtle cross-examination of our star witness.

In a calm, measured voice Gary said, "The team leaders took over, didn't they? They are no longer following orders."

The leader said, "It doesn't matter, but yes. As of now these cells are operating independently."

"Do you know why?" Gary persisted.

"They felt those giving the instructions had become too moderate. In *jihad* it is not simply death to some Americans. All Americans, and their allies, must die. No matter what."

"They don't see the bigger picture."

"No. Of course, it is impossible to kill everybody. Any idiot knows this. A society, its culture, must be destroyed through a combination of forces acting in tandem. The attacks must be carefully planned and executed to create an environment within the society itself that assists in its own destruction. Eventually the society will, in fact, destroy itself from within. It is like setting a house on fire: the fuel which destroys the home must come from the house itself, and not from the forest surrounding it."

Gary inserted, "But once these people got started..."

"Yes. Once the cells determined a method by which

the explosives could be integrated into the foundations of the superstructures during the initial phase of their construction, the soldiers became more committed – more zealous – than anyone could have imagined. They struck out on their own. A means, in their minds, became the end."

"Someone was sent to renegotiate," I guessed. "Someone important."

He nodded.

"Mojab," I said.

He nodded again. "Others were sent before him. He was the last one who went over in an attempt to reason with them."

"He knew some of them, didn't he?" I asked. "He was someone's friend. He trusted that person. Did they give him their word no harm would come to him?"

The leader sighed heavily. "He was betrayed."

"By his friend?" Gary asked.

The leader looked at him. He smiled a resigned smile. "Does it matter? The results speak for themselves."

"I think we can all agree on that," I said. "But who was Mojab? We have satellite images showing his body being transferred in Damascus to a jet belonging to the Saudi Royals. It was then flown to Riyadh. Are the Saudis behind this?"

His eyes became dark pits. "This I cannot say."

"You don't know?" I pressed him.

"The West will be destroyed. Mr. Strickland." He ignored my question. "One way or another, but it is better that its destruction be controlled, not chaotic. Power, as you know, abhors a vacuum."

"You think you can select our leadership?" I was stunned at his audacity.

He returned, "Have you not selected leaders in nations your government has toppled? Is the notion so strange, or are you now being your usual hypocritical selves?"

An uncomfortable silence filled the air, punctuated by my own labored breathing. I didn't understand much about politics. I knew it was a get-down-and-dirty business, and I wondered if he was right. I'd heard the phrase 'puppet democracy' before, but never really paid much attention, thinking it had no effect on me and my life. And yet here I was, all in less than two weeks. The world had seemed so very different back then.

Well, that was then. Now was now.

"Touché," I granted him. "I guess none of us are angels."

"You learn fast, Mr. Strickland," he said. He appreciated my sincerity.

"The explosives were C-4," Javier said. "Both the Americans and the Israelis make it, while the Soviets and Chinese use Cemtex. Was this intentional?"

"Again irrelevant," the leader said quietly. "It is already done."

Meaning the explosives were in place.

He was right, of course, but we didn't yet know how the detonation process worked. Javier had been clever in his attempt to unearth a clue, and I knew Artie McKenzie and the rest of the lab were working on it around the clock; but if we could learn any information as to how the explosives were being triggered, we might be able to somehow stop the process.

I realized we were playing a cat and mouse game. The leader was giving us little. Getting anything from him was painful and slow, but it was clear to me now he had enemies within his own party. Some of his own had run amok and he had an extremely awkward problem on his hands. He had to stop, or at least slow down his own people, without having it appear contrary to the *jihad* in which his people felt they were fully engaged. Mojab, it now appeared, had crossed that line. Either that or he'd truly been an assassin sent to take whomever out. Bottom line was he'd been executed for it, along with the others the leader had referred to. Who the hell had he meant?

I wondered if those had been some of the early deaths of the foundation construction workers we'd managed to uncover. Probably. At least some of them had to have been foreign operatives who'd been murdered for their more temperate approach to terrorism. I guess they hadn't been fundamental enough for the rest of the zealots. So much for moderation.

"How are the explosives triggered?" Nothing else seemed to be working, so I finally tried the direct approach. "We have determined their composition, but so far we don't know anything about the detonators."

My gamble in giving up this information was calculated: I figured the honesty might just be reciprocated. Even a hint as to how the trigger mechanism worked would make the trip to Syria worth it. If we could determine how the explosives were ignited, then perhaps the boys in the lab could do some reverse engineering and somehow shut them down. Maybe it was wishful thinking on my part, but it was all I could think of.

He contemplated me carefully again. Almost on cue, his buddy leaned over to whisper something to him. But this time the leader stopped him with a slight wave of his hand. He'd made up his mind.

"You are a very intelligent man," he began carefully. "Wise beyond your years."

I bowed slightly to acknowledge his compliment.

"My position in this matter is a delicate one. It seems

I am called upon to satisfy more than one master. I noticed you never asked for the location of the doomed structures."

I shrugged, "Without the detonation sequences, if that's how it's being done, what good would they do? Plus, how would we know your information was genuine? I figure we need to eventually match a sequence with a building – that goes without saying. But we need to be able to shut one down somehow. Then we can verify if the building's rigged or not. Once we can confirm one..." I shrugged again.

"Then you can trust the source information to be accurate," he finished for me.

"Something like that. At least we'll know how to jam up the works. Whether it will work unilaterally or not is something the technology wizards will have to figure out. I'm not a scientist."

"But you are very intuitive."

"There's only so many ways to explode a bomb, less if it's buried in concrete. How are you doing it? Is it current, or wave? My guess is the latter. We can shut down electrical grids, even single buildings. It's easy to turn out the lights. Whoever planned this knew this. But waves? Uh-uh. That's a tough one. UHF by wireless command? You could bounce the signal off a satellite using a cell phone, or so I suppose. My guess is you didn't make it easy. Did you even have an exit strategy, in case something went wrong? I guess not. That's why we're here, isn't it?"

A lot of things then happened at once, most of which I wasn't even aware of until after the fact. It began as Charlie moved her hand toward her chest. It was barely perceptible, she'd tell me later, but the gold locket around her neck had begun to warm to the point where it caused her discomfort. She brought her hand to where it hung. It was an innocuous, reflexive motion. Under normal circumstances it would never have been noticed, but these weren't normal circumstances. They were anything but.

The leader's brow furrowed. "What is that?" he said to Charlie as he noticed her finger the pendent beneath her blouse.

At first she wasn't sure he was speaking to her. Then, as he continued to stare, we all followed his gaze.

"Ow!" Charlie gasped. She ripped the pendant from her neck. It was painfully hot to the touch. She looked at the broach in confusion.

"Give it to me! Now!" the leader ordered. He was suddenly on his feet. The rifles around the room were once again leveled at our midsections. He barked a tirade in Arabic, and someone stepped forward to snatch the locket roughly from Charlie's outstretched hand. The thick gold serpentine chain whipped through the air behind the pendant. At the same time all of us began to get to our feet. No one stopped us, but I moved slowly. It was clear to me everyone was agitated as hell, like someone had stuck a lit pole into a wasps' nest.

The leader had closed his hand around the locket. Now he seemed furious.

"What is it?" I demanded, perplexed. "What's wrong?"

He looked straight at me then, searching my eyes for the truth. All he saw was confusion. I could tell he was forcing himself back under control. "You have killed us, Mr. Strickland," he barely managed through gritted teeth. "God help us all."

Chapter 17

"They're killing you, too," he cried, almost in surprise. Then he switched again to Arabic and everyone began to run. I grabbed Charlie.

"Let's get out of here."

My natural reaction was to look toward the door, but something odd in the corner of my eye stopped me.

"Gary! David!" I hissed. My grip on Charlie's shoulder was viselike, but I wanted her right beside me.

They turned and followed my gaze to the spot where the leader and his consigliere had formerly been sitting. We watched as the consigliere threw back the carpet from where it butted up against the wall. He was being helped by one of the armed guards. They worked quickly. Everyone else was scrambling toward the front of the room, leaving from where we had first entered. The leader caught my eye, then, oddly, in a frantic motion he waved me not away, but toward where he stood as his minions located the latch to what was now obviously a trap door near the middle of where the carpet had been.

"This way!" he ordered.

With great effort the guard and the consigliere hefted a piece of the floor upward. It folded over on hidden hinges and stopped about fifteen degrees off center. I noticed the chain holding it as everyone hurried across the wood floor to the entranceway it had hidden only a moment before.

Charlie went first down into the hole. David, almost on top of her, was next, followed by Frank, Javier, the consigliere and the guard. Gary grabbed me under my arm. Without warning, he hoisted me like a crane loading a container onto a freighter and into the cramped entrance. I dropped down and hit a dirt floor about five feet below. I was jerked away from it into semi-darkness just as our host was lowered right after me, presumably by the much stronger Gary.

The mysterious man knew the way. He squeezed past me in the narrow confines of what was obviously an underground tunnel. With relief I heard Gary thump to the floor behind me. I turned just in time to see him reach back up and pull on the chain. The door thudded to a close in time for the hollow concussion of the first explosion somewhere above. Dirt and suffocating clouds of dust cascaded from the shoring around us. We hacked and fought our way forward.

A couple of us already had flashlights out and turned on.

"Quickly!" directed the leader. His voice came from somewhere ahead in the narrow tunnel.

As I scrambled in the direction of his voice in the pitching flashlight beams I realized why I hadn't been able to see him. Within a few feet the sheer walled tunnel took an immediate ninety degree turn. I almost stumbled as I rounded the corner and found that the tunnel began to descend steeply. Everyone groped frantically after whoever was in front of them. Above and behind us, I could hear more explosions, missiles I guessed, although I had no way of knowing for certain.

It finally hit me that the house we'd been standing in

seconds ago was being bombed into oblivion. Somewhere in the back of my mind I was already realizing with equal horror how the target had been located. My mind raced as I ran and stumbled along. Whoever had this kind of technology was on a very short list.

We kept going down for several hundred yards before the claustrophobic tunnel finally leveled off. The only thing I heard now was the raspy, heavy breathing of the people directly in front of me. Gary's breathing behind me sounded like the chug of a steam engine.

I felt like a coal miner, trapped deep in the bowels of a shaft which in my imagination ran miles beneath the earth's surface. I bounced off the walls on either side, and wondered how long it would be before the shoring gave way and tons of dirt tumbled in on us. We would be buried alive. No one would ever know; no one would ever come for us. We would be smothered. I shivered involuntarily in the cool, damp, stuffy air. Suffocation wasn't my first pick as a way to die.

We traveled horizontally for perhaps fifteen more minutes. No one spoke. My own breathing sounded like a blacksmith's bellows. Finally, the tunnel turned upwards again. Yes. Relief washed over me like a cool breeze.

Eventually we were forced to stop. I craned my neck to see around the hunched forms of the guard and the consigliere and caught a glimpse of Javier, who was next in line. That was as far as my vision went.

I surmised this end of the tunnel was probably configured similarly to the other end, and took the same ninety degree turn before the shaft went vertical. The reason for this design was now painfully obvious; it had probably saved our lives. Any concussive force emanating from a mortar or missile attack would be buffered by the walls of the tunnel. The deadly energy never reached us. I wondered now with regret how many of those who'd gone the other way had made it. I'd probably never know. But who was responsible? One thing was certain, whoever it was, they'd made their first big mistake. We were alive, and they'd left their first clue.

"You okay?" Gary had noticed me rubbing the sore spot under the arm he'd used to lower me into the entrance hole. I looked at him with renewed respect. I'd always known he was strong, but this had been a little unreal. He'd tossed me down that hole as if I were a department store mannequin.

"I'll live," I grunted.

"Sorry."

"Don't be. You saved my skin."

Gary grinned. "I was just getting you out of the way, boss. I was the last man out."

I grinned now, too. "Good thing you decided not to go through me."

"It's amazing what you can do on an adrenalin cocktail. I take it this is the exit end?" He tried in vain to see around me.

I turned to follow his gaze, saw it was futile, and tuned back. "That'd be my guess."

"Where do you think it comes up?"

"Somewhere safe, I hope." I had tried to keep track as best as I could as to how far we'd traveled underground, but we were running like rats from flood-waters. "I'd guess we've moved through over a mile of tunnel. We could've been going in any direction, though." With no reference point there was simply no way of determining which direction we'd taken, and I wasn't exactly in the mood for guessing.

"Who do you think attacked us?" Gary asked.

"Not the Syrians. They don't have that kind of sophistry," I said.

"Charlie's necklace?"

I nodded. "Had to be some kind of homing device. They would have needed to triangulate in order to get a fix on our location. I don't think it worked quite the way it was supposed to, though."

"What do you mean?" Gary whispered.

"It burned her. It overheated. I think the device short circuited. It gave us just enough warning to flee. Another few seconds and no one would have left that house alive. Our man up there is smart." I nodded ahead of us. "He doesn't miss a trick. I wonder who he is?"

Gary's eyes narrowed. He remained silent. If he had any idea as to who the leader was, he was keeping it to himself. The walls, as they say, had ears.

The line began to move again. I shrugged at Gary, "This should be interesting."

I was right. There was a right turn, then ten more feet of tunnel before it ended, or at least rose vertically through the ground. A small wooden ladder, perhaps five rungs in height, was leaned against the end wall to announce the way out. I took a deep breath and began to climb.

I helped Gary out of the hole and took a look around. I don't know what I expected to see, but I was still amazed.

One of the Arabs had lit a lantern that must have been left behind. I looked at the hole we'd exited. That in itself was curious, but I now saw why we'd had to wait, too.

A heavy stone, which normally would have looked like the feet of a ten foot high statue, had been forced away from its base. With obvious effort, the heavy stone had been pivoted sideways away from the massive figure above it. We watched as the soldier and the consigliere pushed it back into its original position. It swiveled around, grating on the stone slab under it, until the feet fit snugly back into the statue. It was seamless. No one, without knowing better, would ever be able to tell the statue's feet doubled as an entrance to a secret tunnel.

The rest of the room was awe inspiring. We were in a giant arched hallway, where carved cornices with ledged tops circumscribed the entire ceiling. They marked the end of the walls fifteen feet above our heads and the beginning of a domed ceiling supported by the arches hewn from a single piece of stone. I guessed the hallway itself to run perhaps eighty feet in length.

Smaller versions of similar hallways branched off from this main one. Intricately carved figures of men and women lying in recline were recessed into stone framed alcoves all along the giant hallway. Others reclined in the dim light at either end of the corridor. It was breathtaking.

The leader nodded to the two others who had pushed the stone back into place. They dusted their hands on their robes and squatted next to the feet of the statue. They seemed to be settling in for the long haul.

"What is this place?" my voice sounded hollow as Charlie moved in beside me. I wrapped an arm around her. She shivered, but seemed none the worse for wear despite being uncharacteristically silent.

The leader produced another lantern and retrieved a match. The lantern sputtered to life. The room became a living, breathing coil of carved figures as the lamp brightened, and the shadows became mysterious and ghostly. The leader walked over to the mantle of an alcove and set the second lantern atop it, then turned toward me. His face looked as hollow and cavernous as the face on the statue behind him. The light flickered, and for an instant, as it played across his countenance, I thought his nose and lips had caught fire.

"We are under the surface," he proclaimed. "This site is holy. It is called a hypogeum."

"An underground tomb," whispered Charlie. She shivered again. I massaged her shoulder.

"Yes," said the leader. "We will be safe here for now, until we can return to the surface. No one knows of this place. It is almost two thousand years old."

I heard David whistle softly from where he stood behind the leader. The pilot was examining the stone carving of a beautiful, prone woman who'd lain undisturbed in an alcove for close to twenty centuries. The relief was subtle and intricate, as if ready to come alive.

"We're under the ruins, then." I whispered, yet my voice seemed to carry forever. Soft echoes inundated the far reaches of the holy chamber.

"Yes." He nodded. "There is another vertical passage in one of the antechambers of this hall. It leads upwards through an unknown section of the ruins. The exit is hidden among the foundations of a yet to be restored area. It is not far from where you first encountered the messenger earlier this evening, near the theater. For now, I think it would be far too dangerous for you and your friends to leave Palmyra. I don't believe your helicopter can navigate at night."

"That's okay," I quickly concurred. "Even if it's still there, I wouldn't chance it. Not after whatever the hell it was that just happened." I leaned back, and rested against the wall between two Corinthian columns. The whole place looked like a movie set from an Indiana Jones flick.

Only it was real.

And the mortars, or missiles, or whatever had blasted

the hell out of everything back there – that had been real, too.

"It's still there, Mr. Strickland. So is the pilot. He won't leave without you." As he said it I knew it was true. I just nodded. I didn't need to know how he knew. I was out of surprise for now.

The leader apparently noticed the question on my mind. "It was meant for all of us, Mr. Strickland," he said. "They knew you were here. They waited until they felt we had enough time to be together. It was my fault. I should have known they would have attempted to kill us."

"Who are they?" I asked, moving away from the wall. It was beginning to chill my spine. My shirt was damp under my coat from the exertion of the mad dash through the tunnel. I was uncomfortable and tired and I was becoming impatient, but I muscled the little kid inside me out of the way. I couldn't afford to turn this guy off. I figured we already had enough people in that lineup.

The leader's stare was even. "At the least, it would be a guess. At worst, perhaps a mistake that would cost many lives."

"Many lives?" I issued a short burst of laughter. "I think it's a little late in the game to worry about that, don't you?"

"Perhaps you have a point," he agreed. "The Israelis. The Americans." He was counting the list of possible suspects on his fingers. "The Syrians. The Muslim Fundamentalists, of which I can name three or four who have the surface-to-surface capability."

"Personally, I think it came from the air," Javier interrupted. We both looked at him. "The target was marked by a beacon. May I see it?"

Javier stepped forward to within a couple feet of the Arab. He held out his hand. When Javier saw him hesitate, he explained, "We can reverse engineer it. We can find out where it came from. Chances are pretty good, if we can get out of here and back to New York in one piece without getting blown up, we can find out who was out there tonight. I, for one, would really like to know. I'm sure you'd also like to know, sir. We'll tell you, when we learn who they are. Those are your people back there at the other end of that tunnel. They're dead, sir. My guess is they've been murdered by the same group responsible for the deaths in our tower."

The leader watched Javier intently and dug the pendant out from somewhere deep within his robe. He held it up between himself and Javier's outstretched hand. The light played off the dull gold chain.

"The enemy of my friend is my enemy," he said slowly. He placed the pendant in Javier's open hand. "We will not see each other again after this night. We will not speak again. But you will find who is doing this. And then you will kill them."

"We will bring them to justice," I corrected him.

"No." His voice became irritated. Then, more in control, "They will never be brought to justice. That is not how this works. This is what you in the West have never understood. These people have a very different concept of justice than you. For them there is only *jihad*. Martyrdom. Salvation. You must kill them. This is the only way it will stop." He looked straight into my eyes then. Almost apologetically, he asked, "Have you ever killed a man, Mr. Strickland? Have you ever looked someone in the eye, and then pulled the trigger? It is very difficult the first time, but in no time at all you get used to it. Hate makes it easier."

I ignored his question. Instead of answering, I looked upwards to the hallway's domed ceiling, then along the hallway itself. It appeared the centerpiece was the carved statue of the beautiful woman reclining in an alcove near the center of the main corridor.

"Did you build the tunnel we used to escape?" I spoke to the leader, but addressed the woman.

"Yes. Some of our people were assisting an archeologist from France on a government sponsored dig. Quite by accident this underground tomb was discovered. Part of the stone-reinforced ceiling of another tunnel had begun to decay. The worker's foot sank six inches into the sand in a spot very near here. He was on his way home from work when it happened. He lived in Tadmor. I was called. We repaired the breech, and we built the tunnel from the safe house to the tomb. We sealed the other tunnel so there would be no possibility of the tomb's discovery."

"And then you raided it," I accused him. "There must have been incredible treasure in here. Whoever's tomb this is, they must have been very wealthy. My guess is it's hers." I once again appreciated the tomb's stunning centerpiece. Then, suddenly, it dawned on me. Almost in shock, I swiveled around to face the leader. He was nodding. A faint, knowing smile had formed across his lips.

"It can't be," I said in awe. "She died in Rome."

"Did she?" Now he, too, stared at the head of the beautiful carving. "Two stories emerged, both different, both distinct. Why must one or the other be the truth?"

"She saw it coming," I whispered, asking myself why not. "She had this built. It's hers."

"Yes," the man said. A hint of pride had crept into his voice. "It is an irony that she has reached out across the centuries to help us."

"Queen Zenobia," Charlie said, only now comprehending.

"One part of the historical rumor, it would appear," the leader said, "was correct."

"She committed suicide," Charlie said. "One of the stories says she starved herself to death rather than face the humiliation of defeat at the hands of the Roman Emperor."

I ran my hands along the base of the statue, where Zenobia's arm met the stone base under it. "She's here." I was stunned.

"This is her sarcophagus. She didn't starve herself to death. She was buried alive."

The leader came closer to the carving in the alcove. "History has its secrets, Mr. Strickland. It is possible. Anything, for that matter, is possible. What is fact is that she has provided some means by which once again her people may rise up against their oppressors. With her help we will be victorious."

"By raiding her tomb?" I could only imagine the wealth the Queen had been buried with, if indeed this was truly her final resting place. By today's standards the fortune they'd found inside this tomb would have been incalculable.

"The end always justifies the means," he replied. "The transfer of fortunes is a very dirty business. At least we took it from the dead."

"And that makes it more acceptable?" I was appalled.

"I can live with myself," he replied evenly. "I suppose hypocrites have an even easier time."

"What the hell's that supposed to mean?" I spat back. It had been a long night, and I was finally short on patience. We had come a long way to speak with these people. They seemed long on lectures but weren't offering much of anything else more substantial. I was suddenly tired of it. I began to wonder if they really knew anything about the towers, or were just stringing us along, possibly for the benefit of those who did.

"All right." He suddenly seemed as short as I was. "Since you asked, I will tell you what I know of hypocrisy. Let's start with the Latin American countries in the West, and how an entire section of the world was enslaved for a time by those good, kind people at the World Bank and the IMF who rule over them. Back in the sixties and seventies, like so many others before and since, the people of those countries were impoverished. But they had one thing that made sense to the people with money: oil. Oil meant energy. And energy is collateral."

"Be specific." I was not in the mood. But on the off chance what he was saying was somehow related to why we were here, I was prepared for one last time to let him talk. Then I was going to find the exit and we were all going to do our best to get the hell out of this rat hole. I hadn't heard anymore explosions. I was willing to bet that whoever had tried to kill us probably figured they had succeeded. Under that cover, somehow, we might be able to get back to our jet in Damascus. Even if the chopper we'd come in on was missing, we might be able to hitch a ride across the desert with some tourists. I was beginning to think anything was better than sitting down here and listening to this guy. "What countries?"

He snapped back at me, "I can think of three for starters: Brazil, Bolivia, and Venezuela. You made them loans, Mr. Strickland. Huge loans you called jumbos, ostensibly to improve these nation's infrastructures. These monies were supposed to reach the people so schools and hospitals could be built. Roads could be improved. Hydroelectric facilities were to be built. Very little of these enormous sums ever made it down to the millions of people who needed it most."

"Their governments were corrupt," I pointed out.

"Do you believe for a New York minute, as you like to say, that the lenders did not know this?" I could see he was angry now. "They counted on it. They never wanted to be repaid. That wasn't why those very rich people loaned these countries their money."

"Are you saying –"

"That's exactly what I'm saying," he cut me off. "They wanted the natural resources, which were worth a thousand times more than the loans. And they got them. For decades these nations were bled. Yes, these countries' officials were corrupted, but by whom, Mr. Strickland? How difficult was it to appeal to the people in position of authority? They were greedy, or they learned very quickly. They accepted the bribes. Of course they did. There was no oversight, no accountability. There never had been. Who could turn away from such an opportunity to hand-somely feed his family where before there was starvation?"

"Finally, early in the new millennium, these countries rebelled. I'm sure the twisted irony of democratically elected leaders like Evo Morales and Hugo Chavez having changes of heart was not lost on the capitalists. These men had great courage. They were able to exercise the will of their people when they nationalized their oil and gas industries. The price of oil rose to seventy-five dollars a barrel by early 2006. Instead of settling in some cases for a mere eighteen per cent of the profits from their own natural resources, they took back what had been theirs all along. They were rattled by the capitalists, but what could these hypocrites do? These were American-implemented democracies in action. They were tired of being raped. The world of the poor was behind them one hundred percent. And nothing speaks more loudly than the huddled masses."

"Do you know that at one time, the capitalists sought to own the very water the Bolivians drank? They were going to sell the Bolivians their own water. I believe this was their biggest miscalculation. They became so incredibly greedy they didn't even see what it was they were doing. The people took to the streets, millions of them. Many died, murdered by those who never set foot in Bolivia, but to whom taking a person's water and then selling it back to them made perfect sense. Imagine the temerity. Imagine the hypocrisy." He stared at me as if he was ashamed of what he was seeing.

"How do you fight human beings such as these, Mr. Strickland? Who would take the very water people drink, and wish to make a profit selling it back to them? They have the money to corrupt and buy governments. This is only one way they get this money. And you blame us for taking what is ours from the tombs of our ancestors to fight them? Shame on you and all who think as you do." The man spat onto the floor. "While the stupid masses of the West sleep, they quietly implement their plans for world domination. They want everything. They want to control everyone. We will fight them with our dying breath. They will fail. But we must be smart. We must destroy them from within. The sleeping masses must be awakened, not against us, but against the real murderers: your rulers – not ours."

I looked at him carefully. He believed everything he said; his demeanor left no doubt of that. I had to admit, most of his facts seemed accurate. But world domination, by a handful of super wealthy? It was tough to buy. When I gave it some serious thought, though, hadn't that been the goal of every civilization in history to hold the power cards? I looked at the statue of the Queen again and sighed heavily. What about people like me? Even if there was a grain of truth to what he said, I wanted nothing to do with it.

My country, the United States, had allowed Pop and I a damn good life. I didn't like grabbing anyone's drinking water anymore than the next guy, but surely that had been an isolated incident. Then I realized I definitely knew people who would if they could. They'd feel good about it, too. They would brag to the country club crowd about it, never once understanding how insanely selfish they had become. I began to realize, regrettably, they had spoken to me about just these kinds of deals, and I'd never once spoken out against this kind of atrocity. I, who could, had been so self-absorbed in my own world of high finance that I wasn't even aware of the human side of the equation. Some people I called friends would be going on and on about how much money they were making, and afterwards I couldn't even remember what commodities were involved. And now here was this robed Bedouin who could have just as easily come from another century. He'd had a chance to enrich himself. I imagined the wheelbarrows filled with gold, sparkling diamonds and multi-colored rubies being pushed laboriously through the tunnels they'd built. Not a dime from their sale had gone to self-aggrandizement. It was all going to defeat us.

Talk about commitment.

I doubted if I could find a single American who would've done the same. Looking at this guy, who'd probably just lost a lot of his close friends, I couldn't help but admire and respect him. He must have been holding a lot back. He hadn't even allowed himself time to grieve. I remembered how I'd felt, along with Gary and David, as we'd watched the burning conflagration of our tower. I knew this guy saw similar things on a far more regular basis. No doubt he had ice in his veins. It astonished me that he still cared enough to at least do something to right the injustices he saw around him. Real, or perceived, it didn't much matter. This guy had principle, and an undying belief in what he was trying to accomplish, even if that was to destroy the most powerful nation to ever visit the planet.

"I see you in a new light, sir," I admitted. "I can understand your fight. I don't agree with your methods; I'm a peaceful man."

The hardness left his eyes. "I was once a peaceful man, too. It is, unfortunately, a luxury I can no longer afford."

"The world can always come back to the table," I pointed out.

He sighed heavily. "I wish it were so. But I am afraid that is no longer an option."

"The die is cast? I don't believe anything is irreversible," I said.

"When I was a boy of nine, we lived in a small village in the mountains," the leader confided in me. "One day it began to rain higher up in the ranges. It rained for many days. The river running through our village topped its banks. I never realized the danger until it was too late. I became trapped on a small piece of high ground. My older brother, who was sixteen, came to my rescue. He risked his life for me. He swam against the raging torrent to reach my side. I was crying. I believed I would surely perish. But I remember he smiled at me and told me not to cry. He told me that he loved me and would never let anything bad happen to me. I had to be brave. He strapped me to his body with hemp he'd brought with him. I wrapped my arms around his neck. Somehow we managed to swim back across the low ground. We got to the land on the other side.

"The river was like a beast. It foamed and tore huge chunks of soil away with it as it roared past. I was still clinging to my brother's neck when he collapsed after climbing up the bank and onto the higher ground. Only then did I have the courage to look back. The island of dirt he rescued me from had vanished. The monster flood had devoured it. When my brother finally caught his breath and was able to speak, he smiled. He said, 'I told you, little brother. As long as I live, nothing bad will ever happen to you.'"

"America is like the river that can no longer be contained. The biggest hypocrisy of all is America itself. It has become that which it once fled and despised: the oppressors in England and elsewhere, the people of means whose greed enslaved their own. America was created to be free of this. Now the United States embraces those very same policies it fought against for its independence. It does this in the name of its good forefathers, who are surely rolling over in their graves with shame in the face of such obscenity. I speak of America not so much as a country, but as a metaphor.

"America is the arrogant, selfish, thoughtless greed in all of us, Mr. Strickland. These human qualities, call it the sum of capitalism if you like, are now out of control. Or rather, they are in control of everything, to put it more plainly. The Joshua Effect was 'dreamt up' as you so eloquently put it earlier, as an antidote to this metaphor. You see, all people, deep down, ultimately yearn for freedom. It is something that springs from within each and every one of us. It is self-determination. No one likes to be a slave, not for any reason. So," he quietly folded his hands together, "I will tell you now of the ones who would rule the world. I will tell you who is doing this to your country, to all of us."

I examined his eyes, searching for something in them which would betray his altruism. If it was there, I didn't see it. "Why?" I finally asked.

"Because they are wrong and their methods will ultimately fail. If they are allowed to continue the sheep will rally around their herders. These frightened sheep will continue to give away their freedoms until there is nothing left of what once was. Then America will have won. In the end, those who rule will rule all people, and no one will have a choice."

I stared directly into his eyes. He didn't once blink. "Where's your brother now?" I finally asked him.

He blinked several times. He finally said, "He was killed. My older brother was murdered at the bottom of your tower when he tried to talk some of them into reason. Mojab is dead, and I have only one reason left in my heart to live."

"Vengeance," I said respectfully. I understood the man a lot better now. I realized, too, why he'd looked so familiar to me. I remembered pausing when I came across the picture of the man they'd called Mojab in the file Praveen had sent earlier. I looked into the eyes in the picture and wondered who the man had been. Now I knew.

"No." The leader surprised me. "Vengeance is for God. What I must do, with your help, is stop the madness before it goes too far. There is a line which, once crossed, can never be retraced. We are inches from it. And every day that passes now brings us all one step closer to crossing it."

"And no man will buy or sell without his number," I whispered softly. "The Mark of the Beast."

Chapter 18

I sent an encrypted synopsis to Praveen of everything the leader had told us. I figured now that we'd been killed we had a pretty good chance for survival; we might actually make it back across the Atlantic without being blown out of the sky.

We'd come up through the desert floor somewhere among the ruins like gophers from a hole. In the distance, I could see the glow of the fire against the night sky as the buildings in Tadmor still burned where the missiles had struck. The loss of life I knew had taken place pained me. I didn't know the men who brought us here, but I knew they had families who cared. They were all loved by someone. All of them would be missed.

Khaleb was indeed waiting for us when we arrived back at the tourist helicopter in the parking lot across from the museum. He never saw the leader; the man, his consigliere, and the foot soldiers still with them left us under the Monumental Arch.

If Khaleb knew anything about anything, he never said a word. It appeared he'd been expecting us. He seemed slightly agitated, and was definitely in a hurry. His eyes kept darting along the dark horizon, as if he half expected the roar of military jets to descend upon us at any moment. He was scared. He and David had a hurried conversation, after which both of them disappeared into the helicopter's cockpit. The engines started. David came back out and assured me the guy could actually fly us out at night by using the instruments. I trusted him.

We all clambered aboard and buckled up in the benches behind the cockpit. For the return trip to Damascus, David settled into the seat up front, beside the Syrian pilot. We ran sans lights a hundred feet off the desert floor, all the way back to the capital city's airport.

We didn't bother going back to the Four Seasons. Everything we were leaving could be replaced. Everything was happening so quickly, and it was so early, that I was hoping we could slip out of Syria without being noticed. Fuel wasn't a problem. We'd filled up soon after we'd first landed in Damascus. Our weapons? I hadn't given those a second thought after the missile attack. What good would small arms do against surface to air missiles or an attack from another aircraft?

Russell, David's co-pilot, was working on his second cup of coffee when Khaleb landed the old military helicopter on the tarmac seventy feet from the nose of the Gulfstream.

"Get us in the air as fast as you can, David," I ordered.

I rechecked my pocket for what must have been the tenth time to confirm the papers were still there. Charlie ran across the tarmac ahead of me. Everyone was pale. We moved with a singular purpose. I heard David bark some orders to a slack-jawed Russell. He'd heard the old army chopper land, and had lowered the jet's boarding stairs.

In a barely controlled frenzy, we vaulted up the stairway and into the Gulfstream. The stairway hydraulics whirred and the door closed into its locked position. We taxied out, turned around, somehow managed clearance to take off, and away we went. It was a pit stop that would have made Mario Andretti proud.

I was exhausted, but I couldn't sleep. Not just yet, anyway. My mind was still racing with the unbelievable story the leader had told us.

Gary returned from using the washroom. He plunked himself down in the leather recliner across from me. We were two hours outside Syrian airspace. I looked at him from behind weary, bloodshot eyes. Somehow I felt comforted when I saw that, for a change, his were as bad. That meant Gary was also a mere mortal.

"Praveen got it, then?" he said.

I nodded. "I got it transmitted before anyone knew we left Syria. I'm still nervous, though."

"If Praveen got it –"

"He did," I said irritably, then, "Sorry."

Gary held up a big hand and forced a smile. "Not necessary. No one will do anything, then. By now, they know we know. That makes us safe."

"Unless they think we didn't send it out," I argued.

"They can't take that chance, Jonathan. If they kill us, and that information gets out, we'd become evidence of the truth. Enough people know now that no one can risk it."

"You're talking stalemate."

"Until and if what the Arab said can be proved," said Gary.

"I'd say they've got a problem." I was playing with Charlie's pendant. Javier had given it to me for safe keeping. I was looking forward to getting it into the hands of the guys in the lab. Reverse engineering, I was certain, would reveal a treasure trove of information. As yet I hadn't spoken to Charlie about who'd had access to this little beauty – that conversation could wait a little while longer. But we still had to talk about it soon, before we landed in New York. I appraised the seemingly innocuous piece of jewelry that, when pried open, contained her mother's likeness. If only she could speak, I thought. Soon enough, she would indeed.

"The C-4, these electronics, the trigger codes. These assholes are no longer under the radar, my friend. But we're a long way from connecting the dots."

"True," said Gary. "But at least now we know there are dots to connect."

I sighed and yawned. I'd popped a Valium a half hour earlier. Mercifully, it felt like it was finally kicking in.

"You think Gus is somehow involved in this?"

Gary considered my question carefully. I'd lowered my voice, and he followed suit. We didn't need Charlie in on this part of the conversation. She was, I hoped, asleep. She'd lowered one of the captain's chairs near the galley into its horizontal position, and all I could see was the blanket covering her motionless form. Even David was out in the matching recliner next to hers. Russell was up front. Everyone else was sleeping in different chairs around the cabin. I looked forward to joining them.

"I don't know," Gary hedged. "This thing is complicated. It's got more wrinkles than an old man's face." He yawned now, too. "After what our friend back there told us, I have to believe anything is possible. You've got to talk with her, Jonathan. We need to know the chain of possession on that trinket. Who had access? I'm certainly hoping he's not involved. But I think we have enough to find out more about who is behind this crazy scheme. I wouldn't have normally believed a word of what the Arab said, but if what he told us works..."

"I don't want it to work, because if it does, you and I know what that means. Then what? I can't even think that far ahead. What do we do? Who do we talk to? It's a fucking nightmare, Gary. Even if only half of what he said is true, it's fucking obscene."

"I know. I agree," said the lawyer. "We'll test it, Jonathan. We have to. We can't tell anyone, either. After – well, that's a different story."

"We can't wait until after," I warned him. "We have to trust somebody and set them up now. I'd like it to be Charlie's father. This..." I held up the pendant. The gold chain dripped from my hand, "This will tell us if we can trust him. Now we've done everything we can. I suggest both of us try and get some sleep. We can't afford to get sick. That's what'll happen if we keep running on empty." I yawned again. The Valium was working. I kicked off my shoes, reached down beside me, and felt for the lever to recline the captain's chair. Gary said something else, but I didn't hear him. I hit the light, tucked a blanket in close to me, and was out by my fifth breath.

I opened my eyes a solid nine hours later, groggy but rested. I didn't want to leave the warm recliner, but a kink in my neck pushed me along. I swung my legs over the side of the recliner and sat there for a while, looking around the semi-darkness of the cabin. Everyone was still sleeping as far as I could tell.

I tried to think clearly, but there was no way. I couldn't imagine what time zone we were in; I couldn't even begin to guess where we were.

Careful to remain as silent as I could so as not to wake any of the others, I made my way to the front of the aircraft. I managed the cabin door without much noise. Russell turned to see who it was, and nodded when he recognized me. I closed the door behind me and climbed into the seat beside him.

"Tired?" I asked him.

He smiled. His teeth were perfectly white. With his cropped blonde hair he looked like a poster boy for a fifties Pepsodent commercial. "I was just getting up when you guys stormed the jet. I'm wide awake." His brow furrowed then, and he became serious. "What the hell happened back there?"

I glanced over at him as he re-checked some instruments, but he seemed aware that I was watching. "Every once in a while I like to tweak things myself," he explained. "Don't get me wrong, this is one hell of an aircraft. It practically flies itself. The computer reads everything: altitude, latitude, longitude…it integrates headwinds and tailwinds and makes all the adjustments and corrections before I would even be aware that anything was wrong. It's beautiful." He hit a switch, and swiveled his chair to face me. "She's flying herself now. I won't touch anything again until we move into U.S. airspace."

"When will that be?" I asked.

He checked his watch. "Soon. Maybe two hours, not much longer. We've had to fight a wicked headwind we picked up in the jet stream off the coast of Europe."

I nodded. That wasn't unusual. My head was slowly clearing. "My kingdom for a cup of java," I mumbled.

Russell swiveled back his chair. I noticed the thermos for the first time as he screwed off the lid. He spoke with his back to me. "I snuck back to the galley about an hour ago. This is fresh. Sorry I don't have a clean mug." He handed me the thermos lid, filled with creamy coffee.

"Thanks, Russell."

I realized the young co-pilot knew absolutely nothing of what had transpired back in Syria. I wrestled with what to tell him, pondering while greedily slurping down what tasted like the best cup of coffee I'd had in months. It was funny how the small stuff everyone normally took for granted could end up being so important now. I'd dodged two major bullets in as many weeks; it was time to find another line of work. Next time, I might not be so lucky.

I studied Russell. His lean frame relaxed in the pilot's chair.

"How old are you?" I was suddenly curious. Small things now seemed important. Sometimes they were all we had to get us through. I wondered wryly if this is what they called an epiphany. Was this what Charlie had meant when she'd said I didn't need anyone? Was it just a matter of being so caught up in the moment, and myself, that there just wasn't enough time for anyone else?

"Twenty-nine, Mr. Strickland."

"Call me Jonathan." I admonished him with a slight smile. "There's no room for formalities anymore. You married, Russell?"

"Engaged."

"Congratulations," I said. "I wish you both many years of happiness."

Russell's face changed expression. Suddenly, he was worried.

"What happened to you back there in the desert?" he asked uneasily. "It's something important, isn't it?"

I nodded and took another loud slurp of the coffee. Most of it was gone. Russell retrieved the thermos and refilled the lid. I was beginning to feel like a human being again, and my head had cleared.

"Yeah, it's important all right. They bombed us. It's a fluke that we all lived."

"Bombed you?" He was astonished.

I nodded. "Just missed killing us all. I think they got a bunch of Arabs, though. Ten or twenty, I think."

A lump had returned to the back of my throat. Was this what they called 'the real world'? Was this what the spooks did year in and year out? I hated it. I hated death. Yet they lived with it, out there on the edge, every day of their adult lives — no wonder they sometimes got confused. I could see now how the line between good and evil could become so easily blurred.

I looked at the confusion across Russell's face. "We escaped through a hole in the safe house's floor to a secret tunnel just before the house was blown to bits. It turns out the guy named Mojab was our host's big brother. For that reason alone he had a hard-on for the people doing this."

"The people who rigged the towers are the same ones who tried to kill you last night?" He was scared now, but fascinated, too. "How did they know we were in Syria?"

"How, indeed?" I fingered the thermos lid. "What you're asking is who's who in the zoo. We're not sure. There's been some finger pointing."

"The guy you met in Palmyra?" Russell was trying to follow me.

"He's definitely involved. Or was, in the plot's original incarnation. Now I'm not so sure. I think it kind of got away from the guys who originally planned it. What we have now is an evolution of that first concept, a hybrid, if you will. I think some new guys found out a little more than they were supposed to. Mojab didn't know about this until it became too late to stop the new guys from doing whatever it is they're planning on doing. Neither did his bosses."

"But they found out someone else had taken over," Russell guessed.

"That's what I think," I said. "All the proof they

needed came back in a coffin."

"Did the guy you met last night know who killed his brother?" Russell asked.

I looked carefully at the co-pilot. The more I told him about what was going on, the greater the chances that he, along with the rest of us, would end up the same as Mojab. But not telling him would definitely put him in an even greater jeopardy. I sighed. It was a no-win situation, but at least if I told him there'd be safety in numbers.

As incredible as the Arab's tale may have sounded, all of it seemed to fit. The puzzle was coming together. What he'd said to us, taken in isolation, could be construed as the ravings of a lunatic. But, inserted into the macabre circumstances swirling around us, his story became chillingly believable.

I said, "He had a theory. And interestingly enough, he was kind enough to provide us with a way of testing it – what we in the business world might call a proof of concept. Where does your fiancé live?"

He was momentarily caught off guard. I suppose it was the last question he expected of me at that moment.

"Westchester. Not far from the office on the Hudson. Why?"

"Because she might be in danger. The fellows trying to pull this off have very long tentacles. By now they know who came out here, you included. Is there somewhere safe she can stay for awhile? Somewhere no one knows about except you?"

"You're not serious?"

I measured my next words carefully. "They're playing for the world, and for whatever reason we happen to be in the middle of it. From now on I'm afraid we're all joined at the hip for the duration of this thing. Think of us like we're a sequestered jury. I want you to cease all communications with the outside world. Send a last message to your fiancé through Praveen. They'll use her if they find her, Russell. You're one of my pilots. David has no family. Neither does Gary. Charlie and the others are covered. You're the weakest link. If they haven't already figured this out, they soon will. They'll use you, your weakness, to silence the rest of us. They want us gone. Do you understand what I'm telling you?"

He looked at me with surprising calm. "Thanks, Jonathan." It was the first time he'd ever called me by my first name.

"For what?" I thought he must be demented. Hadn't he heard a word of what I'd just told him?

He smiled. "For trusting me, sir. I guess you forgot. I'm an ex-Marine, Special Forces. No one's getting left behind here, sir. If the bastards want a war, then let's give them a war. Don't worry about my fiancé, either. It's where we met."

Now I was confused.

"She's ex-Navy. Special Ops, just like me. I pity the poor son-of-a-bitch who tries to come in through her door without knocking. That's front or back."

I just stared at his two rows of perfect, white teeth. His smile was becoming contagious.

Chapter 19

It seems I'd forgotten how I'd built the Empire. Russell had reminded me. The Empire was not Jonathan Strickland. Sure, I was its Chief, but the creation of any successful business was always contingent on its ability to put together a team of top professionals who could work together like a finely tuned clock. I had dumped this responsibility onto the heads of the personnel managers after I had assembled my executive core.

I looked around the cabin at Gary, David, and the others. For the first time in a while I no longer took the team for granted. These were good people, all of them. They were the best. I thought that I had chosen them, but in my arrogance it had never before crossed my mind that they may have chosen me instead. The thought was sobering and humbling. If I was a reflection of the quality of these people, then just maybe we stood a chance against the evil we were up against. If these people considered me good enough to lead them, then I felt I might just be good enough for the job – with the caveat, of course, that before last night I'd never even met a so-called terrorist.

Once again, I locked onto Charlie. "I don't know how whoever did it did it, but they did."

She looked down at her pendant, held away like a virus in her hand. I took it from her.

"My father," she finally said.

I sighed.

She immediately began to defend him. "The little gold pin came loose. I happened to be in his office and I mentioned it to him. It was no big deal. I wanted to drop it by a jeweler. Dad knew how special it was to me, so he insisted on looking after it himself. He insisted. There's no way my father could be involved in any of this. My mother died from this kind of shit."

"I believe you," I said.

"You think he'd kill his own daughter?" She was on the verge of losing it.

"He wouldn't. That's why it wasn't Gus. That's the evidence, and his alibi, all in one. He didn't do it, Charlie. He's not responsible, okay?"

I saw some of the edge fade from her demeanor as she absorbed what I said.

"So he's a pawn?" she finally said. I appreciated she had regained control of herself. She was thinking again.

I shook my head, "He's too quick for that. Your father would never knowingly allow himself to be used. He had your piece of jewelry fixed." I fingered the face, sprang the catch, and looked directly into her mother's eyes as the small door of the pendant popped open. Charlie and her mother could have been twin sisters. "That's obvious. It works fine. But someone picked your father's pockets along the way. Someone who knew you. Someone he works with who's seen you with him, and saw you wearing this."

"I wear it all the time," she admitted.

"That certainly narrows down the list of suspects." I was being sarcastic.

"Sorry." She smiled for a moment.

"It might be impossible to find out who did this," I

said.

"Let's hypothesize and start by defining the parameters." Charlie was being optimistic.

I was about to say something to her about this not being a game or some such equally insensitive and trite comment, but stopped before I uttered a word. I must have looked like a goldfish gulping for food, because she laughed.

"What?" Charlie asked me. "What were you going to say?"

"Nothing. Something stupid." I glanced around the cabin. No one was watching us where we spoke at the back of the fuselage, near the kitchen. I lowered my voice and gazed into the most beautiful pair of eyes in the world, smiling in satisfaction. "But I didn't, and that's good, because when this is all over I want you to know how much you, everyone, has changed me. Remember how you told me that night in New York at the townhouse I didn't take you seriously?" I had my hand on her knee. I gently squeezed it. She nodded.

"Well, I do take you seriously, now more than ever before. I take every word you say seriously, Charlie. And I don't know what I'd do with myself if you took that away from me. I can't imagine what life would be like if I couldn't listen to what you have to say and how you see the world. If I couldn't hear your voice anymore; if I couldn't look into your eyes, hear you laugh, hear you cry. My God, my life would be an empty shell if I couldn't catch your scent on the breeze when you walked by. So talk. Tell me what you think. Tell me about your hypothesis. I want to hear everything you have to say."

She stared at me for a moment. Then she leaned over and the space between us disappeared. She hugged and kissed me. I could feel her warm breath against my lips, and then in my ear as she whispered, "I love you, Jonathan. Thank you."

Deja-vu. Hadn't Russell just thanked me as well? I couldn't be changing that much. I began to wonder who I'd been just a couple of weeks back.

"For what?" I had to ask.

Unlike Russell, Charlie simply shrugged. She leaned back into her seat, her face glowing. She had that satisfied look, the one she always got right after we made love.

"I think," she began slowly, "it would have had to be someone, like you said, who has seen me wearing the locket."

"The world," I pointed out.

She sneered at me. I was allowed one. That was it.

"Number two: it would have to be someone —"

"Or a group."

"Or a group of people," she allowed, "with access to and expertise in the kind of technology they planted in my pendant."

"It's obviously pretty sophisticated stuff, clearly cutting edge." I added, "It's not so different, I think, from the kind of stuff necessary to blow the towers."

I knew by now Praveen had our engineers salivating to get their hungry hands on the trinket. I also knew by the time they were done with it they would be able to tell us everything from where it was done, to how it was done, and with what parts. What they wouldn't be able to tell us was who had actually built it. But Charlie's pendant, the smoking gun, would point the way. Coupling it with what our friend in the desert had told us and a few of my own ideas; I felt we just might be getting closer to the lunatics who'd taken over the asylum.

"Thirdly," Charlie said, "the pendant had to have been retrofitted quickly."

"Meaning?"

"Meaning it would have to be done locally. I was in New York when I gave it to my father. It had to have been done there."

I held up a hand to stop her for a moment. "Maybe. But what if they made a duplicate outside the country, and then made a switch with the original when the opportunity presented itself? They could have taken pictures of it beforehand, even lifted film from security surveillance cameras." Even as I spoke I silently cursed, because I realized that's exactly what they'd probably done. Charlie's brow wrinkled. She wasn't defeated, only a little flustered.

"Maybe I'd give you that one," she offered. "But how would you explain my mother's picture in the copy?"

"You don't always wear it," I said. "It would take nothing for someone to have visited your apartment while you were out. A copy of the picture is all they would need. You wouldn't be able to tell it from the original."

"So they switched it," Charlie reluctantly acquiesced. "The engineers will still be able to glean a lot of information from it. And I'll talk with my father right after we land. We might get lucky. Whoever fixed it might still turn out to be the guilty party."

I knew that was going to come up sooner or later. We were still about ninety minutes out over the Atlantic Ocean. I guess a part of me had fooled the rest of me into believing I wouldn't have to deal with it. Now I had no choice.

"I was just in the cockpit," I began.

"I know. I saw you. What's wrong? I don't think I like the tone in your voice."

"Praveen sent something through the computer. It's

a story that Reuters somehow picked up. By now every major news network in the country is running it as their lead story."

"I don't understand," she was bewildered. "What are you talking about? What story?"

I leaned back, folded my hands together, and rested my chin on them, regarding her with keen interest.

"Well," I began, "no one really knows we left Damascus." I saw she still didn't get it. "Uh, they've got some video Charlie. That house we were in last night is no longer there. It and about three others don't look so good." She stared at me with a blank across her face. "I guess someone sold someone the footage. People find that sort of thing interesting. No one's told anyone any different. You can't really blame them."

"Blame who for what?" a man's voice interrupted us. I looked up at my lawyer. I guess Gary was hungry and we were between him and the food. I looked back at Charlie. There was no easy way to say it.

"Sam Clemens phrased it better than I could ever say it," I was trying my best to ease into it.

"Oh. Now I know what you're talking about," said Gary. "Excuse me, Jonathan." He stepped between us on his journey to the kitchen.

"You know?" I frowned up at him.

"Just came from the cockpit," he explained over his shoulder.

I'd missed that, because my back was to the front of the jet. "Gary..." I pleaded for some help.

"Got to get something to eat. I'll be right back. Rumors of my death are greatly exaggerated."

Charlie frowned at his wide back, then looked at me. "What's he talking about?"

"We filed a flight plan under false ID, for security

reasons. No one knows we're here in this aircraft." I shook my head, looked downward, and massaged my temples with my left hand. "I'm afraid we're all dead, Charlie. We were killed in those blasts last night in Tadmor along with the Arabs."

"We're dead?" her voice sounded broken. It would have been comical if it weren't so serious.

I nodded. "Afraid so. We were all blown to kingdom come by missiles. That's the story, and we're using it. Think it through. I know it'll be hard for Gus, but this bogus news story is truly a blessing."

"A blessing? Is that what you call it, John? A blessing?"

"We can test the Arab's story now. They don't know we're still alive, and they can't know it, either. Because if they find out, Charlie, they won't wait. They'll blow those next towers immediately. We'll never be able to prove a thing. Think about it. No one must know we're alive until after we prove the concept."

I watched the different emotions wash across her face like waves on a shoreline. Finally, after what seemed an eternity, she slowly nodded. "I don't like it. My father will kill me when he finds out I let him go on thinking I was dead." She searched my eyes. There was no loophole. No way out. She knew it. "But I understand. I hate it to hell, but I understand." A teardrop rolled down her cheek.

I reached for her and held her. I whispered, "Gus will understand. He would do exactly the same thing if it were him and you thought he was dead. He wouldn't have a choice."

She squeezed me tighter, and said nothing.

Chapter 20

By the time we landed in New York, everyone onboard had been briefed. Not very many of them liked it, but everyone understood the stakes. In the end, we all accepted our new predicament.

In a big way, our being dead gave us a lot more freedom. I didn't think anyone could've dreamed up a better cover story. Eventually people would find out we were all still alive and well, but for now it was a long shot that I'd hoped for but hadn't seen coming.

When I thought about it, I had to wonder. I knew Mojab's brother was smart. This had his fingerprints all over it, but I'd never know for sure. Like he said, we'd never meet again.

General Aviation was tricky, but not as bad as it could have been. We still had official documents that had in essence turned us into government agents. The jet was boarded by customs, but the agent didn't seem too interested in offending anyone. She was courteous and friendly, a true professional. As soon as she saw a couple of seals on letterheads, she became even less interested and more obliging. She never asked for names or passports. Our luck, miraculously, was holding.

I stayed in the back under a blanket feigning illness, but they never asked about me. VIP's and private jets whose value went beyond that of mere salaried mortals were not to be trifled with. No one, customs agents and immigration officials alike, wanted to wake a sleeping giant. Gary told me it was the seals that cinched it. His soothing, lawyerly cadence didn't hurt, either.

I stayed in the jet while Gary and David arranged for ground transportation and a hotel at General Aviation's front office. I watched the two of them return across the tarmac between the building and the jet.

"I did some shoplifting," said Gary when he was back onboard the aircraft. It had turned cold in New York in our absence, unseasonably so; the reverse of what the weather in Syria had been like. He tossed me a gray fedora and a green woolen scarf.

"You'll have to forgive my fashion sense," he smiled. "These were all I could find in the lounge on such short notice."

"I'll go with it," I replied. Anything to obscure my identity was better than nothing.

"Got this, too," he said soberly, as he handed me a copy of a newspaper.

One glance at the front page was all I needed. I groaned as I looked at myself.

"Everybody loves a story about a dead billionaire," said David.

I covered up as much of my face as I could, pulling the hat snugly down over my head.

"How do I look?" I asked no one in particular.

"Like Michael Jackson," Charlie jibed. I smiled under the scarf, glad she still had her sense of humor.

We broke up into three groups this time, taking airport hacks instead of limos. The seven of us reconvened in the living room area of a suite at the Trump International Hotel near Central Park three hours later. They always kept a hospitality suite available for special occasions, and it was dumb luck we found it empty when we really needed it. Gary had reserved it using his encrypted security clearance on the Gulfstream's computer. It was ours for the next three weeks, and no one else in the world would know. It would show up as being reserved for several corporate heads we normally did business with, a totally benign and routine transaction. Room service wouldn't know who had taken up residence, and everything was automatically billed to the comptroller's office in Accounting. They might catch it much later, of course, when an audit was performed – but by then I was hoping all this shit would be long gone, one way or another.

"You gave it to Praveen?" I asked Gary, who was five minutes late and a little out of breath. He arrived carrying a flat case under his arm.

"Personally," he confirmed.

"How was he?" I asked.

"Glad to see me. Glad everyone's healthy, you especially."

We'd spoken by encrypted e-mail. I hadn't wanted to chance a video conference call; someone could have walked in on his end of it.

"What did he think of the pendant?" I asked.

"We met in Central Park, near where the horse carriages line up. We didn't talk for long, but he did say it was no doubt a substitute. Beyond that, he didn't know much else except to say it was an extremely sensitive, sophisticated device. And yes, he gave me the laptop. It's secure and state-of-the-art. He'll call you on it at seven o'clock tomorrow evening, from his home in Catskill. He said to let you know it would be the first time he's been back up there since this whole thing started, but he had a good reason for going. He'll have more for you when you guys talk tomorrow."

Gary handed me the flat bundle from under his arm.

I took it gingerly. We didn't have many of these. Laptop video conferencing was just gaining momentum, and the connections were difficult to secure. I knew whoever felt they'd taken a successful run at us back in Syria was still out there, listening for any signs that we may have escaped. They would take nothing for granted. It was their job to keep looking for us.

"I appreciate everything you've done – and that compliment extends to all of you." I looked around the suite's entertainment area at my other friends.

To my left, Russell relaxed in a comfortable recliner. David had opted for the more solid couch beside it. Gary moved over and sat in the empty space between the pilot and Charlie, who occupied the other end. She sat nearest to me where I'd taken center stage on the edge of an orange corduroy-covered ottoman. Directly across from me was another, larger sofa where Frank sat. Javier lounged on the other half with his legs straight out.

The corporate suite was large. It contained three bedrooms, so we could all live and be fairly comfortable without tripping over one another. As far as I knew there was a television in every room, and until now we'd been glued to the sets. Charlie and I had watched the news in the privacy of the suite's Master Bedroom. What we'd seen was almost unbelievable. It had chilled me to the marrow.

Us against the world, I thought. It was a fleeting moment that passed from my mind in an instant. Us *with* the world was more like it. It was an irony, but if anyone out there knew we were alive and this close to stopping the terror, they would definitely be rooting for the home team.

I glanced at my watch. It was just after five p.m. in New York. Everything seemed to be happening at light speed. Damascus already seemed a blur.

"I caught a little of the news," I began.

"Everyone is scared to death," said Frank. "It's making people crazy."

"That's what good terrorism is all about," Javier replied. "Everyone in this country has been enveloped by a sense of impending doom. They're smothering under the weight of what's going to happen next."

"They've got no one to vilify. The enemy remains invisible," David pointed out. "All the information they get, really, comes from those infernal manifestos. Did you see the story on that group they arrested in Idaho on conspiracy charges? They were nabbed scheming to kill some of the people on the terrorists' hit list."

"The President?" Charlie hadn't seen anything about that one.

"I don't know. The blurb I saw never said who," David clarified. "But the Commander in Chief was conspicuous in the absence of his mention. The report didn't name any of the intended targets."

"It didn't have to," Javier said. "The point is people are beginning to think the government doesn't care what happens to them, as long as all the President's men are safe. And if that way of thinking keeps taking hold, anarchy isn't far behind. The Guard's barely keeping order now. Pour a little more gas on this fire and it's anybody's guess as to where this thing will end up."

"Out of control," said Gary. "It's halfway there already."

"Well how about we see if we can't put the brakes on before it gets all the way there?" I interrupted. "We all know it's not a pretty picture. The beast in each of us is both noble and ugly. Let's find a way to bring out the nobility. It's there. What these people need right now is some hope. Yeah, I'm with them on one thing: I think the fellows at the top of the food chain are doing everyone a disservice right now. The ordinary people who make this country the greatest in the world – the cab drivers and construction workers and everyone in between – deserve better. They deserve to be told the truth."

Gary said cynically, "I think the last guy with that message was FDR."

"I'm not here to talk politics," I reproached him. "I'm too results-oriented for that. In case anyone's forgotten, those next two buildings are going to be flattened by the end of next week. Our job is to stop that from happening."

Gary said soberly, "Is there anything we can do before the lab analyzes the technology in Charlie's pendant?"

"Good question," I said. "I hope we can keep moving in that direction. It's to no one's advantage to sit back and wait for the other side to make the next move."

"Their entire threat, if we're to trust the Arab, is technology based," observed Frank.

"What if the codes he gave us don't override the detonation sequences?" asked David. "Is there any way the military can do a blanket jam? That would stop the forward sequences before they had a chance to initiate themselves."

Now we were getting somewhere.

"I think the answer to that will hopefully surface after the lab has a chance to take a closer look at the pendant," I said.

"Any idea as to the timeline?" David asked.

Gary said, "It's all Praveen is doing. He knows

what's on the line. We need a win, and right now he has the ball. He knows."

"Hopefully we'll know too –" I looked at my watch, "in about twenty-six hours from now."

"Speaking of the news," said Javier, "what's with the morbid fascination about your death, Jonathan? The rest of us barely got honorable mention."

I smiled wryly, "I think they're more concerned about what my death has done to the stock prices."

"No one's resigned yet," Charlie said innocently, referring to some of my senior executive compensation packages. I'd lured some big talent the last few years with attractive options. As our stock plummeted these dollar amounts had been all but wiped out.

The smile on my face stayed there. "Maybe they know something the rest of you don't." I looked around. They were chuckling softly, but I saw no takers.

"One thing puzzles me," said Frank. "Just before the explosions, when we were talking with the Arab, did it strike anybody else as strange how quickly he spotted the homing device? I know everything happened so fast but it seemed to me the guy was grabbing for it even before you said anything, Charlie."

"No. I screamed first. When it got too hot I had to grab it away from my neck. It was burning me. But you're right. He seemed to know what it was almost immediately."

"Like he'd seen one of them before," said Frank.

"Or at least he knew what to look for," Gary said.

"Which isn't so unreasonable," I followed. "But for now, I'm hungry. Anyone else?" I raised my eyebrows. Some nods, some thought about it for a couple seconds, and joined the growing consensus. "Roast beef entree sound alright? Potatoes smothered in southern style gravy and some corn on the cob drooling in butter?" Some groans escaped. "Who wants to order?"

"I'll handle it." Russell quickly volunteered. "As long as I get to pick the dessert."

"You're on. Make it something with chocolate in it," I said. Russell strode to the phone in the suite's front lobby for some quiet. "Now where were we?"

"You were proposing there was nothing wrong with how quickly the Arab picked up on the pendant," Charlie said.

"Maybe he commissioned it," I speculated. "Whoever he is, he's obviously well-financed. Remember, his brother's body was transferred to a jet owned by the Saudi Royals, and flown to Riyadh. He's in their favor. They know each other."

"One big, happy family. You think the Saudi Royals planned this thing?" David asked.

"I think they definitely have knowledge of it. The proposal was probably shopped around. Obviously they must have been approached, maybe even to monitor the operation."

"Something like a capo okaying a hit," said David.

I shrugged. "Let's look at what we do know." I reached into the back pocket of my jeans and retrieved a folded up piece of notepaper. The Four Seasons Damascus logo was emblazoned across the top. "While the rest of you were sleeping on the plane, I made some notes. Right now I think it's important to clearly define the facts. Extrapolation is of course a necessary luxury that's essential to narrowing down the list of suspects, but keep in mind, we may get it wrong. The way I see this thing unfolding, if we do get it wrong, it's going to cost us dearly. We'll lose a couple more buildings, and gain renewed panic. We can't count on luck forever. So here's what we do know."

I began to read: "One. Sixty-three story in New York destroyed by C-4 but unknown detonation. Two. Body leads to Syria. Three." I stopped when I heard Russell. He nodded confirmation of the order to me as he tiptoed silently across the room's plush carpeting and resumed his seat in the leather recliner. "Hebrews 11:30. Four. Meeting with Mojab's brother. Five. Electronic homing device, possibly related to detonation Stateside. Six. Detonation sequences: Real? Phony? Seven." I had underlined the last twice. "Reverse engineering pendant." I folded the paper then, and returned it to my back pocket. "It ain't much, as they say in tobacco country, but it's all we got. Comments anyone?" I looked around expectantly. These were a collection of extremely bright people. I wanted them to keep thinking. I felt like I'd just stoked the fire.

"Why would the Arab leak the strike on his own safe house?" Gary spoke more softly than usual. He was thinking, all right.

"Sympathy?" David suggested.

"Doesn't make sense," Gary said, more like he was talking to himself. He was trying to grab a thought that continued to elude him, just out of reach. "He wouldn't need support, and they don't give a shit if anyone likes what they do or not. Polls don't exist in their world. It's not exactly representation by popular consensus over there. But there has to be a reason."

"I'm with you." Frank leaned forward. "I don't think anything he did was an accident. Remember how quickly he dove for that hole in the floor? We were an afterthought. That tells me he didn't see the attack coming. He was as surprised by it as we were."

"How can you be sure?" asked David.

"He called us there. That means he needed us for

something. He wants to use us. If he wanted to kill us he could've done that outside the hotel in Damascus, but he didn't need to orchestrate what Javier thinks was an air strike. They probably used an unmanned drone, because the Syrians sure as hell didn't drop those nasties on us. And they didn't seem to be big enough ordinances to wipe out everything. They were localized smart bombs with very low collateral damage. Not laser guided, either – the pendant will prove that."

I noticed Gary was listening carefully. He would occasionally nod his head. "The Arab knew that," he said. "He took pictures so the people who did it could see the evidence. He also knew those pictures would appear on the front page of every newspaper around the world. He wanted to convince them their mission had been successful."

Charlie said, "Who would stand the most to gain right now if we'd been killed?"

"Interesting question," Gary said slowly.

"You may have something there, Charlie," David said.

"Who, indeed?" I said, speaking as softly now as Gary had been earlier. I looked at Charlie.

"And would that be figuratively, or literally dead? The Arab seems to want the former. What's interesting is that he told us how to stop the next bombings, but did not give us the who behind them. Which means A: he no longer knows, or, more likely B: he wants us to see for ourselves."

"Why?"

"He must have figured we probably wouldn't have believed him if he told us outright."

Chapter 21

"You're not going to believe this, Jonathan."

"Try me," I invited. Praveen was looking straight at me from the laptop's screen. He actually looked excited.

"When Gary delivered it to me yesterday I was immediately suspicious." His bright eyes were smiling. It was like watching a kid who'd discovered a new candy bar.

"That's when you called Professor Singh?" I guessed.

"No. Not right away. The Professor is a very busy man. It is true he and I have met before. I have great respect for him, and I am very honored he has read some of my own publications. But I did not wish to waste his time. And, of course, I have never actually seen one of these before. I needed to be certain of what it was."

"It's a homing device," I said impatiently. Professional courtesy was one thing, but this was beginning to sound like these guys were in love with one another.

There was a shuffling sound. Praveen stood up. The camera stayed put, now trained on his belt buckle. I heard another voice in the background, and then Praveen said something. Their voices were muffled. I couldn't understand what they were saying. The belt buckle moved out of the picture. Briefly I saw what looked to me like a wall of electronics over the top of what might have been a wooden piano stool. The machines disappeared as another figure moved between them and the camera. The figure sat down on the plain wooden stool. I suddenly found myself staring directly into the eyes of the Nobel Prize-winning, world-renowned Doctor of Electronic Physics, Professor Dunbar Singh.

I was surprised at how young he looked. His frame was slight, his features smooth and almost effeminate. His hair was trimmed neatly and jet black, aside from the few gray wisps that had taken up residence at the lower edges of his almost non-existent side burns. The Professor was expressionless, but his eyes were clear and intelligent. His arm moved and for a moment he was out of focus. Then his image returned, sharper than ever.

"Good evening, Professor Singh," I said, because something told me it was protocol I speak first.

I heard a scratching as the Professor adjusted the microphone this time. He glanced away from the screen, nodded, and came back. "Yes, good evening Mr. Strickland, how nice to see you are alive and well." His eyes sparkled with life.

I thanked him.

"You are very welcome," he replied. "How may I be of assistance?"

"You've examined the pendant?"

"Yes, yes. It is a marvelous device. I did not think anyone had actually been able to build one. Until now, aside from several prototypes with limited success, it existed only in theory."

I nodded, not understanding. "Professor, just what is it we have there? I thought the thing was some kind of homing device."

"At its core yes, but the device is much more."

"It does more?"

From off screen Praveen said something. Singh spoke to him in a low tone. Again I wasn't able to understand them. The professor nodded several times and then returned to our conversation.

"Let me articulate this device in a way you might better appreciate," he began. "This device is to electronics what the Manhattan Project was to physics. In a way never before accomplished, it actually integrates the two fields."

"Electronics and physics," I clarified his words.

"Precisely," he seemed happy I apparently understood. I didn't. I was frustrated, but determined not to let the professor know it.

"I'm amazed at how quickly you reverse engineered it." I stroked his ego. Maybe this approach would work better. I felt Charlie massage my arm. She stood to one side of me. Everyone else was standing as well, hanging on every word.

His expression seemed puzzled. "I cannot imagine why you should be so impressed. I'm the one who designed it."

"Oh," I said, at a temporary loss for anything else intelligent to say. I was obviously in a losing battle. Hell, I'd lost already. "Professor, please excuse me for being so ignorant, but just what does that damn thing do? Aside from finding a location, I mean? It does that very well, I can tell you."

"Of course, of course." He had a habit of repeating certain initial phrases. He'd probably picked the nuance up early on in lecture halls, as he fine-tuned his English along with his teaching skills. I knew from the little I'd read of him he was welcome in any lab in the world. Like Praveen, he'd sought knowledge and developed expertise in coveted areas of science. He'd become the best in the world at what he did. Everyone, including various governments, had tried desperately to lure him into their employ by promising him every treasure known to man.

Like Praveen, Dunbar Singh was not, nor had he ever been, for sale. He chose who employed him and quietly accumulated the awards and accolades that inevitably accompany genius. Not long after he'd been awarded his Nobel Prize, he selected from a private endowment what amounted to a blank check to build and finance a lab in upstate New York. Professor Singh accepted the money on two conditions: one of his own, and the other from whoever was putting up the financing. The Foundation giving him the money was to remain anonymous, on penalty of the immediate retraction of all funding if the identity of those responsible was ever disclosed. Singh had agreed to this condition when his own had been met. His was simple: he would be accountable to only his conscience. The deal was struck immediately and had lasted for the better part of the last ten years.

Professor Singh worked quietly for the benefit of mankind, but that did not stop his work, as was too often the case, from being bastardized for the benefit of a few. It was becoming painfully obvious that had happened again.

Praveen and the Professor were talking with each other again. The Professor returned his attention to the screen. "The device is intelligent. It thinks, Mr. Strickland. It is capable of using tiny pulses of energy to read its immediate environment. It analyzes what it sees, and sends out responses."

I almost couldn't believe what I was hearing. "You called it a machine, Dr. Singh."

He almost chuckled. "Do not allow the size of the machine to mislead you. Parts of this device are assembled with the aid of an electron microscope. Electric charges are injected, creating certain functionality."

"Like installing software onto a hard-drive." I understood that much.

"Not precisely. This is a different technology," he explained. It must have seemed to him like I had the mind of an insect. "But if your analogy allows you to better understand this concept, then I cannot see the harm in it."

"I can understand how this…machine might assimilate information from the environment around it. Things like temperature, air pressure, and the like." I was still thinking in terms of what I knew. The landing of the probe on Mars came to mind. "But it's so small. How could it possibly change to not only accommodate the variables of its immediate location, but then send out instructions to guide missiles? It seems impossible. The signal strength could never be sufficiently amplified. It doesn't even run on batteries. Or was that why the device got so hot just before the explosions began?"

Professor Singh was shaking his head. "The device malfunctioned. It melted. Apparently it was enough warning for you to leave the proximity of your last known coordinates. If the machine had worked the way it was designed to work, I am afraid we would not be speaking to one another right now. As I said, it thinks."

I lost him. "I don't understand."

"Even if you had by some miracle gained prior knowledge of the impending attack," his patience was unyielding, "it would not have mattered in the slightest. The machine would have noticed every change in your environment. It can tell, for instance, what kind of door you open, how large of an opening is present, its location. In this case, it would have sensed the opening was in the floor. The machine is the most sensitive of its kind in the world. Once that trap door had been opened, it would have been able to read the location and direction of the underground tunnel. It would have adjusted the coordinates to accommodate the new location of its target. It would have read the movements of air your bodies created as you moved toward the hole in the floor. It would have noticed as you slowed to enter the hole. It would have extrapolated your exit velocity, and the direction in which you were traveling, and the ordinance trajectory would have been adjusted accordingly. You would not have escaped, Mr. Strickland."

"That thing is small enough to fit in the palm of my hand. Charlie was wearing it around her neck. How is it possible something that tiny can do all that?" I sounded ridiculous even to myself.

"All that and much more, I'm afraid," Dr. Singh continued. "The machine is tiny, yes. It is not powerful in the conventional sense. It works on signal presence, not signal strength. How shall I put this?

"Everything, even our minds, works on electrical charges. There is an endless supply of these positives and negatives, and therefore neutralities all around us. It is how the entire universe as we know it is both held together and kept apart."

"Gravity?" I asked.

"Precisely. And what is gravity except a combination of impulses which variably attract and repulse one another, from all sides, until some quality of equilibrium is reached? It is the very reason we can walk on this earth and not be propelled off into space by the planet's centrifugal force, which is also a product of these impulses. This machine taps into these forces. It uses them to convey fields. Much like the brain uses electricity inherent in the human form to say, move a limb, the machine uses what is already there to redirect a missile. It works on the presence of the medium. The signal is always present, because it is the universe. This machine has infinite power. Unlike its crude and much more conventional ancestors, it does not rely on the enhancement of the medium. It does not rely upon the strength of a signal, only signal presence. Nothing needs amplification. The conveyance occurs, of course, at the speed of light."

"It's a weapon." My voice sounded like fabric being torn.

"It is a machine," he corrected me.

I swallowed hard. I didn't understand half of what Singh was telling us, but I certainly grasped the implications of it, and it scared the hell out of me.

"And you built this?" It wasn't so much a question as an accusation.

"I designed the machine, yes. Too many times, as you are well aware, these technologies fall into the hands of people who are determined to use them in ways that do not benefit the world. They can become weapons." He stared at me from the Catskills.

"This isn't just a weapon, Dr. Singh. If what you say has been developed, it's more than that. It's a fucking doomsday machine."

He continued to stare at me.

"Help me out with something. Please," I continued.

He nodded.

"How does this device fit in with the booby-trapped towers? Are the two related? The superstructures are rigged with C-4, placed in their foundations as far as we know."

"By the very medium which they employ, the machines have a range of utilization we are only now beginning to explore. I designed it for good, Mr. Strickland," he sighed heavily. It was the first and only sign of emotion I'd seen from him. "My heart is broken knowing how it is being used."

"Can we stop them somehow?" I asked. I hoped he wouldn't detect the desperation in my voice.

"Are you asking me if the towers can be saved?"

I sighed. "I don't know what I'm asking you, Professor, other than for your help. The towers for starters, yes. Because now that you mention it, what are they going to do for an encore? My earlier question still stands, though. How does the device relate to the towers?"

"They must be using the machine in the detonation process," he mused. "It must carry the signal to the detonator. That would explain why time and concrete encasement of the explosive material itself had no effect on the initial firing sequence. Of course, this is aside from the inherent stability of the explosive itself. It would have been a greater risk to use more conventional triggers."

"The machine malfunctioned in the desert," I pointed out. I was grasping at straws.

"I am certain whoever is behind this is looking more at the reward rather than the risk," the Doctor said pointedly.

"There must be a way to jam the signal," I said.

"There is no signal to jam," he said. "But..."

"There has to be a way," I pleaded.

"The firing sequence the detonators end up reading works not unlike a series of on and off switches. Pluses and minuses."

"Like binary sequences. Like a computer."

"Precisely, except there are no chips, or rather one big chip – the universe and its infinite electrical power grid. If someone were to process, or initiate the exact opposite switches at precisely the same time as the detonation sequence was being transferred through the grid, in theory the two would cancel each other out."

"They could simply pull the trigger at another time."

Professor Singh shook his head. "In theory the override of the original sequence expands exponentially to an infinite level –"

"Doctor. Please," I interrupted him.

"The machine malfunctions."

"Like it did in the desert."

In a second, uncharacteristic display of emotion, Dr. Singh appeared surprised. His eyes got bigger. "Yes," he said. "Like it did in the desert."

Chapter 22

"How much do we know about lightning, Mr. Strickland?" Personally, I knew very little, and I told him as much.

"You are not alone in your ignorance. Actually, very little is known other than what happens during and after a lightning strike takes place. What initiates the sequence has puzzled scientists since they began to seriously examine the phenomena. It is the universal grid. An incredible surge of power is transferred in an instant through virtually nothing. The molecules comprising the air we breathe are very far apart. There are huge spaces of nothing between those molecules. Yet lightning is one of the most powerful forces we know of. One storm can contain enough energy to power an entire city for weeks. The electricity, you see, feeds upon itself. Picture a snake swallowing its own tail. This is the basic principle of this source of energy. It is everywhere. It is free. It is what we have been working to understand. It is also an untamed beast. My theory tried to explain how it was possible to harness this free energy."

Like a lot of things, it sounded great in theory. I said, "So someone got wind of your theory, and they built a machine which, what? Arranges this universal power grid so it does what it's told? How do we cancel it? If it's been built, then it's got to have an antidote, a cure. Whoever made it's got to have competition. Who do we go to in order to defend ourselves from it? It thinks, therefore it must die."

"Some diseases have no known cure," he said.

Suddenly I was tired of hearing nothing but bad news. Singh almost seemed like he didn't give a damn. He spoke of this visitor from Hell he'd invented as if it was the sparrows that visited the bird feeder out his back door. Like the machine was some kind of personal pet. Mary Shelley had done that already. If this conference was going to be productive in the least, I'd have to get a grip on myself. I had to remain calm, and not cloud my ability to think clearly with raw emotions. I fought to get onto the Doctor's page. I needed to become as dispassionate as he was. Inwardly, I sighed with relief as my murky, volatile mind began to clear. There had to be an answer to this dilemma. Only cooler heads would find it.

"Who finances you, Doctor Singh?" I asked in a monotone.

As I expected, he showed no reaction to a question that had badgered him going on ten years.

"I am bound by contractual obligations, Mr. Strickland. I cannot, nor would I ever divulge details regarding this and related matters." It was a well rehearsed answer.

"Fair enough," I allowed, almost congenially. "I respect your right to privacy."

He blinked, but made no comment. All right, I thought. Obviously I couldn't stroke him. I played another card. "Doctor, do you know the difference between good and evil?"

He looked off camera and blocked the microphone with his hand. He was talking, probably to Praveen. I found it maddening, but I knew I wasn't in control here. As awkward as I found it, I knew I must defer to this man's idiosyncrasies. In the same instant, I realized this was just how I perceived the situation in front of me right now. I was frustrated because I didn't have the kind of control over them that I was used to.

I could fire Praveen, but for what? I realized he was only trying to help. I was sure he'd pulled every favor he could think of just to set up this call. He was probably scrambling right now, trying to explain away my last question the best way he knew how. He'd put his professional reputation on the line for me. This was a big deal for him, as it was to all of us.

I remembered I'd felt this same frustration recently. It had been when Charlie announced she was leaving me. I'd blamed her. I'd been wrong. But back then...I laughed inside at myself. It had been only three and a half months ago. What was happening to me? I was dimly aware I was changing, but I couldn't gauge how much, or how quickly. Or more importantly, was I changing for the better? I was too close to myself for that kind of a determination. I'd have to let others be the judge of that. I smiled inwardly, though. Charlie was still here, and that felt good. As terrified as we all were, she was happier now than I'd ever seen her before. Surely I had something to do with it.

The professor removed his hand from the microphone and turned back to face the camera lens. "There are universal goods and evils, Mr. Strickland. Science sometimes hides behind both. What do want from me, sir? Honesty, in my experience, is always the best policy."

He'd embarrassed me. Not to anyone else, but to myself. Professor Singh was a very humble man. He knew the difference between right and wrong. I didn't have to make some dramatic appeal to his sense of nobility. All he needed from us was the truth. He was still answering only to his own conscience.

In a way, he was the truth. His whole life he'd never accepted a dime to be otherwise. Then I understood. Dr. Singh – older, perhaps wiser – was Praveen's mentor. And that door had no doubt swung back the other way probably an equal number of times. I felt ashamed by my arrogance. I dropped all pretenses.

"I'm sorry," I stuttered. "Please forgive me, you as well Praveen." I knew he was listening off camera. "Sometimes I can be a first class asshole. I guess I can get a little full of myself. I'm trying to be a better person." I felt my face reddening. I could sense everyone looking at me, like I suddenly had no clothes on.

"All of us are upon this same journey." Singh spoke kindly. "It is a quest worthy of the faintest and strongest of hearts alike. No man is without sin."

"Thank you, Doctor," I said with humility, wondering where to take it from here.

He must have felt my angst. Obligingly, he returned to the matter at hand. His own resolve to help became immediately apparent with his next comment. "There are only two scientists I know of in the world today who would be able to help, Mr. Strickland."

"And they could, in your opinion, make this machine?"

"Yes, without a doubt. They have the means, the intellect, and the financial wherewithal. The first is Dr. Vincent Balbosa, an American. His whereabouts are currently unknown."

"I've heard of him," I said, searching my mind for particulars. "And the other?"

"Fortunately for all of us, the other is me," he said.

I was relieved. All we had to do then was find Vincent Balbosa. "I'm glad it's a short list."

I wasn't speaking flippantly. I had already decided that when it came to an honest exchange of information between us, turnabout was fair play. I now knew I could trust this man. "The Arab in Palmyra gave us a code, Dr. Singh. I think it has something to do with what you were trying to explain earlier about the on-off switches."

If Dr. Singh picked up on it, he didn't let on. "Did the Arab give you locations?"

"I asked him. He said it wouldn't matter."

"How much time do we have?" he asked.

"Ten days," I said. "Give or take."

The Professor said, "Fortunately, we are not starting from the beginning. As a child growing up in India, I witnessed poverty all around me. It was then that my dream of free energy available to everyone began to shape itself. It became my life's work."

"I'll provide you with the codes."

"Good. We will work around the clock, Mr. Strickland. But I must warn you, there can be no guarantees. It would be wise for you and your group to remain incognito."

"I agree. We'll work behind the scenes. If there is anything you need, anything at all..."

"I have everything, thank you. With your permission, we will liaise through Praveen."

"Agreed. Please keep us posted on your progress. We'll immediately begin a search for Dr. Balbosa."

"He must be located," Singh impressed on me.

"We'll find him, Doctor. We'll work on our end while you find an antidote and meet in the middle." I was guardedly optimistic.

"Let's hope so," Professor Singh said. "For all of our sakes, let's hope so. God be with you." He leaned forward slightly, and the screen went blank.

The silence of the hotel room replaced his picture. It was eerie. I leaned back from the desk and turned in the chair to face everyone. I noticed most of the color had drained from their faces. My own was probably as pale as wax. But I felt stronger, somehow, knowing that Dr. Singh and his staff were now onboard. The team of good guys was getting bigger.

"You're doing great," Charlie patted my arm to reassure me. Others in the room nodded their support.

"I guess, as far as my understanding of it goes, if Professor Singh finds a way to disseminate the code onto – through – whatever you want to call it – the grid, the location of the detonators becomes irrelevant. For all it matters, the towers could be on the moon. That's what I think he meant when he referred to the signal presence. I think it's something like a whisper. As long as it's there, no one has to hear it. It will fan out across the medium like some kind of ever-widening pulse. That medium, technologically in this case, is the universe. Strength wouldn't enter into it. The detonation sequences on all the bombs would never be initiated. They would cancel themselves out. The machines would all short circuit, if there are more than one – again, I'm not the expert – and that would be that. In essence, every bomb, all the C-4 in however many buildings that are rigged, would be rendered benign. And since whoever's done this used the technology up front, it would be impossible to jury-rig the detonators differently. The logistics wouldn't allow it."

"But the buildings would still be rigged to blow. And we still wouldn't know which ones, or how many," David worried.

"They would be inert, David," Gary injected. "And whoever's doing this would never be able to get near enough to them for long enough to change the triggers.

The C-4 would be entombed in their foundations. Kind of like Queen Zenobia, buried under those ruins in the middle of the desert."

"How would the public react to this?" Frank asked.

"Nervously at first," I said. "But what're they going to do about it? What would you do? You'd go back to work, because you had to. After a while, you wouldn't be so nervous anymore. There would be other things more important for you to worry about. Like being fired, getting a divorce, finding a runaway daughter, that kind of a thing. Oh, sure, there'd be rumors about which buildings were involved. We know some of them already from the deaths which occurred during the site work. They're being x-rayed as we speak."

"Do you think the terrorists know about this?" Russell was thinking ahead. "If they thought we were disarming them, wouldn't they blow the buildings?"

I said, "I'd bet they're probably aware of these counter-measures. But I don't think they're too worried about them. It's going to take a lot longer than the time we've got to find which buildings are rigged and where in the foundations the C-4 is located. And of course, that still leaves the detonators. Who knows what they even look like? I pity the guys working to save those buildings. Those would be the first ones these sick bastards would blow up. They'd do it just to prove a point."

"I think it's safe to say that's pretty much their mind-set at this point. The back door's the way to go. We've got to run with our strengths, and they don't know what we know. They still think we're blind."

"Not to mention dead," Javier added.

"Which means," Frank's soft, southern cadence punctuated the conversation, "we're going to have to be extra careful going after this Balbosa fellow, whoever and wherever the man is. He'll have friends. They'll be on the lookout. That back door we're looking to go in through might just be the exact same one they're looking to use as an escape hatch. I don't think they would ever leave themselves all alone at the back of a box canyon. They're too smart for that. If things get dicey we just might end up meeting them in the doorway on their way out."

Chapter 23

"I'm so proud of you."

"For what?"

We had just finished making love. She felt warm and soft and smelled refined. I smiled in the semi-darkness of the bedroom. The curtains were open. I could just make out the front boundaries of Central Park. The lights from other tall buildings twinkled and shone through the wrap-around windows. A dim halo of orange light enveloped the room. Shadows from the bedside lamps stood guard over us.

Charlie rolled onto her side. She nestled her head into my shoulder and began to massage my chest. "For doing this."

"I didn't see as I had any choice in the matter. The way it happened..." I tripped over my thoughts. It was three in the morning, nine days and counting. "It's like we were all drafted and we are at war."

"You volunteered."

"And you give me far too much credit," I said looking at the ceiling.

"You don't give yourself *enough* credit." Her breath felt warm against my body.

"I'm glad you're here," I said. "With us. With me."

"You almost talked me out of it. Remember? Non-negotiable, was the way I think you put it." She traced a circle around one of my nipples. "That tickle?"

"Feels good," I murmured. "You have a way of making me forget the world."

"Do you realize you're not the same man you were when I first met you?" she suddenly asked.

I thought about it. "Is that what you see?"

"Yes."

"Hmm. And that's a good thing, in your opinion?"

"I'm wondering if it's real. I wonder if this has changed you. I'm scared that once it's over, you'll go back to the way you were. You're alive now, Jonathan. You're in color."

"And before?" I was curious how she saw me. I couldn't remember talking this way with her before.

"More like shades of gray," she said honestly. I could tell she wasn't trying to offend me. I played with her hair in response.

"I'm glad," I said.

"Why?" She was looking at my face.

"Because then there's hope for me. It almost killed me when you left, Charlie. I thought I lost you. I couldn't eat. I couldn't sleep. I was a zombie."

"You didn't look like a zombie on those news reports."

"I'm a great actor," I replied. "The truth is I was dying inside. I remember the helicopter ride we took to the rooftop. The chair you always sat in was empty. I couldn't stand it."

"Then the tower came down," Charlie whispered.

"Yeah. And something began to live again inside me. Then you called." I turned and kissed her on the forehead. "And then everything began to change. Something inside me started to grow. You did that for me."

She shook her head, "Uh-uh. It was you, Jonathan. It

was always you. Sometimes a fire just needs a little spark to get going."

"Well you were that spark, then. I love you, Charlie."

"Hmm," she purred. "I love you, too."

We were silent for a while then, each of us absorbed in our private thoughts. Finally Charlie said, "Why couldn't all this have happened in someone else's life?"

I smiled. "That question gets asked a million times a day, and the answer's always the same. Bad things happen to good people. Your character's measured in how you deal with what comes your way, especially the things you don't want."

"Mm," she replied, non-committal. "Sweetheart?"

"Yes?"

"Did you understand everything Dr. Singh was saying last night? Was it true?"

"What do you think?" I asked her seriously.

"I don't know what to think. I tried to follow what he was saying, but most of it went over my head. I'm not a scientist."

I took a deep breath, and let it out slowly. "Neither am I. He lost me in a few places. What he was talking about hasn't been invented yet."

"Someone invented it. Or was it all bullshit?"

"He was serious. The technology is new. Up until your pendant it was just a theory, but now someone's built it."

"Balbosa."

"Maybe." I wasn't prepared to jump into the deep end without being certain I could swim.

"There's no one else. Unless you think Professor Singh did it."

"Point well taken," I said.

"Why would someone turn such a machine into a

weapon?" she wondered.

"Why not?" I said. "That way they can charge for it. I think Singh's idea was to give it away for free, to everyone."

"He's amazingly selfless," Charlie yawned. She was getting sleepy.

"Right up there with Ghandi," I said.

I was totally unsure of what a world with free energy would be like. I'd been pondering the notion ever since the call with Dr. Singh. My mental gymnastics had failed me completely. What would it mean to a world dependant on fossil fuels? How cheap was free going to be? Was that why someone had turned the technology to warfare? Charlie's own words haunted me: Who stood the most to gain if we, the liberators, were dead? Would this new machine die with us? Maybe for a while, but, as Michael Crichton said in *Jurassic Park*, life finds a way. If we were all murdered in an attempt to smother a new epoch, others would take our place. Freedom was a noble, worthy cause with no shortage of takers. Sooner or later, evil always seemed to run its course. It always lost. The only big problem was that these days, it was getting harder and harder to tell the good guys from the bad ones.

"Are you asleep?" Charlie asked me softly.

"No. I was just thinking." I mused on the changes Charlie said she'd seen in me. I suspected she wasn't alone. My friends were probably thinking the same things she was.

"About what?"

"About what you said earlier. When you said I'd changed. You were right. I think I have changed. I'm still changing. For the first time in my life I'm not working for money. I'm doing this because I care."

"You've always cared." I could barely hear her.

"I know. But this is different. My stock has fallen through the cellar. My business is worth less than half of what it was three weeks ago, and I don't care. I used to worry about stuff like that all the time. Now it all seems so trivial. So pointless. Everything has changed. I can't get the images of my friends on the rooftop out of my mind."

She moved slightly, making herself more comfortable. "I'm sorry, sweetheart."

"No, it's good. It's not like they're ghosts or anything like that. I'm not being haunted. It's more like they're all encouraging me. And it isn't just about the towers. In many ways this country was going down the toilet in a speed boat a long time before any of this stuff came up – the busted unions, crooked executives raping people's life savings from their pension funds, leadership who couldn't tell the truth if their lives depended on it. To tell you the truth, none of what's happening really surprises me. In a way, it seems something like this was inevitable. There's a lot of hate in the world. We brought a lot of it on ourselves. God knows, we could have done a better job. We haven't been very good neighbors. We've bullied our way around the entire planet for so long, it became all we know. That kind of arrogance is enough to piss anyone off. The only reason something like this hasn't happened before is the technology wasn't there."

"They're rooting for you, Jonathan," Charlie said in a dreamy voice.

"Huh?"

I felt her smile. "The ghosts are your friends. Buildings come and go. People are always going to be afraid, no matter what. It's our nature. It's you your friends are worried about, not a bunch of high-rise buildings. Your soul is more important than all the towers in the world."

A lump formed in the back of my throat, and a tear welled up in my eye. "That's the nicest thing anyone's ever said to me, Charlie. Thank you."

"My pleasure. Sweetheart?"

"Yes?"

"Can we get some sleep now?"

Chapter 24

"I don't know how he does it. It's like he never sleeps. He's awake twenty-four hours a day," David marveled.

"More like twenty-one or so," I corrected the pilot. I remembered having this same conversation with Praveen several years back.

"I still don't know how he does it."

"No stress. I think that's got a lot to do with it," I said.

"How can he not have any stress?" Gary came into the living room. It was early in the morning, just after eight. I noticed the lawyer had shaved, but he still wore pajamas. The smell of a fresh onion and green pepper omelet had lured him out of his bedroom. He looked comfortable, as did David. They were now roommates. "If he and Dr. Singh don't find a way to pulse the universal power grid, we can kiss the next two super structures adios, amigos."

He went right for the kitchen, where room service had left carts with enough food and beverages for a small army. Gary dished enough onto his plate for three people, then came back into the living room and plunked himself down on the sofa like he'd lived in the penthouse forever. He started shoveling chunks of the omelet into his mouth, pausing only briefly to wash it down with the glass of fresh squeezed orange juice he'd poured himself.

"Comfortable?" I asked him. "Sleep well?"

He nodded, unable to speak with his mouth full.

David looked on, wide-eyed, amazed at the sheer volume of food going down the lawyer's gullet. "Praveen doesn't sleep and you eat enough for ten men..." He shook his head. "What a crew."

Gary finally swallowed. "Question," he began. "Purely hypothetical at this point, mind you."

"Shoot from the hip," I invited him. I'd been up for an hour. I'd shaved and showered, and put on some clean clothes, courtesy of our own private attendant. I didn't know how he'd done it, but everything I was wearing seemed to fit perfectly. Charlie, on the other hand, was still sleeping as far as I knew. She'd been exhausted. This was a perfect time to catch up on some much needed rest.

"Let's say you're right behind these mad scientists when they're about to pull the next trigger. You can see the blood in their eyes. You know it's them; there's absolutely no doubt it's them. Can't be anyone else. And you've got a gun in your hand. What would you do, Jonathan?" He carved out another chunk of omelet. Watching Gary eat breakfast was like watching a backhoe do trench work.

"I'd command them to stop. If they didn't, I guess I'd have to let them have it. I'd have to shoot them. I'd have no choice," I looked at David. He was nodding his agreement.

We waited while Gary drained the other half of his orange juice. He wiped his mouth with a cloth napkin and burped in satisfaction.

"Wrong answer," he said.

"What? Is this some kind of trick question or something?" He had me curious.

"No tricks. You blinked. They win." He sighed, then continued, "In their minds it's a race. They're not afraid to die, Jonathan. So your threat to shoot them unless they stop means nothing to them. By you hesitating for that split second, you've given them the opportunity they needed. Those next buildings, and every person in them, are now history. Everyone who was counting on you to save their lives is now dead. If you shoot them after the fact, you have nothing, no one you can even interrogate, and no one you can bargain with for more information. Nothing but death and destruction all around you." He reached for more of the eggs.

"Well, what would you do?" asked the befuddled pilot.

"You have a shot, you take it with no hesitation. That's what I would do. Because then you at least have a shot at saving the people in the buildings. If you don't, those people die. That's a certainty. And you're right. I know what you're going to say. It's a very dirty business. I just want you both to know the rules of engagement. There is absolutely no room for compassion. You must shoot to kill. Period."

It became ominously quiet. Gary looked up from his plate. David and I stared at him, not sure what to think. It had been a pretty good morning up to this point. His opinion sobered me into the reality of our situation.

"I'm not trying to be a killjoy, if that's what you think," he said, reading my mind.

"No," I held up my hand to stop him. "You're right."

"I just needed to refresh you guys on that. That's all. These people prey upon human kindness. They see it as our biggest vulnerability, an exploitable weakness." He let the last sink in. Then he said, "I've arranged for the replacement of the firearms we lost in Syria."

A shiver went down my spine. Now I understood why he'd said what he had.

"You think it might come to that?" I asked quietly.

Gary sighed again. "I honestly don't know how this thing's going to play out. But if something like that were to happen, I'd feel a lot more confident knowing each of us could and would do what had to be done. I know that's asking a lot. But Javier and I spoke about this yesterday. We drew straws."

"You lost," I guessed.

"No, I won. I wanted to be the one who set the record straight."

I nodded. "Yeah, okay." I could see it now. Gary and I were close.

"Would you do it? If it came down to it? Could you pull the trigger?" He looked at David, then at me.

David said, "You know my answer."

Gary nodded. Now they both looked at me.

"I...I don't know. The Arab asked me the same thing. I've never killed anyone before. But, I think, given the right circumstances..." Now I sighed. "Yeah, I could do it." Then, more resolutely, "If I had to in order to save those people, I would do it."

Gary nodded slowly. "Good. Remember that, and you'll do just fine. The chances of it coming up are pretty slim. Besides, I'd be in front of you."

"There's probably another lawyer joke in there somewhere," I shot back at him wryly.

"So Praveen dug up a lead on the good Dr. Balbosa?" Gary changed the subject.

"Yes, he did." I was glad to move on to a more palatable subject. "Looks like he's in Miami, of all places."

"How in hell did Praveen find him?" marveled David.

"He followed the money," I said. "Professor Singh helped."

The fork in the road for the two geniuses had occurred about twelve years ago, about two years prior to Singh cutting the deal for his independent financing. Apparently he and Dr. Balbosa originally agreed to a research and development partnership. The disagreements between the two scientists began almost immediately and dragged on for nearly two years. The capital threatened to pull the plug. Reluctantly, and with a broken heart, it was Professor Singh who, rather than see the lab scuttled, finally volunteered to back out and turn the whole thing over to his partner.

What happened after that had biblical overtones. It was the story of King Solomon and the two women who claimed the same baby. When the King offered to cut the baby in half and split the child between the two of them, the real mother pleaded for him to give the child to the other woman rather than see her baby killed. King Solomon then returned the baby to its real mother, the woman who called upon him to give it away to save it. In the case of what would evolve into one of the world's most innovative, progressive laboratories, it was Dunbar Singh, and not Vincent Balbosa, who was finally given the nod.

Any and all pretense of civility dissolved between the two of them when Dr. Balbosa subsequently accepted suspect funding for an almost identical avenue of development. Most of the original theory had been published under Dr. Singh's moniker. Singh took no umbrage when Balbosa claimed a large part of the original theory as his own, which only served to infuriate his already alienated colleague even further. If only from Dr. Balbosa's perspective, they now became bitter enemies, working on the same research, albeit on opposing sides of a basic ideology.

A short time later, Dr. Balbosa's funding seemed to dry up overnight, which in itself was highly suspicious. Praveen, during intense diligence the night prior, suspected Balbosa had simply moved his lab. Operating with this in mind, Praveen postulated the best way to find the missing doctor was to locate and then follow his funding. He successfully hacked into several databases storing some very sensitive offshore banking information. Formerly, Balbosa's research funds had been transferred from a numbered Swiss account to the Chase Bank, headquartered in New York. This changed in the wake of the original partnership's dissolution. Praveen surmised correctly that Balbosa had somehow managed to demonstrate significant enough progress to his financiers to warrant their continued investment. The universal power grid, or UPG, as the doctors called it, had quickly become an extremely hot commodity.

Dr. Balbosa had closed up shop and left New York, heading for Europe. More specifically, Praveen had tracked him to Saudi Arabia. In those days, Balbosa hadn't seen as much reason to hide his tracks as well as he later would. Funds were transferred to his charge cards, and Praveen managed to trace them from their originating accounts. Ten years ago these accounts had been large investment slush funds, not unlike modern day hedge funds. It was a simple task for Praveen to use precedent dollar amounts to trace new transfers of similar amounts forward through Panama, and then on to several Cayman accounts held in trust by the requisite Georgetown lawyers, in this case an established Cayman Islands law firm. Surprisingly, the accounts had not changed much through the years, only expanded. The accounts in the Caymans were used as collateral for loans and then forwarded over the ensuing years to various locations throughout the world. Eventually, and for the last six years, the loans were forwarded to a half dozen accounts held in various banks in the South Florida area. Several numbered, not-for-profit Florida corporations were always the beneficiaries.

"Did he get an address?" Gary had listened intently the whole time.

"Through the Florida Registry of Corporations." I smiled. "It was on the company returns. The names of the directors didn't mean anything."

"They would have been fake," the lawyer suggested.

"That's what I thought," I agreed. "But not the addresses."

"Did Praveen indicate the agent of service?" Gary referred to the information required to incorporate in Florida. It denoted the new company's attorneys, in case the company was ever sued.

"I'm sure he did, but we don't have it – only the confirmation he found. We're in a hotel. The acknowledgment was intentionally vague. He could only go so far."

Gary nodded, seeing immediately what I meant. No security. As unlikely as it might be, any unencrypted transmission could be easily intercepted. We couldn't take that kind of risk with this kind of information.

"One of us would have to go and get it," I said. "Either that or Praveen would have to drop it off. And he's still with Dr. Singh in the Catskills."

"All we need is Balbosa's address," stated David.

I looked at my watch. "Which we'll have in about five minutes. One of the wait staff who wheeled those breakfast trays in here –" A muffled knock on the suite's front door interrupted me. "That'll be him now. One of you guys want to get that? I'll slip in the back, just in case. Praveen's calling on the waiter's cell phone. You weren't the first one up. Javier gave the waiter a fifty buck tip when they delivered breakfast. He promised him the other half if he showed up on time with his cell phone to take Praveen's call."

"Where's Javier?" Gary asked.

"He went back to bed," I said.

"Dirty deeds," said David, smiling.

"Don't worry. No one's seen me without my disguise." I half sneered. I didn't enjoy walking around having to pretend I was dead.

Gary shook his head. He was smiling now, too.

I snuck back in the bedroom to wait for the cell phone, quiet so as not to wake Charlie. I listened from the other side of the bedroom door as Gary received the waiter. He asked the guy if he wanted to wait for his phone. The guy told Gary he didn't need it right away. He'd drop by for it on his next break, about a half hour from now.

It rang as soon as Gary handed it to me. The screen showed it as an unknown number. I flipped it open and listened, just in case it wasn't Praveen.

"Are you there, Jonathan?" came his familiar voice over the line.

"It's me, Praveen," I said.

"It is good to hear your voice."

"It isn't quite the same as the conference center, I'm afraid. But for now, it's all we've got." I sat down in the chair by the writing desk and grabbed a pen and the hotel stationary pad. "Were you able to get Balbosa's current address?"

"Yes."

I jotted it down as he gave it to me. "Thanks, Praveen," I told him.

"It is actually the corporation's address," Praveen reminded me.

"Yeah, but there are no office buildings on Star Island. He's there. I'd bet the farm on it. It's a perfect cover. Cameras everywhere, surrounded on all sides by water, twenty-four hour armed security at a guard house on the only road on and off the island, close to everything. He's there, all right."

"When will you be leaving?" asked Praveen.

I looked at Gary. "As soon as we can. We're not all up yet. An hour. Two at the most. We'll take the Gulfstream."

"Is this a number I can reach you at?"

"No. It's good for this call only. We'll talk again from the jet about the stuff you're working on with the Professor. I want to keep this call short. This line isn't secure."

"Fine. Please call me when you can. I will have more information."

That sounds interesting, I thought. "I'll call you on the way to Miami." I hung up.

I looked from Gary to David. "I'll wake Charlie." I tore the paper I'd written the address onto from the writing pad.

"We'll rouse the others," said David. "We'll be ready to leave in less than an hour."

Chapter 25

I felt a whole lot better once we were in the air. Number one, we were doing something. We weren't just sitting on our hands in a hotel room somewhere, waiting for someone else to make the next move. Back in New York, as Frank might have said, I'd felt like a bloodhound without a scent.

Number two was on the wide screen in front of me. "You look well," Praveen said.

"As do you." He nodded slightly. I felt good, too. We were back on the trail. Charlie and I continued to get closer. I'd had my first decent night's sleep since I could remember. And even though the clock kept ticking, I thought we had a real shot at averting the horror that hovered in the wings. An image of a flaming bat pounding on the gates of hell came and went from my mind.

"How is Dr. Singh?"

"He is working. He understands what he must do. He does not want to fail."

I considered my next question carefully before I asked, "It's personal between him and Dr. Balbosa, isn't it?"

"No," Praveen corrected. "That is not the way Dunbar looks at it." It wasn't lost on me he'd called the Professor by his first name. They were closer friends than I'd imagined. "As far as Dr. Balbosa is concerned, this very well may be true. He was once a good man."

"I guess the competition he felt he was in changed all that," I surmised. "Is he going to make it?"

Praveen studied me before he finally said, "No one is able to predict the future. Dr. Singh is doing everything within his power to stop this. Time is our enemy now. He has brought on more scientists to assist him, people he can trust. Two more are scheduled to arrive this afternoon from India and Pakistan."

It was amazing. It seemed like these two countries had duked it out along the Kashmir flash point forever. Now their best and brightest were working together in this superhuman effort to stop the detonations. It would be a twisted irony indeed, if this terrible calamity actually ended up bringing the world closer together.

"Are you a gambler, Praveen?" I asked him sincerely.

"No."

"Pretend you are. What are our chances?"

Again, Praveen studied me. I realized he was thinking. His complex brain was sorting through a thousand thoughts in a few seconds, searching out the most plausible response. "Find Balbosa," he finally said. "He has already built the machine. The true essence of a man's soul does not change. It only sleeps. At the right time, for the right reason, it will awaken."

"You think if I can find him, this madman might actually help us?" I found it a little hard to believe.

"Dr. Balbosa is not a madman, Jonathan. But he does love money. This means he is just confused. Perhaps, if he is approached in the right manner he may be enlightened."

"They'll kill him before his bosses ever let that happen, unless we can get him out of whatever and whomever he's involved with first. That's only if he can be turned

– if we can even find him. And those are some of the biggest maybes since tomorrow."

"You must still try," he said softly, and I knew he was right. The ghosts came back too, and I remembered what Gary said about everyone counting on me. They were standing on the Manhattan rooftop, waving. I shook my head and the images tumbled in on themselves and vanished from my mind. I needed either a shrink or a shot of tequila, but opted for neither.

"Count on it, my friend," I said with conviction. Options meant everything. One of us, perhaps even both, would succeed. I forced myself to believe it. If I doubted the outcome, if for even a moment I had reservations, it might prove to be just enough of a hesitation to cost us the race. I couldn't let that happen.

"No matter what happens, thank you," I spoke from my heart. "Please tell Dr. Singh the same."

"Thank you. I will contact you the moment we have additional information." He terminated the transmission.

I sank back into the jet's luxurious leather captain's chair. I closed my eyes and tried to clear my head.

"You may need this, Jonathan." It was Gary's voice.

I focused in on the handgun. Gary stood in the aisle beside me, holstering it.

"The thin holster strap fits snugly over your shoulder." He demonstrated the shoulder holster. "The gun's flat, small caliber. Shoots twenty-two longs. It's extremely effective at close and medium ranges. Aim for the head. If they're wearing Kevlar, this'll have about as much effect as hailstones on a tin roof."

I took the holster and gun from him, wondering not only who exactly *they* were, but about our likelihood of running into them. "Thanks. I really hope I don't have to use this."

"Just don't point it at anything unless you're going to shoot, and you'll be fine."

I nodded. Gary seemed to have ice in his veins. "How does a lawyer get to be so good at this kind of shit?" I asked, almost rhetorically.

"It's the company he keeps," Javier said as he joined the conversation. He and Frank had moved into the aisle beside Gary.

"Find a seat, guys." I motioned to the chairs around me. "We still have another ninety minutes before landing."

I had been up front with David right before I'd taken the call from Praveen. There was the slightest of sound, like the beating of a hummingbird's wings, from under the table between the chairs. As they found seats, I retrieved Praveen's color transmission from the on-board printer. I pushed a small button beside the print command. More copies would follow, all of them in color.

I looked at the first eight-by-eleven before I passed it to Gary.

"Not a bad looking guy," Gary commented. "For a mad scientist, that is." He handed the photo to Javier.

"The esteemed Dr. Balbosa?" Javier guessed.

"The one and only," I confirmed. "That photograph was six years ago."

"He could've had cosmetic surgery since then," said Gary.

"Probably has," Frank retorted. I noticed Russell and Charlie join us. Frank rose and gave up his chair to the lady. Charlie smiled her thanks.

"He's on the beach. Aside from the valley out west, Miami's the silicon and Botox capital of the world," she said.

"I doubt he's changed his appearance," I said. "No

one's bothered him in ten years. Besides, the worst amateur personality profile indicates he's vain as hell. The guy's totally full of himself. He wouldn't have any extra lines in his face and he'd look the same now as he did back then."

"Do we know anything else about him?" Frank asked. "Is he into fast cars, fast women? Stuff like that?"

"He was married once." I was reading from a sketchy bio Dr. Singh had provided us. "That was twenty years ago. Divorced three years later. No kids. Seems he was pretty much a workaholic. Never went anywhere, pretty much stuck to his lab. Nothing here about him after his work in Saudi Arabia. He more or less vanished after he divorced Singh."

"But he stayed busy," Javier noted.

"Apparently," said Gary. "Now he's trying to blow up the world, starting with this country."

"All for the money," said Charlie.

"Not just money," I corrected her. "Megabucks. The numbered company owns three houses on Star Island. They're big ones, too. There's probably a good forty-five million dollars wrapped up in that dirt alone, not counting what's inside them."

"That's a problem," said Gary.

I said, "I know."

"What do you mean?" asked Russell.

We looked at him. Javier said, "We don't know which house contains his work."

"What if he spread it out?" Charlie wanted to complicate matters. "In all three houses, I mean."

"Impractical," I explained. "By all accounts Balbosa's very meticulous in his work. A stickler for details. For logistical reasons alone, he'd contain his lab in one location."

"Files?" Gary asked.

"Same thing," I said. "I'm sure they are in the lab or very close to it. It wouldn't matter, anyway. They'd all be on computers. Even if he transferred the data, say, off-shore for instance, and then wiped the hard drives, once we're inside we'll still be able to find them. Praveen can handle the files once we get some kind of password."

Gary scrunched up his face.

"What's the matter?" I asked him.

He thought about it. "We may have to persuade him," was all he said.

"Well, we'll cross that one when we get there."

I let it go. I didn't want to think about what he was suggesting and didn't relish the idea that in order to get what we needed we might have to become exactly like the monsters we were chasing. I wasn't soft-pedaling it, I just didn't have to think that way. I loathed their methods, feared having to use them. I knew what Gary, Javier, and Frank were all thinking. And maybe if I wasn't the boss, they might have mentioned something about me being just a bit too self-righteous for my own good. Thankfully, they were considerate enough not to say it.

I'd told Gary once, and that was good enough. I'd pull a trigger if I had to.

"I wonder what kind of security he's got?" I asked no one in particular. I didn't think we'd be able to just waltz up to his front door and ring the bell. "I know the island itself. A friend of mine built a few of those houses back in the nineties." Could we locate the blueprints for the doctor's homes? They might even have something besides the plat numbers on file with the Miami-Dade Building and Zoning Department. It was worth a shot. I made a mental note to make some calls later, before we landed. There were one or two developers I knew who would be shocked but glad to hear I was still alive. More importantly, I knew I could count on them to keep their mouths shut.

"One road, over water, connects the island to Fifth Street." Russell had either been there, or heard about it. "It's well lit at night, and blocked by armed security at a guard gate twenty-four seven."

We stared at him. He shrugged. "Who hasn't been to Miami Beach?"

"You're showing your age," Gary almost growled at the younger man.

"What? Are you too old to party?" Russell fenced with him.

"I was partying when you were just a glimmer in your old man's eye." Gary sliced him and diced him. Everyone, Russell included, smiled good-naturedly, and some of the tension left the cabin.

Javier said, "I think it's a safe bet to assume he'll have some kind of personal protection. Bodyguards."

"I think it would be a big mistake not to make that assumption," I agreed. "Especially with what's happened in recent weeks."

"You think Balbosa knows what happened in Tadmor?" Charlie asked.

I shrugged. "I can't say for sure. I doubt it, though. He's a scientist, not a spy. I think whoever has those dots connected would have to be some kind of spook. The Doctor just sells his wares."

"No doubt to the highest bidder," Russell injected.

"He's probably never even heard of the Joshua Effect," I said.

"I doubt a whole lot of people have," noted Gary. "But I agree with Javier about the bodyguards."

"Dogs, too," said Javier. "Every home on that island's got something they want to keep the outside world from getting into. Most, if not all of them, have walls. The only side open, in Balbosa's case, will be the back end of his houses. They open on Biscayne Bay. And no one walls up a view of the water."

"What kind of dogs?" Charlie's eyes had gotten bigger.

"Ones with very sharp teeth," Javier said with total seriousness.

"So we check the places out from the water," Russell spoke up. "Easy enough to rent a boat. There's a marina on South Beach, just off Fifth."

I nodded, "It's an option. We'll know about any dogs soon enough. I'm going to call someone I know who's a developer. No promises, but we might get lucky. It will make our lives a whole lot easier if we can get our hands on some prints of those houses." I held up my hand before anybody had time to object. "I know what you're all thinking, but this is someone I trust. He won't say anything to anyone. Plus he knows people on the Beach. He can ask around, and it won't raise any eyebrows."

"I'll give Praveen the heads up. Any change orders on those houses would have to be approved. It'll take him ten minutes to dig those files out of Miami-Dade's database." Russell started for the cockpit.

"Hang on, Russell," I said. "Let's give my guy on the Beach a crack at that one first. Praveen's in the thick of it. Let him keep helping Dr. Singh. What you can do is dig up a map of Star Island from the internet. Zoom in on Balbosa's three houses. Who knows? We might learn something."

"Gotcha, Jonathan." He headed up the aisle toward the cockpit.

"Your guy Thomas?" Gary asked nonchalantly.

"Yeah." I nodded. "Who else?"

"He'll probably want in."

"He's got a boat," I said, tacitly acknowledging Gary's assumption.

"It's more like a ship," he grunted. "We couldn't use it in the Bay. It's too big. Are you sure this is wise? This guy has a reputation."

"I know he can be a little eccentric at times," I allowed.

"A little?"

"He might be able to help."

Gary didn't respond, which was his classy way of registering dissent. I knew he'd never tell me I told you so, even if it turned out to be true.

Chapter 26

Gary and I had been right on all counts. Thomas's boat was too big for the shallow waters of Biscayne Bay, which had originally been formed in large part by a shallow dredging operation. Years ago, when no one knew better, they had scraped off the coral reef under the bay and used it as fill to form Star Island, among others.

Thomas had been surprised to hear from me. He told me he'd just finished a huge party – a wake in fact – in my honor. Now he was grateful to see me once again, and proposed another, larger party to celebrate my miraculous resurrection. He reluctantly agreed to put it on hold, but only on the condition that I'd let him have it later, when he'd have exclusive rights to announce to the world that I was still alive. He made me promise to be the guest of honor.

He loaned us what he called his dinghy. It was a Cigarette boat, which with its shallow draft could navigate Biscayne Bay. Again Thomas had attached a condition: he would be the captain. Initially I refused, but he held the blueprints for ransom until I capitulated. It turned out he had owned the lots Balbosa's houses had originally been built on. As the developer, he had sole approval of the plans for the houses.

Thomas, from what I knew, was like a pack rat. He kept everything. He had the prints, and then some. He'd been pretty sure there'd been add-ons. He quietly called in some favors and was now also in possession of the as-builts on all three of the houses.

"There's nothing more beautiful than the sunset dancing off Biscayne Bay in November," Thomas announced to everyone within earshot. He was holding court and looked regal behind his thin, purple-lensed sunglasses.

We were trolling in calm waters. The engines were quieter than I remembered, but the low rumble they produced still sounded like the not-so distant thunder of what would probably end up being a bad storm.

"It's not the same boat, man." He smiled mischievously when I mentioned the low noise level. These were truly toys for Thomas. The world was one big sandbox, and in his mind God had created it all for his personal enjoyment. "I got rid of the one you and I went to Key West in on that poker run. This one's faster, and a lot quieter. That one was Don Aranow's favorite: the thirty-eight foot Top Gun. They call this one the Tiger XP. It's forty-two feet with twin five seventy-five Mercs, Bravo XR drives. Only I had them rebalance the steps to accommodate high performance number six drives."

I grunted, not understanding any of what he just said. He was an aficionado. I didn't give a shit.

He saw I didn't understand. "More power, higher top end, less noise. It's a faster fucking boat."

I looked across the water. We'd been circumnavigating Star Island for a while, getting a lay of the land, so to speak. I sat in the front passenger seat. Gary, Javier, David and Charlie sat in the chairs behind us. Russell was under the front of the boat, in the air conditioned cabin, talking with Frank and Eric Mizner, an apparent friend of Thomas's. Eric actually lived on Star Island, so even though I wasn't real happy about having one more person in the picture who knew we were here, I let him come along for the ride after he offered us his house to stage the operation. Logistics, in this case, meant everything.

Thomas Schneider had gained weight since I'd last seen him. I know everyone had a tendency toward such as they got older, but Tommy, at thirty-eight, wasn't that old. The extra pounds were a result of his infamous partying. His swollen face was an indication that fast women and Cristal Champagne were beginning to catch up with him. Excess could be a bitch, even if he wasn't yet aware of it. Given his lifestyle, I wondered if Thomas would live long enough to find this out. He wore a loose, blue colored cotton pullover, to match the color of the Cigarette. His Tommy Hilfiger jeans and a pair of inexpensive Nikes rounded out a rather plain ensemble. He was a selfish bastard, who wouldn't think twice about stealing away the woman on another man's arm; he'd gone after Charlie the moment I'd introduced them. She must have said something to him, though, because now I noticed he had given up and was keeping his distance. Knowing Charlie, I smiled. I could only imagine the colorful, metaphoric kick she'd delivered to his juvenile groin.

Aside from that, though, Thomas could be very generous to his friends. For the time being, I fell into that category. A couple of years ago, he'd had a chunk of dirt on South Beach I'd been interested in co-developing with him. We had gone out a few times during the process and chased some skirts together; nothing serious. The vote hadn't gone our way; the development never materialized. We stayed in touch with occasional e-mails and the rare telephone call. Now, I realized, I'd done some changing. Thomas, on the other hand, was still cruising for tail.

"So who is this guy? How much does he owe you?"

He looked at me with a wrinkled brow, his hands resting comfortably on the top of the polished teakwood steering wheel. "Don't bullshit me," he added. "I may be a lot of things to a lot of people, but I'm never a loose-lip. You know that."

I took a deep breath. I looked to my left, to the island, and then back at him.

"And who the hell's trying to kill you?" he threw in for good measure, just as I was about to answer his last question.

"That I don't know," I replied truthfully. "Not for certain."

"But you've got some ideas?"

I nodded slowly. "The usual suspects," I said. "The list isn't very long."

"What'd you get yourself into, man? Are you in over your head?"

"The guy on the island has something we need," I began, ignoring his last salvo. Thomas could also be an alarmist, and although I realized it was probably too late to even think about dousing the fires of his overactive imagination, I certainly wasn't about to fuel it with unnecessary details.

"Is it yours?" It was an intelligent question.

We watched as a smaller cabin cruiser sped by. The wake gently rocked the speed boat. The women on the bridge waved, as they recognized the Cigarette. Thomas wasn't exactly low profile. He waved back.

"Not exactly," I responded coyly.

He laughed, "What's that supposed to mean? You're too fucking rich to be a thief."

"Thomas, if you say a fucking word about any of this, I'll put your nuts in a vise and won't stop squeezing until your eyes pop out of your head. God help me, I'm serious on this one." I stared straight into the ridiculous purple slits of his three hundred dollar Ray-Bans.

"That's the Jonathan Strickland I know and love so well." He grinned from beneath the sunglasses. "I was beginning to think you'd turned into a wuss."

My own cotton shirt wasn't tucked in. I lifted the loose brown cloth just high enough to let him see the holster with the handgun Gary had given me.

"Shit. You're a regular gangster." Surprising me, he lifted his own shirt to reveal the shoulder holstered weapon beneath it. His gun was bigger than mine.

"I guess this means we're all loaded for bear." Gary had been watching the pissing contest from behind us. "If you guys are through trying to impress one another, I suggest we go below to discuss strategy."

I looked from Gary back to Thomas. He shrugged. It was his way of calling a truce.

I headed forward between the seats to the cabin. Thomas weighed anchor as the others followed me below deck. Thomas could be a real prick. I was glad Gary seemed to understand him. I guess I did, too. My dour mood, if I had to be honest, had nothing to do with our new captain, and everything to do with what we'd seen when we had passed by Balbosa's three properties.

"Kennels," Frank said as he moved over to let Thomas, who was last to climb down into the cabin, sit next to him. "That means dogs, and their warehouse is big enough for at least four or five animals. So we've got to assume they patrol the entire property. By the looks of it, all three of those houses are very well guarded. I saw five men dressed in long pants and short sleeved shirts."

"Guards?" asked Russell.

"They weren't tourists," Frank said.

"Did you see the guy who was in the shaded area

under the pool cage screen?"

"The one behind the middle house?" asked Frank. "The guy with the scope?"

"How the –" Russell started to say.

"A flash of light off the lens," Javier answered for Frank.

"Where's your lot in relation to those houses?" I asked Eric. We hadn't been to his place yet.

"Five houses around the bend from the first one he's got." Eric seemed as straight-laced as Thomas was loose. They made an odd pair. But I was one to talk. Money did that sometimes. People who normally would never give each other the time of day sometimes became so bored with their lives they developed odd acquaintances. Sometimes they even became friends.

Thomas had mentioned Eric was an extremely gifted cosmetic surgeon. Miami Beach bared the breasts to prove it. There was no hint that the surgeon was anything but humble, though. He dressed well, spoke well, and looked six or eight years younger than his fifty. I summed him up as a classy guy, and again wondered silently how it was he and Thomas ended up spending what was obviously so much of their spare time together.

"I've had the staff make up the guest wing. You'll each have your own bedroom. There's a bathroom with a shower in each of them." He saw Thomas was about to speak. "You can stay in your usual room."

Thomas had a beautiful home on the water right on Miami Beach. I saw now we'd all be staying under the same roof until this thing finished playing itself out.

"Thanks, Eric," I said. He was an incredible guy. None of us had ever met him before, and yet here he was, opening up his home to us on Tommy's say-so. And he'd never once asked why.

"What're we going to do?" Thomas asked. "Break in? Never mind the dogs and the armed knuckle draggers this guy's got protecting him night and day. If he's even home. Has anyone thought maybe he'll just call the police?" I could see, in his own inimitable fashion, Thomas really wanted to help. I felt myself relax toward him a bit.

"He won't call the police. Trust me. His alarm will be silent, wired into his own security force."

Thomas considered this for a moment. Then he said, "What's he got, Jonathan? Does it have anything to do with the towers? You can tell me that much. Is that why they tried to kill you?" He was fascinated.

I looked at him. Without his glasses his eyes were forthright. I still hadn't taken mine off. I didn't want to chance being recognized – even in a boat on Biscayne Bay. "Technology." I watched him absorb this. "Now do you have the schematics for the alarm system that was put in?"

Thomas nodded slowly. He was still trying to figure out what I meant. "Hand me that cardboard tube over there, will you?" He pointed to the top of the lacquer-coated mahogany shelf between Charlie and Eric. Eric handed it to him across the table we all sat around. Thomas popped off the plastic end of the cardboard tube, and withdrew a set of drawings. He unfurled them onto the table so we could all examine them.

After a few minutes I let out a low whistle.

"This is top notch," Thomas said.

"This isn't the way to get in. Barring a complete power outage these buildings are sealed up tighter than a nun's –"

"I know." Charlie reminded me she was still at the table.

"How about interrupting the power?" Gary brainstormed.

Thomas shook his head. "See these babies right here?" He pointed to a corner of the drawings. "These are generators with batteries. The batteries would kick in the moment the electricity was cut off. The generators would immediately switch on. It looks like this whole system was actually designed with this in mind."

"To accommodate a power outage?" asked Javier.

Thomas nodded. "There are a lot of electrical storms down here. It's not uncommon for a transformer to blow. Generators are common. This looks like it was designed with that in mind. It would definitely protect the integrity of the alarm system."

"So we find a different way in. There's got to be one. Here, what does this mean?" I bent over the engineering drawings. I was curious about a symbol near the water line, at the back of the middle house. It appeared to be a square box with a cross through it.

Thomas leaned forward, squinting. "It's some sort of drainage, I think. Probably a storm drain."

"Here?" I was thinking.

"My guess would be they put it in for a storm surge. In the event of a hurricane," Thomas said.

"That's why you were never a builder, Thomas. Think about it. Star Island's basically a porous coral reef."

"One big sponge."

"That's right. It's sort of like the rest of Miami Beach. It soaks up water until it becomes saturated. Then it floods until the water leaks back out. What the hell good's a storm drain going to do? The water has nowhere to go. Especially in surge conditions," I explained with growing excitement.

"A tunnel, then?" he guessed again.

"Look where it is," I ordered.

"I see where it's marked. It's right beside the pool pump house."

"Yeah, and why would someone do that? Why are just the entrance and egress marked and nothing else?"

"It's camouflaged. Whatever it is, they don't want anyone to know it's there." Thomas was getting excited now, too. He continued, "This Vincent Balbosa has something worth risking everyone's life over. He can't, or rather won't, call the police to protect it. You can't call them to help you recover it. It's a piece of technology. Vinnie's a scientist. He's got twenty-four hour armed security, plus the dogs." He paused, putting the pieces of the puzzle together in his mind. "I can't think of any machine that doesn't require some kind of cooling: air, water, or gas. It's a vent. Usually there's some kind of toxicity involved in the process. Follow the vent..." He raised his eyebrows.

"And find the gold," Gary finished for him.

"Bingo," I said, smiling. "That's why you won't find the flute on any of the drawings, just the hole at the end of it."

"But it doesn't matter," said Thomas.

"No, it doesn't," I agreed. "Because we know it's there. To top it off, we now know he keeps his treasure under the house." I stabbed the middle of the page with my finger.

"What happens when we get it?" Thomas asked. "I'm assuming whatever's there is small enough for us to remove it from the premises."

I sighed again, realizing Thomas was up to his neck in the deep end. "It's information. No doubt Dr. Balbosa has the critical pieces of it."

"Wait a minute. You're not thinking of kidnapping this guy, are you? And take him where?"

"Oh, so now you've suddenly developed a conscience," I accused him.

"I asked where, didn't I?" he corrected me.

I looked at him. He never wavered. "Catskill Mountains, New York."

Thomas nodded. "And if we don't get it?"

I sighed deeply then. I looked around at my friends before I said, "If we fail, then we won't have to worry about New York anymore. Or anywhere else in the United States, for that matter." From the latest news reports the closer the next day of destruction came, the more the country panicked. Civilization was rapidly disintegrating. "I sincerely believe there won't be much of a country left in the next few months. I think there's a genuine possibility that we, the people, can actually lose this one." Sadness came over me as I said this. It felt as if I was being smothered by a cold, damp blanket.

Chapter 27

Time was a precious, clever thief. We had five days. I had been in constant communication with Praveen, frustrated as hell. He was evasive and hard-nosed. And as always, he was polite. But he couldn't tell me a damn thing regarding Dr. Singh's progress. In the end, after every conversation with him, I always ended up thinking the same thing: Praveen didn't know.

I hadn't spoken with Singh. I figured not only would it be foolish to distract him, but absolutely nothing would be gained by it. The Professor would either succeed, or not. I wasn't part of his equation. It gave rise to a feeling of helpless anxiety. Normally I had a pretty good handle on the events that encompassed my life. But this wasn't the case with Dr. Singh. All of what he was trying desperately to accomplish was beyond my influence. So somewhere in the last twenty-four hours of my life I'd said 'fuck it' to myself. I'd do what I could and not worry about the things I couldn't control. I focused all of my attention on Dr. Vincent Balbosa. I decided we'd get him out of Miami, dead or alive. The time for any pretense of civility had long passed. There could only be one end to this deadly game we were all playing, and time was running out.

"You see him?" Gary barely contained his excitement. The past two days on the water around Star Island had been maddening.

We'd gotten a hold of another boat: Eric's. It wasn't a big surprise when I'd learned he'd bought the Top Gun from Thomas. The cosmetic surgeon wasn't all work. I'd pegged him for more of the sailboat type, but who was keeping score? So both Cigarettes had patrolled the waters of Biscayne Bay like two hungry sharks looking for their next meal. We tried not to be obvious, and to a large extent we succeeded; Miami Beach was the capital of ostentatiousness. The only way to blend in was to stick out. Anywhere else and the dull thunderous roar of full throttle of the Cigarette racing boats would have created a big stir. Here, they barely garnered a passing glance. By our third day on the water, we were all but invisible.

I looked down from the Bushnell's viewer to the photo of Balbosa propped up on the ledge under the boat's narrow front windscreen. Then I squinted back into the binoculars. "It's him," I proclaimed. "It's got to be." I looked at the picture one more time to be sure. "He's grown a beard, but I'm certain. Here, take a look." I handed the binoculars to Gary.

It took him ten seconds to say, "It's him. It's fucking him." He was smiling now. It wasn't a happy smile. It was more like a predatory sneer, like he was licking his chops just before he took off after a herd of water buffalo.

"Well, well," I said, gratified. "Patience is indeed a virtue."

"We got fucking lucky," Thomas groused as he climbed the stairs between the front seats from below deck and joined us. "He could've just as easily been in Brazil."

"But he isn't," I said pointedly. "He's here."

"That means we go in as planned. This afternoon." Javier squinted painfully into the glare off the water. He was cleaning his sunglasses. It was still early in the day and there wasn't a cloud in the sky. The deep azure color matched Thomas's boat almost perfectly.

I throttled up, and steered toward the other boat. The boring surveillance had just come to an abrupt end. The waiting was over.

So as not to be overly conspicuous we had split up. The Top Gun was in view, but the boat's occupants couldn't see Balbosa's properties from their vantage point. Thomas, Gary, Javier and myself were in the Tiger XP, while Charlie, David, Frank, Russell and Eric were in the other boat.

The speed boat was lying still in the water. Charlie heard us. She sat up and waved from the front deck, where she was passing some time sun bathing. A tingle went through me as I waved back. I had never gotten used to her body, especially the way she looked in the skin colored thongs. We hadn't had much of a chance to talk about our personal lives lately, but, at least to my reckoning, we were a lot closer to one another now than we'd ever been. I was beginning to believe we might even have some kind of future together. But this didn't take away from the fact that I was still a little gun shy from when she'd left me the last time. What reason was there for her to stick around after this was all finished? What was to stop her from heading out on her own the same way she had then? What had changed? Me? She'd said something to this effect, but I didn't feel any different. When I looked in the mirror it was the same guy I always saw staring back at me.

I throttled down and cut the engines. We drifted the last twenty feet or so. Russell stopped us with a straight arm, and then tied the two boats together so we could talk.

Charlie saw the news in my eyes. "You know what I'll enjoy most when this is over?" she asked me as she wrapped herself in a white terry cloth robe.

"I can think of a few things. Telling your father we're alive?" I thought that would be on top of her list.

"That goes without saying," she said with an audible twinge of angst.

"I'm sorry it has to be this way," I consoled her.

"I know. So am I."

"Hopefully you'll be able to tell him soon," I said. "What else?"

"You can stop wearing all these ridiculous disguises." She reached over to me and smeared some of the white sun screen off my cheeks. "The white under your dark glasses makes you look silly."

"I'm supposed to look silly," I said with mock indignation. "I'm doing my best imitation of a tourist."

"I don't think you have to worry about being recognized," Eric said. "Anyone who is human has been watching Charlie for the past three days. She's the most beautiful woman I've ever seen. All the women around here want me to make them look exactly like her." He smiled at Charlie. It was a professional, almost fatherly appraisal. Coming from one of the country's more talented cosmetic surgeons, it was also quite a compliment.

"Why thank you, Dr. Eric." Charlie leaned over to him and kissed him affectionately on the cheek.

"We spotted him," Gary brought us back to the matter at hand.

Instantly everyone became serious.

"You sure it was him? Even with the old photo?" David asked.

"It's him, all right," said Gary.

A quiet descended on all of us while the implications

of what lay ahead were absorbed.

A gun is rarely used in anger. People kill for any number of reasons, but usually someone is shot out of raw fear. One guy believes the other guy is out to get him, so he strikes first. It explains a lot of the killings in the world. In the case of a sovereignty, one nation believing they're about to be hit, hits first. It's called a pre-emptive strike. At the height of the Cold War everybody was terrified the other side would push the button first. To prevent this from happening, we invented MAD, an acronym standing for Mutually Assured Destruction. The perverted logic behind this policy, which actually seemed to work for as long as it lasted, was that if the idiot pushing the button was convinced he'd be annihilated right afterward, he'd be too scared to start down that road. The upshot of the deal was that everyone lived, albeit in fear.

Once in a while people kill out of spite, or savagery. Or greed. Or, because, plain and simple, they get off on it. But not usually.

What's left is what we were faced with. I got a really weird feeling way down in the pit of my guts, like I might have to throw up but couldn't. It suddenly became very real to me. We – I – might have to kill someone. I told Gary if I had to, I could. I would. That implied a willful, premeditated decision on my part. It was all I could think about: that if I did it, it would be an assassination. The reasons, in my mind, were irrelevant. Murder is murder. I hoped like hell I wasn't going to have to pull the trigger.

Then another thought began to occur to me. We were on our own for obvious reasons. If the bad guys found out we were alive and that we had the codes able to reverse the detonation process on the rigged towers, they'd probably blow every one of them. No way could they chance that we might actually be able to stop it. Be that as it may, Derrick Smith and the people in his world possessed some very sophisticated surveillance systems: everything from the Mir spy satellites to software capable of combing through tens of millions of e-mail and phone communications. We'd been extremely careful, but what if they knew anyway? What if we were being used? What if we'd been followed?

I had to admit, we were doing a damn good job. We were making amazing progress. I didn't think the Arab would have agreed to meet anyone else, much less give someone the kind of information he'd given us. If half of what he'd told us was true, there was a firestorm on the horizon, the likes of which would make previous military exchanges look like a game of rock, paper, scissors. Some of the world's biggest heads were going to roll.

Were they letting out the leash? Were we stooges in a game of powerful interests competing for an ever greater slice of the world pie? These thoughts and more had me and everyone else on edge. But there was no turning back now. We were too close. I might be nervous, but that meant a bunch of other people were, as well.

If they'd followed the Gulfstream back from Syria, we'd taken great pains to lose them after that. Nothing human could follow a taxi in New York. It was too low tech. I brushed aside my uneasiness, and forced myself to concentrate on how we'd get Balbosa to Dr. Singh's lab in Catskill.

We'd spent the last three days planning it. The jet was fueled and ready to go. It was parked on Miami International's tarmac, not five miles straight up Fifth from where we now floated on the Bay.

That Eric was a surgeon was extremely fortuitous. He worked with anesthesia. If Balbosa wouldn't come with us willingly, we had the drugs in the syringes to knock him flat on his ass. He'd wake up twelve hours later on a gurney in Dr. Singh's office. I'd give a lot to see his expression when he finally opened his eyes and looked into those of his former partner. What would go through his mind then?

The anesthetics were the reason I had decided to take Eric into our confidence. Under no circumstances did I want to shoot anybody. With a little luck I believed we could avoid it. Javier, Gary, Frank and Russell didn't have a problem with exercising this option. Maybe I was totally naive, but I thought we could just threaten to shoot them. Then Eric could dope Balbosa's security into oblivion. Either that or we could just grab Balbosa and get the hell out of there without anyone being the wiser.

Calling Homeland Security or anyone else connected to the government wasn't an option. Nobody could find out we were alive and looking to snatch Balbosa. We couldn't risk what might happen if that information leaked out and fell into the wrong hands. The line between friends and enemies was still far too hazy. It was up to us.

I didn't want anyone reading our lips through high powered binoculars, so we fired up the engines and headed to the other side of the island. We tied up to Eric's dock and went inside his home to go over the final details of the kidnapping.

Chapter 28

Gary finally spelled it out for me. I guess it was obvious to everyone but me that I didn't have a clue how to run a paramilitary operation. I was a captain of business, and that was it.

"Jonathan, they'll be coming at us with knives between their teeth," Gary began. He was being politely subtle, but I could tell by the tone of his voice something was bothering him. I saved him his warm up.

"I'm no good at this, Gary." I patted the bulge under my shirt.

The lawyer smiled. He was relieved. "Yeah, this isn't your forte."

Everyone else – even Charlie it seemed – appeared as cool as cucumbers in a farmer's bucket.

"But all you've got to do is get us in there."

I nodded. "That won't be a problem. It's nerves, is all, like you get right before the first game of the playoffs. I'll be fine once I'm in the game."

"When things start happening, keep your head down," he reminded me. "You're on the bench. Second string. Important, but not necessary."

I nodded and took a deep breath, trying on the light jacket we'd had printed the day before. 'Animal Control - Miami Dade' was conspicuously displayed across the back of it. The text also appeared in much smaller letters on the shoulders and under the front chest pocket.

I was the driver of the Trojan Horse. Charlie would be my assistant. I put on the wide brimmed hat, and pulled it down low across my forehead.

"How do I look?"

"You look believable," Gary said seriously. "The first few seconds are paramount. After they believe you're from Animal Control, they'll go along with things. Just remember not to ask them for too much at one time. Take the head security where you want him to go slowly. If you ask him for too much compliance all at once, he'll balk. Remember, we're trying to do this smart, not hard. We'll be in the back of the truck waiting for your signal. Jonathan?"

"Yeah?" I looked back at Gary.

"It's okay to be scared, but don't be afraid. We'll be in the back, right behind you. Just think about what's at stake. You'll do fine. We'll all be fine." His eyes had become slits of dark blue ice. It was like he and the others were transforming themselves, growing second skins of armor around their bodies, both physically and psychologically. Javier had done nothing for three days except disassemble, clean, and then reassemble his firearm. I guess it was his way of dealing with the tedium as we'd spent the hours on the water watching for Balbosa to emerge from hiding. When we spotted the scientist, I noticed Javier had finished putting his weapon back together one last time in the hold of the Cigarette. I hadn't seen it since, but Javier and the others seemed to come alive with intent. They were on a mission. I couldn't help wondering about the possibility I was in the way, and that they were just humoring me.

I did my best to shake off my growing trepidation. Each one of us was linked together along a very fragile chain that was only as strong as its weakest link. And damn it, that wasn't going to be me. I felt a surge of inner strength as my determination grew, and my resolve returned in a flood. I felt my own weapon again under the cloth of my new uniform. In an odd way it gave me comfort.

We had nixed the idea of drugging anyone. There simply wouldn't be time.

I went over the details of my part one last time. If I screwed up, then that was it. The game would be over. We all knew there were no second chances. If Balbosa became alert to the fact someone was trying to grab him, we knew he'd get the hell out immediately. We'd probably never see him again. Worst of all, the wrong people would learn of our survival. Goodbye, towers. Goodbye, country.

I could only imagine the panic in the streets if a dozen or more superstructures imploded, and took the better part of entire downtown city blocks with them as they toppled over onto one another. The carnage was almost beyond my imagination. There would be no warnings, either. It would happen in the middle of the work day, when the body count would end up being the highest.

"You ready?" Gary asked. He seemed like a stranger to me.

I nodded.

"We'll be in the back," he repeated for the umpteenth time. "If we get the jump on the guards like we've planned, they'll throw down. They work for a paycheck. Don't worry. Even mercenaries aren't that stupid. Frank knows them much better than me."

"They're crazy, but not stupid," Frank agreed.

Gary said, "They won't sacrifice themselves for an ideal. They leave that to the others, the stupid ones."

"The suicide bombers," I said.

"That's right. Most of the guys we're about to meet have wives and kids. They work for a living. They don't want to die anymore than we do."

"Even if that work is —"

"What it is," Gary stopped me. "Don't judge them too harshly, Jonathan. We're not so different. They have their god; we have ours."

I nodded, stopping the debate. "I'm ready," I said. I saw everyone else was, too.

We moved from Eric's living room to his four-car garage. It was more of a high-ceilinged hangar; Eric had his pilot's license. He'd knocked out the back of the building, and extended it to where it hung out over the water. He kept his wheels up front, on dry land. The back of the hangar, or garage, was where he kept his boat, and a pontooned Cessna.

"They did a good job." I appraised the official-looking seal on the front door of the five ton truck. "It looks real."

"It is real," Eric assured me. "A Cuban I know works in the office. It's amazing what a new pair of mammaries gets you these days."

I flipped open my new identification and compared the tiny seals to the larger ones on the truck. They were identical. I glanced at Charlie. She was checking her ID in the same way. She caught me looking at her and smiled reassuringly. I sighed. If anything happened to her I knew I wouldn't be able to look at myself in a mirror ever again. I'd known better than to try and change her mind, though. She was tough and independent, just like her father. She looked cute, even in her Animal Control uniform.

The sound of the truck's back door rolling upwards

on its overhead tracks caught my attention. I moved to the back it, where everyone else had gathered.

Right beside the truck, in the next stall, Eric popped open the trunk of a Mercedes sedan that hadn't been there the day before. Thomas reached in and brought out a fully automatic, extended clip AK-47. Frank sauntered over to the Benz and produced an Israeli-made Uzi. It was like watching kids at Christmas around the tree as they opened presents, buy they moved with a fluid purpose.

Javier like most of us, kept a firearm hidden somewhere under his clothing. He picked carefully through the bottom of the trunk. He brought out another fully automatic rifle, this time an M16. It had been the Americans' answer to the AK-47 in the Vietnam conflict. He tested it, sighted down its surprisingly short barrel, and seemed satisfied.

It was a veritable grocery list of munitions. We had ordered the weapons two days earlier. Thomas knew an arms dealer, and in his world enough money bought total, absolute, no-questions-asked silence. Everyone was armed to the teeth with their favorites. I noticed Russell selected a tripod-mountable Bushmaster. It looked more like a cannon than a rifle. These guys knew their weapons.

Together, the firepower we now possessed was a force to be reckoned with. One look would definitely intimidate the most seasoned veterans of any armed conflict. I could only imagine what the local authorities would make of it if they stumbled across us. They'd probably think we were starting a small war. There was virtually no chance whatsoever of this happening, though, because of the operational logistics. We were down the street, a scant half dozen houses from our objective. No one was going to notice us going in. If everything went according to plan, no one would notice us leave the island, either.

"Break a leg," Javier said to me as he vaulted into the back of the truck. The rest of the crew followed him. They looked scary.

Their uniforms had arrived the day before as well. They looked like a SWAT team as they sat down with their backs to the truck walls, cradling their weapons. They wore dark blue, with black leather combat boots laced up to mid-calf. I thought the helmets were a nice touch.

Charlie and I had only our small arms. The idea was for Gary, Javier, Russell, Frank, Thomas, and Eric to swarm out of the back of the truck on my signal. We hoped that surprise, and the aura of legitimacy in our impersonating the authorities, would garner enough of an edge to perhaps bluff Balbosa's small private security force into submission.

We split up the pilots. If the worst happened, we needed at least David to fly the jet. He wanted desperately to come on the raid, but I had forbidden it. Now he was waiting for us at the airport. I didn't envy him. Waiting and not knowing was the worst.

Eric had been a mystery to me up until yesterday. When I learned from Thomas he'd been to the Gulf under the first Bush administration, it explained a lot, such as how he handled weapons. Before that I had suggested to Thomas that it might be a better idea if Eric stayed behind. The doctor, as was his style, had said nothing, while Thomas enumerated on some of the surgeon's other skills. Apparently he had specialized in 'information extraction'. It gave me the willies. I never mentioned anything about him staying home again.

Gary was the last to climb into the back of the truck. He winked at me just before he pulled the door down. It thudded hollowly as it closed. Suddenly I felt alone. I walked back around to the front of the truck and climbed in. Charlie started up the engine. We had decided she would drive. I hit the switch, the garage door crawled open on its tracks, and we moved out along Eric's interlocking brick driveway. I hit the switch a second time to close the garage door. I immediately put my dark glasses back on and pulled my hat lower down onto my forehead.

I punched a second remote and Eric's wrought iron front gate slid silently sideways. Charlie edged the truck onto the street beyond the security gate. She turned left as the gate began to slide closed behind us. There was no one between where we were and the bend in the road which led around to Balbosa's property. As we passed one of the big houses I had a clear view of Biscayne Bay through the servants' side gate. I caught a momentary glimpse of what appeared to be an outrigger and its sole occupant rowing against the current near the shoreline. It reminded me of the sculler as he had rowed purposefully along the Hudson River. That moment now seemed like a lifetime ago.

Charlie eased the truck to a stop at the outer entrance to the big house, which was set back a good distance from the iron security gate. She reached out of the window and depressed the call button on the speaker phone.

A full ten seconds passed. Charlie looked at me, a question mark on her face. I shrugged, suddenly a lot calmer. Charlie moved to press the button again, but the speaker suddenly chirped to life.

"Can I help you?" The voice was crisp and blunt, right to the point.

"Animal Control," Charlie replied, equally detached. "We've had a complaint about your dogs."

She made herself sound bored. We waited.

The response was predictable. "I wouldn't know anything about that."

"Well, we got the complaint. We're here for an inspection."

"You'll have to come back when the owner's home."

Charlie persisted. "Look, I don't want to be a hardass, but if I come back it'll be with a warrant and about a half dozen guys from the Dade County Sheriff's Department. Let's not make a big deal out of this, okay? I'm just doing my job. We have to inspect the animals, make sure they're not being mistreated. It's painless. Won't take more than ten minutes."

"Just a minute," the voice said a few seconds later. All of a sudden the voice didn't sound so sure of itself anymore.

We waited another thirty seconds. Charlie pressed the button again, twice.

"Someone will be right out to speak with you." This time there was a slight edge to the voice. If we hadn't been listening closely we might have missed it. They were keyed up, but not unusually so. Right now we were in the nuisance category. For the time being it's where I wanted us to stay.

Balbosa's groundskeeper deserved a raise. The front lawn was immaculately manicured. It was golf course quality. Palm trees dotted the football field sized yard, some clumped together to obscure clear lines of sight to the home's entryway and others lining the drive in. The driveway was straight, until it neared the house. Then it jogged left and ran for a distance along the front, obscured by shrubs. It curved around the far side of the property and broadened to form a small parking area near some tennis courts. That was at least one location where a turnaround could be made. The lane between the bushes and the house was hidden. I couldn't see how wide it was, so I couldn't tell if we'd be able to turn the truck around without going all the way to the tennis courts. I cursed myself for not examining the plans more closely when I'd had the chance.

Someone was walking toward the front gate. Two people, both men. I took a deep breath and let it seep slowly out between my pursed lips. This was it.

Chapter 29

Their body language as they closed in on the front gate told me they were mostly relaxed. So far this was simple happenstance; maybe a pain in the neck, but given a pack of dogs that no doubt occasionally woke some pretty high maintenance neighbors, not entirely inconceivable.

The wrought iron gate suddenly began to slide open. So far they were buying it. The first guy waved us in when he was still about forty feet up the driveway. Charlie got the whole truck through and about twenty feet onto the property before he stopped us. The second guy hung back, about fifteen or so feet in front of the truck. His lazy eyes looked past us, beyond the gate.

"Who complained?" He was mildly annoyed.

"Can't tell you that." Charlie was on the defensive. "Against the rules."

He nodded, looking across the bench at me. I looked bored.

"You guys got some kind of ID?" he asked, still no suspicion in his manner.

Charlie gave him a hint of a smile. He'd notice her, but pretended not to. She was playing hard to get, reeling the thirty something soldier in over his head. Who was fooling who? I wondered with satisfaction. I made a show of getting out my wallet. I flipped through it, knowing nothing was in it except the fake government documents. I held it open for him to see, and flipped it closed quickly, like anyone with nothing to hide would normally do. I could see his interest in me fading fast, condensing across Charlie. She had him hooked. She held her ID up for him to look at. Even more quickly than I had, she flipped it closed.

"We've got a total of five dogs." He stared at her from under his sunglasses, trying to be friendly. "Three pit bulls, full grown, well groomed, and *trained*," he emphasized trained, "and two rottweilers."

"Those can be a problem," she said. She turned to me and added, "Remember last year? With Humphries?"

I nodded. "At least he can still use his hand."

The guard grimaced.

Charlie smiled. "Do you think you can put the animals in their kennel for us?" She turned to me again. "I think we can do a visual. It'll take less time."

"Whatever." I gave a defeated shrug. The guy must have already concluded I was whipped, and that Charlie got whatever she wanted. The guard was probably already calculating how he could get into her pants without having to pay the same price he thought I had.

I glanced up the driveway as I caught movement in my peripheral vision. The second guy, about the same age as the first but twice as large, was walking toward the truck.

"We going or coming?" he asked gruffly.

"They need to have a look at the dogs." The first guard peeled himself away from where he had been leaning through the driver's side window.

"They can pull the truck over by the side of the driveway. Stay off the grass," the second guard ordered.

Charlie quickly appealed. "There isn't enough room

to back this thing up. Is there somewhere I can just turn it around?"

The first guard smiled. He'd get his shot, after all. He looked at the beefier guy, who seemed to be carefully considering us. I determined he was the guy to watch. His nod to the first man was barely perceptible. That, too, could be trouble. It meant they'd worked together long enough to communicate non-verbally.

"Pull it up to the bend near the house. You can turn around in the lot near the tennis courts." He retrieved a walkie-talkie from inside his pocket and pressed the button on the side of it until it chirped. "Brian, come back," he spoke into the mouthpiece.

"What can I do for you?" a voice came back.

"Put the dogs up, will you? Animal Control's here. They got a complaint from one of the neighbors. Probably Agustus again. They want to have a look, make sure they're eating right." He grinned.

"I'll need about five minutes," Brian said.

"Okay," said the guard. "Pull it ahead, left at the house."

Charlie nodded. She put the truck in drive, and began to accelerate. That's when we all heard it. It wasn't loud, but it was just enough to make everyone freeze.

"Hold it." The first guard was suddenly all business. The second stepped back and eyed the truck with serious intent.

Charlie moved the transmission into park.

"What's in the back?" the guard asked. Gone was any sense of cordiality. "What was that noise?"

Charlie eyed him. "You don't think you're the only place in Miami with an animal problem, do you? It's a dog. We picked it up an hour ago. It might have rabies."

"Then you shouldn't have a problem showing us."

"None whatsoever." Charlie knew if she showed the slightest hesitation this would only escalate the guards' awareness. Right now it was bad enough. It was like watching two lions waking up to the smell of blood. "I wouldn't normally do this, but under the circumstances it's either-or."

"What's that supposed to mean?" the second guard asked from where he stood, a few feet away from her open window.

"Either I show you guys what's in the back of the truck, or I come back here with the Sheriff's Department. If I did that it would give you time to switch out any mistreated animals. Besides –" She cast a glance back at the first guard. "I think I like what I see around here. Maybe you can spring for a coffee after we're done."

A hint of a smile returned to the first guard's face. "Or maybe something a little stronger."

"We're on duty," I said, feigning annoyance.

"Well then," said Charlie, "can you be a dear and open the back so these nice gentlemen can see what we've got?"

"Don't tell me we have to report this." I played my part. I opened the passenger door like it was a big chore and got out. The second guard followed me around to the back of the truck.

"I'm not even sure I'm allowed to do this, you know. It's a rabid dog," I complained. I grabbed the handle and turned it, yanking upwards.

The second guard went for his gun when he saw the first pair of feet. He got it halfway out before he gave up. That was when the weapons came into focus. The door finished its upward slide and there they all were. It was a sight to behold.

Six men dressed in black fatigues, with helmets, all

sighting down automatic rifles aimed directly at the man's head. He froze. Slowly, very slowly, he let his handgun go limp, pointing it at the ground. His free hand stretched out to his side, he carefully squatted, and he placed his gun on the driveway.

I whispered, "Tell your buddy to come back here and see this." I leaned over and grabbed his gun, pointing it directly at him.

"Peter, come back here. Have a look at the size of this dog." He never took his eyes off me.

"Now what?" Peter said from the front of the truck. He must have thought he was making headway with Charlie.

As soon as he saw me, he, too, began to go for his gun. I immediately pointed mine at his head.

"Uh-uh-uh," said Gary as he and the others quietly clambered down out of the back of the truck. He walked over and grabbed the weapon. He looked at it, turning it over. "Nine millimeter semi-automatic. A cop gun. Not bad, if you like pea shooters. But really, if we all started shooting at once, who do you think would be left standing to talk about it?"

Javier finished searching Peter, and then the other man. He found their phones and a couple small caliber weapons they were wearing in ankle holsters.

"How many others? If you lie to me, I will execute you," said Gary. "And I promise you, I will make your death a very painful one." It was as cold blooded a threat as I'd ever heard; a side of Gary I had never seen before. Chills ran down my spine. I knew he would do it.

"Three others, five in total," the second guard offered matter-of-factly. The man was a professional. Gary had been right. I thought they'd at least want to know if they were going to be killed, but they obviously weren't going to ask any questions they already knew were never going to be answered. It came with their job description: assume the worst. Assume if you got caught napping, like they just did, you were going to die. If you didn't make trouble, then it would be quick and painless. If you started to beg, you'd be the first to go, and whoever was pulling the trigger might decide to make an example out of you for no other reason than you annoyed him. Neither of these guys were saying anything. Pros were predictable.

"That's not counting the staff," he quickly added. "Cook, driver, butler, two maids and a cleaning crew Tuesdays and Saturdays."

"What about the other two houses?" Gary lowered his weapon to the man's groin area.

"I have no idea," he said, looking directly into Gary's eyes now. "I've got no reason to lie to you. We've got nothing to do with the other houses. Take a look for yourself. I'm sure you already have. The property's divided on both sides by eight foot high stone walls. That wrought iron on top of the stone adds another four feet to the height of it. It's electrified, too. One touch would fry a steak."

Gary slowly nodded. "I'm feeling generous today," he said in a measured cadence. "I believe you, for now. Tell me about your friends, the other three guards."

"One of them handles the dogs. Brian, but we call him Doogie."

"Go on." What Charlie had done was gold. It was a totally unexpected bonus that the dogs were being locked in the kennel as we spoke. We thought earlier we would have to threaten one of the front guards in order to have someone lock up the animals. That would have been risky. In most cases a paramilitary team working together had a predetermined code which would alert them to a threat. If these guys had one, so far we could be certain they hadn't yet had an opportunity to use it. Our job, in part, was to never give them that chance.

"Arnie spends most of his time inside. Sebastian patrols the grounds. Most of the time he's with Doogie. Peter and I are the point men. We roam, answer any calls, and look for possible breaches or points of vulnerability."

"You missed one," Gary told him.

He continued, "Every three hours, everyone has to have a visual with everyone else."

"No one sleeps?" I asked.

He kept looking at Gary when he answered me, "We sleep in six hour shifts. None of us need anymore than that in twenty-four. It was one of the criteria."

"Who hired you?" Gary grilled him.

"Don't know."

Gary's grip tightened on his machine gun.

"We get cash. Someone makes a deposit once a week in an offshore account. We have someone there verify it. That's all I know. Some guy... he never identified himself. We met in a bar on South Beach. First contact was by e-mail. His money was good. In this business no one asks questions. I don't know who's paying us." He licked his lips.

"Who's senior man on the team?" Gary demanded.

"Everyone's a shooter," he admitted. "We've got parody. The guy offshore gives the green light."

"To kill?"

He nodded. "If we don't get the money...it's our way of collecting."

"Your potato gets baked." Gary meant Balbosa.

The man nodded again.

"When does the contract run out?"

"It terminates with a bonus, a one-point-seven-mil

transfer. If we ever receive that it's our termination no-tice. We leave the day after. If we don't get the bonus, we keep working."

"I'm afraid the bonus is off the table," said Gary. "I hope you haven't already spent your share of it. Who are you babysitting?"

For the first time, the guy looked puzzled. He must have assumed we knew. Now, he realized, either we didn't, or we were on a fishing expedition. Big house, big money. Who knew what was swirling around inside his head right now. He might be thinking we were after property: money and jewels. For the first time, he might even be thinking this was a chink in the armor.

"Don't you know?"

Gary half turned away from him, and then abruptly turned back, leading to the man's midsection with the barrel of the automatic. His full momentum stabbed into the man's stomach with enough force to kill someone. But this guy had been in training. Instead of dying, he doubled over in pain, the wind knocked out of him. He went down, gasping for air.

Gary knelt down with the barrel of the rifle pressing into the man's cheek bone.

"Tell me why I shouldn't blow off one of your knee-caps. Quickly now, before I do it."

The man fought for air to save his leg. "Vincent Balbosa," he gasped. "He's some kind of scientist. That's all I know, I swear to God. I never lied to you."

Gary stood up. He looked around. So far we'd been lucky. We were exposed to the road out front. The tiny island had little vehicular or pedestrian traffic, but sooner or later someone was bound to notice us. They might assume we were a real SWAT team. But more than likely, they'd conclude otherwise and call the actual cops. We might be able to explain our way out of it to them, in a day or two, after the news media got wind of what was going on. That wasn't an option.

Gary glanced at his watch. Then he demanded, "How long since your last visual?"

The man on the ground had gotten to his knees. He was able to breathe now. Gary motioned with his weapon for him to get on his feet. I saw there was a hint of fear in his eyes now. Was he thinking about his family? Did he have a wife and kids waiting for him somewhere? I tasted disgust in the back of my throat. I wondered what kind of a person could do what these guys did for a living. They would leave their loved ones, never knowing for sure if they'd ever see them again. And for what? Money? There was a million other ways to make a living. Were they adventurers? Was it in their blood?

I could try and make excuses for what we were doing. After all, weren't we trying to save the civilized world? It was our country. We were defending our way of life. And yet even as I thought that I knew we'd been the aggressors far more than any of us realized. The bigger the lie, the more likely it was believed. And God knew we'd been lied to more times than any of us cared to admit. To most people, believing was far more preferable than knowing.

The man was recovering quickly. He was compact and in good shape. He massaged his stomach. "We're due," he admitted. Given the reprieve, he wasn't about to test the waters a second time.

"Who's supposed to be where?" Gary asked.

"Doogie's probably just starting to wonder why we're not back behind the house. He'll have the dogs locked up so you can see them. If we're not back there in the next few minutes, he'll probably think something's wrong."

"Will he call first?" I asked.

This time he did look at me. "Probably, but that's not for sure. He might decide to see for himself."

"All right," Gary said. "Get into the back of the truck. Both of you." They started to move. Gary stopped the one he'd been questioning with the muzzle of his gun. "Do you understand that if you make any sound whatsoever while you're in the truck that you will both be killed? You've got air; it won't get too hot to breathe. When this is over a call will be made. The authorities will come for you. They will let you out. Do you understand this?"

"I understand," he said.

"Good," said Gary. "Be quiet, and you might live through this. Make a sound – any sound – and I promise you, I will come back and personally bleed you out. Now get in."

Gary stepped back to let them pass. He said to Javier, "Drive the truck up to the front of the house. Start the turn, but stop the truck halfway through it. Go slow enough so we can come in behind you. We'll use the truck for cover. You and you, stay with the truck. Everyone else, come with me." He pointed to Javier and Eric. We'd agreed not to use names.

Thomas rolled down the truck's overhead door. He locked it with a thick Schlage padlock.

Javier got into the driver's seat. Eric climbed in beside him. The truck began to move up the driveway toward the big house. We jogged in behind it, moving as a single unit, making absolutely certain we couldn't be seen from the house. I would remember when it was too late that we only forgot one thing: the speaker at the front gate worked both ways.

Chapter 30

We didn't want to announce our arrival. If anyone did happen to look out the front windows, or any of the home's several entryways, we could always return fire from behind the vehicle if they did see us coming.

We met no resistance as we stealthily followed the truck up the driveway. When Javier began to make his left turn near the front of Balbosa's mansion we cut and ran for the cover of the house itself. We crouched low among the bushes extending along the side of the house.

Javier and Eric would stage themselves behind the cover of the truck and secure the front of the house. The rest of us moved quietly and quickly toward the back, crouching between the stone fence and the thick foliage. We moved in single file, with me in front. I didn't know the order of the rest of us. My senses were alert, my thoughts in the direction we headed. I listened intently for any sound that didn't belong among the birdcalls, humming pool pump, and the faraway whir of the central air conditioning units. Off in the distance I heard a rumbling heralding the late afternoon storms that would soon be upon us. It dove-tailed with the engines of a jet airliner.

I stopped at the back corner of the house, and held my hand up. A twig snapped somewhere behind me. It sounded like a rifle report.

I carefully craned my neck around the corner of the

house. The back yard was more beautifully manicured than the front. The infinity pool near the lot's shoreline seemed to spill into the Bay. Here and there marble sculptures of Greco-Roman personages littered the landscape. I spotted the dog kennels on the far side of the yard, near the pool's pump house. The showers and changing facilities were on our side of the pump house, near what I assumed were large sliding glass doors leading into the home's back living area. That was our target. Lax security, as we'd witnessed, could be careless. There was little doubt in my mind those glass doors would be unlocked. It's how we could gain entry. The only problem was that from my vantage point I couldn't see into the house. One or more people could be standing on the other side of the glass looking out. If I wasn't careful, they'd see us. So far we had the jump on these guys. If only we could keep it this way, we could avoid the firefight we'd trained for.

I was aware of how much time had elapsed since we'd first spoken to the voice over the intercom. That had been twelve or thirteen minutes ago. I could only assume that our arrival had thrown off the guards' schedule by a few minutes. A dialogue with Animal Control could be expected to drag somewhat. It wasn't the routine they were used to. Their minds would make a mental note to accommodate the irregularity. But then, anytime now, it would be back to business as usual.

We had not met the man behind the voice. Neither one of the two guys who came out to check on us belonged to it. Very soon now, the man behind the voice would become curious, and curiosity was the first cousin to suspicion. Bottom line was we must move quickly. Now. Because the moment someone inside the house called Peter or his buddy on the outside for a report and got no reply was the same instant they'd become aware of the breach. If this were to happen, things would deteriorate quickly. For all we knew, for whatever reason, someone inside may have been given orders to kill Balbosa.

My heart was racing, and my veins quickly flooded with adrenalin. I sprang from my position of relative safety and sprinted for a statue big enough to hide behind. It was about twenty feet away from the home's back wall, about fifty feet from where I'd been hiding. When I made it I felt I'd have a pretty good look around it through the back sliding doors. Hopefully, I'd be able to see into the house.

I crossed the lawn in seconds. The grass beneath my feet seemed spongy. It gave me a kind of buoyancy, almost a spring to my stride. It seemed to take a long time to get to the big statue. When I got there, my firearm drawn, I huddled in behind it, making myself as small as I could.

I was breathing hard, but as silently as I could. I was looking back now in the direction I'd come. Gary was crouched there, staring at me. And that's when I heard the faint, barely audible click of a large caliber rifle's bore being engaged.

It came from another statue, one closer to the pool, on the brick deck surrounding it. With a sickening curiosity, like someone slowing down on the Interstate to have a look at a horrible accident, I glanced over to where the sound had come from. I saw what no one else could see, about half a second before I heard the shot.

I saw the round barrel hole of the rifle, and the assassin who had been crouching on the other side of the statue away from where any of us could see him. The rifle was cradled in his arms, as if he had been either raising it or lowering it from a shooting position. He was only about fifty feet away from me, so I could see the expression on his face clearly. He seemed puzzled.

I was scared shitless. I knew I'd heard his shot. That was good, because dead people don't hear very well. Had I been hit? I didn't feel anything, but sometimes shock did that to you. I concentrated and searched myself, but saw nothing. I looked back at the assassin, dimly aware of sponge sounding footsteps racing across the lawn.

The look of puzzlement on the assassin's face had given way to a wayward resignation, as if time and circumstance had finally caught up with him. He'd expected something like whatever it was that had just happened to him to one day happen, but hadn't really been willing to believe it when the moment had finally come.

Still staring at me, he slowly eased his weapon forward, first the barrel of the rifle, followed by the rest of him. All I could think was what the fuck just happened? I was beyond confusion, beyond terror. I checked my body again, feeling my chest area, still unsure of whether or not I'd just been shot. My head swam. I wondered if I was dying and my last sight was of the son-of-a-bitch who'd taken me out. My mouth was suddenly desert dry. Was this what it felt like to die? I took a deep breath, maybe my last. I felt no pain. In fact, a strange peacefulness seemed to come over me.

I was in the middle of the notion that dying wasn't nearly so bad as I thought it might be when someone lifted me onto my feet with a rude jerk under my elbow.

"You okay?" It was Gary.

I looked at him with a blank expression. "I don't know. I heard a gunshot," I said weakly.

"It was David." Gary pulled me toward the protection of a tree at the back wall of the house.

"David? Our David?" I was dumbfounded.

"He was the last time I checked," said Gary. "You're

okay, boss."

I finished stumbling to the back wall. He propped me up against the tree, a few feet from the adobe wall.

"Better snap out of it, Jonathan," he said, fishing in his pocket for something. "You made it, but we're not done yet."

"He would've shot me. I would've been dead. I heard the bullet go into the chamber, Gary."

"Good. Nothing's wrong with your hearing then, is there? So snap the fuck out of it. PTSD comes later. Are you okay?" He stared into my eyes.

I fought for control with every ounce of internal fortitude which I possessed. Being less than a half a second away from having my head separated from my shoulders had done something to my psyche. I wasn't the same. I was still behind the statue. I still heard the click. I stared back into Gary's eyes, fighting the icy sensation in my veins.

"Hit me."

"What?"

"Hit me," I repeated. "Just do it!"

He shrugged, half turned, and hammered me in the middle of the forehead with the flat of his big hand. It made a smacking noise like a bullwhip. My head swam for the surface. My eyes blurred for a moment, and then as quickly came back into focus. I held up my hand, stopping him as I saw him make a move to slap me again.

My eyes were crystals of clarity as I said, "I'm all right. You don't have to knock me out."

He smiled. I was back. Gary didn't wait for me to ask. He quickly began the explanation of what was going on behind us, near the pool. Unbelievably, only seconds had passed since the loud shot had cascaded across the back lawn.

"David didn't go to the airport. He found an outrigger."

I remembered the rower I'd seen on our way over.

"He never could follow orders," Gary said sarcastically. "He anchored offshore, behind that line of shrubs over there." He pointed along the property line. "He waded in and set up under the dock and sniped the guy who was about to off you. Got him between the shoulders. The guy's going to be all right. He was wearing a bullet-proof vest. Must have been expensive, because it saved his life. It knocked him out cold with the whiplash, though. His buddy was in behind the statue of Apollo. David had a quick bead on him after the first guy went down. The second guy saw he was looking directly into David's scope. It was either throw down or die. He's over there still breathing."

"There's one left then," I said. "Inside?"

"Let's find out," said Gary. He raised the mouth piece of the phone we'd gotten from Peter to his lips. Before he spoke, he glanced across the back lawn and the pool area. It was empty. Frank had hoisted the unconscious sniper onto his shoulders and taken him back the way we'd come, around to the side of the house. I wasn't sure where the others were.

Gary depressed the walkie-talkie button and said, "We have the house secured. Talk to me."

Five seconds passed. Then the voice said, "What do you want?"

Gary looked at me. He seemed a bit surprised.

"You have a package that belongs to us. We have four of yours. We'd like to exchange them. We're in a hurry, so don't fuck around. The batteries in all the toys still work. I'm assuming the same applies to ours."

Ten seconds went by. Then, "See for yourself.

Through the window."

Gary knew where to look. Not at the back sliding glass doors, but in the exact opposite direction, down near the water's edge, next to the dock. A thumb rose up near the edge of the treated wood where the dock's railings obscured the platform on the water behind them. It was David. He was signaling he'd seen Balbosa through his scope. When Gary signaled back to him, the thumb went from pointing up to forming a trigger, which he pulled several times; signifying Balbosa probably had a gun to his head. Then he held up his index finger. One gunman. The odds were in our favor.

David would continue to scope the back of the mansion for as long as this standoff lasted. I was thinking more and more clearly, and my thoughts went to Balbosa's neighbors. They had probably heard the gunshot. This wasn't Little Haiti. They might be inclined to believe what they'd heard as the sound had reverberated across Biscayne Bay had been a backfire from one of the many speed boats; they might also have thought otherwise and called the cops. Or would soon, given enough time for paranoia to set in.

"All we want is what we came for," Gary reiterated. "We're not interested in anything else. Play this thing real, and your guys get a pass."

The response came immediately, "We're all pros. Let's do it. How can you guarantee safe exchange? The Postal Service isn't what it used to be. Things have a way of getting fucked up in transit."

"Send out my package. This line is open. My people are listening on the other phone. We'll drop yours on the doorstep on the way out. Just like Federal Express. Don't fuck it up. Send it out now through the back. We get it, we leave and you stay. Period. Negotiations over." He looked at me, while we waited for the response.

We heard the big glass door begin to slide. Living on a beach, sand in the tracks was inevitable. It grated slightly like the sound of bad bearings and opened just wide enough to allow someone to exit from the darkness within.

Someone did. He wore a beard. He shuffled a few tentative steps through the opening and out into the sunlight. Even though he squinted in the sun, I looked past his facial hair and could tell immediately that it was Balbosa. He seemed scared. His shoulders were hunched over, as if he was about to take one to the head.

"Doctor," Gary hissed loudly. Balbosa turned and saw us. "Walk this way. Do it now."

Balbosa must have been thinking he was jumping from the frying pan into the fire. He hesitated, unsure of exactly what he should do. He must have realized the choice was no longer his. He glanced back, almost ducked, seemed to wince, and stuttered toward us, slowly at first. Then, when nothing happened, after one more glance behind himself, he broke into an awkward ambling gait in our direction, close to a bed of flowers. When he came within reach, Gary grabbed him roughly by the front of his shirt and sucked his face to within an inch of his own. Vincent Balbosa looked truly terrified.

"I ought to put a bullet between your eyes right now and be done with it for all the trouble you've caused, Vinnie."

Balbosa shrank beneath the big man's glare. Gary spat him out, releasing him to support his own weight. "Slow us down and I'll shoot you in the leg. At least then it'll be legitimate."

"Where are you taking me?" Balbosa gulped.

I, too, glared at the man who'd almost cost me my

life. "To see an old friend. Now shut up, and no more questions, or I'll shoot you myself." I waved my handgun menacingly in his face. The small man began to tremble. He didn't say another word until we were twenty-five thousand feet in the air, halfway to New York.

Chapter 31

We never did see the last guard. I guess he figured discretion was the better part of valor.

Everything happened quickly after we had Balbosa. Javier and Eric listened to the negotiations on the other phone from the front of the house. Out manned, out gunned, and out maneuvered, the last guard must have considered himself very lucky to come out of it alive. We left the four other soldiers standing under the house's big front portico. The one David shot was in rough shape. The bullet's velocity had slowed just enough that the projectile hadn't penetrated his vest, but he would come away with one or two broken ribs and very badly bruised lungs.

We went out the same way we'd come in. We heard distant sirens; someone who'd heard the rifle had probably called the police. Since we weren't leaving the island by land, it didn't matter.

We regrouped at the surgeon's house and chucked the fatigues in exchange for more conventional beachwear. The police began to flood the island just as we left through the garage, in Eric's Top Gun. Charlie stayed up top, beside Eric, as we headed out across Biscayne Bay for the mainland, where David had parked a rented van. The rest of us stayed below deck. That way, if the cops were looking for a larger band of brothers, they wouldn't stop the Top Gun. If they tried to hail us, I didn't think they'd be able to catch the Cigarette, anyway. It was one of the fastest production crafts on water. Balbosa kept his mouth shut the whole way.

We piled into the van and got to the airport without incident. We thanked Eric and Thomas profusely, and said some quick goodbyes. Thomas reminded me one last time of my promise to be the guest of honor at my impending resurrection party. The eccentric billionaire had grown on me. In a crunch, Thomas was all balls. Eric, as it turned out, stood tall in the saddle next to him. They both wished us the best. We were in the air less than thirty minutes later.

"What the hell were you thinking?"

David smiled at me good naturedly. His thinning hair played peek-a-boo with his balding pate. One of these days, I thought, he should just get rid of it. Shave his head. I thought he'd look better bald. He leaned back in his seat contentedly.

"Call it a premonition, Jonathan. I just had a bad feeling when I left Eric's place. I can't explain it, can't put it into words. You've heard the stories. A woman is about to get on a flight, gets spooked off it, and the plane goes down. I went straight to the marina. I got that little outrigger, had them take me to a launch on the Bay, and rowed out to the island just in time."

"You saved my life. Again."

"You're welcome. You would've done the same."

"How long before we put this baby on the ground?" I asked, moving on. We both knew what he'd done for all of us. I didn't care if it had been some weird kind of psychic clairvoyance or random chance; David listened to that little voice inside all of us. Most people I knew had ignored it for so long they could no longer hear it. Myself, I called it intuition, but there was a lot to be said for being in the right place at the right time.

"One hour, thirty-four minutes," he calculated. "That's to Dr. Singh's front door. We're fortunate he's got a runway on the property."

"From what I understand he's got everything except dancing girls," I said. "Apparently it's one of the most well equipped facilities in the world. The runway's a necessity. Scientists from around the world visit Singh regularly. They spared no expense."

"I just wonder who *they* are?" David said out loud.

"I've got a funny feeling before this thing's over we're going to find out." I was looking through the jet's windshield at an angry mountain of cumulonimbus clouds.

"You going around that?" The edges of the cloud formation were dark and foreboding.

"It's low enough I can get us up over it. It might get a little bumpy, but it's nothing to worry about."

"All right, I'm going back to talk with the mad scientist. I'll send Russell up to spell you off." I turned to leave the cockpit. Suddenly I turned back, and put my hand on the pilot's shoulder. We looked at each other. David nodded and I smiled. Then I left.

Vincent Balbosa had composed himself somewhat now that he had learned he wasn't in imminent danger of losing his life. It helped tremendously when he found out we weren't leaving the States. He feared that possibility — the unknown. He watched me approach from where he sat buckled securely into a chair near the back of the cabin. Gary eyed him hungrily from across the aisle. Balbosa's eyes darted nervously back and forth from him to me. I sat down in the empty chair opposite the Doctor but said nothing. I stared at him, watching him fidget. Finally the silence became too much for him to bear.

"If it's money you want..." he blurted.

I glared at him as his words evaporated between us. His shoulders seemed to sag even more than they had already.

"May I ask who you represent?" His attempt at civility was trite.

I leaned forward and examined the man's features more closely. It seemed vanity was his strong suit. He actually looked younger in person than his photograph had indicated. His complexion was pale; he had not spent a whole lot of time outdoors. To some extent this explained the absence of heavier lines across his face. The cosmetic surgery was unmistakable, though. He was older than me, his face stretched. His build was slight. It gave him an almost emaciated appearance. His beard caused his nose to be accentuated. No doubt he wore contacts. Real glasses would have made him look a bit like Groucho Marx with facial hair. There was no gray in either the beard or his hair. More vanity.

"You have something we need, Dr. Balbosa," I began.

He squinted at me, like he'd seen me somewhere before but couldn't place where. I'd been in the media a lot lately, especially after the missile attack in Syria. Still, I could see he was fighting to remember. His mind was not an ordinary one. It was like a tape recorder. Given adequate time, he would rewind it to where I'd only been a passing, fleeting sound bite. He'd stop it there, and recognize me. I saved him the trouble.

"My name is Jonathan Strickland, Doctor." Recognition flooded across his face. He was about to say something. I stopped him by holding up my hand.

"I speak, you listen. Those are the rules for now." His mouth remained open, but he said nothing. "Unless I ask you a direct question. Then you'd better not lie to me." I glanced over to where Gary was sitting. Balbosa followed my gaze. Gary sneered at him.

"You invented something," I said.

For a moment he seemed genuinely puzzled. He replied, "May I speak?"

I nodded.

"Not to sound facetious, but I have invented many things. I hold eighty-seven patents in my name, not to mention the others held in various corporations of which I am either a member of the Board, or part owner."

I could see he wasn't trying to brag or be a smart ass. He was simply stating the facts. He was too frightened to think otherwise. If he was being coy, this would stop now.

"Yeah, well, we're interested in the one that's responsible for killing my friends when my tower was demolished. If you want to claim ignorance, Dr. Balbosa, I'm going to get up and spend a few minutes in the front of the aircraft with my pilot. I'll leave you two alone," I jerked my head in Gary's direction, "so the two of you can get better acquainted. I'm in no mood to play games."

"Oh, that one," Balbosa said immediately.

"Yeah, 'that one,'" I said. "Bottom line: How do we stop the detonation sequences for the other buildings? All of them. How does the technology you invented work?"

"You're too late," he said. "You'd need the reverse codes. You would have to –"

"We have them," I cut him off.

"You... have them?" Balbosa seemed stunned. Then he did something I never expected him to do. He clapped his hands together, looked up at the cabin's ceiling, and said, "Thank God in Heaven." He looked back at me, his eyes sparkling like diamonds. He was barely able to contain his excitement as he blurted out, "There may be a way then. I know who you are, I've read about you, Mr. Strickland. Good things. You must get me to a former colleague of mine. Together, we may have a chance. Now I remember. There was a report." He looked at me with curiosity then. "It said you were killed. You and your friends perished in a terrorist attack last week in the Syrian Desert."

"Rumors of my death have been greatly exaggerated," I was getting a little tired of quoting Mark Twain. "Doc, I've got to tell you, your reaction to us being in possession of the codes is a little unexpected."

"Unexpected?" Balbosa seemed insulted. "You don't think I was going along with these people, do you? Were you actually thinking I had something to do with this madness?" he looked aggrieved.

"It is your technology," I reminded him. Things were taking an interesting turn.

"Einstein came up with $e = mc^2$. It doesn't mean he nuked Nagasaki and Hiroshima."

I stared at him. "Are you saying –"

Now he cut me off, "I'm saying I am, and always have been, an extremely unwilling participant in this lunacy. I would no more wish ill upon another human being than hurt my own child." He looked from me to Gary, then back again. It was apparent he'd thought all along we were someone else, perhaps someone who'd been sent to silence his efforts once and for all. Or kidnap him and put him to work for the other side, whomever that was.

"I didn't want any part of this," he continued in earnest. "I didn't invite those gorillas into my home. They weren't my guests. Quite the contrary, I was their prisoner. I was let out once a day. They let me stroll for a half hour in my own back yard. Then it was back to work."

"For who?"

"They never gave me their card." He was exasperated.

"You're saying you don't know who's behind this?" I asked. "Who hired you to," I looked helplessly to Gary, and then back at the doctor, "to build whatever it is that makes whatever it is you've built work?"

I was tripping over my own tongue.

"That's not exactly the way I would describe it, but the answer to your question is yes. Or no. Yes, I'm saying no, as in I don't have the slightest idea who's behind blowing up our buildings. I'm an American. I am not a traitor to my country. If I'd known how my technology was to be bastardized, do you think I would have agreed to work on it for them?"

"Let's hope not," I answered.

"Let's know not." He raised his voice to a level of emphatic conviction.

"You just said 'them'. Who's 'them?'"

"I don't know," he almost yelled. The whole conversation was beginning to remind me of an Abbott and Costello routine.

"Was someone paying you to develop this technology? Someone must have been paying for the research. We checked. You own the home where we found you, and the ones on either side of it. They're not cheap, and it seems you've been collecting offshore trusts."

"I've done nothing illegal. I was forced into that."

"By your former colleague?"

"Dunbar Singh? Do you know him? He's the one I need you to take me to. He's the one person who might be able to help me stop this."

"We're on our way," I said.

"Now?" He was even more overwhelmed.

"Now," I said.

"You're not the enemy, then." His voice faltered. He was beginning to trust me.

"No, Doctor. We're trying to stop them."

"I'll do everything I can to help you," he implored. His eyes were wide open and intent. "I never wanted this. When I first began to suspect how the technology might be used, I objected strenuously in a letter to the Foundation. That's who was paying us into the offshore trusts; a Foundation with a post office box in the Cayman Islands. It was my only point of contact. That's when they sent in those so-called bodyguards. Soon after I realized the real reason they'd been sent."

"To watch you," Gary said.

"I became a prisoner in my own home. They'd wait at the door when I used the bathroom. I've had to live like that for over two years. And then, when I heard about the tower in New York, I knew. They'd pulsed it."

"Pulsed it?" Gary looked at me questioningly.

I sighed. "Free energy. A dream with no end. So big the money flowed into it like lava down the side of a volcano. You're a rich man, aren't you, Doctor?" Nothing could take me away from the notion, aware of it or not, that these scientists sold their souls to the highest bidders anytime they got the chance.

"I don't care about the money." Balbosa's complaint was sincere. "Yes, I'm richer than I ever dreamed possible. And what has it got me? I spent the whole time trying to be somebody else, and I'm miserable. I was always too old, not handsome enough. Then those idiots showed up and I had time to think. I realized I've helped no one but myself. Even that's debatable. My intellect – this gift I have – how have I used it? How has it used me? America is on the verge of collapse. There is widespread panic.

The streets are running red with the blood of my own people because there is no longer enough military to control the panic. In the bigger cities they are shooting people after dark, no questions asked. No one picks up the bodies. They lay there, rotting in the middle of our sidewalks. This isn't America. It's another country, something even Orwell never imagined. And I did it. My invention. Free energy. No more electric bills. Hah!"

Gary and I stared at him.

"Take me to Dunbar," he suddenly demanded. "It's our only chance."

"Don't you mean it's *your* only chance?" I asked him quietly.

He looked at me with an expression that bordered on tears. He sank back into his seat and looked out the window. We were in the storm now. The plane began to shake as we hit the first downdraft.

Chapter 32

"I've missed you. I see the years have been kind to you."

It wasn't at all what I expected, but I liked the idea that the doctors were starting out on a positive note.

"It has been a long time, Vincent." Dr. Singh returned his former partner's salutation. "You look well."

"Who would have dreamed that after all these years our lives would once again intersect under such circumstances?" Balbosa's question was salient.

Dr. Singh was more pragmatic. "We must stop what we have begun. We have not worked so long and so diligently so others may use our insights for such perversions. I once knew you as a brother. Have you changed so much?"

"I've changed back, if anything," Balbosa confessed. "When we separated all those years ago, when you received the Prize, I was incensed. All the accolades, all the money, all of it went to you. I felt completely ignored. It was as if I never existed. You and I worked on the technology together. We were partners. I felt you betrayed me and went insane with jealousy. You were the darling of the press, the 'Scientist of the Millennium.'"

"None of it was what I wanted. They did all that so they could sell more papers. I wanted none of the publicity. We may have needed money, at least enough so our research could continue. My heart was broken when I learned you hated me. We deserved better. We let them hypnotize us."

Private aircraft came and went from Dr. Singh's compound on a regular basis, especially since he had to ratchet up his work week. We filed a flight plan, but under a pseudonym, same as before. So far we'd gotten away with it, but I knew it was only a matter of time before someone figured it out.

I had learned early in life from Pop there were basically two kinds of people: those who could be bought, and those who weren't for sale. The latter group was, of course, in the minority. They weren't any better than all the people who had their price, just different. That difference was always measured by what they did with their lives. Some became homeless. That was their choice. Others went on to great things, which could be a curse or a blessing depending on how they handled the inevitable attention. Right now, in my mind, these two great scientists teetered on that edge. The next few days would determine how history would view them both. Inextricably tied together, they'd either sink or swim in their genius.

Both fame and fortune, ironically, had visited Dr. Singh early. Dr. Balbosa had felt they'd gone to the wrong man. At the very least, he felt the adulation and accolades from both the scientific and public communities should have been shared equally. After all, they had worked together to achieve exactly that. When none had come his way, when Singh had seemed to get it all, some very disturbing aspects of Vincent's personality had fought their way up through the muck of his ego. They had surfaced in an ugly way.

I knew fame. And I knew fortune. I'd achieved both at a very young age. The difference between someone like me and someone like Vincent Balbosa was Pop. I'd had his tutelage. More importantly, though, I'd had his love. That's what everything else in my life had sprung from. It's what made me, me.

I'd be the first in line to admit that from time to time I strayed. Fame and its accompanying emoluments could be intoxicating. I liked to think I had learned from my mistakes, though. Those parties were beyond pompous – all those people fawning over me, telling me how great I was, drinking my booze, filling their fat faces with my expensive caviar. But it wasn't their fault. I had invited them, and not so long ago, either. Why?

So I could get inside their wallets, I realized now with a burgeoning sense of shame.

Why had those people come together on top of my roof? So high and mighty one minute, dust the next. I began to realize in these last few weeks that the higher up I went, the more out of touch with reality I became. It was a long, hard trip back down to the ground.

I just had to look at these two scientists for confirmation. One minute they were going to save the world. Everyone was going to have power. And then what? No one ever stopped to think about that. It seemed like everyone dreamed of doing nothing. I guess they thought they'd spend the rest of their days laying out on a beach somewhere, a cabana boy at their beck and call. They'd spend the rest of their life in a beer commercial.

I had news for them: it didn't work that way. We all had a spirit, a soul. It could actually rot, wither, and die while we went on living. That's when life became hell.

"We're running out of time, gentlemen," I said. "You can discuss what went wrong later." Then I softened my voice. "I might be out of line, but we've got three, maybe four more days until they bring down the next towers. I think you guys should put all that bullshit behind you for the time being, and concentrate on stopping it from happening. It's clear to me we're all on the same team. The twisted irony here is that we always have been. Somehow someone's been able to turn this thing inside out. You two have been so buried in your own agendas that you never stopped long enough to realize what you were being used for, much less who it was using you. Didn't either of you ever wonder who was paying the bills?" I stared at them. I guess when someone gave Singh his Nobel Prize, he never thought to think. And Balbosa never cared. He'd been too consumed with trying to live down the humiliation, or catching up and surpassing the accomplishments of his former partner. I happened to think both were one and the same.

The compound's conference room became still. An embarrassed silence followed.

Charlie was waiting for me upstairs in our room. The others had been assigned theirs. Only Gary had accompanied the doctor and me to meet Singh. Javier and Frank were gone out to check the grounds and meet with the compound's Chief of Security. If anyone had recognized me, so far they hadn't acknowledged it. Singh's group was not much different from what I imagined a cult to be. They were tight knit and tight lipped. Everyone knew everyone else. A stranger among them would be noticed immediately. The compound was fenced and armed security patrolled the perimeter. Gary admitted to me on the way in that he was impressed.

Finally Dr. Singh said, "We have been trying to build the electro-magnetic processor. We cannot get the electronic repeater to work properly. It keeps malfunctioning like the pendant in Syria. The power cannot build up quickly enough in the processor in time to surpass the threshold."

Balbosa was nodding, "It is the same protocol problem which I encountered when I..." He hesitated, then admitted with a sigh, "...stole your theories. I worked on nothing else the first five years. There is a very narrow window of entry between the quantum world and our own with respect to this application. One wrong turn..." He shrugged. "The good news is that together we can fix it."

"What's the bad news?" I had to ask.

The scientists exchanged worried glances. A soft knock on the conference room's heavy oak door interrupted us. It opened and Praveen stepped in.

He must have noticed the solemnity because he politely asked, "Perhaps I should return later."

I quickly waved him in. He closed the door behind him.

One of the first things I'd noticed about the compound was the silence was all around us. On the surface, Dr. Singh's Facilities Center could have passed for some kind of religious retreat for the extra faithful. But it was quiet most of the time for a very good reason: the most brilliant minds in the world gathered here, and they did a lot of deep thinking. They interacted more with machines than with fellow humans.

When I thought about it, this actually made sense to me. Even now, our real battle, our real enemy, was technology. Long ago it had outstripped man's morality and became our master. There were no secrets anymore, thanks to machines. They never slept, they never ate. They had memories that lasted forever. Worst of all, they were never wrong. We'd gotten to the point where we ruined people's lives first rather than admit the fallibility of machines. It was crazy, but it was the world we'd made for ourselves. And now we'd done it one more time. We'd brought ourselves back to the brink of annihilation. Once again we flirted with the destruction of things we'd worked for thousands of years to achieve. I wondered if there was any hope left for any of us. Just as quickly I dug in my heels. As long as I had a breath left in me, there would also be a future. I, for one, wasn't giving up.

"What have you got for us?" I asked Praveen, glad for the intrusion.

"More of the same, I am afraid." Praveen had become our unofficial liaison to the outside world. I didn't have the time. I hadn't caught a news bulletin for what seemed liked months.

"Your memorial was well attended." He seemed to brighten. He was faking it. I knew Praveen well enough to know this wasn't the reason he'd interrupted us. There was something else, and it concerned me, not the scientists. Singh and Balbosa had their role; I had mine. I pretended not to know anything was wrong. We'd talk later, after the scientists left, in private.

"I guess the President wasn't there," I said glibly. Then, "We done?" I looked at the scientists.

Again, they exchanged couched glances. They seemed to share a reluctant secret.

"Let me guess," I said. "The bad news is you may not be able to do this. You may not be able to make a machine to stop it in time, right?"

"We'll do our best," promised Balbosa. It was clear to me no scientist ever got used to working around deadlines. None of them seemed to work well under pressure.

"That's all we can ask," I consoled them. "Remember, if we go down, we all go down together. Have you got everything you need on site? Is anything missing?"

"We have everything now," Dr. Singh looked from

me to his old partner. "Including the most important part."

Vincent Balbosa looked at Singh questioningly.

Dr. Singh smiled, a rare expression of emotion. "We have forgiveness. What do you say, Dr. Balbosa? Shall we go to work? The world is counting on us."

Chapter 33

"You can't be serious," she protested.

"I'm not going alone," I pointed out. "I plan on having as many of us as there are of them."

"He won't see you."

"He doesn't have a choice. What's he going to say? 'No, I'm busy. I'm all booked up until after the superstructures wipe out half the major American downtown metropolitan areas. Give me a call next week. Have your people call mine. We'll set something up.'"

Charlie stared at me in absolute disbelief.

"The press will be there. They're there already. One word about me being alive and they'll descend on his office like locusts on a field of tall grass."

"We still have no proof."

"We may never have it." I thought back to my conversation with Praveen two days ago. "We may never get the evidence we need. They're clever. They're evil incarnate, too. The two go hand in hand. And we're out of time."

"What if the Arab was lying, Jonathan? What then? Do you realize what will happen if we're wrong? Who was he, anyway? For all we know he could be the one responsible. How do we know he isn't?"

"He gave us the means to stop it," I pointed out.

"How do we know that? Even if Professor Singh and

Dr. Balbosa are ready, what if it doesn't work? What if the Arab threw us a red herring? Think about it. We've been occupied. We've spent all our time and resources, not to mention this entire facility's. It would have been a brilliant way to keep us busy while time ticked away."

"So you think the Arab bombed himself, is that it? He sent up a drone to kill his own people, and saved our lives, because remember, he was the one who waved us down into the tunnel; all just so he could send us back here with a bogus decoding sequence. Why would he do that? He could've just killed us and been done with it. We'd be out of the way, and the clock would still be ticking. No, I don't buy it. I believe the man was telling us the truth. He may not have told us everything, but we got enough of it to do something to stop this madness."

She looked at me, considering all of what I said very carefully. "Okay, let's say he was telling the truth. How did he know?"

"Because he was part of it, until this whole thing spiraled out of control. If they bring those buildings down now, who's it going to hurt the most? It's like you once asked: who stands the most to gain, and who's the biggest loser? They tried to kill him once already that we know of. My God, we were there. We almost died alongside him."

"They're not done trying," she said.

"On that we can most assuredly agree. That's exactly why I've got to do this. Once it's out there, it'll be too late."

Charlie slumped into the chair beside the bed in the suite we'd called home since we'd arrived at Singh's compound. She wasn't defeated. She was, however, resigned to the fact we literally had run out of time and options.

I remembered the meeting with Praveen. Maybe

what he'd learned wasn't yet hard evidence, but I was absolutely convinced it was the smoking gun. We would have our proof, but it would take time, precious time we no longer had. We had to act with what we knew now. If we waited, lots of people were going to die a horrible death. The ramifications of the terror about to rain down on us wouldn't just be felt here in the States. I was convinced global assets were being realigned.

Two days ago, Praveen had been very concerned when he asserted, "The C-4 explosives originated from a manufacturer in New Jersey."

"What if we're wrong?" I pleaded. "What if our chemists have made a mistake?"

He just looked at me. He didn't correct me. He knew from experience I'd do that myself. It was wishful thinking on my part. No doubt they had checked and re-checked their findings ten times and ten different ways. We were all looking for a way out, for answers that would make sense to us. It wasn't to be.

"What else?" I had asked. There was another knock on the door. The boardroom was turning out to be a busy place.

Gary poked his head in. I could see Javier over his bear-like shoulders.

"You in the middle of something?" He saw Praveen and nodded hello.

"Come on in," I said, slumping down into a chair near the end of the meeting table. "Some of the tests came back."

"Oh," the lawyer said, entering with Javier in tow. "This ought to be interesting. Does it refute or confirm?" he asked as they found chairs.

"It damns us all to hell, unfortunately. The C-4 is from a defense contractor in New Jersey. Praveen and I just got started. Now you know what I know. Go ahead, Praveen."

I tried to keep myself level-headed.

"The explosives' lot was to be used for live exercises at the naval base in Pensacola. We were able to access the shipping records."

"It arrived in Pensacola," Javier guessed.

"Yes," said Praveen.

"And then the entire shipment was stolen," Gary finished for him.

"That is what has been recorded," Praveen confirmed. He didn't seem surprised we'd guessed correctly.

"That single shipment wouldn't have been enough for the entire operation, though," I said.

"There were four other shipments of C-4 quantities," Praveen said. "They were shipped –"

"And subsequently stolen" Gary filled in.

"In the months leading up to 9/11, before heightened security would become a mitigating factor in such large-scale theft."

"Why wasn't any of this in the newspapers?" wondered Javier.

"Because it would've read as a huge embarrassment to the entire military. After 9/11 there was more than enough motivation to leave it buried. Think of how that news would have played out," said Gary. "No one wanted responsibility for that one getting out of the bag."

"Yeah, then the C-4 might actually have been found," I said sarcastically.

"So they gathered it up from around the country, warehoused it until they needed it..." Javier mused.

"And then shipped it in the shape of specified form boards that were inserted into the bases of our towers," I finished. "I'm almost afraid to ask, Praveen. How much

C-4 ended up being stolen off those bases?"

"Enough to plant the explosives in at least thirty buildings similar to yours," Praveen said.

We stared at him.

"How long –" I started to ask.

Gary cut me off. "It's still good to go, Jonathan. Whatever they've managed to seal into those foundations still works, believe me."

Praveen said, "I am afraid I have even more disturbing news."

I wondered how things could possibly get any worse.

"Homeland Security has asked to inspect these facilities. The entire compound. It is private property. Dr. Singh has told them no, but..." he trailed off.

"They'll get a warrant," the lawyer assured me. "I'm surprised they don't already have one."

"We have to get the hell out of here then," I said emphatically.

Gary held up his hand. "They're fishing, Jonathan. The people behind the people don't know what we know. This proves it."

"But they must suspect something," I worried.

"This might only be their attempt to flush something out," he said.

"Meaning us," I said.

"Not necessarily. I think they've probably moved on. I think they're convinced we got toasted back there in the desert. They're turning over stones, setting some brush fires. Remember what day it is."

He had a point. We were down to three days before the next horror. The nation was already in an accelerated downward spiral. The administration was holding press conferences from an undisclosed underground bunker. They weren't suicidal. No one was about to poke their head out given the present political climate.

The firestorm began when my tower had been brought down, but the front pages of yesterday's daily had said it all: 'Rats Leave Sinking Ship'. The truth was we all had guns. We were armed to the teeth. And with most of them aimed in the direction of the White House, I really couldn't blame our elected officials for going underground. The American people had been trained. We were among the most violent on earth.

In the minds of the average American citizen circumstances had disintegrated. Theirs was a world of survival. If it was them or their leaders, well, isn't that what leaders were for? Isn't that why we paid them all that money? If a sacrifice was called for, if a slaughter was inevitable, it was better 'them' than 'us'. Some had even begun to think that it was downright unpatriotic, un-American, that those named on the manifesto's hit list wouldn't give it up for their country. Insanity ruled. Rule of law was giving way to mob rule.

Like always, the government had its answer, though. They had literally circled the wagons. D.C. was one huge military encampment. Tanks rimmed most of the federal buildings. Military Humvees where the transport of choice. America was no longer America. Strict curfews remained in effect. Violators were arrested and jailed, or, as often, shot on sight.

As I watched and learned, Charlie's question haunted me, because the footprints of who stood the most to gain had began to appear in the crumbling American heartland. The plan was so unbelievable, so diabolical, the lie so huge, that it was beginning to work.

I remembered when we got rid of Saddam. I kept asking the question everyone ignored because no one wanted to believe it: who was getting the money from the sale of the second largest underground oil deposits in the world? It was perhaps the largest cash grab in modern history and either no one saw, or no one cared; at least not until the price at the pumps soared to the penthouse. But even then no one did anything, so after a while I stopped asking. Certainly none of my rich buddies gave a damn; they just wanted to shoot the messenger. And now, albeit on a much grander scale, I was watching it happen again. The people were getting fooled, but this time it affected everyone. Life could no longer be lived in a bubble.

Most of all, it wasn't right. It wasn't American, and I'd be damned if I was going to allow it to happen on my watch. They'd have to kill me first. I didn't have all the pieces yet, but the puzzle was definitely beginning to make a lot more sense to me.

I had instructed everyone to be ready to move out on a moment's notice – then we climbed the walls for the next two days. Frank, Javier, Russell, and Gary spent most of their time on endless patrols of the hundred and fifty acre grounds. Most of it was thick forest, so they got around on horseback; Singh had fully operational stables. It turned out he loved animals, and loved to think on long rides through the forest. It was his only leisure. The forest itself was outfitted with infrared surveillance, and the compound enclosed in a razor-wire fence.

David hung around inside, never far from the doctors and their labs. The technology intrigued and even fascinated him, and he fought hard to understand it. It was, for the most part, way over his head. He'd likened it to the rest of the world being stuck in the Stone Age, while these scientists were traveling among the stars. I only hoped the scientists could somehow accomplish the impossible.

"So when do we leave, then?" Charlie finally asked. She had exhausted all her arguments on me.

I looked at my watch. It was eleven o'clock in the morning on a Tuesday. If they kept their word, they would bring down the next two towers sometime tomorrow, exactly one month to the day my own tower had disintegrated into nothingness.

"Tomorrow morning. I'll tell David to ready the jet. Everyone has been expecting this."

"What do Dr. Singh and Dr. Balbosa think? Can they do it? Will they finish in time?"

"There's no time to test it, if that's what you're asking. That's the one certainty. They said they would be ready by late morning." I sighed. "It's what we have to go with, like it or not. All we can do when we get to the Capitol is stall for as much time as we can get, because I can almost guarantee you of one more certainty..." I left it hanging. Charlie's sidelong glance as she began to throw things into her overnight told me she already knew.

Scientists were no fucking good with deadlines.

Chapter 34

"Why didn't you tell us?" I was astonished. It was beyond anything I could have hoped for.

"You didn't ask." Dr. Balbosa seemed amused. The scientist side of him had taken for granted what to me was an entirely unintended technological consequence with astounding ramifications.

We were leaving for D.C. in two hours. As we talked, David fought for air space in an office down the hall. It was understandably difficult to file a flight plan into Dulles these days. I'd told my skeptical but optimistic pilot I had every ounce of confidence in his ability to get the job done. Be inventive, I'd told him. Once again we were sitting around the large table in the boardroom of the compound's main building, next to one of the labs.

"It leaves a kind of signature," explained Dr. Singh with his usual patience. He offered a metaphor. "Let us say that a small pebble is dropped into a pond filled with goldfish. In this case, we can make an assumption that the goldfish are in motion. At times some tread water, when they feed for instance, but all of them are not stopped completely."

"What if they're dead?" Russell asked.

We all stared at him.

Balbosa said, "Then they're not moving. They're not a part of the model. They are of no consequence. Do you have any other questions, or shall I continue?"

"No more questions," Russell said. From here on I was pretty sure he'd keep his more brilliant insights to himself.

Dr. Singh continued. "The fish all create disturbances — signatures. Each individual goldfish has a unique signature by which it can be identified. These are different from the signature the pebble makes as it penetrates the surface of the pond. There are many other ponds. All are situated in relation to the first, but act more or less independently."

"More or less?" asked Gary.

"They contain fish, as well. Pebbles are also dropped into their waters. But the influence of the signatures created by the movement of the water is so slight on the first pond as to be negligible. Their effect on the first pond approaches zero, so, as in our metaphor, this effect may be discounted. We only need concern ourselves with the original pond."

"Our earth," I guessed. After all, I'd been hanging around David, who'd been hanging around the lab.

"Very good, that is precisely what I was referring to. The other ponds...?" Singh waited like a school teacher for me to complete the analogy.

"Other planets, other stars and solar systems. Anything in space that possesses a magnetomic resonance and gravity."

"Call it what you will, but right again." He went on to explain, "In essence our earth is a giant magnet surrounded by what we call its magnetosphere. Everything is charged. We, of course, as well as all other organic and inorganic material, make up the whole. We are the fish. Mountains would be very slowly moving whales. This technology, as you now know, taps into the entirety of this infinite field, and uses what's already there to magnify itself. When a heretofore nonexistent fish, a pulse, is introduced, it is instantly magnified to a number approaching infinity. It does this because it is connected to everything else, to all the energy in the universe. The receptor of this energy, the detonators in our case, utilizes or drains off exactly the right amount of energy for its encoded purpose. Remember, the energy is everywhere. It is the constant. This technology taps into what already exists. Depending upon the end use, it takes what it needs from the infinite supply. But I digress. We were speaking of signatures. In answer to your question, yes, not only can the detonators be located by their signatures, but in the same manner, so, too, can the machine sending the pulse be found."

"So you'll be able to locate every building that has been rigged, plus the whereabouts of the machine responsible for setting them off?" I confirmed.

"Precisely," Singh agreed.

"What if the protocols for the receivers are different from one another?"

"They won't be," Dr. Balbosa assured us. "That would have taken at least another five years. We're still in the first generation of this technology."

I nodded, understanding. "Sort of like the first computer," I offered lamely.

"Sort of." Balbosa forgave me my ignorance.

"Everything we described just now was given a name," Balbosa added to the sudden quiet of the room. "We called it the Joshua Effect, after the story of Jericho. Jericho in this case being the metaphor for mankind's walls of ignorance, which we had hoped this technology might destroy."

I looked at him with a start. My blood felt like it had

frozen into jagged shards of ice. I tossed glances around the room. It was obvious everyone except the two scientists knew exactly what this meant.

I could see the others were as fearful as I was. They were probably thinking the same thing I was. What would happen when infinite power got into the hands of the wrong people? We were all standing on the doorstep of Armageddon, and those very same people were about to ring the fucking bell.

"When, Doctors?" They knew what I meant.

Dr. Singh volunteered, "We are on track for sometime early this afternoon." He glanced over at his partner.

Dr. Balbosa nodded in agreement. He took a deep breath and let it out in a gush. "We'll certainly be ready. Normally we'd test the different components leading up to the final assembly. In this case…" He shrugged his shoulders and clasped his hands together in his lap. He'd been leaning against the edge of the big table, rather than having found a seat.

"And you think you'll be able to configure the locations? All of them? Including the source of the pulse?" I asked them.

Singh maintained, "With the proviso it works."

"Of course," I returned. "Whatever happens, your effort has been a superhuman one." I approached them and we all shook hands, wishing each other luck. "I just hope we get a chance to write it into the history books. *When* it works," I emphasized the when, "I want to be the third person to know where the pulse came from."

"We should be able to give you an actual street address. Unless, of course, it comes from somewhere like Antarctica. Which is technologically as likely as anywhere else," Balbosa said.

"Let me know the second you get it." I had a hunch

we could rule out the South Pole.

Praveen was the last one to shake my hand on the way out of the boardroom. "Whatever happens, it has been an honor to work with you, Jonathan."

I looked deeply into his dark eyes. "It ain't over yet, my friend." I smiled at him.

"Good luck Jonathan, we will speak soon."

"Thanks, Praveen," I said simply. I turned and walked out the door. I almost got bowled over by David.

"Where's the fire, man?" I asked him. "It's an hour before liftoff." I checked my watch again. I noticed he had a cooler under one arm.

"I've got to get to the kitchen before they throw it out."

"It?"

"The heart." He sounded flustered. "For the transplant." He saw I didn't know what the hell he was talking about. "I'll see you on the jet in an hour. I'll explain then. I gotta go." He brushed past me with strong intent, just like Alice's white rabbit.

An hour later we roared down the compound's private runway. Praveen would tell me later we'd just made it. We were the last of anything to slip out right before the Feds stormed the compound.

Chapter 35

"You said to be inventive." He looked at me. "Where'd you get the white coat?" Gary asked him.

David cocked his head a bit sideways. "Sometimes you worry me, Gary. Some of the guys in the lab wear these. I figured in a crunch they'd pass for a doctor's smock. Appearances. You know; the power of suggestion and all that. We got the heart." He patted the top of the cooler. "They'll believe us. Trust me."

"It's a pig's heart," Gary pointed out.

"What they don't know can't hurt them," David replied.

"As long as it'll get us onto the tarmac at Dulles," I said.

"I'm a little worried about what happens after that," Charlie said truthfully. "The city's under martial law."

I reached down beside the chair where I always kept my files when we flew. "You're forgetting these." I opened one of the folders.

We hadn't actually used any of them since we'd landed in Damascus, but we still had the official identification papers Homeland Security had originally issued us. They weren't that much different, at least in effect, to having diplomatic immunity. I looked at mine and rechecked the seal and accompanying signatures. In my mind they gave us heavyweight status, but there was one problem with them: we didn't know for sure if they had been revoked.

"What if they don't work?" said Javier. "A lot has changed in the last few weeks."

"Plan A: We got the heart. What're they going to do? Let the transplant patient die? If they demand our make-believe patient's medical records, then we'll go to Plan B." I held up our official papers. If these don't work, there's always Plan C."

They looked at me, waiting.

I smiled. "How many people do you know who've come back from the dead? It's not like we don't have friends in high places. I think they'll want to see us. After all, I am one of the richest men in America. Membership has its privileges, you know."

"It's the time line that worries me, Jonathan," said Gary.

I could feel Russell begin our descent into the Capitol.

"If the bad guys somehow find out we're still around, and Singh and Balbosa haven't sent that pulse through the universal grid, there can be only one outcome," Gary reminded us.

Frank injected, "Sometimes you got to have a little faith. Worrying about things we can't change is only going to hurt us. Those doctors won't let us down. They'll do their part."

His little speech seemed to lift our spirits. I rested a hand on his shoulder. "I think Frank has a point. We just have to go for it at this point. All of us have done our best. I'm proud of each and every one of you." I looked around the jet's cabin at my friends. "We've all done a hell of a job. The whole country would be proud. And we're going to have one when this is over. It will be stronger, safer. It won't be the same, it's changed forever, but that's something everyone will have to get used to. It will be worse in some ways but better in others. That's what America is about. It's about change. Sometimes we screw up, but we always fix our mistakes in time. We're good at that. The rest of the world wants to live like we do for a damn good reason. We're the best. It's never come easy, but it's sure as hell been worth the fight. The country's gotten away from us a few times, but we've always taken it back. This time is no different. My America is mine and it's worth dying for."

Russell's voice came over the cabin's intercom: "Twenty minutes, David."

The pilot rose. "Time to bring this baby in." He glanced at the cooler, and said to Gary, "Look after my heart, will you? You just never know."

Gary smiled. "Get us on the ground safely. We'll see if we can find me a brain, and a way home for Dorothy while we're at it."

We all strapped in for the landing. Charlie was in the chair next to mine. She reached over and clasped my hand. I smiled warmly at her.

"I love you," she spoke softly. A lump came to my throat. I squeezed her hand.

"I love you, too, Charlie. I always have. Forgive me?"

"For what?" her brow furrowed.

"For being such a jerk for most of the time we've known each other. I'm sorry."

Now she squeezed my hand. "I suppose I could have been a little more tolerant. We all have our idiosyncrasies."

"Yeah, but mine can make me a real asshole sometimes. How did you end up so smart, Charlie? You make life seem so easy. At least that's how it looked to me before all this." I waved my arm in front of me, indicating what we found ourselves involved with now.

"That's just how it appeared to you. Believe me, my life wasn't all peaches and cream. Before I met you it was pretty damn boring. Nothing much ever went wrong, but nothing ever seemed to happen the other way, either."

"That's when you decided to write my biography?"

She nodded.

"What made you pick me?"

"You were an enigma. No one knew anything about you. Someone mentioned you to me one day. I said why not? I thought you were older. The first time I saw a picture of you I became intrigued. The last thing I ever thought would happen was that we'd end up falling in love."

"And then you left."

"Then I left." She searched my eyes. "Jonathan, you can't imagine how much that decision broke my heart. It tore me in half. It had gotten to the point where I felt we just couldn't go any further."

"You mean I couldn't." I sighed.

"Now you're different."

"In what way?"

"Like just now. You were honest with yourself. A month ago you couldn't have done that. A month ago I don't think you knew yourself well enough."

"You think I was lying to myself?"

"No," Charlie immediately protested. "You just didn't know who you were. The two are very different, sweetheart." She smiled.

"I didn't change," I said, pondering myself. "Maybe there's just more of who I always was."

"That's a big part of it, I think. But you seemed to be always living someone else's life before. It's like you didn't have an identity of your own."

"I was scared," I admitted. "I was afraid I'd disappoint someone: a bank, a business partner. I had an image to live up to. To the rest of the world I was Mr. Success."

"Your own private demon."

I thought about what she said. "I guess my life became grayer after Pop died."

"You really loved your father, didn't you?"

"Yeah," I nodded "He meant the world to me. He taught me everything."

"Except how to be yourself," she said kindly. "That can't be taught, Jonathan. That's the one thing you've got to learn on your own."

"How to live?"

"And in the end, how to die." She saw the hint of fear in my eyes. "It's scary, being on your own, finding yourself."

"It's scarier the other way. Not knowing who you are," I said. "It almost cost me you. I wonder if I would have ever even found out why you left, or whether I would have just kept on wallowing around like a blind man, never knowing what I was missing. Why did I wake up, Charlie? How did I get to see, and other people can't?"

"I don't know," she said. "But I'm glad. You've been blessed, Jonathan. Maybe there was a reason, maybe not. Just be happy with it. Don't think about the ones who struggle with what you once were. You've got too much living to do. You have your hands full right now."

I reached over and kissed her. I smiled. I looked at her delicate hand cradled in my own. "I'm a lucky man, Charlie," I admitted. "When this is over I want to go somewhere. Just you and me. Somewhere no one can find us. I want to get to know you more completely."

She kissed me back. "What about the book?"

"I couldn't think of a better way to write the last chapter, can you?"

"No. Sweetheart?"

"Yeah?" I stroked her hand.

"I'm scared." I could feel her involuntary shiver.

I sighed. "I know what you mean. But it's almost over. Just a little while longer, okay?"

"Okay," she said in what was barely a whisper.

I lifted her face by her chin. "I won't let anything happen to you. That's a promise. And I always keep my promises."

She nodded. "I know. Better fasten our seatbelts."

And reality came crashing back into our lives. David was taking us in for a bumpy landing.

Chapter 36

"Looks a lot like Damascus," Gary observed with a wry wit only an attorney could possess.

We taxied across the tarmac, waved forward to a final stop by a Marine. Military personnel were everywhere. The Gulfstream, normally unnoticed, had garnered the attention of a small gathering of uniformed militia. They waited for us outside the front door of General Aviation. More soldiers began to join the group, all wearing the same shades. The five of them looked like GI Joes. Jeeps and Humvees busied themselves this way and that. I noticed a number of other civilian aircraft, but none of them seemed to be going anywhere. The sky over the Capital was now restricted airspace.

"I think we can pretty much scrap Plan A," I said, looking through one of the aircraft's windows.

Gary nodded. "Might as well go right to C," he suggested. "This isn't the D.C. I remember. This is lock down."

"This is war," I said.

The satellite phone suddenly signaled an incoming message. Almost afraid, I walked across the cabin to where the message would be displayed on the screen. The others watched me, holding their breath.

I read the message and relief washed over me. I deleted it with the click of a key, so no one else could easily recall it if they wanted to read it after we left.

"They did it," I whispered, but it was loud enough for everyone to hear me. "They actually did it."

It was marvelous. I felt ten feet tall. I looked up at Charlie then.

"What else?" She saw something in my eyes.

"Those soldiers out there, the ones standing near the office door? They're friends of your father."

Her brow furrowed. "I don't understand. I —"

"He knows about us, Charlie. He and I spoke last night, while you were sleeping."

"I don't get it," she said, totally bewildered. "You called my father?"

I nodded my head.

She grabbed the back of a chair for support

"I called him from the compound."

"He knows?" She was crying now. "Oh, my God, Jonathan, why didn't you wake me?" Her hand covered her mouth in disbelief.

"He's waiting for us now," I declared. "The Marines are going to take us to see him. I'm sorry. You were sleeping."

She nodded, recovering from the initial shock. She wouldn't hate me for it, but she'd have mixed emotions. This morning I figured everyone already had enough on their minds. I thought no one would mind a good surprise for a change. Even the vigilant Gary had not known about Gus's early morning call. Praveen had awakened me at three thirty to let me know he was on a secured line.

I was wide awake by the time I sat down in front of Gus's digitalized image.

"How long have you known?" I asked him.

"I've had my suspicions for quite a while," he indicated. "How is Charlie?"

"She's fine," I told him.

"You must have gotten out of Damascus in a hurry. No one thought you made it out alive. I don't ever want to go through something like that again. She's my only daughter, Jonathan."

"I understand. It was worse being there. I'll tell you about it later. You were talking about your suspicions, though?" I steered him back to the other reason I'd called.

His image turned, as if someone had come into the room behind him, or he'd heard some kind of noise. He turned back and focused on me.

"When are you leaving?" he asked instead.

"Tomorrow morning." His was a loaded question, a type of code. It was clear to me he either didn't want to get into the details now, or couldn't. Something else, something far more sinister, was preventing him from elaborating.

"Where are you going?" Clearly, Gus didn't know everything.

"D.C."

He seemed relieved, exhaling slowly. "It has to be handled very carefully from here on in. One mistake and they'll go underground. We'll lose them forever. Then it will have been for nothing."

How much did he know? I didn't want to mention anything about the towers and what tomorrow may or may not bring.

"Charlie's pendant, the one with the picture of your wife in it, had a broken clasp," I said, fishing.

He nodded. "I was pleased to learn that someone was able to repair it." His sarcastic inflection was only barely perceptible.

We both knew Charlie had given it to him for this specific reason. In fact, it had been Gus who had insisted on having it fixed for her. But he had just let me know that not only did he know about it and its technology, but also that he hadn't been the one responsible for its substitution.

"It works now." I wanted to see his reaction. Even as we spoke, the scientists worked to perfect their mechanism. And, if Singh and Balbosa prevailed, we would learn everything.

Gus didn't flinch. It made sense. I could be bluffing, in which case at least the next two towers were coming down sometime tomorrow. I'm sure Gus would have given his left arm to find out one way or the other. But he was a wily, patient, clever veteran. The game was still on, its outcome still in question. To blink now would have catastrophic consequences.

"Where will you be landing?" he asked conversationally.

"Why, Gus?"

"Remember who you have with you," he warned. "Appearances are deceptive. I have people I trust. Marines. I know them personally. They'll meet you and bring you in. And Jonathan?"

"Yeah?"

"I am Charlie's father. You must trust me. We have to talk. You've got to believe me. I must see you."

I stared at his image. I could see the resemblance between father and daughter. "Dulles," I said, "Around noon."

"I will smooth the way," he said with relief.

"How can we be sure they're your friends?"

He stared at me from across the void. "One will introduce another by a name you know."

The screen had gone blank the second he'd spoken those cryptic words.

The first five Marines were joined by another ten. For a second I wondered if we should make a run for it. David was at the controls; the engines were still running. But what would it accomplish? We were damned either way, if these weren't friends of Gus.

I tugged my hat low over my brow one last time and crossed the tarmac. A few steps away from the Marines, one separated from the herd. He was all business. Nobody was getting into DC without the proper paperwork.

I acknowledged him with a barely perceptible nod.

"What's the purpose of your trip, sir?" He spoke in a metallic monotone. Suddenly we needed papers to move through checkpoints within our own country.

I tossed a glance over my shoulder at Gary. "We've got a heart for a transplant patient in D.C."

With this, the Marine became interested. He looked past me, at Gary, and the cooler he carried.

"Some VIP at the Pentagon. They've brought the surgical team in from Bethesda to perform the operation."

"The Pentagon?"

"Yes sir," I said. I was still hoping for anonymity.

"Could you come inside please, sir? Follow this gentleman through those doors right over there." Silent, barely discernible exchanges had taken place between the front line security personnel. It was clear they weren't making suggestions. To follow them inside had been an order.

"The heart is on ice." David, in his doctor's smock, was suddenly on the tarmac beside me. The crowd was getting bigger. "The donor died not more than four hours ago. This is extremely time sensitive. If we don't get this organ inside the recipient's chest in the next six hours, we'll lose our window." He was trying his best to sound like he knew what he was doing. I knew the Marine's next move would be to go for his gun. It was intimidating.

"I'm going to have to ask you to come inside, sir." This time he spoke more forcefully. Always with the sir, too. I hated it. Some buck private about to shoot me politely.

About thirty feet behind the checkpoint, the doors of the administration for General Aviation suddenly sprang open. A group of six uniformed Marines in front of a couple of guys in suits, ties, and sunglasses filed out onto the tarmac.

"Private!" the first Marine out of the blocks barked as he walked briskly toward us.

The men in front of us immediately snapped into a more rigid formality. Still, they weren't taking any chances with us. The Marine who'd grilled us kept a wary eye on our group.

"Stand down, Private," his senior ordered. "We'll take it from here."

Gus didn't even look at me. As soon as he saw his daughter he ran past us and they embraced, crying.

"I thought you were gone, sweetheart. It's a miracle," he mumbled.

"I'm okay, Daddy. We're all fine," Charlie assured him.

Everyone now recognized Gus Bakersfield and visibly relaxed. Security was essential, but this was their boss.

Finally Gus and I were able to greet each other. We shook hands. I noticed his trembled slightly. He seemed much older than the last time we met.

"I'm sorry we couldn't tell you earlier," I said. "I know it was hard on you, sir. Truly, I'm sorry."

Gus still had his arm around Charlie. The words cascaded from his lips, "Apology accepted. I'm just so happy, so overwhelmed. I'm sorry." He wiped tears from his eyes as he succumbed once more to the emotion of the moment. I watched as he fought for, and finally regained control of himself. He'd probably wanted to die when they had told him Charlie had been killed. To see her once again, to hold her, to feel her, must truly have been a miracle for him.

"I've got a motorcade waiting in the parking lot. My office at the Pentagon is safe, and it's secure. We've got a lot to talk about."

"Yes, we do," I agreed, looking at father and daughter. I hadn't fully appreciated how rough it must have been for the two of them. Charlie looked like a little girl in her daddy's arms. I shivered slightly as a tinge of edgy, raw emotion coursed through my own body. For the first time since it happened, I realized how close we had come to dying back in the desert.

Chapter 37

"It's not just the Capitol," Gus said, looking slightly more relaxed than at the airport as he leaned back in his big leather chair. "It's the same in nearly every city in the nation. This country's hanging by a thread. No one likes to be occupied, especially if you're an American. We're a free spirit."

"What happened to the plan, Gus?"

He leveled his gaze at me. "The genie got out of the bottle? Absolute power corrupts absolutely. This has been coming down the pike for a long time. Scared people demand scary leaders. You don't have to look back very far: 9/11, the Cole, the Beirut barracks bombing, the embassy bombings. This was a nation ripe for the picking. The people took freedom for granted. We all got fat and lazy. When the media played up the threat, we all bought into it. We started flushing the Constitution down the toilet so we could all keep lining up at the buffet. We wanted McDonald's and we wanted to be safe. This was a black box project from the word go. It would have never gotten legs in any other circumstances."

"Did the President authorize it?" asked Gary, looking out the windows.

"Yes. But he authorizes everything. The President has good intentions."

Javier and Gary rolled their eyes.

"These guys are politicians," Gus continued. "It becomes the age-old dilemma. They're all supposed to represent the will of the people, but there's a problem: they're out of touch with what that will is."

"For good reason," I said.

"For many good reasons," Gus agreed. "One, there's so many nuts out there. They all must have serious protection. They never get a chance to talk to a so-called ordinary person. Even these town hall meetings, Ross Perot's brainchild, are stacked. If anyone doesn't agree with the man on the stage they're simply thrown out of the hall."

"Or arrested," said Gary.

"So when the voice of dissent should be heard the loudest, it's stifled. That's what real freedom rests on. When the chips are down, when the very foundation of the nation is cracking, that's when the beacon – the light – should shine brightest. Unfortunately not true. Congress signed bills, as they do, which they never read."

"Yeah, but not this one, Gus," I said. "No one would have agreed to it."

"They did when they gave all that freedom away. When they gave those powers to Congress, they also gave away the checks and balances."

"No oversight," noted Charlie.

"So this is what happens when no one is looking over the other guy's shoulder." Gary was watching the military out front.

"I'm afraid it was inevitable," said Gus.

"Am I the only one who sees the irony?" I asked. "All of these politicians who promised to make the world a safer place end up making it a far more terrible place to live. And this – this Joshua Effect – is the granddaddy of them all. It's a fucking doomsday machine if ever I've seen one. If it hadn't been for Mojab's brother —"

I was cut off by a loud, authoritative knock on Gus's office door. We instantly fell silent and remained seated while Gus rose.

"Ninth inning, bases loaded," he said quietly. "We shall see what we shall see."

He walked over to the door and opened it. His secretary started to say something from behind Derrick Smith, but Gus waved her off.

"Come on in, Derrick. There are some people in here I'd like you to meet."

Smith strode through the door with supreme confidence. He maintained a cool façade, but I saw the color drain from his face when he saw us.

"Jonathan Strickland," he said. He stole a glance back at Gus. "You're alive."

"Is that good news or bad news?" I smiled.

"Well, of course, it's great news," he fumbled.

"Yeah, it was a tight squeeze out there in the desert," Gary said with no expression, "but we made it. Hard to kill a cockroach, you know."

Smith was perspiring. For the first time he seemed nervous, and a little unsure of himself.

"Well, I'm glad to see you made it." He groped to regain his balance. "The reports we got indicated you'd all been killed in some terrorist blast."

"Like the one that took out my building," I said.

"Something like that. Gus, what's going on here?" He began to take the offensive.

Gus nonchalantly shrugged. "Nothing more than the usual."

Smith ignored him. "I have a lot on my plate right now. Actually," now he looked at his watch, "I'm late for a meeting already. Was there... Is there anything you wanted? I made time for you I couldn't really spare."

Suddenly there was another knock on the door.

"I think you'll want to stick around for this one," Gus said. He moved over to the door. We could see only his secretary through the opening. We heard her say, "He's here, sir."

I could see Gus extend his hand to someone blocked by the door. "Good afternoon, Mr. Secretary. Please come in." Then, right behind the first man who entered, he greeted the next. "Mr. President. Thank you for coming."

We all rose as the Secretary of State, the President, the Homeland Security Director, and a phalanx of Secret Service entered what was fast becoming a very crowded office. More chairs were quickly brought in from the outside foyer. The air conditioning was adjusted. Soon almost all of us were sitting in what could only be described as the strangest round table American history would never record.

"One of you will betray me," the President began. We weren't meeting in the Oval Office because then the law would necessitate the recording of everything spoken. Everything said at this meeting would never leave Gus's office.

"The genie was out of the bottle," said the President, using Gus's words. "Are we prepared to lose more towers? Does anyone know which ones are next?"

I cleared my throat. Suddenly the room was eerily silent. All eyes turned towards me. The military among them were already disconcerted at the presence of what they considered to be rogue civilians. They had no choice in the matter, but their body language made it clear they didn't like associating with people they considered amateurs.

I smiled inwardly. I'd put guys like Gary and Javier up against their best and we'd accomplished what they had not been able to. That was probably a large part of their attitude toward us. And now their Commander-in-Chief was hunting heads. The prognosis wasn't looking good for some of these guys. At the very least, the deck would be shuffled.

The President said to me, "I've heard some good things about you, Mr. Strickland. Not much, but all good, mind you. I hear you and your people had a close call."

"A couple of them," I admitted. "How much do you know, Mr. President?"

"Everything the Assistant to the Director knows," he said unapologetically. Gus had told him much before the meeting. "Why don't you fill me in on the rest, if you would?"

"Certainly," I cleared my throat again. "As all of you know, we were threatened with the destruction of two more of our major superstructures. The deadline to meet certain demands was today." I looked around the circle of men and women. My eyes settled on Smith. "That won't happen." My gaze returned to the President. "Nor will any other of a total of seventeen such superstructures be destroyed. We have stopped this from happening."

"Are you certain?" asked the Director of Homeland Security. He was skeptical; most of them, the uninformed, wanted to believe it was true.

"About as certain as Oppenheimer was with his weapons." I let the surprise sink in before I continued.

"Yeah, we know about the weapon. We know that's how the original technology was twisted. I guess it's not too different from $e = mc^2$. Energy, I suppose, may never come without some form of collateral cost.

"The black box project was ill-conceived at best and

an absolutely horrific nightmare at worst. I can't imagine what you were thinking when you let the Joshua Effect proceed." I addressed them collectively. I knew what happened, how these people lusted after more and more power. My gloves were off.

"Let me recap. It all started with the energy crisis. Only to call it a crisis has always been another way of extracting the most profits from the same old hole in the ground. It involves opportunity first, and then segues on into dependence which eventually evolves into fear which revolves around the inevitability of a dry hole. Scare the hell out of people: tell them it's running out, blame the skyrocketing prices on greedy spot marketeers. The results remain the same: enormous redistributions of enormous wealth. We measure wealth in terms of barrels, not dollars.

"But what if we no longer needed it? What if someone found a way, just like with personal computers for instance, to put that kind of power in the hands of the average person? What if you and I suddenly had all the energy we needed? To fuel our cars, to heat our homes, to power our industries; and all of it was free? What then?

"Turn the page. Someone who knows about this also happens to know about a plot to plant some C-4 in the bottom of a few of our bigger towers. This spells fear. It chills you to the marrow when you think about it.

"So then someone comes up with a brilliant idea. Why don't we let these guys, these terrorists, go ahead with their plan? Fear is and always has been the coin of the realm. And what better way to completely control the American people than to make them afraid? If they're scared, we already know they'll let us do anything to protect their asses.

"My guess is the fanatics were screwing up. I know

the C-4 came from our own military bases. They wouldn't have been able to get it without some help, so we helped them. We made sure they got what they needed, but we couldn't make it look too easy. And that kind of operation is expensive. Someone had to bankroll it. I bet you guys even considered using money from Congress. If something went wrong you could always kill anyone who was thinking about going canary. But what if you actually were caught? Why take that risk, especially if you can find another way. What about a patsy? That's been done before, nothing new there.

"I guess it wasn't too difficult to find a rich American-hating extremist. There's more than a few of those out there. By the way, people are the same everywhere: they don't hate Americans, but they do hate our government. The irony as far as I can see it is that our government is one of the best the world has ever seen. But what makes it the absolute best also makes it the most vulnerable. We are free, and that's exactly why some of the most evil, rotten sons-of-bitches the world's ever seen got in.

"You killed Mojab, or whatever his name was. His family became your patsy. I met his brother in Syria. He wasn't too happy. But when they found out what you were really up to, they hated you enough to die trying to stop it. They wanted to kill the project. But that was no longer an option.

"What you didn't know about was that this same family was also financing one of only two labs in the world developing the energy technology. The Arab was the guy who wrote Dr. Singh his blank check at the same time you guys were financing Dr. Balbosa. It must have really pissed you off after a while when even Dr. Balbosa found you were too slimy to work with. So he began to stall. You put him under house arrest in Miami. Those weren't bodyguards protecting him, they were what? CIA? They were also soft in the middle. They sure weren't expecting us.

"It's actually comical when I think about it. I don't know who the hell most of you are, or what became of who you once were. But we were the ones in the end responsible for accelerating the Joshua Effect. It was the only way to save the towers. In the end it has become the only way to save this country and our people.

"We have perfected the technology, ladies and gentleman. We have stopped the detonation sequences, all of them. None of the booby-trapped superstructures are in danger of collapsing.

"About an hour ago, the detonation of the next two towers was attempted. Our scientists stopped this from happening. For any of you who don't know, one of the towers is in downtown Los Angeles, the other in downtown Chicago.

"The perfection of this new technology has allowed our scientists added benefits. We now know, for instance, the locations of all the buildings rigged for demolition. We also know the exact location where the signal to initiate the detonation sequences originated."

No one said a word. Concerned and furtive glances were exchanged.

"We now have the ability to override all subsequent attempts to initiate altered sequences. The machine has been rendered useless. We incapacitated every circuit on the board. If you look at the hardware you won't be able to tell, but we've done it, nonetheless.

"Along the way we had an unintended, but fortunate consequence. It seems now that the originating processor itself is booby-trapped. I don't know the scientific vernacular, but I've been informed it's sort of like a backed up toilet. Flush it again, and, well, you get the picture. What was going to happen to those buildings will happen at the location of the original processor. The entire network of devices will turn in on itself.

"Gus, I want to thank you personally." I turned to Charlie's father, and winked at him. "If it wasn't for you holding off the troops, we might not have succeeded at the lab.

"I'm told I own everything from real estate to windmills. It's what's in between that's going to make this work. I own a lot of media outlets, and not just here in the States. My holdings are global. I'm poised to tell this story to the world. A big part of me says to do it. I think most of my friends would agree with me. However, I'm a businessman. So I've come to the table with an offer. No one is going to turn my country into some kind of backwater military dictatorship disguised as a democracy. It's by the people, for the people, and it's going to stay that way. Our founding fathers knew enough about greed and the human lust for power, the arrogance in the dark corners of all of our hearts to realize we must maintain checks and balances. So here's one: if whoever's responsible for this doesn't back off, this story will be told tomorrow. That's my deadline. And I, like you, don't bluff. Then whoever's responsible is going down. You'll be lucky not to be hanged for treason from the front portico of the White House with the entire world watching.

"We are in the embryonic stages of a technological revolution such as the world has only dreamed of. Free energy is a reality. No one will be allowed to sell it. As I speak this story is breaking. I'm spreading it around the entire world. By this time tomorrow it will be front page on every newspaper from here to Bangkok. It's already on the Internet. It will take time, but I'm determined our grandchildren will inherit a world better than the one we live in now.

"I've got another request. Gus Bakersfield will be appointed as the new Chief of Homeland Security. The old guy is out." I looked at the current Chief with disgust. "All the other security agencies will report to him. For now, until we come up with a better plan, Gus will make sure everyone is on the same page.

"Come to think of it, we're all here for the same reason, aren't we? We all love our country. Isn't that what it's all about? Each of us wants a better life. I'm here to tell you that there's obviously different ways to get one. I happen to believe the wrong way is when you feel you have to step on your fellow man to do it. That's un-American. And that has stopped, as of today."

I looked at them around the room. They were a somber, thoughtful, scared bunch. Only a short time ago they'd walked into Gus's office with nothing but pride and arrogance.

"Did anyone of you ever serve your country?" I said at last. "Those are not just words. When you got too big for your britches, you lost touch. You lost sight of what this is all for. 'Ask not what your country can do for you, but what you can do for your country.' Don't any of you still have that spark in your heart?

"Make this right," I said sternly. "Undo this. Turn it off, and turn it around. The story about how the towers have been saved goes out later today. It's the sanitized version, but I still want the military withdrawn. I want the tanks off the streets when the story breaks about how you all saved this great country. Don't try and figure a way out. There isn't any. You blinked and you lost; we won.

"We'll keep the proof, just in case. We'll also keep the technology. I'd advise you to lock up the originating processor. I wouldn't want to be within ten city blocks of it if somebody gets the crazy notion of fixing it. Trust me.

"Oh, and I almost forgot. I'm going to need a check for my tower, and an additional ten million for each one of the people on the rooftop who didn't make it. Their families need to feel safe. This is non-negotiable. They need the money by the end of this month. I'm sure Congress won't mind. The America I grew up in looks after its own."

They all stared at me, stone-faced. Most of them looked old and tired. As I got up to leave, so did everyone I loved. Gus stayed behind to assume his new responsibilities. The public would be ecstatic to learn the threat had passed. Not only that, but soon they were no longer going to have to concern themselves with the price of a gallon of fuel. As for the rest of what had happened, well, not much had changed there. Ignorance was still truly blissful.

Chapter 38

"Why does learning take so much time?" She looked beautiful in absolutely nothing.

"Are you talking about you and me, or the rest of the world?" I steered east, toward the Bahamas.

It had been six months since the meeting in Gus's office. So far as we knew, no one had touched the original piece of hardware used to destroy my tower. We already had another tower under construction on the same site as the old one. It would be taller than the first: another ten floors, one for each of the victims. I thought it a fitting tribute.

As a result of the plot, the building codes across America had changed. Now there had to be an inspector on the job full time during the foundation phase. I couldn't fault them for that. Everyone always wanted to be safer and more secure. It had become a balancing act, a give and take: safety for freedom, and then back again. I supposed there was really no way around it, but I preferred freedom.

My friends and I had been prepared to pay the ultimate price for it. But we weren't your average Americans. Sometimes I wished people still had a revolutionary spark, but then I realized they never had it to begin with. It fell to the men and women of vision; the others simply followed.

"I'm talking about everyone, sweetheart," Charlie rolled over onto her stomach. We couldn't have asked for better weather out of Miami. The ocean was as calm as I'd ever seen it. There wasn't a cloud in the sky.

Charlie had stripped down as soon as no other boats were in sight. She always hated tan lines. She smiled at me from the sloop's front deck.

"That's a loaded question," I mused, pretending to give her query on learning the consideration it warranted. I couldn't take my eyes off her. She knew it, too. Even sunglasses couldn't hide that.

"I guess we're never stronger than our weakest link." A sudden gust of breeze pummeled the main sail.

"You learned." She didn't take her eyes off me.

"Yeah, but it was painful. *And*," I emphasized the word as I moved the wheel to accommodate the slight shift in wind direction, "I had a good teacher."

"This country has changed, hasn't it?" she mused.

I considered. "You're right about that. It's better now than it's been in a while. We strayed for a time, but I think we're back on course."

"Why didn't you turn them in, Jonathan? Why didn't you expose them? God knows they deserved it."

"I won't argue that one," I agreed. "I figured we'd gone through enough. The country, I mean. That might have been the straw that killed it. Revenge wasn't the answer. We were better off fixing it, not ruining it. This is the best country in the world. We proved it. I meant what I told them. I want a place where our grandkids can grow up and be free. I want a place where everyone has a voice not just heard, but actually listened to."

"I think they call that home," Charlie said above the creak of the mainsail. The guy wires were tested. They held fast as the breeze picked up.

I smiled. "Home, I like that."

"You're a politician, sweetheart. Why don't you run for office?"

"Gus is doing a fine job," I said. "They don't need me. No one has a winning hand. He'll make sure no one ever does. It works that way. Checks and balances. I'd just screw that up. I'd want to be King. There's no place for a guy like me in a democracy."

As if on cue, my cell phone on the boat's console suddenly started ringing.

"Jonathan, I thought we agreed no phones." Charlie frowned.

"Jonathan, here," I answered. It was Praveen.

"How are you doing?" he asked with his usual soft-spoken politeness.

"Wonderfully," I gazed at Charlie as she rolled back over to sun the front of her body.

"I have just finished processing the last quarter's numbers. The Empire's stock has tripled since last September."

"I'd say that makes you a very rich man," I said to him.

"Jonathan?"

"Yes sir?"

Praveen seemed slightly confused. "I thought you would be happier to hear this."

I took a deep breath and exhaled in the direction of Nassau. "I'm happy, Praveen. I'm happy you're happy. But I guess I'm just not the same man I used to be. You're the one in charge now: you, Gus, Gary, and the others. So long, my friend. Look after the store while I'm gone."

I wound up and threw the phone as far as I could. It made a very small splash in a very big ocean.

I looked up. The sun was beginning its descent behind us. I laughed out loud.

"What's so funny?" Charlie asked.

"I was just thinking. When I was a kid I always wondered what it must be like to sail off into the sunset with the babe."

She turned back over so she could see me, smiling seductively this time. "Well now you know, sweetheart." She got up and came down the short ladder, then pulled me in for a kiss.

"Does this thing have an anchor?" she purred.

"Why?"

"C'mon." She kissed me again, her hold growing tight. "I'd be happy to raise a child in this new country we've made."